I0628781

The future of our civilization has always been in the hands of our children. What you may not know is that many years ago, a few of our young ones fought a quest against evil—an evil unlike anything anyone has ever seen under this sun. They didn't know it, but their sacrifices allowed our forefathers—and us—to maintain our fragile ownership of this world.

In *Seven & Two*, the first book of the *Our Young Guardians* series, we begin the chronicle of one who was brave enough to leave behind what he knew. His faded handwriting not only captures how they struggled through that war, but how they learned to find themselves as they grew up away from their families.

You and I owe them more than we could ever give. And even though there is no word of them ever asking for anything, my heart tells me they would only ask for one thing—to keep them where their friends are.

The least we can do for them is honor their story.

OUR YOUNG GUARDIANS

SEVEN & TWO

1

Rodi Szoke

Text and illustrations Copyright © 2016 by Rodi Szoke.
Cover design by Hiram Cruz.
All rights Reserved.

No part of this publication may be reproduced in whole or in part, or stored in a retrieval system, or transmitted in any form or by any means, electronic, mechanical, photocopying, audio, or otherwise, without written permission of the publisher.

First Edition. 2016

This is a work of fiction. Names, characters, places, and incidents either are the product of the author's imagination or are used fictitiously. Any resemblance to actual persons, living or dead, events, or locales is entirely coincidental.

The text was set in 12 point Garamond, based on the sixteenth-century typeface designs of Claude Garamond.
The typeface used for the author's name is Zapfino regular, designed by Hermann Zapf.

ISBN-13: 978-0-997-56591-1

rodibooks™

TO MY FAMILY,
AND ALL THOSE SOULS
THAT HAVE TOUCHED MY LIFE.

CONTENTS

KHARLO'S LAST KELFIAN PAGE.

*B*eware of these pages.

The words have been crafted in such a way that Malok cannot understand them. The message would be hard to decrypt even with the Eye of Cotifer . . . I hope. The ink on this page carries the souls of the four of us, our flesh and blood, our legacy. In the wrong hands, it could mean the end of an ancient quest against evil, and maybe our world as we know it. Your world.

Tynia says that if you slowly slide your hand over these pages, you might be able to feel it—cold and dry but burning in your palm as a signal, another reminder of the past. In any case, it has been known for ages that the dark mist lives in all of us, frozen, waiting like a shadow deep within our bones, guarded only by the pureness of our hearts. People wiser than us have failed to understand why someone chooses to leave the light and succumb to the shadow realm, so we agreed not to spend more nights on it; we have dropped that leaf. The challenge now is to know who you are before you finish reading these words.

Five hundred and twenty four, if I am not mistaken. About five of them will understand the message on their first try. The rest . . . maybe a few others will eventually get there, *if* they are on the right side of the river, of course.

No riddles, no tests. This is just the way it has been done for centuries. My memory has started to fade; names and places have already left my mind, and barely a few drops of elixir are left, so I had better begin.

I am Kharlo, but no one has called me by this name for a very long time. I am using my last Kelfian page to leave a trail so someone can follow our path. When I was twenty-five, there were seven books—detailed journals written by us to keep track of our part in the quest. I saw one of them burning in the hands of Malok himself, another destroyed by the sun in Minojeb, and the rest were hidden in lands of good and evil, sealed by us but guarded by folk and charms, just waiting to be retrieved.

It is unfortunate that only Jalyena knows which journals were destroyed. We decided not to mark the covers and seals of the remaining books so that no eyes could identify them, not even ours.

You should know that I am yet to meet a soul who can make sense of the riddles she wrote to determine their resting location. Very skillful, our little one. The enemy was close when she gave the last two books to her brother, Artego. They decided to protect the secret with more than swords and spells, so they went into hiding. The siblings traveled to an unnamed town, escorted by Ganthog soldiers and some fairies (Bujetal fairies, I believe). I was told that these magical beings sacrificed themselves in order to change Jalyena's appearance—her clothing, age, and voice. They never returned. Artego must have taken Jalyena's mind into shadows to avoid it being read by Zerkial wizards. By the end of that night, the youngest of us became a stranger to our eyes, bearing a new name and walking a new life. The morning light saw Artego taking her mark and leaving that place in search of his own hiding place.

Tynia is still looking for ingredients in this land to slow my illness. She has tried many times to convince me to go back to Kelfia for more elixir, but it is still too dangerous. In a few days, it will be too late anyway. No recollection of the past will remain in my consciousness, and my role will be over. My spirit is strong, but my body and mind are just too weak to continue. I am leaving behind a list of the remaining tasks and the key. The right soul will be able to complete them, and with spirit and skill, their meaning will be understood. I now see that this road has carried our footsteps far too long, so it is time for someone else to bear these marks.

By now, your fingers must have given life to this page, so never forget these words. Follow your heart. Be humble as you learn, but defend every dream with passion and pride. What you leave behind is the reason; the tears and scars are the price.

The scarlet sky will roar your name with thunder if you are who we hope you are.

BEFORE WE WALK THIS PATH

I am now as old as Kharlo was when he wrote that last page—or at least as old as he looked.

Nowadays, I would venture to say that most people around here know me as an honorable man, a fellow townsperson. In their eyes, I am just another farmer working long hours to bring food to his table. A helping hand for some and a useless nuisance for others. In the end, most content themselves with saying that I am a man who will fade away without adding any color to the history of this region.

I appreciate their simplicity.

Some others go deeper and tell stories about my head not being right, or how a strange illness turned me into a cranky old man that everyone should avoid.

I respect their imagination.

But I know there are a few out there—maybe a handful—who think that there is more to me than I am willing to share. Something untold. Those feelings about who I am and *how* I am don't live in harmony in their heads. They sense it. Something buried deep inside of me that is difficult to grasp. Something elusive.

I admire their senses.

I believe I am a good man, but I think it is fair for you to know that everything that is said about me has some truth in it.

Maybe I should start by introducing myself. My name is Jonek. As you've probably noticed by reading these few lines, I am neither a scribe nor a historian. Even though I've learned many tongues, using a quill and ink for more than a few moments is something I rarely do.

I learned to raise crops from my mother; her hands were gifted in giving life to plants in almost any kind of soil. But she was the one blessed with that ability, not me. I do my best to harvest goods for trading, but I have to confess that farming is not my passion. Now, I say that with the deepest respect, because inheriting some of that knowledge from my mother did save my life on one occasion.

Regardless, after years of fighting with my conscience, I've decided to write what you have in your hands at this very moment. This decision didn't cross my path by mere luck. This morning, four words spoken to me traveled deep inside my mind, making every thought of carrying these secrets to my grave collapse.

 3

Holpoka and his two grandchildren joined me while I was harvesting mushrooms. It was a good day for that; the sunlight could barely filter to the ground through the morning mist, and the smells and sounds were just the right sort of medicine to refresh me after a long night's sleep.

I was on my knees cutting some flatheads when I suddenly felt pain in my hand.

In the beginning, I thought it was just another reminder of my age, but it didn't take long for me to realize it was something different. I desperately rubbed my hands together, trying to dispel that old sensation that my skin wasn't used to anymore, but it was too late.

My body and mind tried to react, but I struggled to keep them focused, so I closed my eyes and rested my forehead on my walking staff. Images, words, and sounds flew by the hundreds through my mind, flooding all my senses. Who? Where? I knew someone was in danger. Is it happening now? The future? Or were they just scenes from the past coming back to haunt me?

"Breathe Jonek, breathe," I whispered.

That blurred flow of colors in my mind slowed until an image finally took shape. I tried to pull myself up, I tripped over my own feet and ended up with my face buried in the grass. Not much I can say about that—I am not young anymore, after all.

I got up and whirled around, looking for Holpoka. He was far away, almost by the road. I had no other choice. I started walking as fast as I could. I glanced at the back of my hand and there it was—the symbol burning bright on my old, wrinkled skin. This was for real.

The children were already out playing in the cool, refreshing fog, so I ventured into the woods just deep enough so they couldn't see me. Somkher and Filvra were sitting on the ground propped up against an old cedar cleaning mushrooms. It felt like a lifetime, but I was able to reach them just in time. A sentinel, maybe six feet long, was climbing the back of the tree and was starting to split. Hideous beast—I couldn't believe there were still some around.

Those instincts buried in me for so many years took over. Pieces of bark and wood splintered into the air as the cracking sound echoed across the valley. I saw the children drop down onto the grass and cover their faces as the light illuminated their surroundings.

Unfortunately, the beast didn't go down quietly. Just moments after, a sharp pain and blood running down my leg alerted me to a deep cut just above my knee. Nothing to worry about—I'd survived worse. As for the beast, it was still twisting headless on the ground when I pushed it aside with my foot.

"Da Jonek, is that you?" Somkher asked.

The little ones were holding each other, covered in bark and grass. They kept shivering but slowly got to their feet as they looked at me.

"Your grandfather is looking for you. Take the mushrooms to him—you have earned your coin."

They put the mushrooms in the basket and started walking back to the field. Then, suddenly, the young girl turned around and softly said those four words.

"Were we in danger?"

Silence was the only thing I could offer. My face probably showed far too well the devastation caused by that question, so they didn't wait for an answer. Her brother pulled her arm and they continued on their way—just in time for them not to see my eyes getting misty.

Many faces inside of me tried to answer that child's question with all the air in their lungs. I felt like I was going deaf listening to those voices, but they slowly faded as the children walked farther into the field. I looked down and watched the beast closing its mouths one last time, two heads twitching where once there had been only one.

"Yes, my child, we were very much in danger." I whispered.

***

I cut a few leaves from a Virkelas bush and chewed them to form a plaster to cover my wound. It's too bad that my blood and the black venom will forever stain those leggings . . . they were my favorites.

Their venom was painful, but it was not lethal for me. I've been immune to it since the time of the great white eclipse. I grabbed the tail of the sentinel and walked into the forest, leaving a trail of blood behind. I think I reached the twin meadows by mid-morning, and even though I wasn't bleeding anymore, burning pain still coursed through my leg.

I hung the beast on a branch and sat down to take a look at my wound. By then, the symbol on the back of my hand was gone, so I couldn't help turning my face toward the sky and thanking my ancestors for that. I let my head rest on the grass and closed my eyes. After a few moments, a distant sound brought me back from that peaceful reverie. What a welcome, healing sound for my soul. His shadow passed over me a few times until he finally landed a few steps from me—my friend of many years and my brother in battle. We risked our lives for each other countless times, and both of us managed to make it out alive. I remember someone saying that when we were together, people could see two warriors—two hearts—but only one soul.

The mighty falcon bowed his head as a sign of respect, so I responded in kind. He moved closer to my wound and cocked his head so that his eyes gazed at me.

"I'll live, old friend," I said aloud, maybe to comfort myself more than him. "I've just gotten slower and clumsier after all these years."

In response, the falcon opened his wings, revealing patches of bare skin, a seemingly humble way of acknowledging that time had taken its toll on him too. Memories were shared in silence as my fingers passed over his feathers and he responded in his own quiet language.

"I was thinking that maybe we should let others know about our secret, just in case there are more of these around," I said, pointing at the sentinel. "Soon you and I will leave these lands forever, and no one will know what to do. Someone must be prepared."

The sun glistened off his feathers as he nodded. Our eyes made contact one last time before he leapt off to the skies, taking that evil snake with him.

I stayed there resting, then wandered in the forest for many hours before heading back to the farm. I didn't think I was walking that slowly, but the sun was beginning to die behind the mountains when I finally saw her standing in front of our house.

She probably felt a thorn in her heart when she saw me limping back to the front step, but she remained calm until I was a few steps from her. We held each other and cried until the night took over the sky, then we went inside to take care of my wound and have something to eat.

She was fairly quiet during our meal, even though I tried my best to distract her with other topics. It was futile. I put two fingers inside my cup and rubbed the back of my hand, trying to drown what remained of that terrible sensation. I leaned into the back of my chair and looked at her.

"You're right. I think it's time," I said softly.

Her face kindly offered me one of those brief, unreadable smiles that always ensnare my heart and she quietly walked into the next room. There, over a small table, she laid out clean parchment, ink, and a few candles. She walked behind me, leaned into plant a soft a kiss on my head, and walked into our bedroom.

Now, you should know that by allowing you to read these lines, I am breaking my word—a promise I made a long time ago when my hair was dark and I was being told my part on the quest.

"Keep what you know to yourself, young man. It is better this way for your people."

That is the last thing he said before blending into the shadows of that cold night. For many years I thought about that promise, but it wasn't until today that I finally realized that you and your children deserve to know how close you were to losing what you have today. All of it.

It is well known that some word of this has been shared with others since the early days. Every generation has poured a few facts into big bowls of imagination, cooking up legends sometimes even more amazing and mysterious than the truth. It has happened before, and I have no doubt it will happen again in the future.

There is just one rule. I will unlock every door but the last one. That one is yours. I honestly wish I could've offered you more than this simple, ungraceful narrative; but unfortunately, my time is running short.

"At this very moment, common folk, warriors, children, creatures, and many other powers are forfeiting their existences to ensure that life can continue for the rest of us in freedom and peace. We, the ones who know, must honor them every time we witness a new morning, feel the touch of a loved one, or are blessed with the briefest sound of life."

Sometimes I close my eyes and can still see the face of that man as he said these words. You should never forget them.

As for me, I now believe that everyone I've known, loved, and even seen die because of my actions is counting on me to embark on this last journey at your side. This is their story.

Now, unlike how it was for me, you have a choice. You can close this book at this very moment and follow your life as you know it. Deep inside, we all understand.

But if you have chosen differently, then you should know that it's safe for you to touch the Kelfian pages, as they were sealed a long time

 7

ago. It is much safer this way. Trust me.

It took only five days for my life and the lives of my friends to change forever, so I think there is no better place for us to start this journey than by reliving what happened during the fair the year I turned thirteen.

Well, we had better begin. As one Zatokam priest once said to me (while standing on my chest, I might add), "Let's start moving, young man. I see many mountains ahead, and I don't think they are willing to move closer to us."

CHAPTER 1. THE INITIATION

Now stay close and let me take you back to the day before.

Five. Just five more days and my thirteenth birthday would've brought me my most anticipated gift—a real bow. That was the time when my clothes remained all dirty and torn regardless of how many times my mother fixed them for me.

I was strong for someone of that age, mainly due to the work I did around the house. My mother and I lived on the outskirts of Ferdhen, a small, lonely town that sprung up just south of the Bhormak Mountains and right at the edge of the Stapian forest. Our ancestors traveled to these lands from kingdoms far away. One day as they traveled, they caught sight of the sparkling waters of our river dividing the grassland and decided to stop there to rest and eat. Twenty-six generations have passed since then, and we are still here. Nobody remembers what their original destination was anymore, but if it wasn't here, then they are certainly taking a very long break in that journey.

Four activities sustain life in these lands: raising crops, hunting, fishing, and trading. Well, at least that's what Yilian's father used to say to his customers back then. But all alone as it was, Ferdhen was by no means a quiet place. We had the largest market, a place where anybody could learn to read and write, and we hosted the most important fair south of the Bhormaks.

Many visitors passed through our lands all year long on their way to other places. It was the perfect layover to replenish food and other supplies before challenging the mountains or stepping into the forest. On those days, my mother bustled over to a place in the market where she sold food, clothes, and clay pottery from sunrise well into the night. Travelers were not only our best customers, but also our main source of news from beyond our lands.

For my friends and I, the real treasure was the folklore and tales that some of them brought from afar. Stories of heroes battling dark warriors, mysterious wizards using their powers to fight good and evil, and countless descriptions of creatures that would make your skin shiver, even in daylight. All of those stories, true or not, nourished our imagination and gave us great inspiration for playing and dreaming.

Unfortunately, my mother didn't share those dreams with me. I'll never forget the day that I took one of her knives and started slicing the air, locked in a duel with an imaginary foe. Everything was fine until I fell off the kitchen chair and the knife barely missed my face. I was maybe eight at the time.

She ran to see if I was alright and quickly snatched the knife from me. She told me that knives and swords were not for children. She was so furious that she pulled a big potato from a sack and put it on the table. Using the same knife, she sliced it in half with one loud stroke and looked at me.

"Jonek, a sword is just as sharp as this knife. I don't think you could even hold the weight of a small sword—even the smallest are bigger than this paltry thing. Now tell me, why do you want one? What would you do with it?"

"I would use it to protect you, mother," I said with my strongest voice.

"To protect me? From who?"

"From wolves and bears."

She sat in front of me and leaned back, exhausted. "You need more than a sword for that, my son. Those animals are bigger and stronger than you."

I remember, at that moment, looking deep into my mother's eyes. "I will fight them for you, mother. I am not afraid."

I never asked my mother what she saw in my face at that very moment, but her eyes filled with tears as she held me tightly in her arms. At that time, I couldn't tell whether she was proud or worried about me. Now I know it was a little bit of both.

The truth is, even today, I am not sure if I would've fought one of those creatures at that age. Maybe not, but that brief moment of foolish bravery did earn something for me. My mother agreed to buy me the best bow she could find—under two conditions. The first was that I would wait until my thirteenth birthday to get it (which certainly felt like a lifetime to me). But it was her second request that made the first one almost unbearable. I had to promise that I wouldn't touch any real weapons until then.

That was certainly a hefty price to pay for a bow, but after thinking about it, I wasn't going to lose that opportunity. I agreed to her terms.

Needless to say, my years between eight and thirteen didn't pass quietly. It is a fact of life that no child can survive the tingling sensation of breaking a few rules here and there, and I wasn't the exception.

Of course, you pay the price for your choices later in life, but this is the way we all learn. Most of my friends got their hands on small wooden weapons while they were very young, so it didn't take long for some of their swords and bows to land in my hands. By mere chance. Really.

Yes, I got used to handling those toys of war early in my life. My friends and I played with them day and night. Of course, I always did it far away from town so as not to jeopardize getting that bow from my mother—a rather unfair situation for my friends, who had to walk long distances just to play with me. Now that I think about it, they almost never complained. Either my words were convincing, or they just didn't want to argue with me. Especially while I was wielding those toys.

So as you may have guessed, I wasn't always a farmer. As you will soon realize, my beginnings were more reckless. It took countless cuts and bruises for me to learn how to defend myself, but I never quit. Instead of playing the usual games of our age, I was always eager to engage anyone in battle using whatever I had in reach, even just sticks.

This passion for the arts of war drove me to go beyond some boundaries that I wouldn't recommend that anyone cross (at any age). In those early years, I used to climb high into a tree close to where Ferdhen's soldiers trained. One day, I was lying on a branch and leaned out a bit too far as my eyes tracked a friendly duel among soldiers. I still remember the sudden rush as I tumbled down onto that large bush and rolled to the ground a good five steps away from the tree. A few guards ran to where I was, brandishing their swords.

"What is your name and flag? Answer!"

"Jonek," I said, waving off the cloud of dust around me.

"Spy! What is your flag?"

"My flag?"

The elder soldier lowered his sword. "You. I've seen you in town. What were you doing up there?"

"I was trying to learn how to fight with a sword, Da Grokpel." I glanced furtively up at the branch I fell from.

"How to use a sword?" he asked.

I realized there was no point in lying, so I told them how I often came to watch them train. One thing was for sure—they weren't pleased.

I wasn't truly worried about being discovered. What I was really nervous about was word of this finding its way to my mother. I stood, waiting silently for their next move, when another voice broke the silence from afar.

"If you are trying to learn from Grokpel, you have a long road ahead, young man. He is a fine soldier, but I wouldn't consider him a master with the sword. And his archery skills? Well, they certainly need some polishing."

A man walked out from behind a tree some twenty paces away from us and took his helmet off. At first, the soldiers lining up in front of me obscured my view of his face as they saluted him in the stoic royal protocol.

"Commander Lobokan! We weren't expecting you until next month."

"I know, Grokpel. That is exactly the reason I am here," he said as he approached. "The king wants to know how well the garrisons are protecting their territories."

Grokpel and the others made way for the commander, who sighed. "It seems that you and your men are skilled enough to capture a boy who has been watching everything you do for months thanks to his slip-up falling from a tree, but I am greatly disappointed in your ability to notice a group as big as mine marching into your region unnoticed. Where are your scouts?" The commander unsheathed his sword and twirled it once in his hand, observing the sun glint off the clean blade.

I was still sitting on the ground, but I was able to see (in between soldiers' legs) a long column of fighters emerging from the forest on the far end of the field. They were wearing the king's seal on their chests and riding magnificent brown and black horses. Once they were close, the soldier riding in front raised his hand, signaling the riders to dismount and form two lines behind the commander. Their faces looked rough and fearless. I counted twenty-four of them.

The commander turned to look at me. "Young man, what did you say your name is? Err, Yanik?"

"Jonek, my liege," I said, stumbling to my feet.

"How old are you, boy?"

"Old enough to be a soldier," I said as I offered him a soldier's salute.

For a moment, I thought the man was going to laugh, but he controlled that impulse and smiled. "Let us rest and eat. We will start the inspection in the afternoon."

The commander grabbed my shoulder and directed me to the far end of the line, where he raised his hand and dismissed the soldiers. As you can imagine, I remained quite silent as the man stared at the mountains while taking his gauntlets off.

"Jonek, I am summoning you back here this afternoon. There is a matter that I would like to discuss with you."

"Am I in trouble?"

"That will be determined later. Just make sure to be back before supper." The man walked away, leaving me alone with my questions.

I left those grounds debating my situation in absolute silence. It was so hard for a boy my age to even comprehend the kind of trouble I was in. My mind rushed in all sorts of directions. What would happen to me if I decided to come back—or not—that afternoon? If I did, would I be taught a lesson? Would I be interrogated? Or worse, would my mother be summoned too?

It was unusual for our town to be visited by royal Wasps, and even more so for a boy like me to exchange words with any of them. The Wasps are elite forces who remain close to the king but are known to be deployed in areas where conflict is imminent. New questions circled in mind. Are we at war? Were they pursuing someone through our lands? Or maybe they were here to make Lord Nutrec—the infamous leader of a well-known band of outlaws in the region—finally pay for their crimes. That kind of information would've been as valuable as gold to me. But what if the commander was just going to teach me a lesson in front of the Wasps and the local soldiers? (In case you're wondering, we called them Wasps because of their outfits. Most of their clothes were tailored in brown cloth and leather, but their armor glittered yellow under the sun). To be honest, even though I knew I was in trouble, being close to the Wasps fulfilled one of my most cherished childhood dreams.

It wasn't until I crossed the river and saw my reflection in the water that I saw the aftermath of my fall from the tree. My forehead and neck were covered in dirt and dry blood. I had no broken bones, but I could feel bruises swelling all over my body. I ran as fast as I could to get home before my mother.

I could've gone to any of my friends' houses to clean up and even borrow some clothes, but there was one slight problem. My mother and I always met at noon to eat together.

It didn't matter whether we were busy, far away, or angry with each other—we always met at midday to share what food we had. That was our unspoken way of reminding us that we were there for each other, together but alone.

That being said, I wasn't expecting a pleased smile if my mother saw my clothes ruined and my skin bruised and bloody so early in the day.

After a short trek, I finally caught sight of our house in the distance. No smoke was coming from the chimney, and I didn't see our wagon anywhere. I ran inside and dunked my head in a bucket of water, then took my shirt off and used it to clean my face and arms. Once I put on clean clothes, I went back to the kitchen and sat down.

My heartbeat was finally slowing down when someone opened the door. My mother and her long-time helper, a young lady named Zilhana, arrived at noon on the dot. To my good fortune, something happened at the market that morning that got the two of them eagerly chatting away for a few minutes too long. They were so immersed in their conversation that my interaction with them was mostly limited to passing food and utensils around. I discretely covered my face and ate as fast as I could. I even left a large piece of my favorite sweet bread untouched so I could gingerly walk away from the kitchen and hide in my room.

My mother left me a list of chores to complete that afternoon before I met up with her back at the market. Honestly, I was thankful for being tasked with all those chores, because they kept my mind away from my main concern—whether or not I should go back to see the commander. Knowing the region as well as I did, I knew I had excellent chances if it came to hiding in the woods (or even the mountains) and never being found.

In the end, my honor overcame my fears; it was the right thing to do anyway. Facing the consequences of your actions is unavoidable in life. You can face them sooner or later, but I learned early in life that time only makes it worse if you wait. I rushed through some of the chores, but I left everything nice and orderly before I started down the road back to the post.

I tried to stay calm along the way, but I felt my heart nearly bursting out of my chest by the time I cleared the edge of the woods and saw the military grounds in the distance.

A large group of soldiers was practicing with swords and shields, others with bows and arrows. It was odd to see them so active at this time of day. The rest were training with larger weapons, mostly spears, maces, axes, and some others I didn't quite recognize. I crept toward the archers and watched dozens of arrows hitting their targets, some accurately, others not so much. I was observing them so intently that I barely heard the voice behind me.

"It takes two or three years for a soldier to master archery. They must practice every day in all types of weather." I turned around and saw the commander standing not too far from me. "It takes thousands of arrows for them to realize the secret. It is not just the stance, or the tension of the string, or even the way your fingers release the arrow." He paused. "It is the wind," he said at last, releasing small pieces of grass into the air. "Everything is important, but knowing how the forces in the air will guide your arrow is what separates an apprentice from a marksman. That and having good eyes, of course."

We stayed there watching the arrows slice the air for some time, then walked toward an area where a large group was practicing with swords. The noise of those blades colliding soon grew too loud for me. We kept walking toward the far end of the main building, where a table and some chairs waited under the shade of a big tree. The commander sat down and asked me to take the chair in front of him. There were many items on that table: maps, parchments, pouches, quills, a few vials with ink, and even some food.

"Jonek, please tell me again why you were hiding in that tree," he said quietly as he poured some wine into a goblet.

"To learn. I've been following how the soldiers train for some time now."

"Learn what? How to become a soldier? It is not common for someone of your age to even be comfortable around soldiers. Most people, young and old, are afraid of them. Wouldn't you rather be spending your time elsewhere?"

"I am not afraid of them. I just want to learn how to fight."

"Why are you so eager to learn these skills? I can understand learning archery for hunting, but it seems that your interests go beyond the bow and arrow."

"How old do I need to be to protect my mother?"

"Is your mother in danger?"

"No, but I think someone should protect her if it comes to that."

"Maybe your father should take care of that."

I turned my eyes away as he finished that sentence. "I never met my father. He died before I was born."

The commander's face briefly lost its strong lines as he leaned back on his chair. "Are you the eldest in your family?"

"I am the only son."

The commander didn't offer another word. He quietly left the chair and walked a short distance away. "Blades are still too heavy for you, so I think the bow is your best option. Jonek, I am willing to make a deal with you, man to man."

I was still trying to understand the meaning of those last few words when he turned around and pointed toward the groups of soldiers sweating buckets.

"I must ensure that these men are at their best, not only when I visit them, but at all times. Grokpel is a good man, but he has grown far too close to his people, and that's creating a serious lack of discipline. No, I need someone else—someone I can trust to keep me informed of what takes place at this garrison. Unfortunately, it is far too difficult for me to visit every town in this kingdom as often as I would like."

"Are you asking me to be a spy for you?"

He walked back to the table and took his seat. "Not a spy, an observer. You will be allowed to visit these grounds and witness the soldiers' training without the need to climb trees anymore."

"I don't think they will respect me if they know what I am doing for you."

"They have no choice. It is by the command of the king, and it will happen whether they like it or not. Make no mistake—I will use any means necessary to ensure that they are ready to protect this town. I've been thinking about this since I met you this morning. Please follow me; I'll make sure Grokpel and his men are clear on this."

He didn't let me say another word. We walked to the center of the grounds and he whispered something to one of his Wasps. This soldier blew a small horn and everyone gathered almost immediately, forming a circle around us.

Just as the last soldier folded into formation, the commander said in his booming voice, "It has been a long time since I visited Ferdhen. Throughout my travels, I've been fortunate to cross paths with members of my family every now and then, but this is the first time I have had one of them fall from a tree in front of me. I want everyone to meet Jonek, my nephew."

My body froze as he said those words.

"I've just learned that Jonek and his mother are living outside this town. In a few years, Jonek will follow our path and become a soldier, but until that time arrives, I am allowing him to visit this post as often as he wants so he can start learning what this life is about."

Some of the soldiers glancing sidelong at me must have noticed the shock on my face, but all of them kept their attention on the commander. The soldier blew the horn again, and four Wasps took a few steps toward the center of the circle. One of them performed a routine with his sword and shield and then returned to the formation. The second took his bow and aimed high into the sky before releasing an arrow. He lowered his bow, bowed to us, and got back in line. Moments later, the arrow came streaking back and landed inside the circle just a couple steps in front of us. The last two soldiers stepped forward and engaged in a duel using daggers. Even though their blades barely missed each other, their faces didn't show any hesitation; clearly they were masters of that skill.

One soldier who seemed to be the commander's right hand, walked closer and stood in front me. "To face the trial, you will need to be initiated." He took a dagger from a satchel and showed it to everyone, then he offered it to me. "Look at it closely, get acquainted with its craftsmanship, but be careful with the blade. Handle it with respect."

It was a flawless weapon, not bigger than a cooking knife but heavier. The blade had some markings engraved on it, and it had a small green gem encrusted in the center of the pommel. I was still feeling the leather on its grip when the commander put his hand on my arm.

"Jonek, use the dagger to draw a symbol on the ground."

"A symbol?"

"Yes, something to identify you. Your own mark."

I felt pity for that shiny blade as it touched the dirt in front of me. I didn't have anything specific in mind, so I hesitated for a moment and finally drew a "J" with a vertical line on its right side, a small circle at the bottom, and three horizontal lines crossing the top of the letter.

The soldier who gave me the dagger called upon an old man standing by the stable. This elder approached and spent a few moments looking at my symbol before taking the dagger from me and leaving. The commander asked me to choose two soldiers from the circle around us. I was impressed by the skill of that archer, so I didn't hesitate to point at him. Then a soldier juggling a dagger in his hand caught my eye, so I thought he'd be a good choice. Both acknowledged by raising their hands.

"Let us welcome Jonek to his initiation!" the commander shouted.

The soldiers cheered as they broke formation and walked closer to me, placing their hands on my head and shoulders, celebrating that moment with me. One thing is for sure—a lot of tension in my ten-year-old body was relieved as that unusual ritual ended.

A bell sounded nearby announcing mealtime, so we walked inside the building. I was guided into an area with no roof where four long tables sat filled with food of all kinds. Each soldier stood behind a chair, and Commander Lobokan asked me to take the seat to his right. Some discreet chuckles caught my ear, and I realized that the soldiers at the tables behind me couldn't see me because the back of my chair was so tall.

The commander motioned for us to take our seats, and the jangle of armor pounded in my ears as dozens of fighters sat at once. A few elegant ladies emerged from the kitchen and poured water and wine while others lit torches and candles around the room. Once the soldiers were busy eating, I took the opportunity to ask the commander about how that odd initiation process got started. Even though I barely whispered my question to him, he chuckled and raised a glass, eager to refresh the story for everyone. He drank some wine and began his tale.

This is how I remember it.

"Thirty-two generations ago, under the rule of King Canodet, the requirements to become a soldier were vast and strict. No one under the age of fifteen would even be considered for service. The king's only son, Prince Komippel, was thirteen years old when he approached his father and requested to be considered for the royal army. He must've been as eager as this young man!" he said, pointing a piece of bread at me.

"The path to becoming a soldier was—and remains to this day—one of the most demanding courses a man could walk in life. No distinctions, no privileges. Our laws command both nobles and commoners to start from the lowest rank. Ours is a path that is survived only by those exhaling devotion, perseverance, and honor with every breath.

"The king knew that if he yielded to his son's request, the prince would have to undergo all the dangers of the process, and that could mean the life of his only heir.

"The king, preoccupied about his son, talked to his closest advisors.

 18

After some deliberation, the three elders recommended that the king expose his son to some of the trials to validate whether the young boy was indeed ready to withstand military life. In the beginning, the king thought about dismissing that proposal, but he ultimately agreed and assigned them to devise such a trial for his son.

"The legend says that the elders summoned both king and prince by the Gate of Spring the following morning, fairly close to the edge of the forest. The elders placed three satchels by the gate and asked the prince to choose one of them. After some hesitation, the prince walked to the gate and made his choice.

" 'Do not open it yet!' an elder said as the other two brought back the remaining satchels.

" 'Let us see which paths you have left behind.'

"Both satchels were opened, and the elders presented two small items: a small silver bow and a golden dagger.

" 'Now show us your destiny, my liege.'

"The prince reached inside the satchel and paused briefly before pulling an unusual artifact from it. Some old scripts contained drawings of a wooden rod, maybe three or four fists long, dark in color, with a peculiar leather grip wrapped around the middle. The prince stared at the elders, begging for an explanation.

"The old men sighed. 'It seems you have chosen the hardest path of all. Your destiny is indeed to become a soldier, but not the kind you have in mind. You will defend your race against a darker evil—an evil born in a place this sky has never seen. You will leave other foes to your father's soldiers; those battles are not yours anymore. Remember that.'

"Our young prince, lost and disheartened by these words, fell to his knees. But the elders had more to add.

" 'You are not alone. There are others who have joined this quest over the last eight centuries. But you must know that you will need to master body, mind, and magic to endure this road.'

"The king was truly concerned after hearing those words, but he remained silent, as he thought the elders were trying to portray a harsh and discouraging picture to the prince in order to make him reconsider his request. The prince was asked to draw a symbol on the ground using that rod. After Komippel finished, one elder took the rod from his hands and walked away with it.

"The king, the prince, and the other two elders remained by the gate

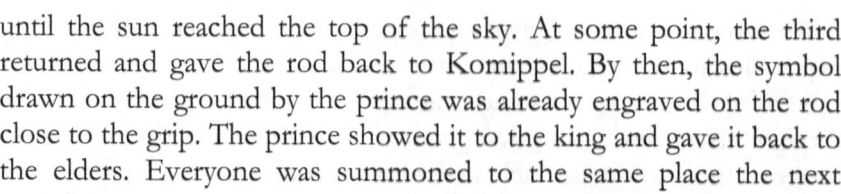

until the sun reached the top of the sky. At some point, the third returned and gave the rod back to Komippel. By then, the symbol drawn on the ground by the prince was already engraved on the rod close to the grip. The prince showed it to the king and gave it back to the elders. Everyone was summoned to the same place the next morning.

"While there were many questions in the mind of the young prince, he remained silent to avoid giving the impression he wasn't ready for the challenge. The next morning, father and son returned to the gate, where two elders were already waiting. Just as on the previous day, everyone waited for the third to return—this time from the forest. Once they were all together, an elder said, 'The weapon has been hidden in the forest. The prince will have to go there and retrieve it. Alone. If he returns with the weapon, we will train him to master the arts of war and magic. If he doesn't succeed or chooses to cease the search, he will have to wait until he turns fifteen to start down this path he has chosen.'

"The elder who had entered the forest stepped forward, placing a wrinkled hand upon the boy's shoulder. 'The road to your weapon's resting place is treacherous, and you will need heart, intelligence, and knowledge to walk through it. We cannot offer any words to help you on this quest, but we can give you three items instead.'

"The old man motioned for the prince to open his hands. The first item he placed there was a small frog of green and blue that briefly stayed on the hand of the prince but swiftly jumped away, disappearing into the grass. The second was soil of a very dark color that felt wet and warm in the prince's hands. The last item was a small, brown and green piece of bark with a very soft surface on one side. Old folklore even says it smelled sweet when it was rubbed with your fingers.

"Komippel was still examining the last two items when another elder retrieved a satchel and walking staff from the other side of the gate.

" 'My Prince, there is food and water in this satchel. The staff will be your only weapon on this journey, so be careful and choose your actions wisely.'

"Centuries have passed and no account exists of the outcome of his trial. Whether the prince found the weapon or not remains unknown. All we do know is that he became one of our mightiest kings." The commander paused. "Unfortunately, his own resting place has no mark on our maps. All that is known is that he disappeared during the northern wars." He glanced at me.

"Since the days of Komippel, an initiation trial is granted to anyone under the age of fifteen who seeks to become a soldier. I believe this to be a great opportunity for a young soul to test both skill and spirit. Today, we don't offer the same choices the elders put in front of Prince Komippel, much less a weapon like the one mentioned in the scrolls, but our craftsmen have created these fine daggers for this purpose."

The old man who had taken the dagger from me shuffled into the room and put the box in front of the commander.

"Times have changed since the days of Komippel, but his legend and tradition have passed from king to king until this day. Not everyone knows that we carry his mark on our flag and shields."

The commander left the table and approached a royal flag hanging on a wall. He pointed to the center and slowly traced the shape of the symbol with his fingers. Even though I had seen our flag many times, I never devoted much attention to the details—the letter "K" with a small circle touching the top of its left side, and a brief horizontal line crossing the backbone of the letter at its bottom. That was the symbol the prince drew on the ground in front of the elders.

The commander returned to his large chair, refilled his cup, and continued his meal while others slowly broke off and regaled each other with their own stories. Descriptions of epic battles and some old poems were also shared that afternoon. Once the plates and goblets were empty and the tables cleaned, the commander called for everyone's attention. He pulled the wooden box closer to him and waited until there was absolute silence in the room.

"The trial begins."

The rest of the soldiers stood up and responded:

"The voice of your heart,
the blood of your soul,
the tears of your mind,
the eyes of our fathers will see."

Lobokan opened the box, allowing the dagger to shine and glitter under the candles. He took it out and carefully passed his fingers over the blade before handing it over to me. My emotions rushed through me and my stomach knotted once I had it back in my hands. As you might suspect from listening to Prince Komippel's story, my symbol was already engraved on the blade. I looked at it for a moment and offered it back to the commander, but he pointed to the soldier sitting next to me, so I passed it to him.

As everyone took turns admiring my dagger, the two soldiers I had selected earlier were asked by the commander to stand by his side. They took their weapons and a satchel brought to them earlier and stood behind Lobokan. Once the dagger made its way back to him, he entrusted it to the two soldiers who then promptly left the room and disappeared into the night.

The rest of the men made their way out, leaving me with just the commander and the two ladies who were cleaning the tables.

"Don't worry, Jonek. These fine women are as loyal as my closest soldiers. They won't share anything that happens here with anyone, much less your mother." The ladies offered a subtle smile and continued their chores.

"Well, Jonek, you have now acquired some benefits—and some responsibilities. A soldier from my personal guard will be waiting for you on the last day of every month. He will be by the green boulder between the cemetery and the forest trail. You will give him a sealed letter containing a full report of the activities for this garrison. Trust me; only my eyes will read what you write, so be detailed and forthcoming." The commander smiled. "Now that we are family, the local soldiers will offer you and your mother special protection; they will make sure nothing happens to either of you. I will leave instructions never to refer to you or your mother as my relatives, for your own protection."

The commander paused, noticing that my eyes kept flitting back to the wooden box that once housed my dagger, so he put his hand on top of it.

"Yes, you've earned the same choices as Prince Komippel. You could search for your weapon, and if you find it, I will arrange for you to become officially enlisted, or you can wait until you are fifteen to do so. Jonek, don't let disappointment dwell for too long inside of you if you fail to find your weapon. Kings and peasants have gone through these trials, and most of them are still searching for their daggers." The commander pushed the box aside and left his chair. "And they are not alone. Even I am still going through the same ordeal. Many years have passed, and mine is still hidden somewhere south of Carudhan Bridge. Well, at least that is where I think it is. Many people throughout the centuries have tried unsuccessfully to find their daggers, and some have even searched for Komippel's weapon but have wasted their lives in the process. Always remember that." The commander walked back to the table and poured himself some more wine. "I'll see you in the morning. You must have a lot to think about, and you need some rest."

I left the post that night not knowing that years would pass before I would see commander Lobokan again.

I always hoped he would feel proud of me for keeping my word and meeting his messengers every month to give them my letters. I can say now that I am also grateful to him for making me practice my writing skills almost every day. At that young age, you never value how important it is to know how to read and write proficiently.

However, not everything was perfect. Even though I did spend many hours learning their moves and techniques, the soldiers never allowed me to touch a real weapon again. In the end, using sticks, poorly crafted bows, and a strong mind helped me become proficient in many of their disciplines, even by their own standards. It took time, but eventually I earned their respect.

You are probably wondering if I ever found my dagger. Well, that night was painful for me. I was so mesmerized by those events that my steps took me back home instead of to the market. I was opening the door when I realized I was in the wrong place. I bolted off as fast as I could, but in the darkness I tripped and skinned my knees on the ground more than once on the way. I finally reached my mother's stall at the market and saw Zilhana packing merchandise while my mother talked to some customers. She cocked an eyebrow when she caught sight of me.

"Well, Jonek, I don't know what time it is in your world, but in ours it's late. Did you forget about us?" It didn't take long for her to notice the dirt on my clothes and face. "Look at you! How will you become a responsible man when you can't even take care of your clothes? Shirts and leggings don't grow in trees, do you know that? Now go and help Zilhana with the crates."

It took longer than expected to load up. My mother received a shipment of fabrics and clay from the south, and even though most of the packages weren't heavy, some of them were big enough to make Zilhana and I sweat as we heaved them onto the wagon.

My mother talked all the way back home; she had this amazing ability to change topics without giving you any warning—and of course she was always upset because you weren't following every word. That

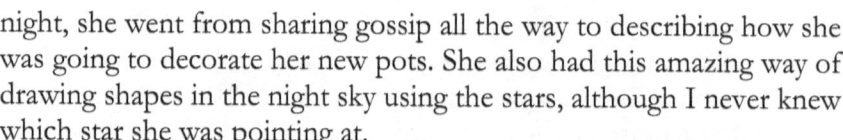

night, she went from sharing gossip all the way to describing how she was going to decorate her new pots. She also had this amazing way of drawing shapes in the night sky using the stars, although I never knew which star she was pointing at.

She must have eventually realized that Zilhana and I were too exhausted to participate, so she kept talking to herself until we got home, unloaded the wagon, and went inside. I always thought that her incessant jabbering was strange, but I later realized that she was probably doing it to stay awake.

Even though my body was slowly drifting off into the comfort of my bed, I was still able to feel my mother leaning over me, playing with my hair as she hummed that beautiful melody she had whispered for me every night for as long as I could remember.

***

I ran to the kitchen without even changing my clothes. There I saw a note from my mother asking me to meet her at the market. I grabbed an apple from a basket near the door and headed out toward the post. Now that I think about it, I ran a lot during those days. (Unfortunately, it was mostly due to my tendency to be late.) Even though the commander hadn't specified a time, I was planning on being there at sunrise.

Once I saw the garrison in the distance, I slowed down and straightened my rumpled clothes with a quick snap. I had no idea what to expect, but I was so angry with myself knowing that I was going to have to start the day by apologizing for my tardiness.

As I got closer, I noticed a lot of activity on the grounds; soldiers filed into formation, and long weapons were being distributed among them. Da Grokpel saw me coming and hailed me.

"Last night we received a message from the king's council," he said, slightly breathless. "There is a threat of an invasion from the hordes of the west, and they are requesting that we come to reinforce the frontiers. Commander Lobokan was summoned by the king and headed out at sunrise. He left this for you."

Da Grokpel tossed a large pouch to me and turned back to his work. Inside were two items: a piece of parchment and a leather glove with the royal seal on it. The parchment no longer exists, but the words written on it will forever live in my memory. "Jonek, the next time someone asks for your flag, just remember the seal on this glove and say the name of your king. For now, just look at the end of the field to the east."

It took me a few seconds to orient myself but I eventually turned my eyes eastward. Out there, very close to the edge of the forest, a Wasp was sitting on his horse, holding the royal banner as if he were guarding the gate of the capital city. I walked briskly at first but ended up running at full speed toward him.

I skittered to a stop in front of the horse, gasping for air. The soldier lowered his banner and dismounted, saluting me before taking a small pouch from inside his clothes. When I opened it, many small white petals fluttered out and were whisked away by the wind. I promptly closed the pouch to save the few left inside. Then, he carefully placed a small patch of fur in my hands. It was gray in color with some mottled tones of white and brown. It was very soft to the touch—from a wolf, perhaps. The last item was a stone that looked like a simple river pebble, but its colors were uncommon. Some thin lines decorated it; they were green or maybe blue. I don't remember anymore.

The soldier bid me farewell following the military protocol. He mounted his horse and quickly disappeared into the forest, leaving me standing there, staring at these items.

Those were the clues to find my dagger, it seemed, and the order in which they were shown to me must have had some meaning. At least that was my thinking. One thing was for sure—from that point on, it was up to me to take the next steps. Needless to say, I spent countless hours talking to people about flowers, wolves, and rocks, after which I took many a trek deep into the woods, doggedly searching for that dagger. As you can imagine, it was both an exciting and extremely frustrating experience.

A couple of years passed, and the boy who once lived that knight's dream had to go back to real life and work hard to help his mother. His muscles grew and his dexterity with weapons became more refined as he practiced. Behind his mother's back, of course.

Anyway, as I was saying quite a while ago, just five more days and my thirteenth birthday would've brought me my most anticipated gift—a real bow. Now, a real bow wasn't just a piece of wood and string to me. It meant something bigger—higher status. People around there had a deep respect for someone with the means for hunting.

Everyone knew that the nomads from the south made the best

bows in our land. Strange people, if I may say so. Nomads tend to move from place to place but are known to stay in the same spot for a few seasons if they like it. The ones from the south would only stay twenty-one days in the same place—not a day more, and not a day less.

Even though some people would say they spoke various languages, they were quiet among others most of the time. It was truly unfair, but most grown-ups considered them drifters—and saw drifters as bad people. It amuses me to think that our parents used to tell us that these nomads would come one night and take us children with them if we didn't behave or finish our food. Somewhat late, but I now value your reasons, mother.

They were the Satolgac tribe. All of them, from children to elders, traditionally wore long hooded cloaks at all times. They only uncovered their faces when they spoke to someone who wasn't part of their clan, mostly while trading. Someone told me once that the color of their cloaks meant some kind of rank in their society, but now that I think about it, most of their robes were fairly dark in color.

Even though they were experts in the art of crafting bows, they never hunted. Rather, they supported their families by trading. That didn't make any sense to me, but I guess my opinion wouldn't matter to them even now.

The Satolgac never followed any particular pattern during their migrations, so my excitement reached the sky when I saw them setting up their tents by our river that evening, just five days before my birthday. They even chose an area close to the bridge, so they were on my way to town—indeed, I was lucky.

At that point, I knew that my chances of getting a Satolgac bow could never be better.

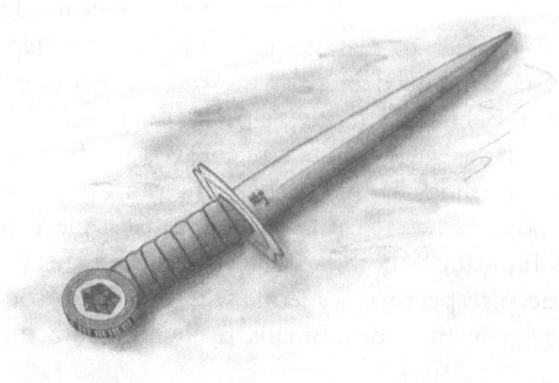

CHAPTER 2. SEVEN & TWO.

*H*ectic is the best way to describe the following morning.

My mother dragged me out of bed and sent me to the gardens to harvest some herbs and vegetables for the market. I slowly made my way through the house, trying my best to avoid being trampled by both ladies in their bustling, then grabbed a basket that was sitting by the door and slid out.

Once I stepped into the garden, I noticed that very few plants were left—likely the last of the season. I wasn't surprised, though. Even though we never had snow, the weather had been just right for it for the last few days. The cold wind was my only real motivation to finish that task and go back inside.

Once I returned, I huddled close to the fire and watched the show for a while. My mother and Zilhana were both running from room to room, parchment lists flapping in their hands as they moved items from crate to crate, counting them over and over again. To be fair, they did stop briefly here and there to cook, eat, change their clothes, and argue about, well, almost anything. Not that they stayed argumentative with each other for long. It was insane. Zilhana finally remembered I was there and put some food on my plate, but my mother took it from me and ate some before I was able to even dip my spoon into it.

Yes, that was a typical first day of the fair.

As I've mentioned before, the town of Ferdhen hosts the most important fair in the region. This gathering attracts visitors from the farthest lands looking to trade their goods—and compete in the games, of course.

Once I managed to defend my plate long enough to actually eat a few bites, I went out to feed the horse and pull the wagon closer to the door. I was ready to start loading some crates when I heard someone whistling by the main road. Perfect timing indeed! I rushed into the kitchen, grabbed my leather bag, and left the house without even a word to the ladies.

"Jonek! Where are you going?" My mother caught me.

"Uh, fishing with Yilian and Tobho," I said, glancing back at her.

"Fishing? But you don't have a fishing rod," she said, heading toward the door.

"I don't need one, mother."

Her face wrinkled into a light frown for a moment, then softened again. "Well, take care of yourself, and please try to come back with clean clothes! I'll see you at midday so we can eat at the fair."

I nodded and then ran as fast as I could to where my friends waited for me. Yilian, the shorter one, was carrying a long leather bag just like mine over his shoulder. His nose was the brightest shade of red in the morning cold. Tobho, the shabby fellow wearing an odd-looking hat, was trying to hold a tune on the ramikha I left at his house the day before. Both were fighting the cold weather but seemed ready to start the day.

"Take your mouth off my ramikha! I don't want to get your diseases," I muttered the last part as I dropped my bag to the ground.

"Thank you, Jonek," Yilian said, rubbing his temples. "My ears have been hurting since we left his house. Tobho, I know you don't want to hear this, but music is *not* for you."

Tobho smiled and blew one last note right toward Yilian's face before I snatched the ramikha from him. I was wiping it off on my clothes when a ray of sunlight made its way through the morning fog and splashed all around us.

"Perfect," I said, closing my eyes and holding my musical instrument as high as I could, making its colors shine in the sun.

"Do you have to do this every time the sun rises? Let's go! I'm cold," Yilian said as he rubbed his hands.

"Just wait. It's something I have to do if I have it with me."

Yilian drooped. "We're wasting time. Just so you know, I finished the arrows last night, and I have them right here in my bag."

That was all I needed to hear to stuff the ramikha in my pocket and pick up my sack. We made our way to the river and headed south until we lost sight of the town. Yilian and I kept stopping every now and then to wait for Tobho to catch up with us. It wasn't that he was a slower walker—he just liked to stop and look at *every single* miracle of nature, no matter how insignificant. A bird, a frog with mud on its head, rocks, and even one piece of bark floating down the river. He always had an explanation for it all, too. I still feel bad about it, but over the years we'd learned to ignore him, mostly. He didn't mind us doing that, though; he knew that deep inside, we respected him.

We kept walking south along the river bed until we arrived at one of our best fishing spots—Dragon's Breath Lagoon.

I have great memories of that place. The water itself was clear and peaceful but quite deep in some areas. The river fed the lagoon from an entrance some thirty steps wide on the north side, and in those days, it was partially blocked by two large trees that fell one on top of the other during a thunderstorm. Oddly, the water in this particular lagoon remained warm throughout the year. No one really knew why, but our ancestors believed that a dragon lived deep at its bottom, heating the water with its fire. Hence the name.

We all knew that dragons were just myths, so that story never stopped us from having some great times in the lagoon.

We could use the fallen trees as a bridge to cross over the entrance, but some of the branches were even better. Two or three were strong enough to hold our weight, so we used them to reach the waters closer to the center of the lagoon. They could hold our weight alright, but if we didn't balance ourselves carefully, we would inevitably end up in the water.

Tobho crouched behind a bush and retrieved a bow that we kept hidden there. Its craftsmanship was crude, and it actually looked more like a long stick, but I remember it being solid and effective. Yilian opened his bag and pulled out the arrows. Tobho and I couldn't contain our chuckles when we saw that Yilian had painted every part of them red—crudely, I might add—even the feathers.

"They look good, don't they? It took me all night to finish them. Let's tie the strings."

"They look . . . colorful for sure," I managed. "Are they sturdy? Do they have the same length as the others?"

"They're perfect, you fool! I even used my father's tools to make them."

"That doesn't make you a Satolgac," Tobho giggled as he used the end of the bow to mess up Yilian's hair.

"Well, there's only one way to find out—let's do some fishing!" I taunted as I grabbed three long strings coiled around some pieces of wood from my bag. Yilian and I tied one end of the strings to the back of the arrows while Tobho tied the other end to the roots of the fallen trees hanging close to the water.

I took the bow and arrows and walked on top of the tree until I was able to reach the second big branch. Yilian followed me but remained a few steps behind, making sure the strings didn't get tangled along the way.

Why a bow and arrow? Well, using fishing rods required a serious amount of patience. Unfortunately, none of us had much of that to spare those days. You could say that our method was more . . . direct. Yilian's job was to lure fish closer to the surface, mine was to put an arrow through them, and Tobho's was to pull them out of the water. Don't get me wrong, the tasks may sound easy, but performing them was not.

Yilian sat on a branch nearby, taking small pieces of bread from his pocket and pressing them with his fingers, shaping them into tiny flakes maybe as wide as a pea. We waited until the branches stopped moving and the surface of the water became clear enough to see the fish moving. Yilian chose a spot and carefully threw down a few flakes of bread.

Two or three gray shadows swam up from the depths and circled the bread still floating on the surface. I leaned forward and pulled back the bowstring. The arrow sliced through the air, and half of its length dove underwater.

"Did you get it?" Yilian asked, leaning forward and making the branch creak a little.

"No, I missed," I said, reaching down for another arrow.

"You missed?" Yilian hadn't even finished saying that when we saw the arrow pop back to the surface. "But how did you know?"

"Well, because I can see. The arrow passed three fingers to the right of the fish. That arrow isn't straight, Yilian."

"Of course it is. All of them are! Nuthek and I chose the hardest wood we could find, and I used my father's tools, remember? Maybe you didn't aim right." I turned around and cocked an eyebrow. He paused. "Well, maybe you aimed right but then the branch moved or the wind pulled it."

"Maybe," I said with a slight roll of the eyes as I walked back to the trunk of the tree. "But probably either the arrow isn't straight or the wood's not as hard as you say. Why did you put paint all over them?"

Tobho pulled the arrow out of the water and brought it back to us.

"You said that our weapons should look mighty. Well, red looks mighty to me."

"Yes, but too much paint could bend the wood! What kind of paint is this, anyway?" Tobho said as he dried the arrow with an old rag. "It's not coming off."

"Please don't paint them from now on, agreed? Tobho, do we have more arrows hidden nearby?"

"Not around here. There may be some by the eastern road, but it would take us most of the morning to get there and come back."

We sat there in silence thinking about our options. The morning was growing old, and we needed some fish before going back to town.

"Three fish will be fine," I said as I stood up. "Let's make these mighty arrows work." Yilian and Tobho didn't say anything, but they probably went back to their posts wondering how I was going to make those bent arrows fly straight. The visibility in the water was still good, but now the fish swam nervously.

Yilian threw more pieces of bread in the water and stayed low on the branch, muttering as if he were casting spells on the fish. I went back to my side of the stump, but this time I moved further away from the trunk. The branch trembled more with each step, so it got harder for me to balance my weight on it. I pulled the bowstring and whispered, "Jonek, they are just fish in a river. You know how they move, how they fight. Just some fish in a river."

My second arrow cut the air like red lighting. This time it plunged deeper, and for a moment, none of us dared take a breath. Everything stood still. Well, everything except the arrow. Yilian's mighty arrow remained vertical and jittered frantically.

"Pull the string, Tobho!" Yilian yelled as he stood up on his branch, dropping the rest of the bread into the water.

I was trying to balance myself on the branch when I saw a larger fish jumping out of the waves right by where the rest of Yilian's bread had landed. I instinctively took another arrow and pulled the bowstring again. Unfortunately, the branch bucked under me with all of our weight, and I was already falling when I released the arrow.

I was truly thankful that the water wasn't as cold as the river. I desperately tried to keep the bow from getting wet, but it went under with me. I rushed to the surface and whipped the water from my face, looking for my friends. My ears were plugged, so I wasn't able to hear whatever they were desperately yelling at me.

Even though Tobho was never fond of taking baths, he jumped into the water to pull the first arrow. I was able to hold onto a branch and noticed Yilian desperately yanking on the string of the other arrow. It was at that moment that I finally heard what they were saying.

"You lucky fool! Help Yilian pull them out!"

"Pull them out?" I tried to shout through a mouthful of water. I'm not sure how, but the last arrow went through the second fish from

31

side to side and caught another near its tail. Now all that mattered was not to lose them.

I threw the bow to shore and swam away from the tree until I was able to grab the string and pull the arrow close to me. It took some time, but as I struggled with the fish, argued with my friends, and swallowed some more water, I was able to grab both ends of the arrow, keeping the fish trapped in the middle.

There was just one problem, though—something I don't usually talk about. I can't stand touching fish.

Yes, that small inconvenience that brought more than enough shame to my otherwise solid prestige as a warrior. All my friends made fun of me because of it, but I can't help it. Even now, as an old man, the very thought is enough to make my skin crawl.

Maybe the fish could sense my distaste, as they kept twisting their bodies along that arrow until they could rub their slimy scales all over my hands. I couldn't stand that torture for long. I was able to feel ground under my feet, so I pushed myself up and threw the arrow (fish and all) out of the lagoon. One of them broke free as soon as it landed and started jumping desperately toward the water.

Tobho and Yilian chased the creature all over the place. They tripped and rolled, tumbling over each other until that slippery thing finally gave up and stilled, lifeless in their hands.

I walked out of the water and collapsed by their side, catching my breath. We struggled indeed, but got what we came for—three fish of very decent size ready to be taken to the fair. The sound of our own labored breathing was the only thing breaking the tranquility of that secluded lagoon. Then, suddenly, a flock of birds crashed desperately from the trees behind us.

I rolled over to take a better look at the trees and there he was. My body still hasn't forgotten the cold sensation that ran through my bones then.

Imagine the head of an enormous wolf, half-eaten by another beast, looking at you from a line of bushes under the trees. His eyes were coal black and he was panting heavily, blood and maggots oozing in thick globs from his gaping mouth.

Tobho froze immediately, and Yilian had just enough courage to whisper, "Looks hurt, almost dying. Think he smelled the fish?"

"Don't move," I said, barely moving my lips. "If he runs toward us, get in the water and swim away as fast as you can. Pull Tobho by his

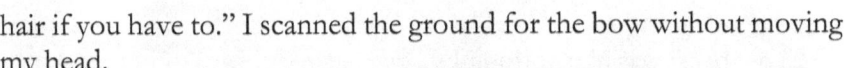

hair if you have to." I scanned the ground for the bow without moving my head.

To my good fortune, the bow was fairly close to me, so I picked it up as I slowly rose to my feet. The closest arrow was the one still stuck in the second fish we caught. Knowing how much I hate to touch fish, I still don't know how I managed to put my bare foot on top of its slimy scales and pull the arrow out in one swift jerk.

The wolf immediately turned his eyes toward me and slowly crept out of the bush.

Have you ever felt fear? Real fear? I certainly hadn't—until that moment. The beast was twice as big as a Stapian wolf with dirty, dark fur bristling head to tail and a white patch on his lower neck just above his chest. His head was scarred and decomposed, and he had large patches of skin missing, and even had bones sticking out in some parts.

But more than anything else, the way he was behaving wasn't normal. Wolves are dangerous in packs, but a single wolf would never try to get this close, especially if it was hurt.

I dug my feet into the mud to get a better stance and slowly pulled the bowstring. The wolf closed his mouth, and his eyes turned as red as fire. He took a few more steps and then stopped. I got a bead on his neck and released the arrow.

Even though it was wet and maybe bent because of Yilian's poor choice in paint, the arrow flew straight toward the beast. Unfortunately, I overlooked one small thing—the string was still tied to the arrow, and it got snagged in a branch. The arrow stopped less than two fingers away from the wolf. But the creature didn't move a single muscle, even after the arrow landed on the ground.

Yilian always said that it was as if the beast knew the range of the string, so he moved closer to challenge us. The wolf kept his eyes on us, his gaze unbending, but eventually he walked closer to sniff the arrow and then touch it with his paw.

Suddenly, the wolf raised his head, howling and growling toward the sky in absolute rage. We caught sight of his long, sharp teeth covered in blood. He looked at us one last time and jumped back into the bush, disappearing into the forest like a ghost.

I am not sure how long we stood there, frozen.

"We're lucky he didn't take the fish," Tobho managed, his voice trembling.

"I don't think he wanted our fish, Tobho," I said as I scanned the far edge of the lagoon.

"That beast was like nothing I've ever seen or heard of before. Have you?" Yilian said as he helped Tobho back to his feet.

"Never. I don't think this creature is even from around here. Let's get back to town. Now!"

Tobho stuffed the fish in Yilian's bag while Yilian brought back our sandals and I cut the strings using the head of an arrow. I told them to walk fast but to avoid running, as I didn't want to show that we were afraid. What a silly thought, really—we would've been easy prey for a beast like that either way.

Yilian and Tobho kept fighting to stay in front while I kept looking behind with the bow ready. We rushed through the forest for several agonizingly long minutes until we saw Ferdhen far in the distance. Without a doubt, the most beautiful sight of that day.

Once we joined other travelers making their way along the southern road, I realized that I was still holding the bow in my hand. We didn't have a hiding place nearby, and I was certainly not throwing it away, so we stopped by a creek, untied the string from it, wrapped a piece of cloth around one end to disguise it as a walking staff and brought it with me.

***

The sun was already high in the sky when we walked into town. In previous years, the fair took place mostly at the market and the open grounds around it. In that year, the fair had grown so big that it took over the entire town. Merchants and performers of all kinds were stationed in every street and corner of Ferdhen. Even though the day was still young, music filled the air wherever you walked, and endless chains of people were weaving through any open space, making it impossible to walk from one side of the street to the other.

Food and treats of all kinds exchanged hands, and tents offering all sorts of merchandise were already crowded with customers. Even the illusionists started early that day, playing tricks for young and old trying to earn some coin.

No words can describe how exciting those five days were for boys like us. Yilian was always eager to practice the trading skills he inherited from his father. Tobho waited all year to welcome those who offered food. For me, it was something else that captured my senses—the people. Those faces, their clothes, the strange accents and words with no meaning to me were gifts that still live in my memories even now. That year, the theater was built behind the bell tower. It didn't matter what kind of play it was—the theater was something we never missed.

As we had just finished enjoying some of the festivities, we caught sight of a few of our friends pushing through the crowd.

"Are you rich today?" one of them yelled.

"Not yet, but we will be shortly!" Yilian shouted back as he opened his bag and brandished the largest fish.

"Not bad," one of them said with an approving nod. "We already got our coins, so now we're waiting for Nuthek to come back. He's trading with some merchants in those tents." They pointed off to a section of canopies and then started their own little conversation among themselves.

Yilian looked at me. "Jonek, you better stay here while Tobho and I pay a visit to your favorite merchant. I don't think he's forgiven you yet." The two chuckled.

Yilian picked up the fish bag and followed Tobho. I kept an eye on them until they disappeared inside that large tent where Da Klarismek sold food and ales during the fair—mostly to travelers staying in one of the many rooms in his house.

I turned around to talk to the others, but something passed them— a glimmer and a whirl of motion—caught my attention. A man wearing a dark cloak was standing in front of a tent looking through the items on the tables. His head wasn't covered so his long red hair reflected the sunlight. I am not sure why, but I instinctively walked toward that tent, leaving my friends behind.

The man was reaching across the table to take an old piece of parchment, but he quickly withdrew his hands back inside his cloak as I approached. I pretended to be interested in the merchandise, so I looked closely at a few pieces, as if trying to judge their quality.

The table was full of a menagerie of trinkets, baubles, and even some weapons. I kept pretending to look at various pieces until I noticed a strange object buried under a pile of metal scraps. It took some digging, but eventually I pulled out a rusty piece that looked like a metal disk. It was slightly smaller than a food plate and had a few holes radiating from its center. Some markings were crudely carved on both sides but were completely unfamiliar to me. Its edge was dull; the whole thing was dented. It reminded me of one of those round seashells that sailors traded in the south but a tad bigger. I asked the merchant behind the table what the thing was, but he just shrugged dismissively.

I asked again, and he sighed. "Look boy, I don't know. I traded it from a beggar in Gafardem. It looked valuable to me back then, but nobody has shown any interest in it. You could have it for five coins. What do you say?"

I silently put the disk back on the table and the merchant responded with another short sigh. I didn't have any coins just then, so I kept looking at other items, pretending that the price just wasn't good for me.

None of the other customers paid attention to my actions, but the man with red hair followed every step of my failed negotiation. I knew, of course—I had been looking at his reflection in a smooth steel shield hanging behind the merchant. The man eventually turned his eyes back to the table and slinked his hand from inside his cloak to grab a small, ornate pebble. This is when I saw his ring—a golden snake with two red gems as eyes, twisting its body around his finger. Only the members of one tribe are known to wear those rings. He was a Satolgac.

"Seven," he said as he held the small rock in his hand, almost at my eye level. The merchant huffed. "Eight."

The Satolgac took another pebble from the pile and dropped it next to the first one. "Two."

Both the merchant and I paused. He was going to pay seven for the first one, but he was offering two coins for both?

The merchant scratched his head, probably thinking the man knew more about rocks than him, or that maybe he was just a tough negotiator. After a few moments, the merchant finally said, "Three and not a coin less."

Now the Satolgac seemed to be the one intrigued. He hesitated but ultimately took three coins from inside his robe and paid the merchant. By that time, I wasn't pretending anymore; my eyes were focused on the man and his actions. He glanced at me as he turned around, and we briefly made eye contact.

The man walked a few steps away from the tent but stopped and turned around. "Will you trade?" he said, looking at me.

"Trade what?"

The man put the two pebbles in a small pouch and offered them to me. "I will give you Seven and Two for your bow and one arrow."

Well, maybe I hadn't done a good job disguising the bow, but the reason we made our long leather bags was to make it *not* obvious we were carrying arrows—especially for my mother.

Yes, I was intrigued by the offer, but I knew it wasn't a good deal for me. Trading a bow for some rocks was far from Yilian's stringent bargaining standards, but after thinking about it I decided to do it anyway. Even if it was a bad trade, I thought it would be a good opportunity for me to become friends with a Satolgac.

I set my bag on the ground and looked around to see if someone who might knew my mother was nearby. For a moment, I felt like a thief selling stolen goods on the street.

I gave the bow to him and then cut the string off one of Yilian's arrows and offered it to him. The man passed his fingers along the arrow and noticed the small piece of string still attached to it. He concealed the arrow inside his cloak and put the pouch on my hand.

"Use them wisely," he said as he pulled the hood over his head.

I looked at the small leather pouch and noticed a strange symbol painted in faded golden ink. I emptied its contents into my hand, and to my surprise, there were not two but three stones inside. I raised my head, looking for the Satolgac, but the man had already vanished into the crowd. I looked everywhere, but the only ones I was able to find were Yilian and Tobho, who were already walking back toward our meeting place.

"What a fool! I didn't even ask his name." I dropped the stones back in the pouch and rushed to meet my partners.

"Are we rich or not?" I asked.

"Rich? We are more than rich! Klarismek knows how to bargain, but not only did Yilian make him agree to our price for the fish, but he also begged us to sell him the wild boar we caught last week. We'll have to bring it to him tomorrow. It seems we'll have good sales supplying Klarismek during the fair. Yilian, show him the loot."

Yilian opened his hands to reveal three gold pieces and more than forty coins.

The fair was the best place to buy food, tools, weapons, and rare items that in other times are difficult to find. I must confess that out of the countless items my friends and I bought during the fair over the years, only two or three items were of real value. The rest were useless trinkets that held our interest for a moment and were surely lost or forgotten soon afterwards. What can I say? We didn't know better.

Other than paying for our ever-growing stock of useless items, those coins were also destined for a greater purpose—the games.

No, I am not talking about games of chance. I am talking about warrior competitions. These events were the main attraction of the fair, and even though you could observe them from many places, there were special areas built closer to the competition grounds where people could enjoy the events without anyone obstructing their view.

Of course, gaining access to these areas wasn't free; two coins each was the price in those days. It was a high price for boys like us, but we never complained. It was certainly worth it.

Swordsmen and masters of every combat discipline came to Ferdhen every year to compete in these contests. At the end of the fair, most would leave town silently, dragging honorable defeats behind them. Others would earn prestige and treasures as they won in their disciplines, but one—just one—would bring home honor and recognition beyond the ordinary. Every year, the champion of one category was honored with the title of Olikant Warrior. This title was the highest honor anyone could receive in times of peace. There were two higher titles used to honor individuals in times of war (Paldokant Warrior and Hero of the Land), but they could only be awarded by the king himself.

Other than the title, a unique piece of treasure was also awarded to the Olikant Warrior. This token was of significant value, either in gold or history. To everyone's surprise, the council chose a bell as the reward for that year. It wasn't a common bell by any means; it was cast in solid gold and was the size of a big apple or maybe even bigger.

Why was that a surprise? Well, the unspoken tradition was to give a weapon to the Olikant warrior. Usually a sword or shield used in a legendary battle, but it could also be a newly crafted piece with jewels and precious metals.

Someone told Yilian's father that the bell was found by divers in the Garpodian Sea, so it must have been part of a hoard of treasure carried by one of the many ships that sank in those treacherous waters.

"Well," I said, "let's split the coins. You wait for me here, alright?"

Yilian gave me my share, and I walked back to the tent where I traded with the Satolgac. I moved some things around the table, took that metal disk, and held it up to the merchant.

"I'll give you three coins for this trinket. This is my last offer."

Either the merchant had a slow morning or he just wanted me to disappear. Whatever the reason, he muttered something I couldn't understand and nodded. I slipped the disk inside my clothes, and once we'd reconvened, we all headed toward the competition grounds.

Yilian led, and we lined up single-file behind him past the rowdy crowd at The Two Moons, Ferdhen's tavern. Someone bumped a merchant who dropped a large cage of Vhunsek lizards; they scattered in all directions, climbing on top of people and grabbing onto their hair. They love hair.

Those lizards were wicked fast—they could run and grab onto your hair faster than lightning. We loved them. They weren't dangerous (they didn't even bite), but they could stay glued to your hair for days if you didn't know how to take them off. Dozens of people, including my friends and I, ended up with lizards on our heads, and even some patrons burst out of the tavern with lizards hanging from their beards. The best part? They were free.

Five or six soldiers turned the corner and approached us as we continued on. Those days meant hard work for Da Grokpel and his men as they walked the streets day and night, making sure no one broke the law. The first soldier in line saluted me as they walked by, and I responded to him as discreetly as possible in front of my friends.

"Did he just salute you?" Tobho asked.

"No, I think he was just letting me know that I had a lizard on my head. Good man. Well, let's move on. I can see the grounds from here."

The arenas were already full of contestants practicing their skills, and observers crowded every open spot. Flags and banners decorated everywhere south of the market, and hundreds of tents sat pitched on the west side, providing a place to sleep for merchants and visitors for the duration of the fair.

Our sky was no exception. We couldn't believe how many falcons were already flying in every direction chasing Vothras. This ancient game was one of the most popular events of the fair and the one with the largest arena—my favorite without a doubt.

Even though some of the rules have changed throughout the centuries, the basic objectives remain the same. Crathim falcons are trained by their masters to fetch small wooden balls covered with thick leather. These balls are called Vothras and have a thin cloth ribbon hanging from them. The players use these balls to hit metal plates hung at various heights around tall wooden poles to earn points. It may sound easy, but you'll see that it isn't.

My friends and I took a long walk around the grounds, looking over every contestant. Some of them were new, and others were already famous warriors thirsty for more glory. Their strengths, experience, and style were all taken into consideration as we chose our champion.

Now here is where we played our own game of chance. Every day, each of us offered a coin or trinket as a wager, and whoever chose the warrior with the highest points of the day would keep all the bets. Simple but entertaining. Of course, you need something valuable to bet, which was another reason we worked so hard running errands, fishing, or hunting on those days.

To be honest, winning or losing was inconsequential to us. In the end, the winner always shared the spoils with the group. But choosing a champion has always been an art. A good eye and a good ear were essential to have an edge over your friends. That talent was even more valuable at the end of the games, because whoever picked the most champions was named among us Olikant Master. It was certainly glorious for any of us to carry a title—even a fake one—for a whole year.

We selected our champions for that day and gathered by the river to watch the swimmers one last time. Yilian collected the bets and put them inside my bag; I remember most of us betting a coin on that day. Tobho was chosen as the keeper, so he wrote the names of our champions on a piece of parchment, and I handed my bag over to him.

Moments later, the bells in town and the horns around the competition grounds announced it was midday. We agreed to get together again at two in the afternoon by the entrance to the main arena, and then we went separate ways.

***

"Why on *earth* are you carrying a lizard in your hair?" my mother asked the moment I stopped by her tent. "You know I don't like those creatures."

"It won't let go, and I was going to find a cage to keep it."

"Oh no. I won't have that thing crawling in the house. Zilhana!"

Zilhana marched straight toward me. She grabbed the lizard with one hand and poured water over its head, making it release my hair.

She put the lizard in a small bowl and covered it with some wood, then she came back and gave me a rag to dry off.

"Jonek, I'm glad to see you," my mother said breathlessly. "Would you untie those crates and get the pots out? Bring browns and greens to this side and the rest on that table."

I sunk to the ground and pulled the two crates closer to me—not exactly how I was planning to spend my day. One thing was for sure—whoever tied those crates thought they were meant to stay that way forever. I tried my best to loosen the knots, but there was no way they were coming undone.

I looked around for something sharp to cut the ropes, but nothing was at hand. The only metal object in my possession was that disk I bought that morning. I pushed the package to the back so the ladies couldn't see what I was doing and took the disk from inside my clothes. I passed my fingers along its edge, trying to find a sharp side, but it was too smooth. Still, with nothing else to use for the job, I put my fingers through some of the holes and gave it a try.

I clearly remember barely putting the weight of my hand on the rope, but to my surprise, the disk sheared right through it and into the wooden crate, almost reaching the jars. I turned my head to see if anyone saw what just happened, but no one did. I quickly put the disk away and threw the ropes and damaged wooden cover aside.

I crouched in front of the second box, slid my fingers through the holes again, and pressed the disk over the ropes. It didn't even make a mark. I tried to cut in various sections, with different angles, pushing with all my strength or barely tapping, but I just couldn't make it happen. Frustrated, I grabbed the disk in both hands and held it up to the light. I followed its shape with my fingers and noticed that the holes followed no obvious pattern for my hand to hold. Maybe the first time was just a fluke with weak ropes. I tried my hands again, but needless to say, it was impossible for me to untie those knots. I was considering biting the ropes when I heard my mother behind me.

"Wait, Jonek, let me cut that rope for you."

***

My mother and I sat on top of a crate to enjoy the stew she had made for lunch while Zilhana took care of the customers. For a while, we chatted about the fish I'd caught and how much I sold them for. I reached into my pocket and offered the gold piece to her. My mother forgot about her food for a moment. She took the coin gingerly and put it in a pouch she always carried by her waist, then hugged me.

"I'm so proud of you sharing the fruits of your work with me. You are a good son." I smiled and hugged her back. I was fortunate to have someone like her—even if she wouldn't let me use weapons or keep my lizards. We finished off our stew in contented silence, and when I noticed she was getting ready to put her bowl away, I braced myself and spoke.

"Mother, have you ever seen a big wolf with a white patch of fur on its chest?"

My mother froze. "What happened?" she said, turning back to me. "Were you in danger?"

"No, but some friends were talking about such beasts, and I think they were just making up stories to scare us."

She slowly put a piece of bread in her mouth. "You scared me, Jonek. A big wolf with a white patch on its chest? No, I haven't seen anything like that." She paused. "But I do remember hearing stories about wolves almost as big as a bear when I was your age. In those days, hunters talked about animals with fur as dark as night roaming the deepest parts of the forest. Some even said they were responsible for missing children back then. Lots of men spent weeks looking for those poor boys, but neither they nor the animals were ever found. I haven't heard anyone talking about such creatures in a long time, so it seems it's just as you said—stories to scare people."

***

Many years have passed, but I still remember the scents that floated in the air that day as I headed back toward the arena. As you can imagine, my mother wasn't the only one selling food. Many others offered rare dishes brought from every corner of the kingdom and beyond. Delicacies, sweets, and drinks of all kinds changed hands, but not all the food was as appealing as you'd think. Some dishes were just too exotic for my taste—at least the ones that used ants, snakes, or live worms as ingredients.

Animals of all kinds were also sold or traded. Birds, cats, dogs, horses, and various types of reptiles were favored by the community for domestication, but I also saw people walking with rats, crows, and snakes on their shoulders, and some even had bats hanging from inside of their clothes.

I was almost back to the competition grounds when I saw Lord Nutrec saunter by, a long black cape dragging behind him and his favorite falcon, Criokan, sitting proudly on his left arm. A dozen of his ruffians made sure everyone moved aside as he made his way toward the arena. Knowing his reputation, I couldn't help but cringe when our eyes briefly met through the crowd.

Yes, it was common knowledge that Nutrec was never on the side of the law. Unfortunately, no one ever got close enough to catch him in the middle of something illegal. He was just too clever for that. Unfortunately, many of his lackeys were *not*, once you got a few ales into them. That's how everyone knew.

I ducked into a back alley to avoid being crushed by the crowd. I was halfway through the line of tents when the music ceased momentarily.

"I don't need your help!" I heard someone shout in the temporary silence. "Stay away from my tent!"

A merchant selling wooden artifacts was pushing away two families, almost shoving the children to the ground.

I pushed through the crowd until I was standing behind them. I knew their tribe very well; they were Tromzils. It makes little sense to me, but many thought Tromzils were the lowest of the low because they look different. Both male and female adults had no hair and they all had the same birthmark—the skin around one of their hands was dark red.

Just writing that makes me ashamed of my own kind.

Tromzils migrated throughout the lands, taking their chances in groups of two or three families at most. To me, they were honorable, caring souls that could be as hard-working and intelligent as anyone around here, if not more. My mother always gave them work farming our lands, she allowed them to stay as long as they wanted, and she often traded their share on their behalf to negotiate better prices for them. They weren't warriors, and they would never use a weapon against anyone—not even to defend themselves.

So what did they do to make that man in that alley angry? They just asked for work. Those men could've carried heavy items, the women could've cleaned the merchandise . . . who knows? Their work could've been of higher quality than any other helper at the fair, but no one would give them the chance.

I reached out a hand and helped one of the Tromzils to his feet. "What's your name?" I asked.

"Zatioke," he answered as he took his old hat off.

"Do you know how to clean fields?"

"Indeed we do, master," he said.

"I'm not your master. My name is Jonek, and my mother and I need help cleaning our fields before the winter." The small group seemed to perk up. "We can't offer much pay until the harvest next summer, but you can stay on our lands until then. We have plenty of wood and tools if you want to build shelters for the winter. If you stay with us the whole season, we'll share the harvest with you. So, can we count on you?"

A boy saying those words might have been difficult to believe for a grown-up, but then I took all the coins I had and put them in the hands of one of the women. Her eyes filled with tears.

"Can we count on you?" I asked again.

The man closed the woman's hand holding the coins with his own. "I speak for Zatioke and all the Tromzil blood in front of you, you can count on us."

I nodded. "Follow the eastern road, cross the bridge, and then go south through the woods until you leave the pine trees. You will see our farmlands and our house on the right side of the road. You can start setting up your tents or building shelters if you need them. If anyone bothers you or you need any help, just tell any soldier that you work for Jonek and his mother. Remember that."

I left the alley and ended up in front of one of the largest tents in the fair. Just outside were two or three wooden racks stacked with bows on one side of the door and dozens of swords and other weapons on the other.

Satolgac bows, I thought to myself. I walked closer to look at them. Their craftsmanship was good, but they seemed old—some even had battle marks. I extended my arm to take one when I heard a voice coming from inside the tent.

"What you seek is not out there."

I pulled my hand back. "How do you know what I seek?" I responded hesitantly.

An old man slowly made his way out of the tent, supporting himself with a walking staff. Just behind him, a girl probably my age walked out and tossed a cape onto his back.

"It's too cold for you, grandfather," she said. He chuckled.

"You don't know what a real cold day is. I once survived for weeks walking in the snow in the northern peaks. Let me remind you that I also floated on the Garpodian Sea for days holding onto a barrel and I am still here . . . with all my limbs. Today is not my day Zilhien. I know." The man glanced at me and lowered his voice, a faint smile touching his lips. "Don't mind my granddaughter. She thinks my old age has turned me into a sack of illnesses."

The old man walked closer, grabbed my face, and moved my head from side to side. "You look familiar. Your eyes are sad, but they show your strength. You have a warrior's eyes. You remind me of someone I knew a long time ago. What did you say your name was?"

"Jonek."

"Jonek? No, I haven't heard that name before. Is anyone in your family a soldier?"

"No."

"Hmm, how strange. How old are you?"

"I'll be thirteen in four days."

"Well, maybe you are his son or a distant relative. He was about your age when I met him, but one day he left and we never heard from him again. A strong boy indeed, very good with weapons and an excellent hunter. Your faces are different, but your eyes were made from the same mold." He turned around and walked toward the wooden rack. "These weapons are relics of past wars. They are not for sale; they are part of my collection, and I use them to bring color to my stories. I am not a merchant, I am a historian." He smiled and pointed at his head. "Wars and battles live in here with great detail, so I go from town to town sharing them with others to honor the warriors lost in them."

"Do I have to pay for that?" I asked naively.

"Only if you want to," he said laughing. "I don't do this for gold—that I have plenty of. I do this to feed my soul. For me, there is nothing better than to relive our past glories and give respect to those who fought and died for all of us. That is the nourishment that keeps my mind and body going."

I tried to peek behind him. "So, can you tell me what you have inside the tent?"

"Inside the tent? I don't understand."

"You said that I wouldn't find what I seek out here."

The man looked intrigued. "I don't recall ever saying that to you, young man. What makes you think I did?"

I hesitated for a moment, but then I remembered something my mother told me once. Some older people have great recollection of old memories but have problems keeping track of recent ones. I changed topics.

"So when are you going to tell a story?"

"Today is a special day; I will give a full account of the Siege of Norkomas at the theater. I'll also share other stories with smaller groups here by my tent for the rest of the fair."

The bell in the tower announced it was two in the afternoon, so I said farewell to the old man using the royal protocol. With a smile, he responded accordingly. I was really glad I learned to do that from Grokpel's men.

No more distractions for me (even though the fair is full of them, clearly). I had to get back to the competition grounds. To my surprise, none of my friends were at our meeting place. Just as I'd begun to scan the crowd for them, I noticed Nuthek waving his arms in the distance, just by the line to enter the arena for the Vothras.

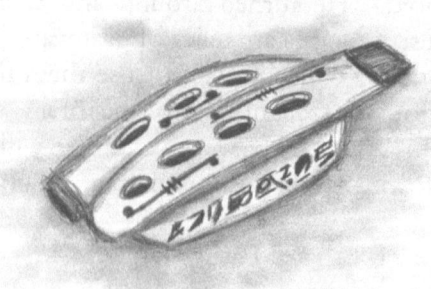

CHAPTER 3. TEARS AND FALCONS.

I made my way over to him, and the crowd carried us inside.

We ended up with scratches and bruises, but we were lucky to find a spot right in the middle of the arena. Long wooden benches were roughly assembled to accommodate about two hundred people in four layers. In most years, the arena for the Vothras had eight or nine of these stands around it. That year, there were twelve.

Even though Nuthek knew the large fellow collecting coins at the entrance, we ended up paying not two but *three* coins each in order to sit on the lowest bench.

Thankfully, Yilian found us just as we were about to enter, because he had to pay for me since I'd given my coins to the Tromzils.

"Not bad. There aren't many browns or blues around us," Yilian said as he tied a green ribbon around his wrist and handed one to me.

"Yes, but look at the other side of the arena! The entire town of Gafardem is there," I said, pointing at the crowd waving their flags and letting their brown ribbons play in the wind right across from us.

Even though people from many towns and regions attended our fair, champions from three areas harbored the most entrenched rivalry for generations: Ferdhen, Gafardem, and the towns along the Garpodian shores (like Rovhos), which always used blue to represent their lands, since they were by the ocean. Tobho whistled as he sat down with us and some vendors came closer to show us their treats. Food and drinks of all kinds were offered to us, and after some bargaining, we got enough to feed us for the entire day. I wasn't really hungry after eating that stew, but I did get one of those sweet beverages made with berries (paid by Tobho, of course).

Suddenly, the banners and flags began to make their way into the arenas. Groups assisting their champions walked around the field carrying their colors and weapons to their places. Once the last contestant walked into the field, one of the oldest rituals of the games began.

Twelve wooden poles as thick and tall as a forty-year-old pine stood scattered around the competition grounds. These poles had a round cage at the top filled with wood and cloth soaked in oil. I always thought of them as enormous torches. They were so tall that you could see them from almost anywhere.

Before the poles were brought to the fair, members of the council carved a symbol representing one competition on each pole and covered them with metal plates, all in absolute secrecy. The ritual was simple. An archer was selected by the city council. This warrior was responsible for lighting up the poles in any order he or she wanted. Every time a pole was lit, the metal plate at its base was removed to reveal its symbol. This process determined the order in which the final contest for each category would take place on the last day of the fair. I have to say that everyone—and especially the contestants—felt excitement, anxiety, and frustration during this ritual. Only the winner of the category hidden on the last pole would become the Olikant Warrior for those games.

I always thought this method was fair, because everyone had a chance to compete for the highest honor, even if they were in a category not popular with the masses.

That year, an archer from Rovhos earned the privilege of lighting the poles. The warrior walked to the center of the arena where the members of our council were already standing. A lady from that group raised the golden bell that would be this year's prize, and all of us cheered.

The archer lit an arrow, walked toward the northern edge of the field and aimed at the top of the pole that was closest to the market. The crowd went silent as the arrow left his longbow. The wind tried to play with it, but the skill of that man was impeccable. Dark smoke briefly painted the sky as the fire roared to life.

Two soldiers standing took the metal plate off its base. That one had a gauntlet carved underneath, so hand-to-hand combat with no weapons would be the first event on the last day. The second pole had a bow and arrow, and the third one the river.

It was when the archer released his sixth arrow that this year's games became famous. Just as the bowstring sliced forward, a peal of thunder shook the ground throughout the valley, and everybody went dead silent. You could even hear the water from the river hitting the rocks far in the distance. The thunder faded away but bounced back on the Bhormak Mountains, passing us on its way south moments later.

"What was that?" a man whispered behind us.

"I don't know. Thunder with no clouds isn't natural," his friend said.

"Look!" someone said, pointing at the top of the sixth pole.

The arrow was firmly stuck in the cage, but even though it was burning brightly, the wood in the cage wasn't. We all waited for the oil to catch fire, but it never did. A few soldiers even shook the pole at its base, making the flames dance over the cage. Nothing happened. The fire just refused to go beyond the arrow.

The archer hesitated at first but then lit up another arrow, aimed again at the sixth pole, and let it loose. That arrow hit the cage just to the left of the first one. Nothing.

"Maybe they didn't pour oil on it," Tobho whispered.

"Not likely," Yilian said. "Even without oil, the timber in that cage should be burning by now."

"No," I whispered, rising to my feet, "this is something else. Look at the falcons."

Even though the birds had their eyes covered with hoods, they were flapping and screeching frantically on the arms of their handlers.

The audience began to grow uneasy. Many were deeply superstitious, and not finishing the ritual would've been seen as a bad omen for the games. A member of the council whispered something to the archer and he promptly shot an arrow at a different pole. That one caught fire as soon as the arrow hit it. Behind its plate was a carving of a fish.

The archer kept lighting the rest of the poles until there were only two left. The man looked at the one that was reluctant to catch fire and aimed at it again. By then, the first two arrows had crumbled to dust. He pulled the bowstring and held his stance for a moment. Just as we thought he was going to release his arrow, he slowly let the bowstring go slack and walked toward the other pole.

That settled it—the category on the pole that didn't catch fire was going to be the last and main event of the games.

Just as he was going to pull his bowstring, it happened again. A faint echo of thunder came back from the south, making a big cloud of smoke and flames explode at the top of the sixth pole as soon as it reached the grounds—well, by then it was the eleventh pole with fire burning at its top.

No one could explain what had just happened. The soldiers hesitated, but eventually removed its plate. The archer paused to hear the category behind its plate. The Vothras.

Many celebrated when they heard that the last pole had the symbol of the sword carved on it, as that category hadn't been chosen as the final competition for almost twenty years by then. Others didn't like that outcome, but the rules were absolute. My friends and I knew there was one person in particular who was truly fuming after that turn of events—Lord Nutrec. He would've loved to win that golden bell chasing Vothras, but now if he wanted to claim it and be called Olikant Warrior, he would have to use a sword.

Once the ceremony was finished, the banners were removed from the arenas and the competitors began to perform their last training routines before the competition began. The falcons were released, and everyone cheered as the birds flew right over our heads, fighting each other to dominate the skies.

***

Understanding the game of Vothras might seem complicated at first, but it is actually fairly simple. The arena is a long rectangle, and the edges are marked with white sand. On one of the narrow ends of the rectangle, usually toward the entrance to the arena, is a circle filled with green sand called the starting point. This starting point is moved every day along that edge to make it harder—or easier—for the player to enter the field.

The field itself is about a hundred and fifty paces long by seventy paces wide and houses three poles maybe forty feet high. The first pole is rooted on the left side of the field from the edge where the starting point is. The second is about sixty paces away from the first pole, but it's on the right side of the field. The last one is called the halfway pole, and it stands right at the center of the far end of the field.

There are four metal plates hanging on rotating arms at various heights on each pole. These plates circle around the pole depending on how hard they've been hit or if the wind is strong enough to move them. The halfway pole at the other end only has two plates very close to its top. Finally, a circle filled with white sand, maybe twelve paces across, is made around the base of each pole to mark safe zones.

The objective is to gain points by hitting the metal plates with the three Vothras each warrior has. Players earn points depending on which plate they hit, and they are allowed to stand inside the safe zone of a pole where they've scored to throw their next Vothra. Once they cross the entire field and hit the halfway pole, they have two choices—

they can stop there and wait for another turn to start at the green circle, or they can choose to play the course backwards, gaining triple points with each hit.

That might seem like the best way to play, but doing the course backwards is extremely challenging; a warrior would have to fight for the plates that others behind them are fighting for, and if he ends up at a pole with two other players at the same time, he loses the points he has earned so far and has to give one of his Vothras to each of the two players he is sharing the pole with. Going backwards is a game of risk versus reward.

But it wasn't really the Vothras and the metal plates that make this game challenging (and dangerous). The rules say that warriors are allowed to use a falcon to play (and I've never heard of someone doing it without one). The falcons are trained to hunt the Vothras the moment they are in the air. If your Vothra is caught by someone else's bird before it hits the plates, you lose your place to the owner of that falcon, and he gets to keep your Vothra. If you were already at a pole when you lost your ball, you have to go back to the starting circle and wait for another turn to play again. If the owner of the falcon that caught your ball has lost any of his Vothras to you, you could trade with him to get yours back.

One last thing. The falcons are trained to leave alone any Vothra that lands outside the field or inside the white circles around the poles. The area in the field where they *can* pick up Vothras is known as "gronsvoh"—red soil. It's the most dangerous area on the field, as falcons will dive from the skies and fight both other birds and men in order to get the Vothras.

As a player, fighting another warrior for a fallen Vothra that your bird didn't catch wasn't what you feared the most, it was the falcons. Crathim falcons are two or three hands larger than regular mountain falcons and are trained from birth to hunt Vothras. Believe me, they will show no mercy to anyone. Even though the players were skilled and most wore light armor, I remember a handful of them being dragged out of the field, leaving a trail of blood behind them. That's why it's called "gronsvoh."

I still remember years ago, a warrior named Rhalok was lying on the ground between the second and the halfway pole. The blood from his forehead was blinding him, but he kept that Vothra in his hand. To everyone's surprise, his diamond-headed falcon dove down and battled to keep both birds and players away from his master. Even after that mighty bird was mortally wounded, he just stood on Rhalok's back while his master dragged himself into the last circle.

Rhalok, the warrior from the forest realm, became the Olikant Warrior that year. His prize was the shield of Gerteba, a legendary shield forged with blue steel from the Kolikuj Islands. It had protected heroes in many wars and was ultimately brought from the western planes to be the prize for those games. No one could argue that it is still one of the most valuable prizes ever offered. Some say that Rhalok buried his falcon and covered him with the shield somewhere along the Dragon's Back at the top of the Bhormaks. The man was never seen again.

***

The horns sounded around the grounds and everyone took their places. A competitor wearing the colors from Gafardem stepped into the starting circle, a brown falcon perched on his arm. He uncovered the bird's head and sent it flying with the others. One long brown and gold ribbon skimmed the ground as he passed his first Vothra from hand to hand. He pointed toward the plates in the middle of the closest pole.

Warriors used different techniques to throw their Vothras. This warrior was the first I ever saw holding the ball by its ribbon and spinning it over his head before throwing it. When he let it fly, more than one falcon tried to grab it, but it was just too fast. The metal clang announced the first two points of the competition, and the warrior ran into the white circle, avoiding birds the best he could.

We were celebrating that great throw when the second contestant approached the starting circle. This player's falcon was already in the air. The man whistled, and his red falcon began circling the pole.

The middle plate was still moving after the opening shot, so his eyes focused on the plates above. He was rubbing a black Vothra with his left hand, and for some reason, we couldn't see its ribbon at first.

He backed up a few steps, careful not to touch the outside of the circle. The man whistled again, ran toward the first pole, and threw his Vothra as hard as he could. His falcon flew toward the ball, and it wasn't until half way to its target that the ribbon on that Vothra extended behind it.

Two other birds went after it. Their speed and direction were perfect to intercept the ball, but at the last moment, the player's falcon flew right in between, allowing the Vothra to continue its path.

The ball hit the outer edge of the plate to enthusiastic applause. As the competitor ran toward the circle, the first player was still struggling to get to the second pole. He had already lost one Vothra by missing the plates, and now the wind was moving the plates around the poles for the first time. He took his chances and ran a few steps outside the circle to throw his second ball. The ribbon on that Vothra painted a good trajectory, but various birds quickly changed direction and went after it. Even though most of the falcons had followed his Vothra, one noticed the player stepping outside of the circle with the Vothra in his hand; it dove and shrieked as the man released the ball. The ball barely touched the middle plate, but it was good enough for him to advance. He rolled and stumbled all the way to the next circle fighting the falcon, but the bird managed to leave some cuts on his armor and hand.

The crowd celebrated the man's boldness, and even the other contestant in the field paid respect to him.

Only a few bystanders noticed that Lord Nutrec was approaching the starting circle, and I can assure you, he wasn't pleased about missing out. Nutrec always fancied being the center of attention. A green and black ribbon trailed on the ground as he pulled out a golden Vothra. He raised his right arm and the crowd lowered their voices. All he was doing was calling his falcon, but his smile proved the pleasure he took in manipulating the masses.

Criokan flew over Nutrec's head as he ran to the other end of the starting circle. It was hard to believe, but Nutrec threw his Vothra toward the first pole, and for the first half of its journey, the falcon flew over it as if he were escorting it. Two other falcons changed direction toward the ball, but just as they were going to reach it, Nutrec's falcon grabbed the ball, closed its wings, and plunged down. Just when we thought the bird would hit the ground, he opened his wings, flew away from the first pole, and skimmed around the second pole. Criokan dodged other birds as he gained altitude and finally turned down into a steep dive, slamming the Vothra on the top plate of the first pole.

Even though most people despised Lord Nutrec, that shot deserved every round of applause he got for it.

"It is like throwing dry leaves into a fire," Tobho said as the audience fed Nutrec's ego with endless cheers. The man was enjoying the moment so much that he even slowed down as he made his way to the first pole. By then, the first player managed to finish his round with single-digit points and chose to stop there to heal his wounds.

The player in front of Nutrec was making his best attempt at the top plates on the next pole, but unfortunately, his Vothra hit the pole itself and bounced off, landing outside the white circle. Various players alerted their falcons, and a swarm of birds descended from the skies toward that Vothra. The warrior decided to risk it all after seeing Nutrec's shot, so he took his chances. Most of us stood up as he left the safety of the white sand and ran toward his Vothra.

Suddenly, I felt some liquid splatter all over my feet. I briefly took my eyes away from the arena, but then Yilian's voice made me look back.

"Look at the white one!" he called out.

Bunches of feathers tumbled down from above, where a snow falcon was now flying erratically. The bird tried to stay in the air but ultimately collapsed close to the second pole.

"What happened?" I asked.

"I don't know," Yilian responded. "It was as if the bird crashed into a wall in midair."

That moment was so confusing that even the warrior who ventured into the gronsvoh stopped abruptly and went back a short distance. A few contestants hesitated, but others kept calling their birds, directing them toward the ball. Then a gray-headed bird screeched loudly as his body hit the ground close to the first pole.

Most of us were used to seeing falcons getting hurt and even losing their lives in this game, but these birds were falling from the sky for no reason.

Many falcons flew away, as if they sensed something wrong in the field. Even the players waiting for their turn left their shaded area and searched the skies for an explanation. Suddenly, a red falcon and Nutrec's bird engaged each other in a steep dive from the skies toward the Vothra still lying untouched on the gronsvoh.

Criokan suddenly screeched in pain.

The other falcon flew away just as the feathers from Nutrec's bird filled the air around the second pole. Criokan tumbled to the ground and hobbled there until he heard Lord Nutrec's call and flew back to his master's arm. He wasn't happy as he looked at his falcon's injuries, but he sent it back to the sky moments later. At this point, there were two players sharing the first pole; now both would have to compete for the next one.

"What happened to you? A falcon crashed into your drink too?" Yilian said, looking at Tobho.

He didn't answer as he flicked something off his fingertips. His face and clothes were drenched in some purple liquid.

"What happened to you?" I asked.

"I don't know. I was holding my cup when it suddenly broke into pieces."

"You must have a very strong grip," Yilian said, and we all laughed.

I felt bad for Tobho losing his drink, so I picked up the pieces of clay from his broken cup and stood to go get him another. I put a finger inside to taste what he'd had so I knew what to buy, but as my finger hit the bottom of the cup, it bumped something smooth. I poured the rest of the drink into my hand, and there it was—a small gray pebble losing its invisibility in front of my eyes.

I put the pebble in my pocket and pulled Yilian with me to the area where the vendors gathered.

"Something's not right," I said to Yilian.

"Of course!" he said, not turning his eyes to me. "Nutrec just moved to the second pole with another four points."

"Not that," I sighed. "Open your hand."

I took the pebble from my pocket and put it in his hand. To our surprise, the rock was starting to turn invisible again. Portions of it were still gray, but most of it was already transparent.

"What's this?" Yilian said. "Where did you get it?"

"This is what shattered Tobho's cup. He's lucky it didn't land on his head. Rocks don't just fall from the sky; someone is throwing them."

Yilian looked up. "The only thing falling from the sky is feathers, Jonek."

"Two birds are on the ground, and a few others are injured without an explanation. Who could benefit from that?" We gave each other a knowing look, but then Yilian shook his head.

"I don't know, Jonek . . . Lord Nutrec is powerful, but I don't think he can manage this kind of magic."

"I'm not so sure about that. Let's see if we can find out who's throwing these rocks."

"But Nutrec's falcon was injured too, Jonek."

"True, but that could've just been a mistake. Did you see him complaining to the judges after his bird was injured? You know he makes a big fuss over anything he doesn't like. No, I'm not convinced he's innocent. Let's look around."

We walked around the arena a few times, but it was futile. Trying to keep track of anyone's actions in that crowd was close to impossible.

"Let's go back," I said, "but don't say anything about the pebble. We'll show Nuthek later. He always liked magical trinkets, so he might know something."

We watched the rest of the competition but kept our eyes open for anything unusual. The last Vothra in play was caught by a falcon that belonged to a warrior from our town, so Ferdhen would have the privilege of starting the competition on the second day.

The horns around the grounds announced the end of the games for the day. The long shadows under the trees meant that we only had a couple more hours before nightfall. If I wanted to find out more about this odd stone, I'd need to show it to Nuthek.

***

We all followed Tobho to the Wall of Honor—a long, flat rock entrenched in the side of a hill that was used to keep track of the scores for the games since the early days. It was without a doubt a place of glory and tradition, as every Olikant Warrior had his name permanently carved into it.

The area near the wall was crowded, so we waited for Nuthek and Tobho to bring the final scores.

"Jonek, Tobho says you've won the pool," Nuthek said as they joined us. Tobho looked over the piece of parchment we'd used to write our names and champions earlier.

"Let me see that," Nuthek said, taking the parchment from Tobho and walking under a torch already burning nearby.

Tobho chuckled. "He's always been a sore loser. Well, I'll see you later. I have to go home," he said handing me my bag.

I gave Tobho a quick nod and walked toward Nuthek.

I stood by his side pretending I was also interested in the list. I took the pebble from my pocket and dropped it onto the parchment. Nuthek wasn't holding the parchment tightly, so the pebble fell to the

 56

ground.

"What was that?" he said, looking at me.

"Don't move. It landed by your feet."

I leaned down, took a handful of dirt and put it in my pocket, then grabbed my bag and asked him to follow me. Yilian joined us as we headed toward the streets. We didn't stop until we reached the back of Da Klarismek's place. I took the metal disk from inside my clothes and put it in the bag.

"What is that thing?"

"Nothing Yilian, just a trinket. Nuthek, do you see that plate over there? Bring it." He picked it up and threw away the scraps of food that were still on it. "Hold it steady. Don't drop it," I said as I put my hand in my pocket.

I put the dirt and rocks on the plate, then I scooped water from a barrel nearby and poured it all over it.

"Now watch this."

Slowly, one gray pebble took shape on one side of the plate. Nuthek's hands began to shake, so I took the plate from him before he dropped it. It took some time, but eventually he touched the rock with his finger and moved it around the plate.

"A tear from Althizam. I think."

"A tear from who?" Yilian asked.

"Not who, *where*."

"What are you talking about?" I asked as I took the pebble and put the plate on the ground.

"It's just a story I heard before. There is a city called Althizam that lies deep in some mountain range. Most of its dwellers were miners and were deemed the wealthiest race that ever existed. I don't remember the details, but I know they were betrayed by an army that previously swore to protect them, in order to steal their riches. Somehow, the people from Althizam and its allies defeated that evil army using invisible stones just like this one. The people from Althizam were still mourning the loss of hundreds of innocent souls slain during the first attack as they crafted these stones, so many of their tears spilled over these pebbles. That's why they're known as Tears of Althizam."

"Who in the world told you this story?"

"You'll never believe it, Jonek—it was the old man who lives east of the cemetery."

"You talk to him? Is your head not working? My mother told me to stay away from that man."

"He isn't dangerous. Somewhat odd maybe, but he knows great stories."

"The one thing he may know is how to eat you alive and bury your bones," Yilian said, poking Nuthek in his belly.

Nuthek snorted. "That man is not a bad person. He's just different."

"Yes, maybe he's from another place—a place where grownups eat their young after telling them stories." Nuthek couldn't stay serious and ended up laughing.

"I've never heard that old man say a word," I said as he caught his breath again. "How did you make him talk to you?"

"One day I was swimming in the lower lagoon of the waterfall and decided to climb to the top one. As I was getting over the first rocks, I heard a voice coming from the edge of the water below me. 'Be careful young man. Who knows if someone might be crossing today.'" We all gasped. "I turned around and saw the old man staring at me. He slowly walked away and sat under a tree nearby. I didn't want to show I was scared of him, so I kept climbing and swam in the big lagoon for a while."

"So what happened?" I said.

"First I thought he was sleeping, but then he started writing something in a book. I thought that was the right moment for me to leave, so I climbed down, picked up my shirt and sandals, and walked toward the road. 'Don't be afraid; they don't know we're here,' he said as I walked by him. I was meaning to ignore him and walk away, but I was too curious. 'Who doesn't know we're here?' I asked him. 'Not you,' he said. 'Us.' "

***

We sat and listened to Nuthek talk about Drukhol—as we learned that odd man was called—and how he apparently used to be a soldier in his younger days. It grew dark, and even as we started to head over to the theater for the play, Nuthek wouldn't stop talking about the man and his stories. We all agreed that Nuthek was the oddest of us all (not that he didn't have some fierce competition), and Yilian playfully punched him perhaps a bit too hard.

Even though the play wasn't starting until later, we quickly realized we were already late. Hundreds of people got to the theater before us, so the whole area was filled by the time we arrived. We ducked in and out of the crowd looking for places suitable for short people like us, but there were none in the main area. Then we saw some large wooden crates piled against a wall and decided to climb on top of those.

That spot was even better than we thought. We were high enough to see the whole stage without any obstruction, and we caught sight of huge platters of snacks wending their way through the crowd. Some people wearing gold-colored vests made their rounds collecting coins for the entrance fee to see the play.

"Two coins for one, three for two," said a voice from below. I looked down and saw the granddaughter of that old man I had met that afternoon—the one who'd covered him in a shawl for fear he'd get sick. She was also collecting coins.

She halfway smirked when she saw me. "I should charge you three coins each since you have a much better view from up there."

"How much for the three of us?" Yilian asked, ever the barterer.

"Five coins."

"Isn't that too much? We could pay four."

I briefly smiled at the girl and pulled Yilian back. "Let's not get her in trouble. She's just collecting coins for the owners."

We climbed down from the crates and gave her the coins. On those days, once you paid your fees, you received a wrist band made of cloth with threads of special colors to acknowledge your payment. She tied one on Nuthek's wrist and one on Yilian's. She rummaged in her satchel for another one, but unfortunately for me, those two were the last ones she had.

"I'm sorry, I don't have any more bands. Give me a minute and I'll go get one more."

"But what if someone thinks I haven't paid my fee?"

"Tell them you paid your fee to me but I didn't have any more bands. My name is Zilhien. And just so you know, my grandfather owns this theater, so you are actually talking to one of the owners." She flipped her hair indignantly as she turned to leave.

I didn't really like being with girls at that age, but something happened during those brief moments that started to change those feelings in me.

"My name is Jonek," I said as she was leaving.

"I know. The kid with warrior eyes, right?" She smiled and kept walking toward the stage. Meanwhile, a hand knocked on my head a couple of times.

"Come on, climb up, Warrior Eyes," Nuthek drawled.

I sat back on top of the crate just as the sound of a horn announced the beginning of the play. Soft music emanated from one side of the theater, traveling far into the streets of Ferdhen. Two large curtains were pulled to the sides, revealing a young lady, not older than twenty, sitting on the floor in front of a mirror. As she lifted her face, my surroundings became empty. Every angle, every tone on her face must have been touched by angels. Some accents of her long white dress danced bashfully with the wind, guiding us mortals through a river of sparkles and dreams. Slowly, she opened her hands and pushed a piece of parchment against her lips.

She was a princess. Her loved one had followed her father into battle, and she had just received news that even though their odds were unfavorable, they were going to face the enemy in one massive battle. For over an hour, we watched how she traded dress, jewels, and comfort for armor, weapons, and the hardship of a journey to find the one she loved. We rarely took our eyes from that stage.

Eventually, she reached the front lines. The main battle had just ended, and its gruesome aftermath colored the landscape with crimson. There by a river, her loved one was still fighting a handful of enemy soldiers, but he was seriously wounded. The princess stormed in.

It was incredible. The actors were highly skilled, but the way that princess used her sword was unreal. She swiftly moved around them, delivering blows and slicing the air all around her. She was so fast that neither her opponents nor the audience could keep track of where her sword was. She didn't belong in the theater—she belonged with the Wasps, or at the very least, competing in our games.

It was obvious by the sound of those blades colliding that the swords were real. She took the lives of three of them, wounded another one, and the last two fled the scene. She had saved her loved one.

***

A man blew a horn, letting us know we had a few minutes before the next presentation, so we got down from the crates to stretch our legs. Two men wearing golden vests saw us climbing down from the crates, so they walked closer and asked us to show them our wristbands. Nuthek pulled up his sleeve, and Yilian had his arm already extended so the men could see his.

"Zilhien is bringing mine shortly. She just ran out of wristbands when I paid her," I told the men as I searched for Zilhien in the crowd.

Both men scowled. "Listen kid, why don't you just pay the two coins and continue enjoying the theater?"

"I already did. I paid my fee to Zilhien."

"Who's Zilhien?" one of them asked.

I paused. Did that girl actually fool me? Or were these just a few bullies? It seemed that nothing in my life was destined to be simple— some of Da Grokpel's soldiers standing nearby noticed the commotion, so they approached.

"What's the problem here?"

"This boy doesn't want to pay the fee for the theater."

"That isn't true! I've already paid. A girl collected our money earlier and gave my friends wristbands, but she didn't have one for me. She said she was going to come back to give me mine during the play."

"If Jonek says so, then it is true," the soldier said as both my friends wondered why that soldier knew my name.

"The kid didn't pay! Make him. You're supposed to protect us against thieves!"

"Are you calling Jonek a thief?" the other soldier muttered, his hand gently settling on the hilt of his sword.

In a matter of moments, the tone of that discussion turned completely aggressive. One of the men in the gold vests made a signal, and a few others rose from the crowd and stood behind him. As those men joined the scene, more soldiers made their way to where we were.

And so my day at the theater turned from a slight misunderstanding to a full-scale fight. And of course, both my honor and my twelve-year-old body were right in the middle of it.

The men with golden vests grabbed anything within reach to defend themselves (which meant that one of them was brandishing the back end of a straw broom), and just when I thought they were going to start fighting, the theater's horn sounded loudly by the stage. Everyone paused.

The next few moments seemed to pass very slowly, and the only sound I could hear was my heart pounding against my chest. So where was that fearless warrior in me at that moment? Great question.

"He paid his fee. Leave him alone!" Zilhien yelled from beside the huge man holding the horn. She sprinted over and placed herself between me, the soldiers, and the would-be coin collectors. "I can't believe all of you are ready to fight each other for a matter of two coins. Really? I ran out of wristbands, so I went back for more and the play started."

Zilhien unhooked a silver bracelet she was wearing and put it on my wrist. "Here. Now he has an heirloom that belongs to the owners of the theater. He owes us nothing."

It's hard for me to accept this, but this wouldn't be the last time a woman defended my honor.

The coin collectors began to blend with the crowd again, and Da Grokpel showed up and dismissed his soldiers to other areas. Zilhien, Yilian, Nuthek, and I remained there with our backs against the crates. We were very quiet.

"That was a close one," Yilian said.

"It's my fault," Zilhien whispered. "I should've come back with your wristband sooner."

As people moved away, a woman emerged from the crowd in front of us. She had a sword in her hands, and the tip of the blade was dragging on the ground. We all recognized her as she put her sword away and walked closer to us. She was the princess from the play.

"Well Zilhien, you do know how to start and end a fight."

"It was just a misunderstanding. No one got hurt."

"Clearly it wasn't this boy's fault, it was yours. You should've given him back his coins in case the others asked to see his band. He could've paid the fee to them." The lady sighed. "What are your names?"

"Nuthek."

"Yilian."

"I'm Jonek."

"Jonek is the one our grandfather was talking about today, Min," Zilhien said.

"Is that so?" she said, sizing me up. Then, she smiled. "Why don't the three of you join us backstage? I think you'll like it."

***

At the center of the stage behind the curtain, Zilhien's grandfather was reading from a book preparing to face the audience. The princess approached the old man and whispered something in his ear.

She waved at us, asking us to join them where they were. The man greeted us and then focused his eyes on me.

"I see that you've met my granddaughters, Minhiala and Zilhien. Good. I just want to tell you that I realized what you were looking for in my tent. So many years have passed that I've almost forgotten about it. It also took some time for me to realize who you are."

My friends and I traded glances. Yes, this man was certainly an odd one, we silently agreed. (Perhaps he'd be good friends with that Drukhol by the cemetery.) The only thing I could offer was a smile and plenty of silence. The man closed his book and looked at me. "You were looking for me." He paused. "We'll talk about that later. Right now, I must go out there and take the audience back to that time when our soldiers gave blood and soul defending the city of Norkomas."

After he'd captivated the audience with his tales, we applauded the old man's performance until the palms of our hands turned red. Coins of many colors landed by his feet as he walked to the center of the stage to thank the audience. The curtains closed, and our two lady friends quickly ran to assist him.

"This was the best play I've ever seen!" Yilian said.

Zilhien nudged me.

"Jonek, my grandfather is inviting you and your friends to eat with us tomorrow in our tent. If you can't join us, then just make sure you visit him before the end of the fair."

"I think this is yours," I said, reminding her of her bracelet.

"You can give it back to me tomorrow. Just don't lose it. It was my grandmother's," she said before disappearing into the crowd.

We left the theater and walked back toward the market. "Well," Yilian said with a yawn, "I think I better head back to the store. Don't lose that invisible stone, Jonek. I'll see you in the morning by the road."

Once we walked into the market, Nuthek and I parted ways. When I reached our wagon, my mother and Zilhana were already packing for the night. The wagon was almost empty, so I asked my mother if she wanted me to start loading it. She smiled.

"Jonek, there's nothing to load! Look, we sold everything—even most of our crates. Aren't you happy?" I smiled back at her; it was rare to see her this energized and excited this late in the day. No doubt the first day of the fair was a great success for both ladies.

I threw my bag in the back of the wagon and loaded the few things lying on the ground. I was ready to climb into the back when, oddly (and for the first time in my life), I was asked to take the reins and take us back home. My mother and Zilhana climbed in and laid down on some empty sacks. I believe they began to snore even before we left the market.

I went slowly through the streets, but once we left town, I goaded him a little faster. I stopped by the entrance of the bridge to light a torch, but suddenly, the horse spooked and took off. I pulled the reins as hard as I could, but instead of slowing down, the horse veered to the side and slammed the wagon into the bridge.

The last thing I remember is the wagon hitting one of the rock pillars at the far entrance of the bridge and seeing everything in the air. The wagon slid along its side, and I was lucky to land on soft ground just a few steps away from it.

The horse was desperately trying to pull the weight of the toppled wagon, but he couldn't make it move. Exhausted, he stopped pulling and stood still, grunting out puffs of vapor through his nose and mouth.

My family. I stood up and looked around. Even though the lights from our wagon died in the crash, the two torches on the pillars illuminated my surroundings. I remember seeing the lights from the town in the distance and the fires from the Satolgac camp far off in the north.

"Mother! Zilhana! Are you alright?"

"Jonek, here . . ." someone said from a ways off, almost by the river. I grabbed one of the torches from the bridge and stumbled down to the river. My mother was huddled there by the edge of the water, soaked and covered with mud.

"Are you alright?" I called out. "Are you hurt?"

She coughed. "I'm hurt, but it's nothing serious. Are you alright?" She ran her hands all over my arms and face.

"I'm fine, mother. Where's Zilhana?"

Mother took my torch and turned it toward the water. "Go get the other torch and look up there." She headed under the bridge.

I slowly made my way up. Just as her torch vanished behind the stone arch and the shadows of the night covered me, I felt a hand holding my shoulder.

"Zilhana, is that you? Are you alright?" I whispered.

Silence and long fingers sliding over my forehead is all I remember of those few moments in darkness. My shoulder was released, so I moved my arms, trying to touch the person in front of me.

"Stop playing games, Zilhana. Is that you?" I whispered.

No answer. I kept walking until I reached the entrance to the bridge and took the other torch.

I was making my way back to the river when I saw Zilhana leaning on my mother, both hobbling out of the water. I shivered—who had touched my face, then?

It took some time but we gathered our belongings and made our way back home. Both ladies went inside to tend to their wounds while I unhitched the horse and unloaded the wagon.

This is when I realized something was missing—my bag.

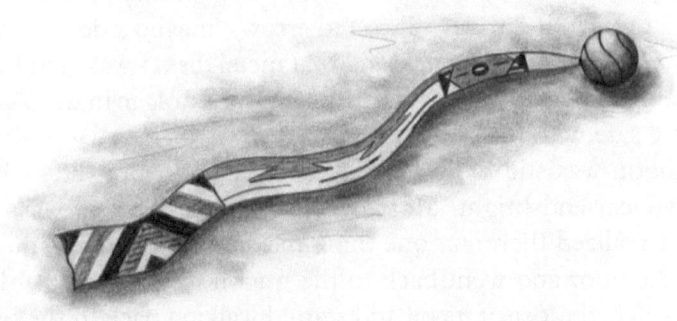

CHAPTER 4. THE WITCH OF BARKREK.

I couldn't find it anywhere.

I unloaded everything from the wagon and searched underneath it. Twice. I even went back to the main road but found nothing. The house? I searched every corner of the place in case my mother or Zilhana might have taken it inside with them. I was avoiding the thought as much as I could, but after running out of options, I had to accept my fate—we left my bag somewhere around the bridge.

I walked into my mother's room again and saw her snoring, still wearing those mud-covered clothes. Zilhana was sleeping so deeply that she didn't notice when I covered her with a blanket. It was too late to get them involved, so I sat down outside the kitchen door and debated whether it was a good idea to go back for that bag.

So what was in it anyway? Two red arrows, maybe a dozen coins, a few trinkets I won in the games, and that metal disk. I was glad I didn't put my ramikha or the stones I traded with the Satolgac in it, so at least those were safe with me.

The moon was still hiding behind some clouds, but the night sky was fairly clear and bright. Most of what was in that bag wasn't too dire, but I realized there *was* one thing making me hesitate—the disk. I closed the door and went back to the wagon to get a lamp. I lit the one that still had most of its oil and started walking back to the bridge.

Now, if walking alone in the woods late at night terrifies many adults, imagine how it was for a boy of my age. That journey became a serious trial of my courage. I really didn't mind walking alone at night, but that part of the forest always made me uneasy. Any sound, any shadow could betray your senses. And what of that rotted wolf-beast we'd seen? Your biggest enemy was your mind. Your imagination could make you lose control quickly, and on that night, the road back to the bridge seemed longer than it really was. I walked most of the time, but I have to confess that I ran through some areas, agitated by fear and anxiety. The pounding of my heart and the noises of the wind weren't loud enough to drown out the whispers and footsteps I thought I heard behind me all the way there.

Finally, the torches on the eastern side of the bridge appeared in the distance. I sprinted the rest of the way there and leaned on one of the pillars, trying to catch my breath. Then, taking a torch from the bridge in one hand and my lamp in the other, I started looking for my bag.

The first thing I noticed was the swatch of huge gouges the wagon had made in the ground as it landed on its side. Among the footprints near the edge of the water, I found the small box my mother used to carry vials of paint to retouch her pottery. That box, one empty pouch, and a few pieces of rope were all I could find around the bridge. At that point, I started thinking that my bag probably landed in the water and got carried away by the current.

I walked downstream along the edge of the river until I could no longer see the bridge. There was no sign of my bag, and I couldn't just spend the whole night searching the river's edge, so I decided to go back. I slid the torch back into its sconce and walked down to the edge of the water to sit on a rock. The air was getting colder, so I pulled the lantern closer to keep me warm.

Slowly, the clouds began to move away. The moon was so bright that you didn't need a lamp, and I was tempted to put out the flame to save the oil, but it was too cold for me to be without it.

It was no use—I'd never find that bag. I stood and headed downstream, intending to take the trail over the hills to stay away from any suspicious-looking shrubbery. I didn't even make it that far. I was jumping over a fallen tree when I accidentally hooked my toes on a branch and stumbled, one hand splashing into the water.

I stifled my yelp, but I couldn't help but mentally scold myself. The lamp splashed into the water with a hiss. I was able to grab it before it sank too deep, but it was useless. I had to empty the oil and water and carry it upside down to dry.

I sat still on my muddy knees for a moment to allow my eyes to get used to the moonlight. I was filthy at this point anyway, so I waded into the water to go around the rest of the big tree blocking my path. This was when I saw the light coming from the water. At first, I thought it was the reflection of the moon, but the light didn't move as I kept walking.

As I looked closer, there was definitely something glowing intensely at the bottom of the river. I left my mother's paint box and lamp on top of a flat rock and walked back into the river. The water was frigid, but fortunately for me, the light was close enough that I only needed to wade out waist-deep to reach it.

My hesitant steps sank deep into the river bottom, then suddenly, they touched something soft. My bag. The light emanating from it helped me illuminate my way back to the rocks, where I sat down and rubbed my legs briskly to warm them up. I reached inside and grabbed the disk. The thing was bright enough to glow through leather and cloth, sure, but out in the open, it illuminated my surroundings better than a dozen torches.

It was dripping wet, so I rubbed it over my shirt. To my surprise, the area I dried stopped glowing. My leggings were wet, so I ran the disk over them and it started glowing again.

"What kind of trinket are you?" I asked, shivering.

I gently put the disk by my side and scrounged through my bag to see if everything else was still in there. As any good archer would do, I pulled the red arrows out and dried them with my clothes.

If they weren't bent before, they're certainly useless now, I thought.

***

As I slowly made my way home, I caught sight of a dim light hidden away in the trees off the path. I was hesitant to venture into the forest so late at night, but what sort of others would be out at this time? I had to know.

I sat my jangling sack of objects under a bush at the tree line and quietly crept into the forest, drying off most of the disk to keep from being spotted. Soon, the smell of burning twigs and the crackle of a fire reached me, and I ducked down. Slinking low, I peered through a bush and spotted them—Satolgacs. An old man and a young girl.

They sat by the fire and talked, using both my language and theirs, while the man carefully inspected a bow and pulled its string a few times. He eventually gave it to the girl, and both sat in silence, looking at the fire and glancing at the sky from time to time.

I don't know how much time passed, but I was just about ready to give up and head back to the trail when suddenly, the man took one torch and walked to some trees maybe fifteen or twenty paces away. He placed the torch on the ground in front of a tree and hung something on a branch right above the torch's dancing flame. The man left the torch there and walked further into the woods; I lost sight of him as soon as he walked beyond the tree.

Soon, the man returned with two arrows. He threw a few logs on the fire, and the girl took an arrow. Both waited in silence, looking at the sky again. Looks like we weren't the only ones hiding arrows in the woods.

"It is time. The choice is yours," the man said.

The girl stood and walked in the opposite direction of the tree with the torch. After ten or twelve paces, she turned around, pulled the string, and released the arrow. It was hard to see through the bush, but the arrow sliced into the forest and all was quiet again.

I looked through another hole between the branches and noticed that there was no arrow stuck in the tree.

The girl rejoined the old man and knelt down in front of him. He sighed, reached down, and hugged her softly. It was a bit odd to witness, as the Satolgacs are known for not expressing any kind of emotion.

The man got back to his feet. "Now tell me, what is your choice, Khatzika?"

The girl didn't say a word but offered the bow and the last arrow to the man. He took them and put a pendant on her neck while saying some words I couldn't understand. The girl covered her head with her hood, took the other torch, and started walking back toward the place I was hiding.

I ducked down into the bush, but not before I saw something that broke my heart. The man threw the bow and the last arrow in the fire.

A real Satolgac bow turned to ashes. What a waste! I rested my head on the ground and remained still to avoid being discovered. I tried to breathe as softly as I could, but the girl stopped right by the bush where I was hiding. I was able to see her through the branches, so I'm sure she never looked down.

"You have no choice," she said, facing the darkness of the forest. "They are already here. Remember, they are just fish in the river."

She left me with those words and kept walking without looking back. I don't know how much time passed after she left (and the man followed shortly after), but I didn't move for a while. Honestly, my inexperienced brain was having trouble understanding what I'd just seen, and not even the cold wind made me move from that spot until much later.

At some point, I crawled out from underneath that bush with a realization. I was a stranger in my own life. Events and voices were trying to tell me something, but I was having a hard time understanding their message. Only one thing was clear to me—the life I had always known was long gone.

***

Long after they were gone, I approached their dying fire.

What a waste! I thought as I walked toward it. The image of that Satolgac throwing the bow into the flames was still fresh in my mind. I passed the disk over my leggings, trying to get some more light than just the dying embers, but my clothes were dry by then.

Some pieces of wood were still burning, so I gathered more to revive the fire. Then I noticed that the man didn't take the torch he left under the tree, so I went over there to get it.

As I got closer, I was finally able to see what the Satolgac had hung from the branch. I pulled the torch from the ground and raised it to illuminate a flat piece of wood with some carvings on one side and a small white circle on the other.

"This would've been a great shot," I said as I briefly glanced back at the place where she was standing when she released the arrow. Then I noticed something else out there, maybe fifteen paces farther into the woods.

When I walked closer, my torch lit up a similar piece hanging from another tree, only this one was half the size of the first. An arrow hung stuck in the center of its white circle. A perfect shot—and this target wasn't illuminated. I thought about taking the arrow with me, but I chose not to as a sign of respect for their traditions.

When I walked back to the fire, the high flames made me notice something I'd missed before. The bow was still there. The fire did burn its string and the arrow, but the bow itself was untouched.

I moved it away from the fire and searched for more wood. It didn't take long for me to rustle up a good fire, giving me plenty of heat and light. Instead of taking the bow and heading back to my house, I sat down and started admiring its craftsmanship.

I carefully untied the burned pieces of string and searched my bag for the one I took from the bow from the lagoon that morning. To my good fortune, the string was long enough for this bow.

I tried my best to tie the string the same way, but Satolgac knots are fairly difficult to make. The one thing I remember is the moon already on its way down before I finally had a working bow in my hands. I pulled and released the bowstring several times to feel its tension. I loved its sound.

Even though the string wasn't of good quality, what I had in my hands was the best bow I'd ever touched in my life. I thought about testing it using one of the red arrows, but a bent arrow wasn't worthy of that bow.

By that time, I was barely able to keep my eyes open. A nice divet in the ground by the fire seemed to fit me perfectly, and before I quite realized what was happening, the bow slid from my fingers and I was asleep.

***

My dreams that night felt very real. Some were old memories, others mere artifacts of my imagination. Familiar faces and others I no longer remember guided me through many moments that twisted and converged into a deafening mass, then suddenly, silence. A voice said, "It is time, Jonek."

I jolted awake, the morning mist was already making its way through the woods. Everything slowly came back to my mind as I saw the remnants of the fire and the bow at my side. I grabbed the beautiful weapon, kicked some dirt over the ashes, and headed back toward the trail. I still had a good chance of getting back to my house before my mother and Zilhana woke up, so I hurried uphill as fast as I could. Even though the sun was maybe an hour away from cresting the hills of the Stapian forest, there was enough light for me to rush through the woods.

I eventually reached the trail and switched from a jog to a run. I was just about to pass over a small hillock when, suddenly, I heard a terrible sound coming from the depths of the forest—some kind of dreadful, howling growl.

My first reaction was to stop and grab an arrow. Yilian's red arrows had remained by the fire most of the night, so at least they felt dry to the touch. I stayed low behind a bush, looking downhill toward the area the sound had come from, but I couldn't see anything moving.

I paused, taking one last sweep, then continued down the trail. I didn't even make it as far as the next hill when I heard more growling from the south. This time, some voices were caught up with it.

My instincts took control of my actions. I knew someone was in trouble, so I charged downhill toward the sounds. I ran as fast as I could until I slid to a stop behind an enormous tree lying on the ground.

"Run! I'll hold them! Run and don't look back!" someone yelled on the other side of the tree.

A loud growl swallowed up the end of that sentence. I climbed the fallen tree as fast as I could. What I saw next changed my life forever.

There were two Satolgacs on the other side. One was running uphill around the far end of a very large pit maybe twelve feet deep. The other one was downhill, standing with his back against the edge of the pit facing two wolves; both as mauled and terrifying as the beast we faced at the lagoon the day before.

Bright red eyes glowed on their grossly disfigured faces, and one was making awful grinding noises with his teeth. The Satolgac in front of them was slowly moving backwards, pointing a small rod at them. A wolf lunged at him, but some kind of lightning streaked out from his rod and knocked back the wolf in the air. The Satolgac threw the wolf against a tree, and even though it lay stunned on the ground for a moment, the beast quickly got up and joined the other with no less ferocity than before.

The Satolgac uphill was having trouble climbing some large rocks, so he changed direction and followed the edge of the pit toward the fallen tree where I was. One of the wolves caught sight of him, though, so he jumped back into the woods to cut his escape.

Not good, I thought.

The beast was charging toward my tree, so I was going to end up exactly in between the Satolgac and the wolf. The man with the rod lost his balance as he reached the edge of the pit, and the wolf took this opportunity to expel something from its mouth directly at his face. The Satolgac cried in pain and fell backward into the pit. It didn't look that high from where I was standing, but the man didn't move after the fall.

Oddly, the beast didn't jump into the pit to finish the Satolgac. Instead, he made his way around it, following the other Satolgac, who was now running in my direction. Time was running out. I took both arrows, left my bag hanging from a branch, and stepped on top of the tree. I pulled the bowstring and took a deep breath.

"Remember, they are just fish in a river," I whispered.

I released the arrow just as I heard a noise nearby—something was creeping onto my tree. I snagged the other arrow I'd left stuck by my side. By the time I whirled to my left, my bowstring was pulled and the arrow was ready.

Suddenly, there he was. The other wolf was crouched maybe ten paces away from me. The beast was drooling profusely, his eyes aglow. We both held our stance for a few moments, gazes locked. My fingers, still pulling that string, started to hurt, but I didn't move a muscle.

Just when I thought he was going to spring forward, a loud howl came from below, just by the face of the hill. I didn't turn my head to see where it was coming from, but the wolf in front of me did. His red eyes looked at me again and slowly turned black. I could feel his anger physically burning my face. He stepped back and swiftly jumped off the tree, disappearing into the woods.

I quickly whirled to my right, looking for a target, and there he was, lying inside the pit. My arrow didn't hit the wolf where I'd aimed, but it pierced through one of his back legs.

The beast was trying to drag itself out of the pit but wasn't making any progress. Something wasn't right, though. By the way that wolf was shaking and the sounds he was making, it seemed like he was dying. *One arrow in your leg can't kill a beast like you that quickly,* I thought.

Both Satolgacs were now lying on the ground unconscious—one in the pit and one uphill by its edge—and they were too far away for me to see if they were still alive.

I slid my bag off the tree limb and climbed down into the pit where the first Satolgac had fallen. I moved the body but quickly stepped away when I saw the old, wrinkled face. It wasn't a Satolgac, or even a man. It was the Witch of Barkrek.

At least, that's what we used to call her. That old lady was well-known in Ferdhen. Many people said she lived about an hour away in the Barkrek caves (hence the name), but no one really knew exactly where. She visited the market from time to time to trade items, mostly herbs. My mother told me once that she saw her trading live squirrels for a handful of mushrooms—an odd trade, if you ask me. She rarely talked to anybody and had no family; therefore, my friends and I concluded that she was a witch.

She was still breathing, and other than the brown drool from that wolf dripping from her face, she looked unharmed. A small satchel was lying close to her, so I slid it under her head and left my bag by her side. I picked up the wooden rod she had been using to defend herself and put it inside my shirt, then focused my attention on the wolf sprawled on the ground uphill.

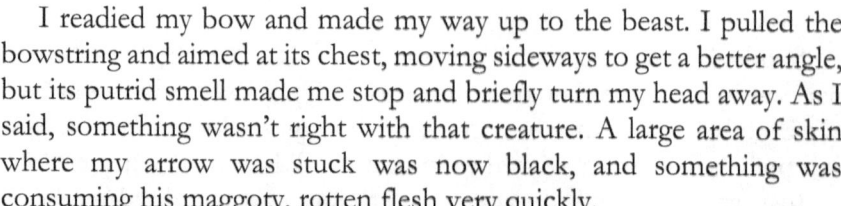

CHAPTER FOUR

I readied my bow and made my way up to the beast. I pulled the bowstring and aimed at its chest, moving sideways to get a better angle, but its putrid smell made me stop and briefly turn my head away. As I said, something wasn't right with that creature. A large area of skin where my arrow was stuck was now black, and something was consuming his maggoty, rotten flesh very quickly.

The beast kept making horrible sounds, but he turned his head toward me and his eyes began to glow red again. Suddenly, a sickening chill passed over me. He began to shake profusely. His fur retreated into slick pink skin and his body took the shape of a man. The white patch on his chest morphed into a black symbol burned onto his skin—a terrible scar for anyone to bear.

"What poison did you give me, animal?" He screamed at me, his face contorted in pain. I didn't say a word. I just kept moving uphill, pointing my arrow at him. "Your insignificant race will not survive this war! You must be the other one . . . . Artego. We will find you, animal, and you will pay for your crimes!" He rested his face on the ground and began to spit blood and breathe heavily.

I crept past him until I reached the second Satolgac. I knelt down and rolled him over to see his face—it was the old man from the cemetery that Nuthek talked about the day before. He was still breathing, but his forehead was bleeding badly. As I moved him, a book slid from his hands and landed by my feet.

The man with my arrow stuck in his leg kept laughing, and his bloody cackles made my spine shiver. I turned toward him again, bow ready. His face and body grew dark, and the scars on his chest glowed red. Suddenly, he stopped laughing.

"I've seen your face. You can't hide anymore."

Those were his last words. His eyes turned black and his body crumbled into ash. Just as I was lowering my weapon, another voice came from down in the pit.

"Help me, young man."

The old lady was trying to move but couldn't quite find her feet. I made my way down and helped her onto a rock.

"Are you alright?" I asked as I eased her down. "Are you hurt?"

"My face is burning and my leg hurts, but I'm fine," she said as she rubbed the brown spit onto her sleeve. When she was a little cleaner, she glanced uphill. "Is he alive?"

"One wolf escaped into the forest, the other one is dead, and the man has a bad wound on his head."

Hobbling to her feet, she pulled her pendant from inside her clothes and pinched it between her fingers, closing her eyes.

It seemed to me that of all the times to stop and pray, this wasn't it, but suddenly the rod inside my clothes grew warmer, and a humming sound emanated from it. I pulled it out to see a symbol glowing on its shaft. She opened her eyes and took it from my hands.

"Don't worry, young man. It won't harm you unless you have too much dark mist flooding your veins. What's your name?"

"Jonek," I said as she leaned on my shoulder.

We pressed on until we reached the place where the wolf had died. His ashes burned all the plants, leaving a swath of dry soil behind. Curiously, my arrow and something that looked like a wolf's claw hanging from a long leather string were also buried in the ash.

She asked me to go get the arrow, and then we kept walking until we reached the old man. The lady knelt down, touched the man's head, and then listened to his heart. She searched his clothes and took another rod like hers from him, placing it inside a fold in her robe-like shirt.

"He is too weak. We need to stop this bleeding."

"I live behind that hill in the distance," I offered. "We can take him to my house if you want. My mother could help."

She pursed her lips, looking around. Retrieving a piece of dead bark from the ground, she leaned in and placed it on the old man's forehead, then passed her rod over it, muttering something unintelligible. To my surprise, the bark changed, taking the form of the old man's forehead. She tried to move it, but it was tightly attached to his head.

"This will stop the bleeding for now. Please bring my satchel; we need to leave this place."

I rushed down and brought back her satchel, my bag, and even the wolf's claw. I stuffed the man's book in my bag and we started dragging him. She helped as much as she could.

After what seemed like hours, we reached the trail and covered most of the distance. I slid my ramikha out and let it catch the morning sun for just a moment—even now, I had to keep that promise, at least. We stopped at the top of the hill to catch our breath. I can't describe how happy I was to see our house down in the middle of the valley. Not a moment later, loud howling and the sound of what must've been a huge horn echoed from the distant woods behind us. My breath hitched, and despite her solid composure, I thought I felt the lady tense.

"I can run to my house and bring the wagon."

"Yes, go get it. I'll hold them here. Just leave me your arrows."

We carefully placed the old man on the side of the trail, and I offered her my bow and arrows.

"Only your arrows. Keep your bow."

I didn't waste more time. I threw my bag over my shoulder and ran as fast I could to my house. As I got to the bottom of the hill, I briefly turned around and was nearly blinded by a very bright light shining where the old lady was. It didn't last long, so I kept running as fast as I could. As I got closer to my house, I realized we had another problem—parts of that trail wouldn't be wide enough for the wagon.

Without time to find other options, I decided to leave the wagon and just bring the horse with me. I skidded around the house and nearly crashed into Zilhana, who was carrying two pots.

"Jonek? We thought you went fishing."

"Zilhana, tell my mother that there's a pack of wolves attacking some people on the hill to the west. They need help!"

Zilhana probably saw the desperation in my eyes, because she dropped the jars with a clatter and ran back into the house. The horse was already tied to the wagon, and to make matters worse, the wagon was already loaded with merchandise for the fair. I had to do something fast. I dropped the bow and my bag, nearly tearing it open to look for the disk.

That was the only sharp thing I had to cut the ropes that kept the horse and the wagon together. I put my fingers through some of the holes, took a deep breath, and shoved it over the ropes. I don't know why, but this time the disk didn't fail me. The ropes tumbled to the ground, cleanly cut. I pulled the horse out, took the reins, and started back toward the hill.

I was holding the reins with one hand and the disk with the other, keeping it just over my chest. I never turned back to see if my mother or Zilhana ever came out of the house. I just needed to get back to the hill as soon as possible.

Now, a twelve-year-old boy riding a draft horse bareback at full speed might sound dangerous, and it certainly was, but I managed to cling onto the beast's mane as we started uphill. In the distance, the old woman drew back a bow, aiming at the other side of the hill. It was a silver bow so shiny that its glare made me close my eyes for a moment.

I pulled the reins to slow down but it was too late—the horse was out of control. The old lady was standing on the narrowest part of the trail, and even though I yelled at her a couple of times, she never turned around to see that I was going to run her over. Just when we were a few steps from each other, a black wolf leaped from the other side of the hill directly toward me.

Oddly, my only reaction was to raise the hand with the disk in front of the wolf.

I'm not entirely sure how to describe what happened just then. Imagine some kind of shield made of round waves of light emanating from the center of the disk and converging into a shiny silver edge. Something like that appeared in front of me just before the wolf's massive body collided with it, making me fly off the horse and roll downhill into a bush. Lucky for me, it didn't have any thorns.

I still don't know how the old lady managed to avoid my horse, but once the world stopped spinning and I looked back at the trail, two wolves were down and she had the bowstring knocked with a strange silver arrow, ready for another shot.

Well, she really knows how to use a bow, . . . for a witch, I thought. I pushed the shield away from my body and stumbled to my feet.

"Jonek, are you alright? Can you walk?" the woman yelled as she crouched in front of the old man. I was in pain, and my horse was nowhere to be found, but I hobbled back onto the trail. The carcasses of two wolves lay sprawled near the incapacitated man. "Jonek," the lady said without looking up, "get your fingers out of that shield and take the arrows from the wolves. We need to keep moving."

I heard the words, but my body was slow to obey. I pulled a finger from the disk and the shield disappeared. I slipped it inside my clothes and approached the beasts.

Pulling the first arrow from that wolf tore something inside of me. I now knew that those animals were in fact men—evil folk, but men no less. This wasn't a boy's game anymore. Fighting evil feels vastly different when you see the faces of your foes lifeless in front of you. Remember these words. Taking the life of another, even if it is to defend good from evil, will scar your soul forever. Sometimes you have no other choice, and it is the only way for you to protect what is good in this world. So don't hesitate, ever. They won't.

The wolf turned into a human as soon as I pulled the arrow from him. He had the same black scars on his chest, but this one had one eye missing. As I walked closer to the other wolf, I heard my mother's voice.

"Jonek, is that man dead? Are you hurt? Speak to me, boy!"

My mother and Zilhana were standing a few paces behind the old woman, and both of them looked decidedly disturbed.

"These beasts are no men. They are dark warriors. Assassins," the old woman responded.

"The old man—"

Zilhana never finished that sentence. Her voice caught in her throat as the first man turned into dust and I pulled the arrow from the other wolf and he turned into a man.

My mother pulled Zilhana closer and hugged her as both witnessed those terrible transformations. Well, Zilhana didn't see the whole process—she fainted in my mother's arms before the wind swept away the ashes of the second one. I picked up the pendants and put them in my pocket with the other claw.

"Listen!" the lady hissed. "We are still in danger. Your mother and I will drag Drukhol to your house while you help the girl." It occurred to me that by "the girl" she meant Zilhana, but I was preoccupied watching her silver bow changing back into the wooden rod.

My mother hesitated but ended up taking the old man's arm and hoisting him up, noticing the piece of bark on his forehead.

"My dear lady, don't be afraid. This piece of bark is nothing compared to the evil out there searching for us," Tynia said, looking into my mother's eyes.

My mother couldn't offer any response, so they both dragged the man downhill in silence. I crouched and fanned Zilhana's face until she came to and could walk with me. Just as I was closing the door to the kitchen, those awful sounds broke out from the woods beyond the hill. They were still distant, but the message was clear. They were coming.

I barred the door with a table and went straight to my room. The old lady was peeling the bark from the man's forehead while my mother kept sopping up the blood on his face and neck. He was still breathing, but his condition wasn't good. My mother saw me standing there holding the Satolgac bow, but she didn't say a word.

"I think there are more wolves coming," I said softly.

The old lady looked up from the old man to see both my mother and I staring at her. She knew we were on her side. We were trying to help, but we were in no position to understand the situation we had just been pulled into. She realized that this new reality was beyond our comprehension, so she put her hand on the man's forehead to apply pressure on his wound, steadying herself in the process.

"I regret with all my heart that you were dragged into this." She paused. "My name is Tynia. This man's real name is Kharlo. We are guardians—warriors fighting an ancient battle against evil. Evil from another world."

My mother and I remained silent.

"As you can see, times are difficult right now. Far away, under a different sky, is a place connected to this land by pathways created thousands of years ago. A massive war has swallowed the souls of that world for countless generations. Lately, our forces have been failing on many fronts, and the conflict is now spreading into this world.

"For now, the only thing you need to know is that saving this man may be our only chance to change the tide in our favor. We, the guardians, are the protectors of what they ultimately seek. It doesn't matter to them how long it takes or how many legions they lose—they will never stop until they find us."

"Well, it seems they already know where you are," my mother said as she knelt closer to Kharlo, dabbing up more blood.

Tynia opened Kharlo's shirt and pushed a golden pendant on a thin leather string out of the way. My mother couldn't stomach the wounds on his chest, so she turned her eyes away.

"Jonek, take your bow, the red arrows, and the shield and find a high place where you can target anyone that comes close to the house," Tynia said.

"My dear lady, my son is no soldier, nor a guardian like you. He's twelve!"

"Almost thirteen," I felt the need to interject.

Tynia glanced up at my mother. "He has the skin of a boy with the heart of a man. He could be twelve, thirteen, or thirty-five. All I know is that this young man saved our lives this morning by facing two of the deadliest creatures this world will hopefully ever see. I don't know how, but he did. Believe me when I say this—he knows how to use a bow, and his blood carries more courage than most warriors."

For all their flattery, I think those words destroyed any chance I had to get that bow on my birthday. Not that it mattered at that point, but

I still think that something broke inside my mother's heart when she realized what Tynia was saying. She kept cleaning Kharlo's wounds, a frown on her face. Finally, she said, "Jonek, do as the lady says, but please be very careful."

"I'll climb on top of the house and hit the roof three times if I see someone coming. I just wish I had more arrows."

My mother stood up, left the room, and came back moments later with a quiver full of arrows.

"I bought these Satolgac arrows for you as part of your gift. I was going to buy your bow today, but it seems you don't need one anymore." She briefly hugged me and went back to help Tynia.

"Wait," Tynia said. "These arrows won't help. There must be something on the red ones that is deadly for the dark scouts." She held the shaft close to her nose, examining it carefully before handing it back to me. "Yes, it has to be the red paint. The rest of it looks normal. Do you know what kind of paint this is?"

My mother took the arrow and smelled it. Then she bit a small piece from it and spit it out almost immediately. "This paint is very common around here. We make it using petals from the Jikhol flower. We dry them and mix them with oil to make the red color. I have some in my box."

"Oh, I have your box, mother!" I said. I'd forgotten shoving it in my satchel during the night. She opened one of the vials of red paint and compared it to the color on the arrows.

"Yes, this is the one. This is all the red paint I have, but we can buy or make more if needed. I just need to get the ingredients in town."

Tynia opened the vial and scooped out some paint with her finger. She pulled her pendant from inside her clothes and painted a small portion of the leather string with it.

"Jonek, cover the rest of the arrowheads with this and be ready. Stomp on the roof as you said if you see anyone coming."

As I left the room, I saw Zilhana looking through a small hole in a corner. "Do you see anyone out there?" I asked.

"Are they going to hurt us?" she asked, shivering.

"Don't be afraid. I won't let them get near the house. Push these crates against the door as soon as I get out and make sure the table stays against the kitchen door."

I slowly opened the door and looked around. I ran a few steps away from the house, threw the bow and arrows on the roof, and circled

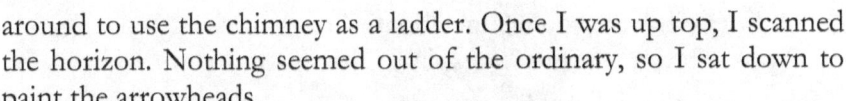

around to use the chimney as a ladder. Once I was up top, I scanned the horizon. Nothing seemed out of the ordinary, so I sat down to paint the arrowheads.

I pulled a few arrows from the quiver and couldn't help but notice how perfect they were. Their heads were sharp, the wood was smooth, and they were definitely straight.

Out of the corner of my eye, I caught sight of something moving on the top of the hill in front of me. I picked up the bow and walked to the edge of the roof, focusing in on the place where Tynia killed those wolves.

I was waiting for some sort of beast to jump over the hill when I heard someone whistling by the road on the other side of the house.

"Yilian," I whispered.

I walked to the other side of the roof and saw my two friends in the distance standing by the road. Yilian and Tobho were ready to go fishing and were play-pushing each other. They knew nothing.

I whistled back a few times until I got their attention. They slowly walked toward the house, probably wondering what was I doing on the roof. Once they got closer, I realized why they were walking with such hesitation. Both were carrying bows (and most likely a few arrows) inside their leather bags.

"Go to the other side and use the chimney to climb up!"

"Are you crazy? Your mother will see us!" Tobho said as he showed me his bow.

"Don't worry about your bows! We have bigger problems right now. Throw your bows and bags on the roof!"

"What's going on?" Yilian asked.

"Remember the black wolf yesterday?"

"Of course."

"That beast wasn't alone. There's more than a few out roaming, and they're not wolves. They're men. Assassins."

"What are you talking about?"

"Yes Tobho, *men*. And I had to kill one this morning."

I remember Tobho and Yilian's eyes opening wide when they heard that. They didn't say anything else and they climbed straight up. Before they were even all the way onto the roof, the questions started.

"You killed a wolf or a man?"

"Well, you could say I killed one of each. They were the same. The wolf transformed into a man and then turned into ashes."

"Ashes? What are you talking about? Are you alright, Jonek?"

"Look, there's no time to explain. Take your arrows and dip the heads in this vial. Trust me."

"This is the same paint I used on my arrows. I thought you didn't want us to paint them anymore!" Yilian said.

"I know. Just do it, please."

As they took care of their arrows, I turned my eyes back to the hill to the west, but now everything was quiet.

"Yilian, do you see the top of that hill?"

"Mhmm."

"Keep your eyes there. Let me know if you see anything moving. I'll take a look at the other side and come back in a minute."

"But what am I looking for?"

I took the three leather strings holding those huge wolf claws from my pocket and dangled them right in front of their faces. "Something really bad," I said.

Tobho grabbed the claws, looking at them closely. Yilian peeked over his shoulder.

"Jonek, are you sure these came from a wolf and not a bear?"

"Unfortunately, yes."

Yilian took his bow and some of my Satolgac arrows and stood by the edge of the roof, staring at the hill to the west. I took a few arrows and went to the other side to watch the area close to the road.

I heard the door opening below me. I leaned forward and saw Zilhana slinking a few steps out of the house. She looked at me, threw something on the roof, and scurried back inside before I was able to say a word.

I couldn't believe it. Even at a time like this, my mother was worried about me not having something to eat. She'd sent Zilhana to bring me bread and two apples. I left some arrows on that side of the roof and returned to Yilian and Tobho. I sat down with Tobho and noticed he was still looking at the pendants.

"Here, Tobho, eat some bread," I said, taking the pendants. "Don't worry, we'll be fine."

I was going to lighten the mood by sharing a grandiose retelling of my adventures over the last few hours, but suddenly, we heard growling just beyond the hill in front of us. It was so loud that we heard its echo reverberating across the hills behind us. Our gazes met.

"Here they come."

CHAPTER 5. COLD FLAMES.

*W*e didn't have much time.

"Yilian, Tobho, listen to me! Don't think too much. If we hesitate, we won't make it." I grabbed the vial of paint. "I don't know why, but this paint is poison for them. When they touch it, they turn into dust." I painted a line on my forehead and put some on my arms and hands. Yilian and Tobho didn't say a word. They slung their bows over their shoulders and painted themselves as I did.

"This paint is burning my lips," Tobho said as he spit some of it on the roof. Yilian stayed by my side facing west, and Tobho stood a few steps behind us.

"I hope he doesn't faint when he sees them," I leaned in and whispered to Yilian.

"I hope I don't faint too," he said, glancing at me. "Do you know how many there are?"

"I don't. I killed one in the woods, and Tynia killed two on the top of that hill."

"Tynia?"

"Oh, right. You haven't met Tynia and Kharlo. Well, you actually know them both. She's that witch in the Barkrek caves, and Kharlo is the crazy old man Nuthek was talking about yesterday. Both are hiding out with mother and Zilhana for the moment. Don't worry, you'll have a chance to meet them . . . if we make it through this."

Yilian just stared at me. "It finally happened. You've really lost your mind. Did you fall on your head again?"

Even in those tense moments, I couldn't help the brief smile creeping onto my face.

A sound in the distance made us look west again. A flock of birds took off at the top of the hill as my mother's horse finally reappeared, galloping wildly toward us.

"Get ready!"

Yilian was going to say something, but his voice failed him.

Two wolves and a black bear bounded over the top of the hill toward the house. I stomped on the roof three times and moved to my left to cover more area.

"Tobho, take a few arrows and go to the other side," I said.

Yilian and I settled into our best stances, pulled our bowstrings back, and waited for the beasts to get closer. Tobho later said he heard the front door opening and saw the Witch of Barkrek emerge. He didn't understand a word she said, but a burst of flames erupted from her rod. She pointed the spell toward the ground and a wall of fire maybe ten feet high surrounded the house. Yilian actually fell backward from the blast of heat.

My mother's horse briefly stopped but kept going around the fire toward the road. The beasts slowed down and circled the wall a few times.

"Tobho, Yilian, if you have a clear shot, take it!"

"They're moving too fast, Jonek!"

"Just aim and release."

The bear stopped in front of the chimney and stood on his hind legs, trying to reach us over the fire. The wolves ran around, changing directions, looking for a way to cross the wall. I moved backward and glanced at Tobho. We didn't know how long the fire would keep burning, so we had to do something quickly.

Their howling and growling was taking a toll on our ragged nerves, but Yilian and I managed to keep track of them. Tobho, however, was beside himself. He was slowly backing up, pointing his bow toward the roof.

"Tobho! Wake up!"

"I don't want to die, Jonek," he said, shivering uncontrollably. His eyes watered, and I doubt it was from the smoke.

"Tobho, look at me!" I took a few steps toward him without turning away from the bear. "Look at me!"

Tobho slowly turned his head and made eye contact with me, his breath coming in shaking gasps.

"You will live through this and whatever other ridiculous things we'll get ourselves into. Now shoot some arrows."

Yilian ran over and stood by Tobho's side. After a few moments, the wall of fire started to lose height in some areas. I was following one of the wolves moving away from the fire when I noticed something in the distance. Someone was standing on the hill, just below where Tynia killed those two wolves. He was far away, but I could clearly see a red cloak and some beasts standing by his side.

I stomped on the roof again to let everyone know that our situation wasn't improving. The fire was dying; suddenly, the wolves charged straight toward the house and made it over the flames. I released an arrow and immediately pulled another one from the quiver, but just when I thought the arrow was going to hit the wolf, the beast disappeared. I stepped back and glanced at my friends, wondering if they'd seen it too.

"What's going on?"

"I don't know," Yilian said from behind me. "The wolf and bear stopped moving. They're just staring at us."

"Don't waste your arrows. How far away from the fire are they?"

They didn't even have the chance to answer. When I heard them gasp, I whirled around, even though I already knew. The beasts had vanished in front of them too. I took a few steps forward to stare through what remained of the fire and suddenly, there they were. The person wearing the red cloak wasn't at the top of the hill anymore; he was standing a few steps from the fire holding a long, crooked staff in his right hand. A bear stood in front of him, and two wolves circled at his side.

I didn't realize what had happened until then—that man was clever indeed. The beasts running around us had been nothing more than an illusion. They were sent to make us waste our arrows and expose our strengths to the man on the hill.

"Yilian, Tobho, come to this side. Now!"

I slowly stepped closer to the edge of the roof. The man's hood obscured his face completely; the only flesh we could see was those long, dirty fingers holding the staff. The beasts kept making horrible grinding sounds with their teeth, their eyes following our every move.

I took another step forward and aimed directly at the man's chest. I thought about releasing the arrow and rolling backward to take cover, but I wasn't sure whether any of them were real or just another illusion. I let the bowstring go idle and lowered my weapon.

I took the disk from inside my clothes, threading my fingers through its holes. The man moved his head for the first time. Even though we still couldn't see his face, I knew he was watching intently.

He lowered his head, and a deep, low voice reverberated from inside those robes. "Your kind are extinct. My father and the father of my father all the way back to Sulibhor's time have hunted and exterminated your people. I see that you are now protecting these animals—a demeaning job for you, elite. You will die. I will see your blood staining the hands of my servants. Look at them! They hunger for your suffering, and they will make you suffer. But they will do it as warriors." The man tapped the ground with his staff, and the three beasts transformed into humans. All of them carried swords and daggers pointed at me. It was obvious he had mistaken me for someone else.

The fire was dying, so the dark scouts crept a few steps closer to the house. I took this opportunity to stomp on the roof again, begging for help. No response. My eyes met an assassin's.

Those few seconds passed slowly; the assassins stepped over the fire easily, and I was running out of options. Perhaps it was a poorly contrived plan, but it was all I had. I took a deep breath and dropped the bow at my feet. I took the three claw pendants from my pocket and threw them down to the warriors.

"How many more of you do we have to kill before you realize that you will never subdue us?" I said, feigning confidence. "Hear me when I say that each one of you will pay for the innocent lives you have taken in the name of your master. Go and tell your people that this time, war is coming to you. You'd better leave and bring more if you want to win this fight. But if you all want to turn to ash this fine morning, so be it."

The assassins paused. "Vothik and his men," one said, turning back to look at the man in red. He wrapped his bony fingers around the edge of his hood and uncovered his face. He was an old man, barely skin and bones with patches of long white hair and a beard. He had many black symbols burned on him, and he was blindfolded with a filthy piece of cloth. He took a step forward, and the assassins parted for him.

"You say some brave words for a guardian about to die. I will see your bones burning on this ground in front of me. Vhivrok!"

His shout jolted us, and Tobho was so on-edge that the man's loud shout made him jump, and his fingers slipped from the bowstring. I remember feeling the arrow barely missing my arm as it flew toward them. The three assassins hesitated. Maybe some of my words had disturbed them.

That arrow certainly took the old man by surprise. Even though he ducked sideways at the last moment, the arrow sliced a deep cut into his neck. The man screamed and lost his balance, tumbling to the ground. The scouts regained their composure, hurling their daggers toward us. I barely had time to push Yilian aside.

That was the second time that disk saved my life. Yilian and I were falling when the shield appeared again, blocking two daggers. The other one barely missed Tobho's leg. I somehow managed to stay on the roof, but Yilian landed on the ground, hard.

The old man put a hand on his neck and pointed his staff toward us. Some kind of red lightning crackled our way, leaving a trail of fire along the wall of my house. Unfortunately for him, that lighting also killed two of his assassins, barely missing Yilian and the third scout, who managed to roll on the ground to avoid the beam.

"Tobho, target the old man again! I'll cover you!" I said as I got on my knees.

"Again? I didn't mean to the first time!"

"Just do it!"

Maybe by fear, maybe by instinct, he released another arrow. Of course, he didn't hit anyone—in fact it flew closer to the third scout than the old man. That actually helped Yilian, as the assassin was crawling toward him and he had to move back to avoid Tobho's arrow.

"Again, Tobho!"

I could hear my friend's ragged breathing and almost feel him trembling, but this time the last assassin couldn't avoid the arrow, and it lodged into his shoulder with a dull *thwack*. The old man tried to stand up but fell back to his knees, clutching his neck and wheezing.

"What kind of magic is this?!" the old man yelled as he clawed at his neck, almost as if trying to tear the skin off. He waved his staff at us again, but the pain threw off his aim and arcs of lightning splintered in random directions. At some point, a bolt from his staff actually hit my shield, and a rain of sparks cascaded over Tobho and me. The shield turned red for a moment, then released the lightning back toward the old man. Tobho and I were blinded by the light, but Yilian said that the lightning turned the man's staff a molten red and he threw it down a few steps away, his hand blistering.

Without his staff, the old man began to act as if he was really blind. He crawled on his knees, patting the ground in search of it. We never even saw Tynia come out of the house but there she was, kicking the staff further away from him just as he got close to it. Her rod briefly shined as it turned into a long, silver sword.

"Jonek, you and your friend can come down now. There are no more wizards or scouts nearby."

Tynia waved her sword, hurling chunks of earth toward the side of the house to put out what was left of the lightning fire. She slowly approached the old man and began to circle him.

"Look at this old blind mage. A greedy soul who betrayed his own race to swear allegiance to the Zerkial cult. And for what? A broken promise?" She pointed her sword toward the last scout who was writhing on the ground, a painted arrow lodged in his quickly decaying skin. "And you—you are not a man anymore. You are nothing more than a beast with no soul and no peace."

The old man remained on his knees as Tynia stopped in front of him. It seemed like she was ready to actually use that sword.

"We will find you, old witch," the man said as he lowered his head, waiting for her final blow. "Your time is coming."

"You are old," Tynia said as she raised her sword. "I just *look* that way."

One part of me wanted to see that evil wizard leave this world, but the other wasn't so sure about seeing an unarmed man slain.

Just when I thought she was going to do it, the last assassin threw a dagger toward her. Even though she wasn't looking at him, Tynia swiftly moved to one side and sent her sword flying, piercing his chest. The man made a brief, almost inaudible sound as his head hit the ground and his body turned to ashes.

At the same time, the wizard's body began to shake violently, and his skin turned dark. The man said two or three words in a tongue that none of us understood. His body froze and disintegrated, leaving that strip of cloth covering his eyes partially buried in the ashes. Neither the ground nor the wind took those remains away. They sat there, unwanted by anyone or anything in this world.

Tynia picked up her sword and an arrow lying close to Yilian. She made a small cut on the skin of the other two scouts burned by the wizard and looked at us. "We don't have much time. Jonek, pick up their weapons and bring them inside. I have to see how Kharlo is doing."

Tobho gathered the arrows while I tossed our bows to Yilian, then I put the disk and the vial of paint inside my clothes. By the time we joined Yilian, he was holding six claw pendants in his hand. We gathered the staff, swords, and daggers and brought them inside.

Zilhana was in the kitchen, sitting in a corner. She was sobbing traces of tears carving tracks all over her dirty face. She was just staring at the floor and said nothing as we passed. My mother and Tynia were still in my room working on a wound on Kharlo's leg that was bleeding badly. We put the weapons on the table and sat on the floor with our backs to the wall still smoking from the wizard's fire.

My mother came out for water and saw us sitting there. She sucked in a breath when she saw our skin covered in red, but she almost smiled when she realized that it wasn't blood. She never said a word—she just knelt down and hugged me as if she hadn't seen me in years. To be honest, I felt the same way.

After a long, long hug, she left us there and disappeared into the kitchen. I looked around to see family and friends tired, disoriented, but mostly afraid. I decided it would be best if we kept our minds busy.

"Tobho, go to each room and look through the holes in the walls. Let us know if you see anything moving outside." Tobho quietly got up and walked into my mother's room.

"Hey, what happened to the old man from the cemetery. Is he alright?" Yilian whispered.

"I don't think so," I said, leaning further back. "They were attacked by those beasts and he was seriously wounded. They must have fought them for hours."

"Where did you find them?"

"In the forest to the west. When I found them, Tynia was fighting the wolves and he was trying to run away."

"Did he have a weapon?"

"He had a wooden rod like Tynia's, but he wasn't using it. The only thing he had in his hands was a book."

"A book?"

"Yes, I have it here in my bag."

"Well?" Yilian said, glancing at the satchel.

I hesitated but ended up pulling my bag closer and taking the book out. It wasn't big—maybe a hundred pages between brown leather covers.

I opened it, and to our surprise there were no words or symbols on the first page. I turned to the next and found another blank page. I flipped through the entire book and couldn't find a spot of ink.

Yilian took it and flipped through the pages too. Why was he protecting an empty book?

"Maybe the book is magical or the ink he used was invisible," he said.

"Or maybe he took the wrong book," I answered with a shrug.

We sat in silence for a few minutes. Yilian glanced over at me, opened his mouth, closed it again, and then pulled his legs up to his chest and wrapped his arms around them.

"That round thing you used outside. What is it?" he asked.

"I don't know. I bought it yesterday from a vendor thinking it would be a great addition to my collection, but it turned out to be more than just a trinket. Yesterday its edge turned sharper than a snake's fang. Today it turned into some kind of shield. Who knows what else it can do."

Just then, Tobho returned and sat back down. "I looked through every hole, and there is nothing out there. Your horse came back, though." He heaved a deep sigh, his face still pale. After resting with his eyes closed for a few minutes, he looked across the room, and his brows furrowed when he noticed Zilhana. Tobho did something then I never really expected. Walking over to her and gently placing a hand on her shoulder, he sat by her side.

"Zilhana, I know you're listening to me. I understand what you're going through at this very moment." He softly pushed the cup of water toward her. "I have lived afraid all my life. I'm not strong or fast or even skillful with any tools or weapons. Some people make fun of my size and how much I eat, but I've learned to live with that. Only my friends—Yilian, Jonek, and Nuthek—make me feel respected or even important."

Tobho looked down at the cup. "Am I afraid to die? Every day of my life. Do I feel ready to face those creatures outside? Not in a hundred years. Am I going to let them take my life without a fight? Never. I have learned that big or small, everyone's role in this life is important. You are important. We need you. Please eat or drink something."

I had never heard any of my friends speak that way toward anyone. I grew to deeply respect Tobho that day. Those words were more powerful than any magic around us.

Zilhana moved her head and looked at Tobho. She slowly took the bread from his hand and nibbled off a small piece.

Knowing that Zilhana was in good hands, I stood and headed to my room. Kharlo was lying on my bed, most of his body bandaged. My mother and Tynia were sitting by his side, and by the way they looked, it seemed like they had just been through a battle themselves.

"How is he doing?"

"Come here," my mother said, offering her arms to me. "This man is clinging to life by a very thin thread. We managed to stop the bleeding, but he is extremely weak. It is difficult to say if he will see tomorrow."

"I've known him since we were nine or ten," Tynia said out of the blue, expressionless. "We were chosen to follow a path that separated us from our families since we were about your age, Jonek. Too many memories cross my mind as I see him lying there. He was the strongest of us. The warrior. Our leader."

"Where are you from?" my mother asked.

"We are from a place not far from here, just west of Ferdhen. Our story is not easy to follow or be understood. It took many years for us to comprehend the rules ourselves and learn to live with the consequences."

"You were born around here? Do I know your family?"

A twinge of sadness crossed Tynia's face. She furrowed her brow, her eyes tearing up. Her lip quivered slightly, but she fought it back. However, after a few moments, she stood and knelt down in front of my mother. She couldn't hold back the tears this time, and she covered her face with her hands and began to sob.

"This old lady crying in front of you is just thirty-five years old."

My mother and I paused and traded glances but remained silent while Tynia cried. Mother ran a hand gently over her back, and Tynia sniffled.

"My friends and I have probably lived seven lifetimes as guardians in the other world, but our bodies haven't aged more than a few years since we joined this quest. I know this doesn't make any sense to you, but my appearance is just a consequence of traveling between both worlds."

That was a complicated moment for my mother and me. It just didn't make sense. None of this did.

My mother didn't know what to say, but at some point she must have realized that even though she looked significantly younger than Tynia, she was in fact the oldest in the room. My mother slowly put her hands on Tynia's head, whispered something in her ear, and allowed her to cry for a while. When Tynia's sobs turned to exhausted breaths, my mother used her skirt to dab away the tears on Tynia's face.

"You said you are thirty-five and were born here; I must know your family."

"I know some people around here," Tynia said, "but I don't think anyone will ever recognize me. I left these lands as a child. I spent most of my time in Kirolcan, the other world, but Kharlo and I have lived here in hiding for the last three years."

"Everything is so confusing. If what you're saying is true, we must've seen each other when we were children," my mother said.

"I don't remember you. It's true that I didn't have many friends, but I knew one other girl that lived across the river from my house, her name was Viarali. Unfortunately, I lost track of her a long time ago."

"You knew my mother?"

We turned toward the door and saw Yilian standing there wide-eyed, Zilhana and Tobho behind him. Zilhana was holding a bowl in her hands, and Tobho had bread in his.

"You are Viarali's son?" Tynia asked.

Yilian barely managed to nod as his eyes got misty. Tobho quickly jumped in. "Well, . . . err, we brought some food for the lady and we were wondering if we should bring something for the man."

"Come with me," my mother said, helping Tynia to her feet. "Let's have something to eat. My son will stay with your man and watch him. Later, we'll come back and try to give him something to eat."

"Kharlo is not my 'man' nor my husband. He is my best friend."

"Oh, my mistake. Well, let's go to the kitchen. I need these two young men to watch the doors while Zilhana, you, and I have something to eat. Jonek, let us know if this man is having trouble breathing, and make sure you pass the wet rag around his neck and face to keep his fever down."

They left me there and closed the door halfway. Only a candle and a hole in my wooden window lit up my room. I walked closer to look at Kharlo's face and see if he was breathing—thankfully, he was. I pulled a chair closer to the bed and sat there.

Are you also thirty-five years old? I thought as I watched the old man breathe. *What is a guardian anyway? Guardian of what? What is the quest Tynia talked about? What kind of weapon is that thing you're carrying? Are these like the one prince Komippel was looking for?* I had enough questions to keep my mind more than occupied.

The house grew very quiet. I could hear muffled voices from the other room, but I couldn't really understand anything.

The ray of sunlight coming through the window was on my lap at the moment, so I took the disk from inside my clothes and traced its details in the light. I counted nine holes and many symbols carved on both sides of the disk. There was still some dirt and rust on it, so I put my hand inside the bucket of water and tried to clean it.

I noticed that the water on the disk was slightly red—some of Kharlo's blood. I put my fingers in various holes and moved the disk around, trying to make it work.

I extended my arm and asked for a shield with my mind, but nothing happened. I put my fingers in different holes and tried again. Nothing.

"How do you use this thing?" I whispered, looking at Kharlo.

I tried a few more times with no success and then thought that if it didn't respond to thoughts, maybe it would to feelings.

I stopped for a moment to pass the wet rag over Kharlo's neck and face. As I was moving away from him I noticed the thin leather necklace he was wearing. My curiosity had me running my fingers along it to the golden pendant at the end.

The pendant depicted a circle with a vertical line crossing its center and two lines in the shape of serpents crossing sideways. I really didn't question whether it was right or wrong—I just instinctively touched it.

Well, it didn't take long for me to realize that I shouldn't have done that. I tried to pull my fingers away, but suddenly his hand grabbed mine, holding my fingers in place. He never opened his eyes or said anything, and no other part of his body moved. The disk started to vibrate in my other hand. At first there was a dim light emanating from it, but it suddenly exploded into a bright glow moments later. Even though I imagined my heart was going to burst out of my chest, I managed to keep myself from screaming.

"Mother, something is happening!"

Everyone rushed in but froze when they saw the brilliant light. I held the disk as far away from me as I could—the light was becoming too bright for my eyes. None of them, not even Tynia, knew what was happening.

Suddenly the light from the disk projected an image. A rainbow of colors coalesced like droplets of water until a human figure took shape in the center of the glow. A young man with long black hair was leaning on a rock, drawing something on the ground with the tip of his sword. The background seemed like a forest, but it was hard to tell as it was constantly in motion, like a reflection on the water.

"How are you, Tyn?" the man said, taking his eyes off the ground.

Tynia walked closer. "Kharlo?"

"Yes. Forgive me for doing this, but my body is beyond healing with the medicines of this world. There isn't much time. Before the wizards found me this morning, I was on my way to see you. I think I've found the last clue. I don't have the skills to decipher it, but you and the others will know how to do it. It's time for us to find Artego and Jalyena and bring them back into the fight."

The man in the glow walked closer to us. "Only Artego knows where Jalyena is, and Artego's location is hidden in the pages of the fifth journal."

I remember turning my head and looking first at the Kharlo lying on my bed, then at the one talking to us. You could almost say they were father and son.

"Tynia, it's time for me to get back to Kelfia. I need to get there, even if my heart is the only thing that remains alive as we do it. I can temporarily defeat my illness by crossing to Kirolcan, and now that I've found the last clue, we should take that risk since I'm the only one who can open the fifth journal. We have no choice."

"But how?"

"Cast a Jiretal spell on my body."

I remember the color draining from Tynia's face after hearing that. No one had any idea what they were talking about, but it sounded dangerous.

"Kharlo, I'm not even sure I can do it! I never completed my training."

"We have no other choice. You need to do it and go back to Kelfia for more elixir and anything else you might need to help me survive the trip back."

"But who will protect you while I'm gone? The dark army knows we're here."

"We will," I said. I have no idea where those words came from, but I felt confident in them. "We just need to get more help and red paint."

"They are not prepared, Kharlo!"

"Were we prepared?" he asked, smiling. "Don't you remember our faces when we accepted this task? Don't fight it, Tyn. We don't have much time, so let's not waste it. Do as I say and we'll meet again soon. And I know you have felt it too."

"Felt what?"

"The cold flames burning inside this young man. This is why you have to take him with you and bring him in front of the elders in Kelfia."

The young Kharlo put his sword against his forehead. He muttered something, and his weapon glowed green. I started sweating, and the last thing I remember was a wave of very intense heat traveling through my body before darkness swallowed me.

Years after, my mother and Yilian described to me what happened. The pendant hanging from the neck of the old Kharlo also glowed green. Then, a bright light burst from it, and my body began to shake until I fainted. My mother and Tynia caught me as I fell, and noticed that I had Kharlo's symbol glowing on the back of my hand. As soon as Tynia convinced my mother that I wasn't dead, they carried me to my mother's room and left me there with Zilhana.

Tynia had no time to waste. It seemed that Kharlo's life was reduced to just a few minutes after what he did to me, and in that time, she had to perform a magical ritual called Jiretal to save him—a ritual that was later described to me as "freezing somebody's life inside of him." Not his body, his life. How long would a person last after that? Well, that depends on the abilities of the wizard and the state of that person.

My mother said that Tynia took her weapon with both hands, there was a brief flash of light, and she ended up with two rods, one on each hand. She left one on Kharlo's chest and held the other a few inches above his body. She started the incantation and then took her hands away from the second staff and left it in the air as it swiftly changed colors.

She placed one hand on Kharlo's chest and asked everybody else in the room to touch her other hand. A humming sound began to come out of her weapon as the colors changed faster and faster.

A sudden, huge gust of wind knocked everyone backward as both staffs rejoined and ribbons of light tendrilled down and clung to Kharlo's body. The lights grew dim until the room went dark, leaving Kharlo's pendant and the cracked wood of the window as the only sources of light.

Tobho and Yilian helped settle Zilhana and my mother in the chairs while Tynia checked to make sure that Kharlo was alive. He was. Kharlo's pendant shifted between colors slower and slower until it settled on one.

"Blue. Better than I thought," Tynia said. "The elders would be proud of me."

"What does that mean?" my mother asked.

"His life will be frozen inside him for three or four days."

"Three or four days? That's not enough time to do anything!"

"Days of this land—your days. Time in Kirolcan is different. A few days over here are like a few months over there. We just have to use our time wisely or our chances of saving Kharlo might grow slim."

"Only you know what you're talking about," my mother said. "I'm just wondering how these boys, Zilhana, and I will be able to protect this man while you're gone."

Tynia frowned. "I'm sorry. Jonek has to come with me."

"You can't think I'll let you take my son!"

"Unfortunately, I don't think we have a choice. Kharlo almost gave his life to give us a good chance of making it back. This quest is against evil—evil that doesn't discriminate by gender or age. Evil eager to make people suffer. I am truly sorry for saying this, but Jonek will have better chances with me than he would staying here."

"Thanks for the good news, lady," Tobho whispered.

"We need to find a place for you to hide and maybe bring others to help you. People you can trust." Tynia placed a hand on Kharlo. "Jonek and I will face other challenges. Kharlo had the key to cross back to Kirolcan. I know how to reach the door, but I can't open it without the key."

"And where is it?"

"I don't know. Hopefully Kharlo passed that knowledge to your son, but we won't know until he wakes up."

My mother told me later on that Kharlo's body wasn't truly "frozen." He was breathing normally, and his skin was warm. Two things were unusual, though—his wounds remained open but weren't bleeding, and his pendant now seemed to be embedded in his skin just below his neck.

"There is something you should know," Tynia said as she softly passed her finger over Kharlo's pendant. "Nothing can harm Kharlo's body while he is under this spell. If he is wounded, any new cut or bruise on his flesh will heal by itself in moments. You can move him around without putting him in any danger. Even though he seems to be breathing, his lungs don't need air right now. The color of his mark will slowly change from blue to green, then to yellow, and ultimately from yellow to white. Once it reaches white, his mark will detach from his skin and turn golden again. At that point, he will die within minutes unless he's back in Kirolcan."

"What's a mark?" Tobho asked.

"The pendant, you fool," Yilian answered, punching his friend in the arm.

"These pendants are the symbols we chose to identify ourselves as guardians," Tynia said. "The elders say that they mark your skin and your soul once you accept this fate. These pendants are made from a metal that looks like gold but is almost impossible to destroy. Guardians also see their symbol glowing on the back of their hands and on their weapons whenever the enemy is nearby." Tynia grabbed Kharlo's staff and pointed to the symbol carved on it, very close to the grip. "It remains your mark even after your role is taken by someone else or you die."

"But that symbol was glowing on my son's hand. What does that mean?" my mother asked.

"Kharlo must've passed his knowledge and abilities to your son. I don't know how long they will last inside of him, but at least he should be able to use Kharlo's weapon on this journey."

"You mean he will have to use swords and spears and I-don't-know-what-else?"

"Yes. Kharlo is probably the best warrior guardian both worlds have seen in several lifetimes. I just hope Jonek can use these skills to help us complete our journey and come back."

Everyone remained silent as Tynia placed Kharlo's weapon by his side.

"Well, swords and bows are no strangers to him," Yilian said.

"What do you mean?" my mother said with a frown. Yilian gulped.

"He'll never forgive me for saying this, but your son is the best swordsman and archer of all of us. He's learned by watching our local soldiers for the last few years. He's never owned a real sword, but he knows how to use them."

Tobho told me later that my mother didn't say a word, but there may have been a tear or two welling up in her eyes.

"Can I see your weapon?" Tobho asked. Tynia offered a brief smile and handed her weapon to him. Tobho looked it over and moved it around as everyone else watched. When he waved it near Zilhana, she skittered backward.

"Don't worry," Tynia said. "It's just a useless stick for anyone but the owner. These weapons are made by the elders—wizards from the

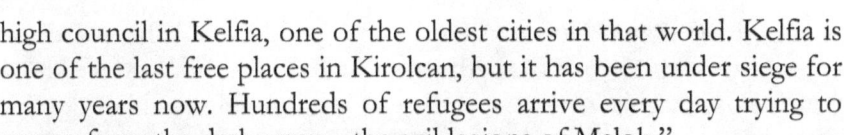

high council in Kelfia, one of the oldest cities in that world. Kelfia is one of the last free places in Kirolcan, but it has been under siege for many years now. Hundreds of refugees arrive every day trying to escape from the dark army—the evil legions of Malok."

Though they'd never heard it before, everyone somehow knew not to speak when she said that name.

"He calls himself King Malok, but we know he is only a prince. Jalyena gathered a lot of information about his history and ancestors."

"Who is Jalyena?"

"My apologies, I keep forgetting who I'm talking to. Jalyena is one of us; she became a guardian a few years after Kharlo, Artego, and I. She is a fair warrior, but her mightiest weapon is her mind. Not only can she remember every word she reads or hears, but she can control the behavior of most men and beasts at will. Jalyena is the youngest of us and is the creator of all the locks and riddles that protect the most amazing treasures in Kirolcan—including our journals.

"As you know, Kharlo is the warrior. He's a master in combat disciplines and a very effective leader. He could be stubborn sometimes, but his heart is as soft as flower petals. I'm the wizard in the group; even though magic flows in all of us, it has rushed through me more intensely than the others since my early days. Rubzilet, the second highest elder in Kelfia, took me as his apprentice. Even though I haven't completed my training, he says my progress outpaces any other mages he's seen with similar experience."

"So why can't you cure this man?" Zilhana said in all but a whisper. Tynia sighed, not in frustration with Zilhana, but with herself.

"Kharlo's illness is beyond my skills. He is dying of a dark spell that Malok cast—against me. Kharlo protected me, and now he is the one dying instead of me. When I see Kharlo suffering, I think that somehow that dark spell still cursed me. Seeing him dying consumes my soul every day." She paused. "I can't imagine the pain he has endured to remain alive and keep his mind focused. Only a magical elixir that I brought from Kelfia has been able to slow down the effects of this curse. His body is decaying rapidly, but the worst part is that Malok's black magic is taking away his memory. Even if Kharlo survives these wounds, his mind will be empty in a few more days."

"Someone else must be able to help," my mother said.

"Only the elders have the power to cure him. Unfortunately, Malok found us just as we were crossing back to this world, so we barely managed to escape. No one other than the elders and the guardians knew of the existence of the pathways that lead here, but now we know that Malok and his Zerkial wizards can send people to this side. We don't know how they do it, because they're not using the Lost Path, but we believe that none of them have been able to return to Kirolcan."

Suddenly, something blocked the light spilling in from the hole in the window.

CHAPTER 6. THE EYES OF AN OWL.

*E*veryone took cover.

Tobho and Tynia put their backs against the wall just under the window. Yilian stayed with my mother in a corner, holding a chair in front of them. He grunted as he shifted his weight; the paint they'd smeared over themselves earlier was starting to burn more by the minute. Tynia's weapon briefly illuminated the room as it transformed into a long staff. No sound other than their breathing broke the silence.

Tynia signaled Yilian. "Go with Tobho to the other rooms and try to see who's out there. Stay away from the doors."

My friends crawled out of the room and looked through cracks and holes in other parts of the house, but they couldn't see anything moving outside. Yilian crept inside my mother's room and saw Zilhana sobbing by my side. He briefly stopped to see if I was breathing, then kept walking toward the window.

Someone whistled outside. Even though the sound was familiar, Yilian paused for a moment to compose himself before carefully opening the window just enough to see Nuthek walking toward the front of the house.

"Hey, come here!" Yilian urged him quietly from the open window.

"Yilian? What are you doing in there? Where's Jonek?"

"He's here. Go to the kitchen door, quick!"

Yilian closed the window as Tobho walked into the room. "Who was that?"

"Nuthek. I think."

"You think? Was he Nuthek or not?"

"Well, he looks and whistles like him, but what if he's another illusion or someone's controlling his mind?"

They both pursed their lips, looking at each other. Finally, Yilian sighed. "Well, there's one way to know. Follow me."

Yilian gave the vial of red paint to Tobho and picked up his bow and arrows before walking into the kitchen. "Tobho, open the door and throw some paint on Nuthek as soon as you see him. I'll cover you from here."

Tobho nodded. Yilian pulled his bowstring and aimed at the door. "Open it." Tobho pulled the table away from the door.

"Is that you, Nuthek?"

"Tobho? What's going on? Open the door!"

"Nuthek, I can't speak too loud, so get closer to the door. I have to tell you something before you come inside."

Tobho waited for a moment and then flung open the door. Nuthek, who had put his ear to the door, lost his balance and stumbled in. Tobho splashed a streak of paint over Nuthek's face and pushed him back outside. Everyone must have jumped when they heard Nuthek's piercing scream. He fell down the two steps out front but never turned or used his hands to break the fall. Actually, his hands went directly to his eyes.

"Take the shot, Yilian!" Tobho yelled, reacting instinctively to Nuthek's scream and sudden hand movements. Yilian released the arrow just as he heard Tynia's voice.

"Wait!"

When I listen to my friends describe those moments, it's obvious they didn't have much time to think. No one could blame Yilian and Tobho for making that call.

Nuthek was falling, and if Tynia hadn't cast that spell, Yilian's arrow would've landed in Nuthek's body without a doubt; he was just too close for him to miss. Nuthek disappeared right before their eyes, and Yilian's arrow zipped through thin air until it lodged itself in the ground.

"What happened?" Tobho asked as he got to his feet.

"That wasn't any dark warrior," Tynia responded.

"Oh no! Nuthek . . ."

"Don't worry, Yilian. He's still alive."

"Alive? I don't see anyone dead *or* alive out there!" Tobho said.

Tynia raised a hand. "He's not here anymore, but he's fine. See if there are more of your friends out there, Yilian. Just be careful."

Yilian dropped to the floor, the bow clattering down beside him, and put his head in his hands. Tobho looked at him, and realizing he was in no shape to go outside, went out himself. A minute or so later, he came back and closed the door, pushing the table back against it.

"I found Nuthek's bag and his bow, but there's no one else out there."

Tynia picked up Yilian's bow and offered it back to him. "Your friend is fine. Well, he probably landed hard where he is right now, so I can't say he isn't a little achy. But he's alive."

"I . . . could've killed him."

"Listen to me, Yilian—sometimes we have to make decisions on pure instinct. You didn't have much time to think, and your hands followed Tobho's call." She paused and sat next to him. "Never be afraid to make these choices. One day, they could mean your life or the life of someone you care about. It is true that you will carry the consequences of your actions until your last day, but with time and help from your loved ones, you'll learn to live in peace with yourself."

Yilian struggled to keep tears from rolling down his cheeks. "But how did you know he was Nuthek?" he asked, reaching out a shaking hand to take the bow.

"Our marks let us know," she said, showing the back of her hand to him.

"I walked into the kitchen to let you know we were safe for now, but you were faster than me."

***

Imagine a glue-like liquid covering your eyes—in this case, a dense paint intended to stay on clay pots for years. Tobho wasn't lying when he said the red paint burned his lips that morning.

Unfortunately, Tobho managed to get so much paint in Nuthek's eyes that he couldn't open them by the time he crashed into that wooden floor. He didn't even question all the objects falling and shattering around him. His only instinct was to desperately try to peel as much paint from his eyes as he could.

He tumbled across the floor until he reached the wall, and even though he managed to dig most of the paint from his eyes moments later, the damage was done. There is no doubt in my mind—the pain he endured must have been unbearable.

"Tobho! Yilian!" he cried out, breathless. "What happened to me?"

The burning from his swollen eyelids was too sharp for him to even touch them anymore, so he leaned forward, keeping his head between his knees. He'd begun to sweat, but amid the haze of agony, he realized. Silence.

"Yilian? Tobho? Are you there?"

He passed his hand over the old wooden floor, touching a few objects lying close to him. A cup, some parchments, and other pieces he didn't recognize. He knew he was indoors, but where? He slowly stood up, leaning on the wall behind him as the pain made his stomach turn. Fortunately for him, that nausea kept him weakly leaning on the wall; toward the center of the room, a dense black brew dripped from a table. A brown beetle crawling out of the remains of a broken pot suddenly stopped as it passed through the black puddle, making a crackling noise as it turned into stone. Nuthek heard the noise and slowly moved away, dragging himself along the wall. Blind, lost, and alone, he decided to sit on the floor again. What else was he to do?

***

Tobho returned from looking again through every hole he could find.

"Nothing. Other than the horse, there's no one else on the other side," Tobho said. "I think Nuthek was alone."

"I hope he's not too badly beaten up," Tynia said. "Let me try to talk to him." She stood and made her way to the main room; everyone followed. She made them push everything against the walls and put out all the candles and lamps. Tynia placed her hand a few fingers above her staff and closed her eyes. It didn't take long for some thin ribbons of light dancing between her hand and the staff to illuminate the room. Her lips never moved, but everyone in the room could hear her voice.

"Nuthek, can you hear me?"

If I would've been Nuthek, I would've wet my leggings after hearing that voice. No response, though.

"Yilian and Tobho are here with me. Can you hear me, Nuthek?"

"Here?" Nuthek's voice echoed softly. "Where? Who are you?" His words seemed distant, as if he were speaking from the depths of a cave.

"We are not there with you. We are in Jonek's house."

"Who are you? Where am I?"

Tobho approached Tynia. "Nuthek, I'm sorry for painting your face," he said.

Tynia opened her eyes and looked at Tobho. "He can't hear you. He can only hear my voice," she said. She closed her eyes again. "Tobho is apologizing for painting your face."

"Painting my face? He threw fire into my eyes! I can't see anything, and I feel like I have thorns stuck in them."

"Yilian and Tobho thought you were someone else. They did what they did to protect us. Don't worry about your eyes—I can heal them. My name is Tynia, and you must be somewhere inside my house."

"Your house? How did I get here?"

"That may take some time to explain, and right now we don't have a moment to spare. I'm going to bring you back to Jonek's house, so please stay still for a moment."

Tynia grabbed the ribbons of light and wrap them around the staff's head. She muttered some words, and the ribbons just faded away and appeared again between the staff and her hand. Tynia frowned.

"Not good," she said, glancing at the ribbons. "The orb is not aligned." She closed her eyes once more. "Nuthek, what happened when you landed in my house?"

"What do you mean? When I fell? I don't know—I landed on my back and things started to fall all over me. So now I'm sitting against a wall with a lot of pain in my eyes thanks to Tobho."

"You must have hit the table and threw the orb apart. Is there anything close to you?"

"Lady, I don't even know what an orb is," Nuthek said, patting the floor around him.

"An orb is just a stone with a hole in it that looks like a drop of water on a flat surface. We use it to mark places."

"I can't *see*, in case you've forgotten," Nuthek snarled. A strange object was glowing under the table in front of him, but he had no way of knowing.

"The orb needs a binding stone for it to work as a marker. The stone I used to bind my staff with the orb must have fallen out of the hole when you hit the table."

"Wait, just wait! You're going too fast. I don't know where I am, who you are, and whether my friends are really with you. The only thing I know is that I'm in a lot of pain and that I'm blind. So please excuse me while I decide if I should believe your story or not." Nuthek took a deep breath. "Give me some time, please."

Yilian got closer to Tynia. "Tell him that I still think his story about the Tears of Althizam is just a sack of lies," he said.

Tynia looked at Yilian after hearing those words, but she continued, "Yilian says that your story about the Tears of Althizam is just a sack of lies." She paused, waiting for an answer. None came. "I don't know how both of you know about it, but I can assure you that Althizam and those invisible stones are real," she added.

Nuthek raised his head after hearing that, then answered softly. "I didn't make up that story. Da Drukhol told it to me."

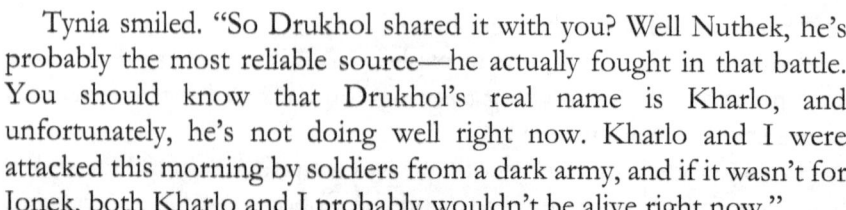

Tynia smiled. "So Drukhol shared it with you? Well Nuthek, he's probably the most reliable source—he actually fought in that battle. You should know that Drukhol's real name is Kharlo, and unfortunately, he's not doing well right now. Kharlo and I were attacked this morning by soldiers from a dark army, and if it wasn't for Jonek, both Kharlo and I probably wouldn't be alive right now."

Nuthek tried again to open his eyes, but the pain was just unbearable. "It's useless. I can't see anything, lady. And I don't even know what I'm looking for. And I don't know if you've noticed, but I'm not in the best mood right now."

"Calm down, Nuthek. Let's see . . . there should be a door and two windows in the room. Walk along the wall and try to find them."

Nuthek stood and palmed his way along the wall, trying to find a window or door. Eventually, rammed his knuckle into the door's old wooden lock. He tried to force it open to no avail. He passed his fingers along the edge of the door, trying to see if there was something keeping it from opening, but he couldn't find anything.

Everyone at my house remained silent, trying to recognize the sounds that came from the staff.

"I think he found the door," Tobho said.

"Don't waste your time with the door, Nuthek. I don't even remember how many nails I used to close it . . . permanently."

"So what I am looking for then? You said find the door."

"There's a wooden crate full of clothes on the floor just to the right of the door. Underneath those clothes, you'll find some vials. Look for one that has a cap shaped like an owl."

Nuthek extended his leg and touched the wooden crate with his foot. He knelt down and reached inside. "I think I found it."

"Just be careful. Sometimes my pets like to hide in it, and I don't want them to bite you."

"Great. More good news. Thank you, lady." Nuthek reluctantly put his hand in the pile of clothes and slowly burrowed deeper until his fingers reached the vials. "How do I know if I'm touching the head of an owl or some other bird?"

Yilian chuckled. "You fool," he mumbled, almost to himself. "Owls have big heads." Tynia gave him a sidelong glance.

"I don't remember having many vials with owl caps, so it should be rather distinctive, but Yilian says you should look for the one with the biggest head."

"Just like his own," Nuthek muttered. "I wish he was the one putting his hand inside this crate." Everyone waited, unwilling to move for fear of making noise that would obscure the sounds of Nuthek's rummaging. "I think I found it!" he said at last. "It's a small vial with a cap in the shape of a bird. It feels like an owl to me."

"Good work, Nuthek. Now here's what you have to do. Rip a long strip of cloth from anything in that crate and keep it with you. Lie on your back and keep your eyes closed. Pour some of the potion from that vial all over your eyes. Grab onto something, and, well…just open them. Make sure the potion gets in your eyes as much as possible."

"Did you just say grab onto something?"

"Nuthek, I won't lie to you—this is going to hurt."

"More than it's hurting right now?"

"It will hurt more at first, but the pain will go away after a moment. Here's the problem, though—the potion will only let you see for two or three minutes. But that's all the time you'll need to find three things: the orb, the binding stone, and a chain that has a pendant with a gem in the shape of a triangle. I'm not sure where I left that necklace, but I think it's in the bedroom."

"My dear lady, you can't be serious."

"Nuthek, there's no time to lose. We're all in great danger, including you. Remember, the orb looks like a sphere that's been cut in half, and it has a hole in the center of its flat side. It's probably glowing as we speak. The binding stone is a small pebble that looks like a red egg. The necklace is a thin silver chain holding a blue triangular gem." She paused. "I don't want to make this any more stressful than it has to be, but time is something we don't have much of right now. There are dark wizards roaming these lands, and they probably sensed when you traveled from here to my house. They must be on their way there."

Nuthek didn't say anything else. He ripped off a long piece of cloth, got on his back, and opened the vial. He poured its dense contents over his eyes, covering everything from his forehead to half of his nose.

He tossed the vial on the floor and tried to find something to grab onto. He touched everywhere and ended up sliding his fingers under the door and holding onto it. "One orb, one egg, one pendant," he repeated as he tried to open his eyes.

I say "tried" because he couldn't actually open them. His eyelids were too swollen. Mustering his last drop of courage, he used his fingers to open them one at a time, forcing the potion into his eyes.

All they heard in my house was feet stomping and kicking the door. Many sounds of pain echoed throughout my house until Nuthek's voice slowly merged with his heavy breathing.

"My eyes are burning again," he gasped.

"Calm down! Stay still and breathe. It will go away in a moment."

He slid down against the door, holding his head between his knees as he had before. He sat there in silence until a cooling sensation soothed his eyes.

"I think it's working. The pain is going away."

Tynia smiled. "Go ahead—open your eyes."

The blurred image before him slowly came into focus. He was indeed in the main room of a house, and there were only two sources of light partially illuminating his surroundings. One was the top of a broken window, and the other was the light coming from under the door behind him.

"Move, Nuthek. You don't have much time!"

"Wait, there's something wrong. I can't see clearly! Everything is green."

"This is not a permanent heal, so it won't get any better than this. Just don't try to clean the potion from your eyes. Leave it there. Now get up and find the orb!"

Just as he was trying to focus his vision on the items on the floor, he noticed a shadow briefly blocking the light under the door. His heart began to pound, and he crawled away.

"I think there's someone outside," he whispered as he threw the piece of cloth over his shoulder.

"Stay quiet and find the orb. Move!" Tynia whispered.

He got to his feet and carefully made his way to the table. Even though Nuthek couldn't see any color but green, he saw the stone glowing under the table. He picked it up and continued away from the door (and the many shadows now blocking the light under it).

"One orb, one egg, one pendant," he whispered.

I can't imagine what thoughts crossed his mind when he saw all those pebbles, metal nuggets, and strange-looking gems lying on the table and most of the floor. Even though many of them looked like tiny eggs, the worst part was that all of them were green to him. In the end, he did what most of us would've done—he took as many as he could.

He put every pebble within reach in his pockets and carried a few more in his hands. Then he kept walking toward the two doors in the back. Nuthek and everyone else in my house jumped when they heard a loud bang on Tynia's door.

"Open the door, witch! We know you're in there!" Tynia and the rest heard those men laugh almost as clearly as if they were outside my own house. "We came here to do business with you. We waited for you by the road, but you never showed up. So we thought it was best to visit you here, in your palace," the man said, laughing. "Open up, and if you're good to us, we might be good to you later." The laughs of the others quickly followed that last statement.

"They're just brigands," Tynia said as she opened her eyes to look at my mother.

"Keep moving, Nuthek. Let me know when you have all the items."

Another bang rattled Tynia's door. "Is it too early for you, old witch? Let me make a deal with you so we don't have to see your ugly face for long. We'll give you fifteen gold coins if you give us a vial of that magical paint we borrowed from you last time. What do you say? Take your time and think about it. We aren't going anywhere."

Tynia frowned. "Lord Nutrec's men," she whispered.

Nuthek winced. "My eyes—the pain is coming back." It was too late. His eyelids were swollen again, and his sight was gone. "What should I do now? Should I go back for more of that potion?"

"That won't help you anymore," Tynia said. "Wrap the cloth around your head to cover your eyes. Just don't tighten it too much."

Nuthek sat on the floor. He tried his best to clean the rest of the potion from his face and covered his eyes with the cloth. Another loud blow echoed all the way to my house as Lord Nutrec's brigands threw something at the window.

"We want to make this deal a good one for you, so we'll give you *twenty* gold coins for the potion and we'll leave you alone . . . for today."

Tynia scowled. "Don't make me go out there and make you pay for stealing my potions! Nothing would heal the wounds I'll leave on all of you!"

Nuthek pulled the orb closer to his chest. "Lady, are you crazy? Remember that I'm the one here with them, not you."

"Don't worry—they can't break down the door. Any luck with the pendant?" The expression on Tynia's face suddenly changed. "Oh no. Hide! Quickly!"

***

Those were the last words anybody wanted to hear from Tynia. Tobho and Zilhana ran to the kitchen and Yilian to my room. My mother stayed by my side, and Nuthek just sat on the floor between the two doors.

Suddenly, the voices and laughs outside of Tynia's house turned into something vastly different. Nuthek and everyone at my house couldn't do anything but cringe as they heard those terrible screams among cacophony of howling, growling, and weapons clanging against the walls of the house. Someone outside fired a volley of spells that rattled the house.

"They've found you, Nuthek! Forget the pendant. Go to the room on the right and look for a barrel in a corner. There is a trap door underneath that goes into the mines. Get in there as fast as you can!"

What Nuthek didn't know was that one of those spells left a hole in the window big enough for a sentinel to slowly creep its way inside Tynia's house. A Gozikro viper with red and black scales is the beast of choice for Zerkial wizards wanting to track living things. Even though they're slow, sentinels are cold-blooded killers. These beasts not only have fangs but also a stinger on their tail that is usually hard enough to pierce light armor. A sentinel will remain as a single serpent while tracking prey, but it will separate into two vipers, one black and one red, when it's ready to kill. There are even some places in Kirolcan where prisons have no guards—just these hideous beasts living on their outskirts.

Nuthek crawled his way toward the trap door as fast as he could. The sentinel spotted him immediately, splitting into his black and red twins to mount an attack from two sides. No one really knows what happened next, but we believe that an iron ball shattered the window and the sentinels tumbled down into powders and potions spilled everywhere. It was that black brew dripping from the table that ultimately saved him. Both snakes darted through it and managed to bare their fangs less than two fists away from Nuthek before turning into stone. Our friend just kept crawling, completely oblivious of their presence.

Nuthek was terrified of putting his hands on anything, but the carnage outside gave him the courage he needed to make his way to the far wall. "Lady, you better tell me how heavy this barrel is. Will I

 110

even be able to—"

Tynia didn't have a chance to answer as a loud blast deafened everybody, cutting off Nuthek's words. To this day, we still don't know what hit Tynia's house, but something rather large crashed into a wall and the entire structure shook and cracked. Debris cascaded onto Nuthek's shoulders, making him fall. And even though hitting the floor must have been painful, he was certainly more worried about the pebbles he dropped as he fell. He desperately passed his hands over the floor, picking up as many as he could. This is when he touched a thin chain.

At first, he didn't know what it was, but he wanted to pick it up anyway. He pulled on it but quickly realized it was stuck. He put his back against what felt to be a rather large chest pinning it down and pushed as hard as he could.

"KARKOON TIKHO MOKSTUNO." A deep, loud voice emanated from the orb in Nuthek's pocket, making the ground shake around Tynia's house. The dark beasts stopped their raging and knelt at the sound of those words. Everything became silent.

The orb must have burned Nuthek's skin the same way the symbols on Tynia's, Kharlo's, and my hand did at that moment. Tynia knew she had no other choice. She grimaced as she held her staff with both hands and kept speaking those words.

"KARKOON SETKOLHA MOKSTUNO." These words made the walls of Tynia's house crack even further.

Tynia exhaled as if she had been holding her breath for minutes. A faint whisper was all she could manage next. "Nuthek, get in the trapdoor."

Nuthek's body was buried in dust, spider webs, and debris, but he clearly heard her. He jostled himself free and shoved the chest off the chain. His fingers quickly followed the chain to touch a pendant—a smooth gem cut in the shape of a triangle.

"It's here! I found the pendant," he whispered as loud as he dared.

Tynia heard, but she couldn't answer. Moments later she collapsed, bringing complete darkness and silence to the room.

Nuthek picked up as many pebbles as he could and put the chain around his neck. He probably didn't feel when the pendant changed its shape into a sparkling round gem, but the storm of lights it created certainly dazzled his brain. An image slowly came into shape in front of him. A colorless image of a room ready to fall apart.

"What's happening? This can't be true," he said.

The image remained still as he moved his head, and he furrowed his eyebrows. It wasn't until he moved the pendant and saw the image of the room following the jewel's movement that he realized it.

"The pendant . . . *is* my eyes?" He lifted the pendant in front of him and moved it around. He found the barrel in the corner, but it was torn to pieces.

"KARKOON MALOK THERKOLAH," a deep voice said outside.

There was no time to play dead in there. Nuthek kept moving pieces of the barrel away from the corner until he uncovered the small door in the floor.

"KARKOON MALOK THERKOLAH," the voice said again, just on the other side of the wall where Nuthek was.

Nuthek threw a piece of wood through the door into the main room. Voices and footsteps rushed to the other side of the house, and he used that moment to open the trapdoor. A long ladder stretched further down than he—or rather, the gem—could see, and even though there was no light, the pendant was able to show him a picture without it. He slid in and closed the trap door just as a massive blast crushed the walls. The rumbling intensified and he nearly lost his grip; it was likely the whole house had collapsed. The wizards must have realized Tynia's deception and ordered the beasts to destroy and burn everything.

Nuthek's ears were ringing after the blast, but he descended that ladder as fast as he could, skipping rungs and sliding down. He had entirely forgotten about the pain in his eyes. Those last sounds of the house falling apart must have echoed deep inside his mind, so getting away from there was his biggest motivation.

Tired and with his hands full of splinters, he made it to the bottom of the ladder about a hundred feet underground. He stood there catching his breath, then took the pendant and pointed it up the ladder. Up at the top, dancing shadows from flames indicated that everything above ground was burning. He stepped away from the ladder and pointed the pendant around to see where he was. I recall him describing the place as a small, humid cave no more than twenty steps from wall to wall with a single exit on the other end and old mining tools lying everywhere.

Nuthek walked closer to the exit and sat down against the wall.

"I made it. I'm in the caves. What's next?" he said as he carefully passed his hands over the cloth covering his eyes. Silence was all he got in response. "Lady? Are you there?"

His hand immediately reached inside his pocket. He took the orb out and confirmed his fears. It wasn't glowing anymore. He rubbed it furiously with his hands, but nothing changed. "Did I break you? Oh, please work," he said through clenched teeth.

Nuthek held the orb out in front of him with one hand and examined it with the pendant in the other, but a crashing sound jolted him from his thoughts. The last burning pieces of the trap door landed by the bottom of the ladder. He scrambled to put away the orb and grab a wooden staff leaning by the door, then quickly left the room.

It was a great advantage for him not to need a torch or lamp to walk in the darkness. The Barkrek mines were abandoned two or three generations before our time, so finding oil or a good torch in there would've been as lucky as finding gold.

Nuthek followed the long tunnel until he reached a cave with a water well in the center. Entrances to six other tunnels dotted the edge of the room. He knelt down and softly rubbed his head, trying to mitigate the pain and dizziness from this whole ordeal. This time, tears of a different kind escaped from the cloth covering his eyes.

"Where are you, lady?" he sobbed quietly.

***

Tynia couldn't hear anyone standing around her, much less Nuthek. Something about those words she spoke in that other tongue drained all the energy in her body. The situation certainly wasn't improving for my mother. She now had Kharlo, Tynia, and me lying unconscious. Add to that Zilhana, who was unhinged in her usual state of despair. Yilian and Tobho kept running from room to room looking through the holes and hoping that nothing moved outside.

My mother soaked a rag with water and passed it over Tynia's forehead and neck. This is when the burning sensation on the back of my hand finally woke me. The room was dark, so my eyes took a moment to adjust. I tried to rub the hand where Kharlo's symbol glowed, but someone was holding my other hand. I couldn't see anyone next to me, so I looked down and there she was—Zilhana was hiding under the bed, holding my hand tightly.

"Zilhana, what happened?" I asked.

Instead of answering, Zilhana just yelled, "Jonek is back!"

Back from where? I thought as I rested my head on the bed.

My mother rushed to my side. "Jonek, you're alive! My chest has been hurting since you fainted. Your friend Nuthek is stranded in this lady's house, and now she's unconscious too! We don't know who or what is outside waiting for us, and you haven't said anything about it. Talk to me, boy!"

"I'm still here," I said as I rubbed my eyes.

My mother was just too spent; she put her head over my chest and cried. Tobho and Yilian peeked through the door and offered me a smile. They didn't hold those smiles for long, though. The expressions on their faces clearly communicated that we were still in danger.

"Where's Tynia?" I asked.

"She's on the floor in the other room, but she's still breathing," Yilian said.

"Kharlo?"

My mother lifted her head. "He's sleeping," she said through a sniffle. "Tynia did something to keep him alive, but don't ask me what."

I slowly peeled myself out of Zilhana's grip and sat on the bed. I pulled my mother's candle closer to look at the back of my hand. There was no symbol on it, but a burning feeling was still bothering my skin.

"I feel heavier," I said, looking at my mother.

"Let me bring you some water," she said.

Zilhana and my mother left the room, and my friends rushed to my side.

"You fool!" Yilian snarled. "Don't ever do this to us again."

"Do what?"

"Leave us."

Tobho sat by my side, and the paint on his face reminded me of the wizard and the dark soldiers.

"What happened? Are there more outside?"

"We're safe for now, thanks to Nuthek," Tobho said.

"Nuthek? Is he here? What happened?"

Yilian sat down on my other side and sighed, head hung low. "It happened so fast, Jonek. Nuthek probably got worried that we didn't meet him by the river, so he came to your house looking for us. We didn't know if he was another wizard or assassin, so Tobho threw paint

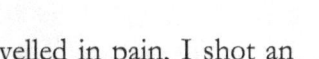

on his face and it got in his eyes. When he yelled in pain, I shot an arrow."

I raised my head and looked at him.

"He did it because I made him do it," Tobho interjected.

"Where is he?" I said, putting my feet on the floor.

"Tynia made him vanish before the arrow hit him. It seems that he's in Tynia's house, somewhere close to the Barkrek mines."

"So is he alive or not?"

"He's probably alive, but he can't see," Yilian said. "The paint blinded him, but the witch—I mean, Tynia—says she can heal him."

"Those beasts went after him, but now we don't know how he is doing since we lost connection with him when Tynia collapsed," Tobho said.

I slowly made my way to the door. Tynia was lying on the floor, and my mother and Zilhana were doing something in the kitchen. I dropped to my knees in front of her and saw her breathing softly.

"Where is her weapon?" I asked.

Both searched around until Tobho found her rod lying by the wall and brought it to me. I pulled Tynia's pendant from around her neck and passed the rod over it. Her golden symbol briefly turned silver in color, so I left the rod by her side and stood.

"She's fine," I said.

My friends looked at me with hesitation. "How do you know? Are you a healer now?" Yilian said.

"No, her mark turned silver. She isn't hurt."

"Really? And how do you know that?"

"I'm . . . not sure. I just know," I said as I scratched my head. Tobho took Tynia's staff and passed it over her pendant again, making it glow silver.

"Is this magic?" he asked, looking at me.

"I'm not sure, but I know that red or black are not the colors you want to see when you do that."

Zilhana rushed to our side looking more terrified than ever. "There's someone outside," she whispered.

I quickly glanced at my friends. "Get your bows and the red arrows. Where's mine?"

Yilian handed me the Satolgac bow and a few arrows. Tobho went back to the kitchen, my mother and Zilhana sat on the floor by Tynia's side, and Yilian and I ran from hole to hole trying to see what was happening outside. The horse kept whinnying and rearing up, but we didn't see anything or anyone around him.

"Look at your hand, Jonek," Yilian said.

That was the first time I saw Kharlo's symbol glowing on my skin, almost by my wrist. Without quite knowing why, I closed my eyes and saw many images flowing through my mind; they moved so fast that I couldn't keep track of them. I dropped the bow and knelt, putting my hands on my head. My mother pulled me closer to Tynia just before we heard two blows strike the window.

The blows weren't loud, though—maybe as loud as an arrow hitting a tree. There was a brief silence, and then we heard two more by Tobho's head. He ducked away from the hole in the wall just before a black stinger made its way through. Tobho stepped back as the beast pushed its tail deeper, and they were able to see the red and black scales of the snake.

"Sentinels. Two of them," I said.

Yilian charged at the hole where Tobho had been standing and stabbed a red arrow through the serpent still writhing to get in. The beast tried to escape, but it was too late. Its body disintegrated into dust, dropping the stinger and the arrow on the floor.

"Stay away from the walls! Don't look through the holes!" Yilian said, grabbing another arrow.

"The other one separated," I said as I opened my eyes.

"Where? Where are they?"

"I don't know, Yilian. Everything is moving too fast!"

Yilian huffed. "Tobho, put some arrows through the holes and use what's left of the paint to mark around the others."

As my friends plugged the holes with arrows, my mother brought the red paint from the kitchen, painting a line by the door. Tobho and Yilian drew back their bowstrings, one aimed at the door and the other at the window. Everyone remained silent. Suddenly, a column of dust hissed down to the floor. Someone was on the roof.

"Where's the shield?" I asked softly.

"Shield? What shield?"

"The disk, Yilian. Where is it?"

"I think I saw it in your room," Yilian said.

"Wait here," I said.

"Jonek! Stay here," my mother scolded, but I ignored her.

Just as I entered my room, a sentinel finished sliding in through a broken piece of my window. I slowly leaned down to pick up the disk.

You'd better work, I remember thinking as I squeezed the holes in the disk. "Shield!" I commanded, but nothing happened. "I need a shield!" Still nothing.

The long serpent wound its way inside without ever taking its eyes from me. I hesitated and slowly stepped back. I glanced at Kharlo and noticed that his staff was by his leg, so I moved closer and took it.

The sentinel attacked us both at the same time. The shield never appeared, but I was able to block its first blow with the disk itself. My other hand swiftly flew toward the viper's body, and the room burst into light as if I had created a star. I stepped back and covered my face with the disk.

I didn't feel another attack, but I heard blows by my bed. I opened my eyes and saw the now-headless beast sticking its tail into Kharlo's body. In my hand was a long, thin sword with dark blood staining its silvery finish. I walked closer to the beast and cut off its tail with one swing. Its body kept writhing on the floor, leaving a dark pool of blood around it.

"Jonek? Are you alright?" Yilian said from the other room.

I turned around and kicked the head of the sentinel into the main room. Everyone gasped as they saw the red head bounce across the floor, leaving a black trail behind. I walked out of my room holding the disk in one hand and the sword in the other. My face was almost white, though—this was just too much for me. Suddenly, a screeching sound came from above.

The black side of the sentinel dropped from the ceiling. I don't know how, but my hand guided the sword into a flurry of arcs all around me. By the time the beast hit the ground, it was cut into four pieces. Kharlo's sword was stuck in the floor, keeping the tail from stinging anybody. I dropped the disk and landed on my knees, gasping for air.

"I told you that Kharlo was a great warrior," Tynia said, barely audible.

"Tynia! Are you alright?" my mother asked.

"I feel weak, but I'll survive. Impersonating Malok will drain even the strongest wizard's strength." She shakily pulled herself up. "Welcome back, Jonek. I see you now carry the skills and powers of a guardian. Now it's just a matter of teaching you how to use them wisely."

"I feel sick," I said as I pulled the sword from the floor and saw it turning back into a wooden rod.

"I remember the feeling. It took some time, but we eventually learned how to manage the effects."

"We're worried about Nuthek," Tobho said, approaching Tynia.

She took her rod and stood in the center of the room. Once again, her weapon turned into a long staff as she put her hand on top of it and closed her eyes.

"Nuthek. Can you hear me?"

Her voice echoed loud and clear in our house, but silence is all we got.

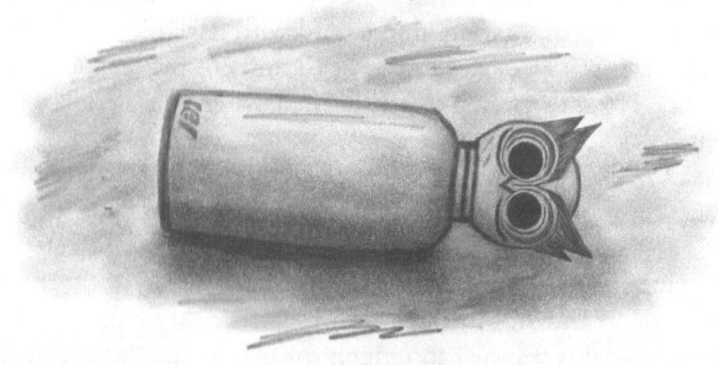

CHAPTER 7. THE PATRIARCH TREE.

If all of us would've stopped moving and making noises, we would've been able to hear that faint sound coming from Tynia's staff as Nuthek rushed, breathless, into the deepest levels of the caverns. What luck—a whispering stone, the only pebble capable of blocking sounds coming in or out from the orb, was the one stuck inside the hole. But the orb wasn't Nuthek's main worry at the moment.

I sometimes remember his eyes and the tremor in his hands as he described that day. The loneliness and desperation he endured in there probably haunted him for years—but it never brought him down. He never faltered. His skills and moody ways were core to the soul of our group. I miss my old friend.

But let's go back a little. By the time the burning sensation on my hand woke me, Nuthek was still sitting by the water well waiting for his dizziness to fade. Then he had one of his curious ideas. He took the cloth covering his eyes and put the pendant on his forehead, right between his eyebrows. Even though he probably noticed it as he touched it, he never questioned why the gem was round by then.

He carefully wrapped the cloth around his forehead, trying his best to keep the gem from moving. Not even the cloth itself could block the sight of the pendant. It wasn't perfect, but at least his vision now followed the movement of his head.

He stood up and walked around the cave, getting used to his new form of sight and determining which way he should go next. He noticed some strange markings on the walls by the entrance of each tunnel—symbols completely unfamiliar to him. He brushed the dust and spiderwebs off a few and noticed that the markings were the same on some of them. He was looking at the symbol just outside the entrance tunnel when he heard a distant blast rumble from the far end of it.

Nuthek instinctively stepped aside as he felt the flow of air pushing him backwards. He put his back against the wall but held out his hand, feeling the wind rush out from the tunnel. He didn't keep it there for long, though; the air became hot quickly, and he jerked his hand away just before the flames burst into the cave. He stumbled into the next tunnel to avoid getting scorched. That was a clear reminder—he had to keep moving.

Loud growling echoed throughout the mines, and chutes of dust cascaded down the walls at the sound. Nuthek trekked for quite a ways before he had to stop to catch his breath and put a hand on the wall. This is when he felt it. A distant but fast-paced pounding was making the walls shake more and more every second.

Having never seen the beasts, Nuthek had no idea that the pounding was coming from dozens of dark warriors marching into the mines looking for him. He took his hand away from the wall and looked into the depths of the tunnel. He knew that his only chance to stay alive was to go deeper, so he kept moving as fast as he could.

The tunnel widened as he kept going. Suddenly, Nuthek spotted a line of old wooden stakes blocking the center of the tunnel marking off a gap in the path. It was maybe thirty feet long and almost as wide as the tunnel itself. He got closer to the edge and looked down; even though the pendant allowed him to see in the dark, he couldn't find the bottom. This was no pit, it was a chasm. A very narrow ledge along the wall on his left was still intact, but stepping on it would be suicide.

He knew it wasn't the best idea, but the terrible sounds coming from the tunnel behind him motivated Nuthek to get closer to the ledge and hug the wall. His feet slowly slid along, and he grabbed onto any rock or hole he could get his fingers on. His body trembled, and a drop of sweat dripped from the tip of his nose.

He kept going, even though the rumbling swelled and the ground shook. He briefly glanced at the other side and realized he was just three or four steps away. Softly placing his forehead against the wall, he took one long, slow breath.

Another blast crackled from the tunnel behind him. The wall shook, and his sweaty fingers slipped from his handhold. His stomach lurched, and he used all the balance he still had to launch himself toward the far edge.

Rocks and dust flew everywhere, shot out from under his feet and exploding from the blast in the tunnel. By the time the echo died, Nuthek was clinging onto one of those rickety, ancient stakes marking the edge of the abyss on the other side. His legs and feet were digging desperately into the cliffside, trying to find some support on the wall, but he only knocked loose the rocks and dirt below him.

A feeble creak greeted Nuthek every time he tried to use the wooden stake to pull himself over the edge. Finally, he decided that it was now or never and hefted himself up with all his strength. The wood groaned loudly but never broke, and Nuthek rolled his body onto the cliffside. He acknowledged the favor that old stake had done for him by patting it a few times.

He waited a moment to catch his breath before standing up. He glanced at the bottom of the chasm once more but turned around and kept walking. Sure that the trench would slow his pursuers for at least a little while, he grabbed the orb from his pocket. Noticing the whispering stone stuck in its hole, he popped it out. "What were you doing in there?" he whispered.

Those words came through loud and clear in my house. Nuthek was cleaning the orb over his clothes when Tynia's voice startled him and made him drop it on the ground.

"Nuthek! You're alive!" We all smiled widely.

"Lady? Where *were* you? Why did you leave me?"

"We had our own problems, but we're fine. You've got everything you need. Let's try to bring you back. Where are you?"

"Deep in the mines somewhere. I don't know who's chasing me, but they're getting closer. I barely survived being burned alive, I almost died falling into a bottomless pit, and just so you don't forget, I'm still blind! Well, almost—I'm using that pendant now. Slapped it right on my head."

"Sounds like him alright," Tobho said.

"Indeed," I responded.

"Did you find the binding stone?" Tynia said.

"The one shaped like an egg? Well, I found a lot, actually, but I can't tell if any of them are red."

"Don't worry, let's try one at a time. Just let me know before you put them in the hole. If you can't hear me, just pull the pebble out."

Nuthek sat on the ground, dumped the stones out of his pockets, and made a pile in front of him.

"Here's the first one. Should I put the orb on the ground?"

"No, just keep it in your hands."

Nuthek blew into the hole to get the dust out and pushed the stone all the way in. "It is in there. Now what?"

The lights dancing around Tynia's staff turned blue, but nothing else happened. "That's a water stone. Put it aside and try another."

Nuthek put another pebble in the orb.

This time, the ribbons from Tynia's staff blended and projected an image all around us. There he was—even though Nuthek's surroundings remained dark for him, we were able to see his face above us and the details of the tunnel all around our room. His skin and the cloth around his eyes still had remnants of both the red paint and the green potion.

"We can see you, Nuthek!" Tynia exclaimed. "That's my star stone. Keep it separate from the others; it might be useful later. Now try another one."

Suddenly, a thunderous blast shook our walls. For a moment, we didn't know if that sound came from outside my house or from where Nuthek was.

"The cave!" Tynia said. A cloud of dust engulfed Nuthek. "Nuthek! Are you alright? Nuthek!"

There was no response.

I could feel my friends and family tense around me as we waited, but then we heard someone coughing in the background.

"They're close," Nuthek said, waving his hand to dispel the dusty fog. "What's chasing me?"

"Get away from there," Tynia said. "Take the stones!"

Nuthek looked down the tunnel on the other side of the pit and saw lights. Grabbing the orb and the pebbles, he pressed further onward. Hopefully that chasm would keep them occupied for long enough. He soon found a spot where a large boulder was protruding from one side of the tunnel and sat behind it.

"I'm ready to try the next one," he said as he put the pebbles back on the ground.

"I'm ready too," Tynia answered, raising her voice so Nuthek could hear her over the stomping of the soldiers. "Wait!" she said suddenly. "Leave the star pebble in the orb and pass each pebble close to it so I can see them. It will be faster this way."

Nuthek held a pebble close to the orb. "How about this one?"

"No. That isn't the one."

"This one?"

"No, keep going. . . ."

Nuthek showed three more useless pebbles, and all of us started to worry that he might have left the binding stone in Tynia's house.

"How about this one?" he nearly shouted as the sounds in the cavern rumbled so loudly that we thought we were in those tunnels with him.

"No, that's a mirror stone," she said, looking at the silver-toned pebble. Nuthek passed another pebble by the orb, and Tynia's opened her eyes momentarily. "That one! That stone in your hand is my binding stone, Nuthek. Don't lose it!" She paused. "Wait. Look around; I sense something moving close to you."

Nuthek looked up. "There's light coming from the other end of the tunnel." His voice quivered slightly. "I'm trapped."

Tynia snarled to herself, frustrated. "We don't have time to let the orb and stone bind again. Rub the mirror stone on the wall behind you and then put it in your mouth. Whatever happens, don't move. Do you understand? Stay still and don't talk!"

Nuthek put the binding stone in his pocket and quickly touched the wall with the mirror stone before putting it in his mouth. Even though his face, arms, and legs started to itch, he didn't move a muscle. His entire body and everything touching his skin took the shape and color of the rocks and soil around him. Nuthek became just another pile of rocks that blended perfectly with the wall. He carefully moved his foot to cover the pebbles on the ground just before a sentinel cleared the top of the boulder and passed its slimy scales over his chest.

Two other serpents made their way over him, and Nuthek regretted not taking the pendant off. He saw everything, even though he had his eyes closed.

A bear, five or six wolves with burning red eyes, and twenty or more assassins on foot followed the sentinels, passing their swords and maces a couple fingers away from Nuthek. Finally, two Zerkial wizards muttering in a strange tongue walked by him, following the rest.

Nuthek slowly turned his head to watch the wizards. He had no idea how they had managed to make it into his tunnel across that gap, but he realized at that point that the orb was his only way out. He stood still, breathing quietly for quite a while after they had vanished from sight. Suddenly, a bloodcurdling howl pierced down the tunnel—they must have realized that Nuthek had slipped through their fingers.

Two blasts echoed through the caves, but there was no fire. Nuthek slowly sucked in another breath as he noticed the scouts walking back to where he was. They grunted and huffed furiously, blasting the walls with their weapons. He knew he might not make it through that march if they kept scorching random holes in the wall.

The beasts got closer and closer, and suddenly he saw a large mace coming his way. His nerves tensed, but he didn't flinch. The soldier would've certainly hit him, but a sentinel slithered over Nuthek and the beast stopped his blow a few fingers away. The scout growled at the snake, bathing Nuthek in an awful stench. The serpent responded by hissing and showing its enormous fangs to the soldier. They kept moving.

The rest of the soldiers and wolves passed by Nuthek, and the men in red cloaks followed a few steps behind. Zerkial wizards are no fools, though—their ability to sense what others can't has always been one of their defining traits.

One of them stopped two or three paces away from Nuthek and said something to the other. The second one turned around and pointed his staff at the highest point of the tunnel and cast a spell.

Tynia's eyes snapped open. "Oh no. They know someone's in that tunnel, and they're going to destroy it."

"Tell him!" my mother said.

"I can't. They would hear what I say."

The wizard left his staff leaning on the boulder, and it started emitting a pulsating light. Both men promptly hustled out, allowing Nuthek to take a deep breath.

"Hey lady, the old man left his staff next to me, and it has a strange light glowing on the top," Nuthek whispered.

"Run! The whole tunnel is going to cave in!"

Nuthek leaned forward to run, but his body was still made of rocks and he lost his balance. He spit the rock from his mouth and his body returned to normal. The staff behind him began to vibrate.

"Where should I go?" Nuthek said as loud as he dared. "I'm trapped here!"

"The binding stone, Nuthek! Put the stone in the orb!" Tynia said as she put her two hands over her staff, which floated in place when she let go.

Nuthek took the pebble from his pocket and put it in the orb. Both the orb and the pebble glowed together as Tynia took the ribbons of light and wrapped them around her staff's head, making a perfect circle. "Keep the orb in your hands!" she shouted.

Nuthek turned around and saw lights coming back from the deep end of the tunnel.

"They're coming back! Get me out of here!" he begged as he made his way back to the edge of the chasm.

"It'll take a moment, Nuthek! Don't lose the orb."

Nuthek crouched down and curled himself around the orb, trying to mask its light. A wizard appeared in the distance and lashed out with his staff, summoning an arc of light.

"Lady, it's now or never!"

"Keep hold of that orb!" she answered.

A flash of lightning burst from the wizard's staff, sending a ball of fire toward Nuthek. He didn't remember if he jumped or the blast pushed him over, but Nuthek said that he was falling when he saw the fire swallowing the air above him.

**

For years after, we avoided talking about those moments. Everything was so unclear—the forces we faced on that second day were beyond our comprehension. And that was just the beginning for us.

It was difficult to say whether Nuthek lost consciousness as he fell or when he landed, but either way, he remained still after he crashed onto the floor of my house, scattering stones all over the place.

"Nuthek!" we all shouted. Everyone rushed to his side. Tynia opened her eyes as her long staff turned into a rod once again.

"Don't touch him," Tynia said. "Please bring water and clean rags." She knelt down and made sure he was breathing. She touched his arms and legs and then passed her weapon all over him. "He has many broken bones, as well as some wounds on the inside. But don't worry. His body is not cursed like Kharlo's—it will take my magic. He will be fine." Tynia looked at me. "Jonek, we need to leave this house. Malok's army knows where we are, and this time they won't hesitate."

I took Kharlo's staff and the disk. "Mother," I said, turning to her, "take only what's important to you. We might not see this house standing again."

"The only thing important to me," she said as she brushed the disheveled hair from my face, "is what I am touching right now."

I wrapped my arms around her neck and whispered into her ear, "I will protect you, Mother, from wolves and bears. I'm not afraid."

"I know," she whispered. I could feel her tears.

I pulled away to look at Yilian and Tobho. "Let's tie the horse to the wagon and throw all the weapons on it. Where's my bow?"

"You won't need it anymore," Tynia said, peeling the cloth away from Nuthek's eyes. "You have one in your hand."

I looked at Kharlo's rod and thought about my failed attempts to bring the shield out. "How do I use it?" I asked.

"It will appear when you need it. As long as your hand is on the grip of the weapon, a sword, a bow, a battle axe—it doesn't matter what. Your weapon will become what you need . . . if you believe in it."

"How about this one?" I asked, showing the disk to her.

"I've never used one of those before. They are ancient. Artego learned how to use them, but the rest of us never had the need to. I'm sorry, but I can't help you with that."

Tynia turned her attention back to Nuthek as Zilhana and my mother ran around gathering clothes and food. Yilian and Tobho took the arrows from the holes and put them in their bags and my quiver.

"Mother, the wagon is full of merchandise. We might need to leave it behind."

"Push everything off the wagon, Jonek. Those things don't matter. But be careful going out there!"

"Don't worry, there's no one around. I know because my hand is not burning."

Just a day had passed since we first saw that wolf at the lagoon, and it already felt distant. The time when we thought Lord Nutrec was the most evil person in this world. My friends and I lost that unappreciated innocence on that morning; the second day of the fair. All of us, without a doubt, have missed the warmth of our nests ever since—like baby birds not ready to be grown yet.

Tobho and Yilian joined me, heading to the side of the house toward the wagon. He threw his bow on top and started pushing everything off. The sounds of those pots breaking must have pained Zilhana's heart. I know they did.

***

"I'll hold the horse while you tie it to the wagon."

I took the piece of rope and looked at Yilian. "And how am I supposed to cut it?" I looked around for a moment, then paused. "Yilian, hold that end of the rope." I took Kharlo's staff and swung over it. No blade appeared.

"You're just trying. The lady said you have to *believe*," Tobho said as he jumped off the wagon.

Yilian pulled the rope tighter. "Cut the rope, Jonek! We don't have all day."

My inability to command the disk—and now Kharlo's weapon—was even frustrating others. I closed my eyes and focused my mind—*There is a sword in my hand.* I swung again, and this time, a bright light burst from the weapon as it transformed into a small sword and cut the rope cleanly.

The silvery blade was flawless and sharp as a viper's fang. Kharlo's symbol was glowing on the blade like molten iron, but it was cold to the touch. "Let's try something," I said, offering the weapon to Yilian. "Hold this for me."

Yilian hesitated but eventually put his hand on the grip. The sword turned back into a wooden rod the moment I took my fingers off it.

"I wish it would work with me too," Yilian sighed.

"No you don't," Tobho said. "Those beasts would be hunting you too if it did."

Yilian frowned, but I know he agreed with Tobho's words. My friends could probably get lost in a crowd and never be recognized as enemies by dark soldiers, but with Kharlo's mark on my hand, I became prey they could track.

***

Tynia was cleaning Nuthek's eyes, and we saw for the first time how swollen they were. Tobho couldn't even stare at Nuthek's face for long; he just quietly walked away, swallowing his guilt.

"His ribs and legs are healed. Now I need to work on his eyes."

Tynia poured water on her hand and cast a spell over it. The water turned blue and dense. She put her weapon away and spread some of the blue liquid over Nuthek's face.

"His eyes will heal in a few hours," she said as she cleaned her hands. "But we can't stay here for long. Let's put Kharlo on the wagon first."

It was a team effort, but soon enough both Kharlo and the still-unconscious Nuthek were both safely tucked into the back of the wagon. Tynia gave the vial of red paint to my mother. "You'll need more of this. Keep some with you at all times."

"Keep the vial; we can get more at the market," my mother said.

Tynia nodded. "Leave the doors open," she added, looking at the house. "They may not destroy it if they can roam inside freely."

Our house was badly damaged by the fire—I had no doubt the roof was going to collapse in a matter of days—and we didn't know what the dark army would do to it once they saw we weren't there. We all got on the wagon, and my mother whipped the reins. She never turned around to look at our house one last time, but I noticed her eyes watering by the time we got to the main road.

"Where should we go?" she asked.

"The wizards and sentinels won't be able to sense Kharlo in his current state, but they will certainly find Jonek and me, so we have to go our separate ways as soon as possible. Let's go to Ferdhen. You'll have to find a place to hide Kharlo and take care of Nuthek while Jonek and I make our way to the Lost Path."

My mother took the road toward the bridge. Yilian and Tobho stayed on the back with their bows in their hands while I sat by my mother's side, the disk and Kharlo's weapon on my lap.

No one said a word for quite some time. Then, as the wagon crossed one of the smalls creeks in the woods, Tynia asked my mother to stop.

"Wait here," she said as she jumped off the wagon. "Keep your eyes open." She followed the creek downstream until she got to a place where a few large boulders diverted the water to one side. She walked behind them and disappeared for a few moments. Then she came back carrying a leather satchel in her hands. The unmistakable sound of coins jingling caught our attention when she threw it in the back of the wagon and climbed on.

"You might need these," she said, looking at my mother. "Spend it all if you need to."

My mother whipped the reins and the wagon moved again. Some lonely rays of sun broke through the dense forest, illuminating the ground here and there. We saw many travelers on the road, but we were careful to hide our weapons to avoid making anyone suspicious.

Only Zilhana noticed when Nuthek shakily moved his hand toward his face. "Everything hurts. Where am I?"

"Welcome back," Yilian said, grabbing his hand before he could reach his eyes.

"Yilian?"

"Jonek and I are here too," Tobho said as he softly kicked Nuthek's leg.

"But . . . I was falling."

"And you did. But you landed in my house. You did well."

"Where are we? I'm really thirsty."

"We're riding on my mother's wagon heading to town."

Tobho raised Nuthek's head and poured a bit of water in his mouth. "Nuthek, I'm really sorry for what I did to your eyes. I wish I would've been the one getting painted."

Nuthek slowly moved his hand and grabbed Tobho by the foot. "No you don't. You should've seen the abyss I had to cross."

"You're a brave young man," Tynia said. "You won't need the pendant anymore. Your eyes will be fine before sunset."

"That voice . . . I thought you weren't real."

"Oh, I am very real," she said, grabbing Nuthek's hand. "Try to rest, and don't touch your eyes."

Nuthek lowered his hand and touched Kharlo. "Who is this?"

"The man you know as Drukhol," Tynia answered. She smiled. "I know you would want to know that his sword defended the people of Althizam for days until that evil army was defeated. It was by mere coincidence that Kharlo ended up there in the middle of those dreadful events, but his name is honored by them even now."

Nuthek slowly took his hand away from Kharlo. "Is he alive?"

"Barely, but he is," Tynia answered.

***

We sat in silence, listening to the wagon wheels thud through rivets in the road until we reached the edge of the woods. Seeing the bridge in the distance made me remember the beautiful moon amid the chaos the night before.

"This is where we will go our separate ways," Tynia said. My mother stopped the horse. "Jonek and I have to reach the door before midnight. Remember, nothing that happens to Kharlo's body will harm him as long as his mark is glowing any color other than gold. He doesn't need water, food, or air."

My mother ran her fingers through my hair, eyes welling up with tears. "Take care of my boy," she said, looking at Tynia. "He's all I have."

I stood up and hugged her, my eyes stinging from my own tears. Then, I turned to my friends.

"You must protect my mother, Zilhana, and Kharlo. Promise me!" Yilian and Tobho nodded. "We promise."

"With our lives," Nuthek said, raising his hand.

"Bring others if needed, but be careful not to say too much. Some may not understand how serious this is," Tynia said as I took my bag and put a few painted arrows in it. Tynia took the orb, the triangular pendant, and some of the pebbles Nuthek brought with him, giving him a single gold coin in return. She slipped an identical coin over the head of her staff, which—oddly—absorbed it like liquid metal.

"Nuthek, keep this coin with you at all times. When you feel it heat up, pour some water in a bowl and drop the coin in it. Touch the water and close your eyes. We will be able to talk and see each other. Zerkial wizards might be able to sense it, though, so we can't do it for more than a few moments."

I gave each of my friends a sturdy slap on the shoulders. "Be strong, but most of all, don't do anything foolish," I said as I jumped from the wagon.

"Pull those empty sacks over Kharlo and Nuthek," Tynia said. "Keep going and don't look back. You have your own battles to fight."

The horse began to pull the wagon once more. My mother looked into my eyes one last time, then turned back toward the road. Yilian and Tobho stayed on each side of the wagon keeping their hands on their bows. The last thing I saw was Zilhana bashfully raising her hand and offering us a smile as a token of good luck.

***

"I know how you feel, Jonek. Believe me, I do," Tynia said as she put her hand on my shoulder.

"I will see them again. I know I will," I said. She nodded.

"Now let's go. We have to get to the cemetery."

In those days, the road to the cemetery passed right by the Satolgac camp, so that wasn't an option if we wanted to avoid being seen as much as possible. We ducked into the tree cover and began blazing our own trail.

"What is the Lost Path?" I said after a mile or so of walking in silence.

Tynia slowed down and walked by my side. "It's one of the ancient doorways that connect this world with Kirolcan. No one really knows who built them or how old they are. The elders in Kelfia are endowed with long lives; some have even lived for thousands of years. In order to allow younger generations to become part of their council, some choose to exile themselves every few hundred years and come to this world through the Lost Path."

"They come here? Who are they? *Where* are they?"

"Most of them live their lives in secrecy, mainly as common folk. Some become apprentices of the arts of this world and travel." Tynia changed her satchel to her other shoulder. "Others are not that discreet and use some of their skills to help people. They are known as healers in some towns, wizards in others. Some live the rest of their lives secluded in remote locations, but we've also heard of some that have risen to high places in societies. They've even become advisors to kings."

"I've heard about evil wizards. Do they come from there too?"

"It's hard to say. I don't believe that someone who has served on the high council of Kelfia for hundreds of years would come here and become evil. It's just not in their nature. I lean more toward the idea that Malok has been able to send some of his own people to this world, and they've allied or served people of bad nature from here. Remember, though, that what we call "bad" may not really be so— being different or unexplainable doesn't make a thing bad. Unfortunately, that's the way our kind thinks."

"I'm sorry," I said.

"For what?"

"What you're saying is true. We used to call you a witch."

"Is that so?"

"Yes. The Witch of Barkrek."

Tynia smiled. "I know," she said glancing at me. "It is not a name I like, but it's been helpful keeping people away."

We kept walking in silence. Tynia stopped from time to time to look at the top of the trees. We were following a narrow trail when suddenly she stopped and put her hand in front of me to keep me from walking any further.

"Take out your weapon," she whispered. "Focus and trust your instincts."

My heart pounded hard as I pulled out Kharlo's weapon. Considering I'd started learning to fight for my life *yesterday*, I wasn't sure which instincts she thought I should be trusting.

"What do I need? A sword? A bow?"

"Don't worry about that. You will know." She motioned for me to hide behind a tree nearby.

I lowered my head and made my way over. I looked around but couldn't see anything, so I dropped the bag and kept my back against the tree. Behind a large wall of bushes came a guttural rasping. Whatever it was, it wasn't moving quietly. I glanced at Tynia and saw her weapon slowly turning into a sword. A cloud of birds flew away from the trees in that area, and I begged for the sounds to be some animal running away from hunters.

Naturally, it wasn't.

Three men burst from the bushes, tripping and rolling over each other, their skin and clothes covered in mud and blood. One of them was holding a sword and a broken piece of shield still hanging from his other arm. Tynia stepped in front of them, but they didn't even stop. They went around her and kept running toward the road as fast as they could.

"Jonek, you are stronger than them! Remember that," she said as she dropped her satchel on the ground and put the other hand on the grip of her sword.

A cacophony of howling and growling confirmed my fears. Three scouts jumped over the bushes a moment after. Two of them slid across the ground and transformed into men. The last one kept running around us as a wolf. I followed him with my eyes as the other two approached Tynia, weapons ready. The wolf paused mid-stride and glared at me with those burning red eyes. He began to approach, creeping slowly, ears flattened back.

Two sentinels peeked their heads through the bushes, but a scout stopped and directed them back to where they came from.

The wolf before me contorted into a man holding a sword still stained with blood. This time, they didn't hesitate—the three attacked us at the same time. The next moments are still a blur in my mind, but some images have returned to my memory over the years.

The scout sent his sword flying toward me. I clearly remember the blade whistling through the air a couple feet from my chest.

At the last moment, I turned sideways and swung my sword, breaking his blade in two. I couldn't believe I'd actually done it, so I didn't even notice him running toward me. He turned back into a wolf in his last two steps and jumped over me, ripping through my shoulder and back with his claws.

Tynia was blocking their blows and swinging her sword even faster than the princess in the theater had. The beasts managed to corner her against a tree, but she dazzled them with a blast of light from her sword. Somehow she vanished and appeared behind them, cutting the legs off one of them just before parrying the sword of the other one inches from her neck. The man on the ground kept swinging his sword even though he was bleeding profusely.

I had my own problems, though, so I couldn't attend to Tynia for long. The wolf once again turned into a man, slamming an iron ball attached to a long chain into the ground in front of him. He threw the ball toward me, but I knocked it away with Kharlo's sword. I dodged sideways and behind a tree, but the scout was quick; he sent his chain flying around me, pinning me to the tree. The chain was so tight it almost made my skin bleed.

I looked down, trying to shake myself from the sharp bite of the chain when suddenly it went slack and clattered to the ground— Tynia's weapon, now an axe, clung to my tree trunk. I couldn't see the scout who'd pinned me, so I wrenched Tynia's axe from the tree and threw both it and Kharlo's weapon toward her.

I was still thinking about her axe, so my weapon changed into one at the same time that Tynia's turned into a rod. Tynia caught her weapon in one hand as she tumbled backward, turned it into a bow, and released a silver arrow that whistled by my ear and stuck itself in the mouth of the scout standing a few steps behind me.

Tynia quickly rolled on the ground, stood up, and pulled her bowstring toward the scout behind her. She didn't have to. The scout was gasping for air, Kharlo's weapon pinning him to a tree.

I slowly sank to the ground. I couldn't believe how far I'd thrown that axe. Those weapons felt light in your hands, but you could stop even crushing blows with them. That axe flew twice as far as I could've ever thrown a normal one. Clearly there was still a lot I didn't know.

Tynia stood up and pulled Kharlo's weapon from the scout's chest. "Cut that one with a red arrow!" she shouted as she walked back to the tree where she left her satchel.

I went back for the arrows in my bag and made a cut on the man's arm. This time, I didn't even wait to see him turn to ashes. I just walked away.

Tynia opened the vial of red paint. She dabbed a finger in it and let a drop of paint land on the face of the scout. The man turned to ash as she walked toward the one lying on the ground with no legs.

"I can't use my bag as a quiver. Should I keep the arrows in my hand just in case?" I asked as I walked toward her.

She turned around to answer me, but the scout lying behind her used his last breath to swing his sword one more time. Even though she backed away as soon as she noticed, the scout's blade tore her satchel and cut into her leg.

Tynia slammed a foot down on his sword and swiftly passed her finger over the man's face, leaving a brief line of paint on it. The scout turned to ashes moments later. Everything Tynia had been carrying lay scattered around her. She even dropped the vial of paint and rolled to the ground, spilling its last drops on the soil stained with dark blood. Tynia sopped up as much paint as she could with her fingers and painted more of the thin leather string holding her pendant.

"Jonek, bring your bag here. Hurry!"

I rushed to her side and opened my bag. We both picked up as many of her items as we could, but there were still many pebbles and other trinkets on the ground when we heard a horn in the distance. Tynia's eyes widened.

"They found us!" she said as she tore a long strip from her skirt and tied it over the cut on her leg. "Let's move. We're not that far away." She began to hobble away, but I noticed a patch of Virkelas plant at the base of a tree near the scout who'd wounded her. My mother used the leaves of that plant to heal minor cuts, but I saw her once use the sap of its fruit to close a deep cut on Zilhana's hand. I rushed over and grabbed a handful before catching up with Tynia, hoping to treat her wound as soon as we found some cover.

We made our way through the forest as fast as we could. I kept a red arrow in my hand at all times, though I wasn't sure how useful I'd actually be with it if it came to that.

A symphony of pounding, howling, and the crackling of falling trees echoed in the depths of the forest as we reached the cemetery. We circled around it toward a small house on the east side of the meadow.

"The key, Jonek," Tynia said, glancing at me. "Do you know where it is?"

Even today, I can still distinctly recall the feeling of my stomach leaping when I realized I had no idea what she was talking about, though she was clearly counting on me for . . . something.

"Key?" I said, feeling a little bit of cold sweat welling on the back of my neck. "What key?"

Tynia put a hand on my shoulders. "We need a key to open the door to the Lost Path. Kharlo had it, and he must have passed that knowledge to you. Think!"

All I could do was nod mutely. We kept a steady pace—as fast as Tynia's leg would allow—until we reached Kharlo's (or at least in those parts, Da Drukhol's) house beyond the cemetery. Tynia took out her weapon, transformed it into a staff, and passed it around the doorframe.

"It's safe. Let's go inside."

The entire house was just one room with a bed, a table, and a small chimney. A few tapestries and knick-knacks hung from the walls and ceiling, and countless books were piled everywhere. Tynia took rope, bread, and a few candles and put them inside my bag.

"Think, Jonek. Where is it?"

"My mind is empty. I have no memory of a key."

"This is no ordinary key. It looks like a round stick as thick as my finger, maybe two or three fists long. It has an iron ring on one end and lines carved around it. It looks like this." She took a charred piece of wood from the chimney, opened a book from the table, and drew on a page. I was following the lines she drew when I saw a flash, as if someone had hit me hard on the nose.

I looked at Tynia with amazement. "I just saw things I've never lived before. The key that Celkhora gave to Kharlo isn't in this house—it's buried. There are three rocks marking its place; one's white and two are brown."

"Sounds like the grave of an unknown warrior," she said. We didn't say another word. We left the house and ran toward the cemetery. "I'll start on the lower side!" she shouted as we parted ways. "You go uphill!"

Many stories were shared among our people about ghosts and other beings dwelling in that place. To our good fortune, Tynia and I had the daylight on our side, so it wasn't as frightful as it could've been at night. Unfortunately, being in the sun also meant that people could see us roaming over the hill from a good distance.

Two brown rocks and one white, I thought as I kept moving, trying to duck low behind the gravestones. Tynia was stopping from time to time to tighten the cloth over her wound.

CHAPTER SEVEN

The horn sounded again by the edge of the forest.

I turned my eyes toward Tynia, and she signaled for me to stay low and follow her. Even though our wounds were bothering us, we didn't stop until we reached the other end of the cemetery.

Then we saw them—four wizards escorted by thirty or forty scouts. Some prowled forward as wolves and bears, some walked as men. They were all being led by no less than a dozen sentinels sliding their bodies over our footprints, hunting us. In the back, an enormous warrior carrying two swords was holding a horn in one hand and a shield in the other. Black armor covered his body, and he had a single red mark on his chest.

"There are too many," Tynia whispered the moment I was close enough. "I don't know how Malok managed to send so many here."

"What do we do now?"

"We need the key. Can't you remember anything else? Think." I closed my eyes and put my forehead on my arm as I tried to remember more. "Breathe, Jonek. Breathe," she whispered. I felt her soft but sturdy hands rub my back.

Soon, the flashing lights behind my eyelids slowed and I was able to once again see those hands placing rocks over the spot where the key was buried. This time, through the eyes of the one who buried it, I saw a sharp rock protruding from the wall of the mountain a few steps away from that key.

"It's by the wall of the mountain," I whispered, opening my eyes again. "We need to look for some sharp rocks coming out from the base of the wall."

Tynia crawled back a short distance and looked up, spotting a place that fit that description almost immediately. Unfortunately, those rocks were at the highest point on the hill where it would be very easy to see us.

"We have to get there," she said as she put a hand on her wound.

"Why don't you heal yourself?" I whispered.

"I can't. The wizards would sense the magic."

"Then at least let me see what I can do," I said, pulling the Virkelas out of my bag. I used the head of an arrow to slice a handful of them in half. Tynia hesitated, but she must have seen something in my eyes that made her take the cloth off her wound and turn her head away. It was a deep cut. I closed it with my fingers and squeezed the fruit's juice into it.

Even the stalwart Tynia winced, but the bleeding stopped almost immediately. She tore another strip from her skirt and covered it again.

"I'll leave my bag here and crawl to those rocks," I said, pointing uphill. "Have your weapon ready just in case."

Tynia didn't argue. She pulled my bag closer and kept her weapon in her hand.

I was thinking about the sentinels tracking our steps, and I quickened my pace as I dragged myself between graves. Just as I reached the top of the hill, I saw the soldiers tearing apart Kharlo's house. I couldn't help but think about my own house.

I turned my attention toward the face of the mountain and the sharp rocks. I crawled closer and dug my hands into the dirt. I tossed away rock after rock, finally happening upon a white one. I glanced back at the house and noticed a few sentinels already making their way toward the cemetery. Burrowing just a little deeper, my fingers got stuck in a large iron ring.

There it was—a long, round piece of wood with a ring on one end. I put it inside my clothes and started crawling back. In my clumsy haste, I nudged a rock, which rolled downhill. The sentinels perked up.

No more crawling. I leapt to my feet and ran as fast as I could, leaping over and ducking around graves. As the arrows began to fly by me, I took cover behind the taller gravestones. Chunks of rock showered past my head as the enemy's sharp arrowheads cracked pieces of the gravestone free. I glanced back to see where they were, but oddly, they refused to enter the cemetery. They kept circling around the grounds, shooting a rain of arrows toward me. I turned the other way, looking for Tynia, and in one brief moment on that hill, an image was carved into my mind so deeply that I still dream about it nowadays.

There in the distance. Ferdhen. The town itself, the market, the tents, and all those falcons flying around the competition grounds became one of the most cherished images my soul still carries—besides the ones of my mother, of course. As you can imagine, that moment didn't last long. An arrow flew right in front of me, waking me from that dream.

Tynia was waiting for me behind a tree, but I ran by her without even stopping. Tynia followed as close as she could. The horn rang louder and louder behind us.

We never looked back. We ran around the lower lagoon and then south, along the eastern bank of the river. Tynia cast a spell and insects oozed from the ground by the thousands, walking in all directions and covering our tracks.

We paused just long enough for Tynia to put her hand on my forehead and wave her staff above us, making three more Tynias and Joneks appear. She directed them to run in opposite directions and pulled me toward the river.

"Try to stay in the water to avoid leaving tracks," she said.

We ran about two hundred paces in the water until Tynia stopped in front of a trail of flat rocks that headed back into the forest.

"Walk on top of these rocks and stay close," she said as she jumped from rock to rock. I followed her lead, and with a quick wave of her staff, she helped me along by whisking me into the air so that I was walking on nothing. We didn't stop until we reached the tallest tree in that part of the Stapian forest. This tree was well-known by my friends and me—it must have stood there for thousands of years. I remember people saying that you could walk more than a hundred steps and still not make one circle around it. But it was forbidden for us to even walk close to it, because it had very poisonous weeds with red thorns all around its base, maybe as high as eight feet from the ground.

"I can't risk using more magic," Tynia said. "Can you climb a tree?"

"Of course I can, but I'm not touching those weeds. If any of those thorns even graze our skin, we'll die in minutes. You know that, right?"

"I know," she said. "The thorns protecting the Patriarch Tree are deadly even for us. But we have to get to the top."

"But how?"

Tynia said something, but the sound of the horn coming from the river swallowed her words.

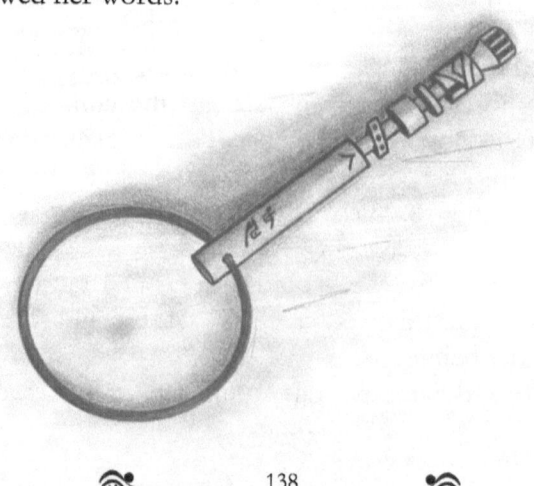

CHAPTER 8. SILENT HEROES.

The dark army briefly lost our tracks somewhere by the river.

Walking on top of the rocks, running in the air—all those tricks gave us a few minutes, but their sentinels tracked down our scent faster than we could run.

"Look at my weapon!" Tynia called as a chain erupted from her staff and a small metal ball covered with thin spikes took shape at its end. "Step away from the tree, swing the chain, and throw the ball as high as you can toward the tree. Once it's attached, pull the chain once. When you feel the chain pulling you, run toward the tree and jump as high as you can to clear the vines. Don't even look down. Keep climbing and hide on top of those branches."

That was it. No more explanations. She stepped away, swung the metal ball a couple times, and threw it to the top of the tree. The chain kept stretching out of her weapon until the ball stuck in some branches maybe thirty feet high. She swiftly pulled the chain and ran toward me. I barely had time to lower my head and let her feet fly above me.

"Hurry up, Jonek!" she shouted as she climbed.

Fear was my immediate reaction. Fear of not being able to make my staff transform into a chain. All those times when I wasn't able to use the disk and Kharlo's weapon rushed through my mind as I walked away from the tree. I turned around and saw Tynia pulling herself over the first branches. Suddenly, I noticed someone in the distance coming our way.

I didn't even look at my weapon—I just convinced myself that a chain was already hanging from the staff. I ran a few steps and threw it to the top of the tree. That moment felt endless, but my heart started beating again when I saw the ball at the end of my chain getting stuck high in the branches. I noticed two or three groups of dark scouts storming their way through the forest in the distance, so I rushed toward the tree. It didn't take long for me to realize I had forgotten a critical step.

I desperately pulled the chain and ran to one side, trying to keep the tree between the dark scouts and me. I remember taking my hands off the grip and grabbing the chain itself as I jumped. My feet landed just above the vines. A few thorns tore into my bag, but I didn't move until the chain shortened and the grip of the weapon slid into my hands

 139

again.

I stepped on anything I could until I made it to the first branch. I quickly softened my grip on the weapon to make the chain disappear. At that moment, the scouts and sentinels reached the tree.

I laid on my back on top of the branch and put my bag between my legs. Tynia was looking at me from a higher branch, but she didn't say a word. Slowly, she hid her face behind the leaves, and I immediately understood why. We were already surrounded by the dark army. That branch was wide enough to hide me and nothing more. I closed my eyes and lay still, holding Kharlo's weapon over my chest.

Scouts and wizards shouted commands right below my branch. Some words sounded familiar, but most of it was meaningless. Drops of sweat rolled down my face and landed on the branch; I'm just glad they didn't land on top of some beast on the ground. I didn't even try to look down. I knew I had better chances if I just stayed still, so I closed my eyes, quieted my ragged breath, and froze every muscle in my body.

I heard the beasts moving around the tree looking for a way to avoid the vines. Some made the mistake of trying to charge through and ended up lifeless, deadly thorns stuck in their bodies. After a few minutes of fruitless searching, they shot a volley of arrows to the top of the tree in a desperate attempt to hit us by chance. I knew it would be hard for them to find a way to climb to where we were, but the wizards surprised us both. Slinging their staffs forward, they threw a few sentinels over the vines, allowing the snakes to grab onto the tree. I felt something land on my chest.

It took a moment, but I was able to find Tynia's face among the sea of leaves. I was glad to see that she was unharmed, but I wasn't happy about the expression on her face.

Her lips were moving, but I couldn't understand anything she said. She careful made some gestures, and then it clicked. Sentinels were making their way up, and by the time she hid again, the red and black sides had split and were already taking different paths up to where I was.

I wasn't sure what to do. I hesitated, but a moment later, Kharlo's staff slowly transformed back into a sword. It turns out that almost no light comes out of those weapons if you let them transform slowly. My plan was simple—I was going to slice at anything that reached my branch. (Of course, I didn't know that more than thirty warriors were waiting below, arrows pointed at the top of the tree.)

One of the wizards below tried to burn the vines down, but the tree defended itself; the dark warriors tried to run away, but their voices turned into screams and I decided to look down. In that brief moment, I saw two unforgettable things—dark soldiers being torn to pieces by the roots of the tree and the slimy scales of a red sentinel sliding under my branch.

The last thing I remember was Tynia's voice.

"Take cover!"

A crackling blast echoed through the woods and the tree stopped shaking a moment after. Deafened by the time I reopened my eyes, I tried to stay still even though I had no idea what was going on. Then I saw Tynia signaling me to climb to where she was. Utterly confused and lightheaded from the loud ringing in my ears, I started making my way up. When I glanced down, I couldn't believe what I saw in that world of silence.

Thousands of red thorns were stuck everywhere. The roots of the tree disappeared underground, leaving the bodies of the dark soldiers and a number of wizards covered in thorns. The sentinels under my branch were still moving, but the thorns kept them stuck to the tree. It took some time for me to get rid of the thorns stuck everywhere as I climbed up, but eventually I was able to reach Tynia.

"Jonek, you got lucky!" Tynia said with a sigh of relief. "I was worried you were out in the open when the tree threw thorns everywhere."

Well, at least that's what I thought she said. My ears were not at their best just then. We kept climbing far beyond the canopy of the forest. My friends and I had always wondered how tall that tree really was, because its branches and the dense forest were so thick that we couldn't see the top from the ground.

Tynia climbed up to a branch that was flat on top and waited for me to join her. Once we were together, she took her weapon and drew her symbol in the air in front of the trunk. The thin rivers of light from her staff floated before us until she softly pushed them with her other hand into the tree. Suddenly, the bark on the trunk turned to dust, and an entrance appeared in front of us.

Tynia took a small hourglass from my bag and hung it from her waist. She walked a few steps to find the sun, then turned the hourglass upside down. Its sand changed color as it flowed down to its bottom chamber.

"Please remind me to turn the hourglass every hour or we will lose track of time," she said. "Now try to stay close. It's easy to get lost in here."

The sun illuminated the first few steps into the woody cavern, but we had to stop when a new layer of bark closed the entrance, leaving us in complete darkness. Tynia transformed her weapon into a long staff with some kind of bright blue flames burning on its top. The flames bathed our path, illuminating a long staircase spiraling down.

"We're safe for now. Let me take care of your wounds." She reached over and slid the bag from my shoulder.

Tynia healed our wounds, soothed the pain in my ears, and left me to rest while she looked through everything in my bag. She was very disappointed when she realized that we left many of her belongings back in the forest.

What I remember most from being inside that tree is how lonely you feel in there. No light, no sounds, and certainly no life. Other than Tynia and me, there were no other living things disturbing the emptiness of that space.

"Let's start heading down," she said as she stood up. "Just one thing—you'll see doors opening on the wall as we go down. Don't mind them. Just stay behind me."

We didn't descend more than twenty steps when a light illuminated the wall and an entrance was revealed. I thought my eyes were deceiving me. Even though we were inside a tree, a torch in there illuminated the first few steps of a long underground tunnel. A thin flow of water quickly rushed from the depths of that tunnel toward our feet, eventually spilling over the edge of the stairwell.

"Jonek, I need you to stay very quiet from here on out."

The door closed and its light slowly died as we went further down. I don't know how long we kept going, but many doors opened and closed as we ventured deeper and deeper. From time to time, Tynia touched the wall with her staff, leaving a small red or green flame burning on it.

After a while she stopped, left two flames on the wall, and made us walk back until she finally stopped in front of one of the doors we'd already passed. To me, it looked exactly the same as the rest. Water rushed again from inside, so I stepped aside and looked at her.

"This is it," Tynia said. "I hope we have enough time to reach the

Lost Path before the moon rises."

"But I thought *this* was the Lost Path."

Tynia smiled. "Those same words have broken the silence of this place many times before. Unfortunately, we haven't reached it yet. This is just one of the three entrances that lead to the door. Be careful where you step—these rocks are slippery."

We walked through that old tunnel for more than three hours. Tynia finally stopped by a huge flat rock that offered us a dry place to sit.

"I am hungry," she said, leaning her staff on the wall. "Let's eat and rest." I handed my bag to her and sat by her side. She stretched her legs and leaned back, hands behind her. "I haven't used this entrance in ages," she said as she offered me a piece of bread. "The other routes will challenge your strength and prowess with your weapon, but this one tests your mind. It's fairly easy to get lost in here. You use the wrong door and you could walk for weeks in these tunnels only to end up back at the stairwell—if you had enough food to survive."

"But how do you know which door is the right one?"

"You learn that from the elders."

"Is the rest of the way as wet and dark as it's been so far?"

Tynia smirked. "Would you prefer to battle the dark army on dry ground and in broad daylight?"

"Nope. I just feel uneasy not knowing what's waiting for us ahead."

"Well, rest assured that we won't face enemies in here. But there *is* a part of this tunnel that might become a challenge for us this time of the year."

I didn't want to ask anything else. After everything I'd experienced over those two days, I didn't want to know what could possibly lie ahead that would make someone like Tynia worry.

"Let's rest," she said as she leaned back on the wall and closed her eyes. I was tired too. I tried to sleep, but I couldn't quiet my racing thoughts. In my sleeplessness, I rolled over and noticed that all the thin rivers of water flowing through the tunnel were coming out of tiny fissures along the bottom of the walls. Interesting. It also didn't take long for my thoughts to turn toward my mother, Zilhana, and my friends. Were they able to find a safe place? Were they unharmed? Alive?

I don't know why, but at some point I took my ramikha and softly played my mother's lullaby. Tynia didn't open her eyes, but the fire from her staff gracefully followed my melody, tiny embers floating away into the darkness of the tunnel.

***

Tynia and I weren't the only ones resting. Hiding just beyond the edge of the forest to the west of the competition grounds, my mother and friends waited in silence. My mother offered her place at the market to some merchants she knew, and they gave her plenty of coins, food, and even some clothes for it. Other than Tobho and Yilian, who were standing by some trees nearby, the group was sitting quietly on the back of the wagon.

Zilhana was soaking bread in a bowl of soup and giving some pieces to Nuthek. Lucky for them, their journey was far less eventful than ours. Their biggest challenge had been to navigate through the endless swarm of people as they passed through our town and the competition grounds.

At some point, Nuthek reached into his pocket and pulled out the gold coin. "Maybe we can use this to talk to them." Everyone looked at my mother. She hesitated but ended up agreeing. "The lady said we have to be brief. Those wizards may find us if we use this for too long."

Zilhana opened a crate, took a large bowl from it, and placed it in front of Nuthek. Tobho and Yilian climbed onto the wagon as my mother poured water in the bowl. Tobho took the coin from Nuthek, put it in the water, and looked at the others. Everyone hesitated, but my mother slowly leaned forward and put her fingers in the water. Zilhana and Tobho did the same, and Yilian took Nuthek's hand and guided it into the bowl.

"Let's close our eyes," Yilian said.

The rest didn't see or feel anything at first. Only Nuthek, who'd kept his eyes closed since that morning, saw the darkness devouring the faint glimmer of daylight he'd just begun to notice for the last hour.

"Is it night already?" he asked.

Yilian opened his eyes, looking out over the beams of sunlight streaming through the trees. "What do you mean, Nuthek?"

"I could see some light a moment ago, but it all went dark after I put my fingers in the water."

"Let's just keep our eyes closed," Yilian said.

One by one, they began to see the shadow covering the light until

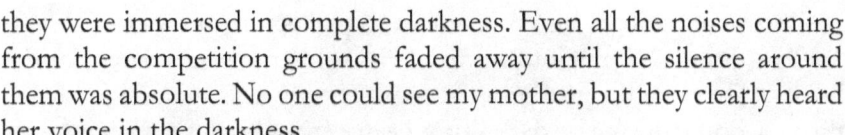

they were immersed in complete darkness. Even all the noises coming from the competition grounds faded away until the silence around them was absolute. No one could see my mother, but they clearly heard her voice in the darkness.

"Jonek? Can you hear me?" A few moments passed with no answer.

"Maybe we're doing this wrong," Tobho said.

"Jonek, where are you? Please answer me. . . ."

***

A strange sound hummed out of Tynia's staff. I stopped playing my ramikha, and Tynia opened her eyes and took the staff. She subdued its flames, leaving us in complete darkness.

"Jonek, stay where you are. Nuthek is trying to talk to us."

Tynia touched the water running by our feet with her staff. A flash of light dazzled me. There, in the middle of the darkness, a small, glimmering star floated in midair, almost as high as my face. As I got used to its light, I was able to see my mother and the rest standing around it, blocking its light with their hands.

"Lower your hands. We don't have much time," Tynia said as she made the light dimmer.

"Where are we?" Nuthek asked. "Where is this darkness?"

"You are still where you were before you touched the water. This is just how we communicate between Kirolcan and this world. Jonek and I haven't gotten there yet—we're still a few hours from the door."

"Are you alright, Jonek?"

"Yes, mother," I said with a smile. "Where are you?"

"Hiding in the woods west of the competition grounds. I wanted you to know that Nuthek's eyes aren't fully healed, but he's getting better."

"If my eyes are not healed, how come I can see you?" Nuthek said.

"Because you're using your mind, not your eyes," Tynia said.

My mother took a deep breath. "We haven't found a place to hide."

"It's probably best if you stay where others can help. Jonek and I saw many dark soldiers and wizards roaming the forest to the east, but I don't think they were the only groups looking for us."

"Tobho, Yilian, where exactly are you?" I asked.

"Just behind the trees where the bees stung Nuthek last year."

"Well, maybe you should ask the local soldiers for help. Da Grokpel has instructions from his commander to protect my mother—"

"No, Jonek," Tynia interrupted. "His soldiers are no match for the beasts. They would just provoke unnecessary carnage if they faced them. I don't think the dark army even cares about Ferdhen and its soldiers—at least not yet. My guess is that they'll keep searching for you and me in small groups, slaying only those unlucky enough to cross their path."

My mother looked at me. "Why would a commander ask Da Grokpel to protect me?"

"Well, it's a long story, mother. Don't worry. Just forget it."

"No, Jonek, I'm not going to 'forget it.' I haven't stopped praying for you to come back safe, but you and I will have a serious talk about this—and a few other things your friends kindly shared with me—when you come back."

"There's no time for this," Tynia said. "You have to find a safe place before nightfall. Where can you go from there?"

Nuthek stepped closer to the light. "Well, if we're by the trees where I shot that beehive, then we've got some choices. To the north is the main road that goes to the top of the Bhormaks. The western lands aren't an option—they're swarming with Lord Nutrec's brigands, and our wagon would be an easy target. The south has a smoother landscape, but the open fields would make us easy for any beasts to find. And everyone knows the competition grounds and Ferdhen are east of here."

"And beyond that, a large group of beasts roaming the Stapian forest," Tobho said.

"We should go south and hide in the farmlands," Zilhana said.

"Even a blind dog could find us there," Yilian retorted. "We should get more food and warm clothes and head to the mountains."

"No, Yilian," Nuthek said. "We'll run out of food by the time we reach the Dragon's Back. And once we're there, the snow will do us in."

"I'd rather stay close to the warriors," Tobho said. "We have the best gathered in town for the rest of the week." One by one, they all realized that Tobho's idea was probably their best hope for survival. "We'll find a tent in the center and—"

Those were the last words I heard before Tynia turned around, looked into the darkness, and then suddenly slammed her staff down and made the star disappear. She swiftly reconjured the blue flames again.

"There was someone else in there with us—maybe a wizard. Only you, me, and the ones touching the coin should have been able to understand what was said in there . . . I hope." Tynia put her feet back in the water. "Don't worry, Jonek. I truly believe they'll be fine as long as they stay together. Don't let your mind dwell too much on it."

"Well, now I have two things to worry about—their well-being and the long conversation that awaits me when I see my mother again."

Tynia offered me a brief smile and started walking. That tunnel didn't change much for the next three or four hours. Sometimes it felt as if we were going uphill, but most of the time the ground was fairly level. Tynia's blue flames were still the only source of light we had, though I was deceived many times when it reflected off the many crystals, gems, and metals embedded in the walls.

I kept wondering what the miners would have paid to walk through that tunnel. I have no doubt that those digging holes inside the Barkrek mines would've built an underground city using that tunnel as their main street if only they'd known about it.

Suddenly, the tunnel began to go downhill until we found it blocked by a wall made of porous black rock. There was a pool of water covering almost half the height of the tunnel below, so we left my bag on dry ground and walked into the water to reach the black wall. Tynia passed her hands over it and put her fingers in every hole she could.

"Use your weapon to make some flames like mine," she said as she sloshed back out of the water to get something from the bag. I took Kharlo's weapon and looked at Tynia in hesitation. "Don't think about it too much. Just believe that you can."

I kept staring at her.

"Jonek, you have to find your own means to make it happen every time. All guardians develop a routine to ensure their weapons transform every time. Kharlo squeezes the grip when he wants it to transform, Jalyena closes her eyes, and Artego thinks about a secret word. It's between you and the weapon to make that connection, but don't think about it too much—just do it."

I knew that moment wasn't the best time for me to devise my own routine. Knowing it was Kharlo's weapon, I squeezed its grip slightly and raised it over my head. Suddenly, large blue flames burst from it, flooding our surroundings with more light and making Tynia grin at me proudly.

She went back into the water and turned her staff into a long, sharp spear. She muttered something, and the tip of the spear became as red and hot as molten iron. Slowly, she inserted the spear in a hole just a few inches above the surface of the water. She kept pushing her staff until it went all the way through. Then she pulled it back out and stared at the hole for a moment.

"Great. We may still have a few hours."

"A few hours for what?" I asked nervously.

"A few hours before the next flow of molten rock heads up to the top of the mountain."

"Are we under the Bhormaks?" I asked.

"Yes, just under the Dragon's Nose." She took a pebble from her clothes, passed it over the flames of my staff, and threw it into the water. "Put your flames out and don't move."

After just a few moments, the entire pool was glowing as blue as the sky.

"Well, we can't blast this wall; the entire tunnel may cave in. We'll have to dig a path ourselves." Tynia turned her staff into a silver mining pick. "We have to be on the other side in no more than an hour."

I walked closer to the wall, squeezed the grip of Kharlo's weapon, and hit it with all my strength.

The sound it made was very different from the one coming from Tynia's pick.

In fact, the tool I was holding was nothing even close to a mining pick. It actually looked more like a mace with thick spikes. Tynia turned, wide-eyed, then shrugged.

"I've never seen one of those before. Whatever it is, it did quite a bit of damage to the wall, so keep swinging it as hard as you can!"

***

While our tools were chipping away at that wall, my mother, Zilhana, and Tobho were walking between long lines of tents, having a hard time finding one to use. The great success of the fair made it almost impossible for anyone to find an empty tent by then. Zilhana even heard that travelers arriving late to the fair were offering two or three times the usual price for a small tent.

It wasn't until Tobho overheard someone inside a tent saying they would leave to treat someone's wounds in their hometown that their luck changed. Tobho ran and told my mother, so both ladies promptly went inside the tent while he stood outside.

The negotiations lasted for a while, but eventually both parties agreed on a price. After the coins exchanged hands, the previous owners gathered their belongings and left the tent. Tobho briefly saw the face of the wounded man being carried to a wagon nearby. He was the contestant who threw the first Vothra the day before.

Unfortunately, no falcons went back with him that day.

Zilhana stayed in the tent while Tobho and my mother went to the market to buy more food and other necessities. When they got back to the wagon, Yilian was standing by Kharlo's feet with his bow in his hand while Nuthek walked slowly around the wagon, holding onto it to avoid falling.

"Nuthek! You can see!" Tobho shouted as he threw the sack he was carrying on top of the wagon.

"My eyes aren't as sharp as usual, but they're getting better."

"Tobho can put more of his red medicine on them if you want," Yilian said, laughing from above.

"Not even amusing," Nuthek said, throwing a small stick at Yilian.

My mother put her sacks on the ground and stopped to catch her breath. "We need to put this armor on Kharlo. We'll disguise him as an injured warrior and take him to the tent."

If it's difficult to put heavy armor on a healthy warrior while he's standing, imagine what they went through to put it on Kharlo. Yilian told me the competitions ended and the sun was long gone before they'd finished. They even wrapped his head with some bandages to enhance the act. Once Kharlo was ready, they put some weapons by his side and made their way around the tents.

They left the wagon behind the tent and carried him using a cot. One benefit of doing this at night was that there wasn't enough light to see his face, and most others were either celebrating their triumphs or trying to forget their defeats. No one paid attention to a woman and some boys carrying one more wounded warrior.

Once they'd arrived, Tobho and Yilian placed a tall torch in front of the entrance with a white cloth tied to it so that people would stay away and not bother the "injured" warrior inside.

Tobho sat by the entrance to keep an eye on what was happening outside. The rest gathered by my mother as she lit a clay oven to warm up food and milk.

***

Tynia and I, on the other hand, were in direr straits. We kept hacking off large pieces of the black wall until we finally broke through to the other side. Bright yellow light illuminated our surroundings, and a draft of warm air blew past us. The water from the pool spilled over to the other side. Tynia retrieved the pebble from the water and put it back in her clothes.

"We may have less time than I thought. I knew it wouldn't be easy this time of year," she said. "Go get the bag. There's no time to waste."

I squirmed through the hole and back, then joined her on a ledge built on the wall of an enormous cave—a cave big enough to fit another mountain inside. The temperature difference was like night and day. No ceiling above us, just the walls of the cave converging around a big opening at the top. Several hundred feet down was a sea of molten rock that was making its way up. Quickly.

Standing where we were, we had three options. The first was an open bridge of shiny bricks in front of us. It was maybe four feet wide and took us directly to the other side of the cave, right over the sea of molten rock. The second was a much wider path to our left that led to the same place, but this one took us the long way along the wall of the cave. Of course, our last option was to go back to the safety of the tunnel.

Tynia looked at some of the symbols carved into the first section of the bridge and glanced at the molten rock at the bottom. "We either cross this bridge and open a hole to the tunnel on the other side in less than three hours, or we go back and reach the Lost Path some other way."

"Why?"

"In about three hours, both the bridge and the path around the cave will be covered in molten rock, and it will take a few days for it to go down again."

"Should we go back?"

"I would've said yes any other time, but right now, I'm not sure the dangers we'll face on the other routes are any less deadly."

"This bridge looks too narrow, and it doesn't have any protection on its sides."

Tynia glanced at me and nodded. "That's why we don't use this entrance often. It has no enemies, but it's more treacherous."

I shook my head. "We don't have a choice. We can't afford to lose even one day. I'll follow you," I said, slinging my bag over my shoulder.

Tynia used her weapon to cut her skirt off from the knees down and turned to me. "Don't look down, and keep your balance when you see the towers of vapor rising from below."

Our clothes were dry after just a few steps. Walking on such a narrow bridge with no handrails was nerve-wracking, but I kept my composure well enough to notice that even though heat was rising all around us, the bridge itself was cold. I even lay down a few times so the stone could cool my face and clothes.

"Don't let the bridge slow you down!" Tynia shouted when she noticed me staying behind lying on the bridge.

"I can't help it," I said as I caught up with her. "When I lie down, the bridge shields my body from the heat."

"I know, Jalyena—I mean, Jonek," she said as she got on her knees, all sweaty. "There are many things in life that will lure you away from your quest. Some of them will even make you forget what's important by offering false comforts. Wise is the one who knows which ones those are and stays away from them." Tynia allowed her hands to cool down on the bridge and then passed them over her neck and forehead. "In this case, if you lie on the bridge too long or too often, you'll die." She pushed herself up again with her staff.

Not even the comfort of the bridge allowed me to disregard those words. I got back on my feet and kept walking.

"Who built this bridge?"

"No one really knows. Some think it was built by the elders, but others talk about another civilization that used to live in underground cities in Kirolcan. Very few know where those cities are, because the dark army destroyed them long ago. No one has seen survivors from that race since."

"But what were they doing here?"

"Who knows? Everything people say about this place could just be legends and folklore."

"Well, they could've built this bridge a bit wider! Either they were small or they ran out of bricks," I said as I changed my bag to my other shoulder.

Tynia turned and offered me a brief smile through cracked, dry lips. We kept going until the bridge sloped upward and finally let us off on a ledge similar to the one we started at. I dropped my bag by the wall and poured the last few drops of water from my waterskin in my mouth. Tynia sat down in front of me and looked at the wall.

"Oh no," she said as she leaned forward and put her hand on the wall.

"What? What's wrong?"

"Where's the symbol?"

I rolled my eyes. "What symbol?" She never explained anything before I had to ask.

"There's supposed to be a symbol marking where the tunnel is."

"Are there markings on the bridge like on the other side? Maybe it says there."

"No, those just talk about the molten rock and its levels. We need to find it ourselves."

I walked in front of the wall from side to side, and indeed, there was no symbol or any visual indication of a tunnel. Even the colors of the wall were the same end to end. Tynia turned her weapon into that long spear from earlier and started making holes in the wall as fast as she could.

"Is the tunnel there?" I asked every time she pulled her staff out.

She didn't even answer me. She kept walking along the wall making holes while I kept glancing at the molten rock getting closer and closer. I can't even describe the relief I felt when she pulled her staff from the last hole and saw water pour over our feet.

"Here!" she said.

My mace was flying toward the wall even before she finished speaking. We didn't stop, didn't even look back at the bridge as it vanished in the rising sea of molten rock. I never would have believed that a boy and an old lady could have opened a hole like that in such a short time, but we did. Tynia and I crawled into the hole just as the molten rock began to flood the ledge.

The scorching heat we felt died abruptly when we tumbled into another pool of cold water. We didn't even care about getting the bag wet at this point—all we wanted was for our bodies to cool down as quickly as possible.

"Don't drink this water. Let's keep moving," Tynia said as blue flames lit up the top of her staff once more. We hadn't walked more than ten steps out of the water before we heard rocks cracking and a loud hissing behind us.

"Sounds like the molten rock reached the water," Tynia breathed as a cloud of vapor wafted by us. "We barely made it." Tynia strode over to a rock with a small trickle of water pouring from the top. She tasted the water and said, "This seems clean. Let's fill our bags here."

I'm not sure how much water we drank, but I remember filling our bags more than once. We kept walking until we reached a round room where everything—floor, walls, and ceiling—was covered with thin brown bricks. A very old lamp illuminated the room from the top of a small pedestal in the center, so Tynia put her staff away. Eight or nine doorways dotted the wall around the room.

"So, which tunnel is it?" I asked.

"Well, only one of them will take us where we want to go. Many guardians have devised some creative ways to determine which one it is, but Jalyena's method hasn't failed us so far. We just need to wait for the light to go out."

I didn't understand what she meant by that, so I quietly followed her closer to the lamp. Four large iron rings hung around the roughly carved stone pedestal, and water flowed from a crack on its base. Tynia cleaned the glass around the lamp so it could provide more light and looked at me.

"When you see this light dying, grab onto one of these rings and don't let go."

Tynia couldn't finish her sentence. The flame inside the lamp dimmed, and everything around us began to move. I couldn't tell whether it was the room or us spinning around, but our feet were in the air for quite some time.

Eventually we stopped and the lamp illuminated the room again. Even though Tynia must have felt as sick and dizzy as I was, she crawled to one side of the room and looked at the floor.

"Look at the floor. There should be a small flow of water going from this room into one of the tunnels. Quickly! It won't last long."

I couldn't walk. I stayed on the floor, crawling like a dying lizard. There was water all over it, but I noticed specks of dirt and tiny rocks being carried away by a thin trickle of water into a tunnel nearby.

"There's some water here," I said as I rested my face on the floor and pointed at a doorway. Tynia got closer and looked at the bricks in front of the tunnel.

"Yes, this is the one."

"Ok, let's go," I said dragging myself into the tunnel.

"Where are you going?" she said. "Not this one. The one on the left."

"I don't understand."

"The left side of the river."

"What river?"

She waved her hand in front of her face. "Don't worry. I'll explain it to you some other time."

Tynia turned her hourglass twice as we walked through that tunnel. We were making our way around some large rocks when we noticed a wisp of a breeze playing with the flames of Tynia's staff.

"We're not far now."

"I sure hope so," I said with a sigh. "I would love a change of scenery right about now."

The tunnel made a sharp right turn and we found ourselves in front of a mass of plants and vines blocking our way.

"Try not to hurt or step on these plants," Tynia said as she put her back against the wall and slid her way out of the tunnel. I slowly followed her into a much brighter area, and my eyes took some time to adapt.

As the images became clear, I realized I was standing in a place that looked like a large, dense forest blooming in spring. There were trees and plants of all colors everywhere around us, and even though my mother had taught me to recognize many varieties, most of them were unfamiliar to me.

The best way to describe where the light was coming from— because it was certainly not the sun—is to think of how flames dance around a cauldron when it's put on a fire. Imagine those flames moving slowly down an immense curved wall that acted as a natural roof hundreds of feet above us.

Once my eyes got used to the light, I looked up to see an enormous opening in the center of the roof, and through it, the night sky.

"I hope this change of scenery is good enough for you, Jonek."

"Indeed it is, but where are we?"

"We call it Tumjule Garden. The door to the Lost Path is here, right in the center. The other two paths we could've used also bring you to this place, but their tunnels are on the other side. Try to stay close, and remember not to hurt the plants or other living things in here. This is a sanctuary, and we are just guests passing through."

What other living things? I wondered as I picked up my bag.

It was true—we were far from alone. Once our steps took us away from the wall, many bashful insects, birds, and other beings slowly emerged from their hiding places, infusing life into our surroundings. Some of these creatures gathered along our path, some running around us and others even climbing on Tynia's arms and shoulders as if they were happy to see her.

Tynia took our last pieces of bread and the rest of our berries and scattered them as we walked. Many tiny animals rushed to pick up the tidbits as I wondered what she and I would eat later that night.

"Don't worry, Jonek," she said, as if reading my mind. "We can't take this food with us anyway."

We kept walking. The path led us through some beautiful meadows covered with green and blue grass. By the time my faraway friends had come back from asking their families if they could spend the night in our tent, Tynia and I had reached a vast opening at the center of the garden where a graceful mountain stood proudly.

The clouds parted enough for the moonlight to touch our faces, and Tynia looked at her hourglass.

"This path is certainly shorter than the other ones. We're slightly ahead of time."

"It didn't feel short to me," I responded.

Tynia smiled and took two small lizards who'd been quietly traveling on my shoulder and carefully put them in the grass.

"It's odd that they trust you during your first time through their realm. Maybe it's because they sense Kharlo in you," she said as she kept walking.

"Well, at least they didn't chew on my hair like their Vhunsek cousin did yesterday at the fair," I whispered. Tynia shook her head and giggled.

The trail took us to a bridge over a lake that encircled the entire mountain, only this lake had no water. It was full of tiny red rocks moving continuously, like how the waves lift and move the sand of the Garpodian shores. Once we crossed the bridge and stepped onto the island, a brick path led up to a long staircase that weaved back and forth on the mountainside all the way to an archway. Tynia stopped at the base of the staircase just in front of a large statue of a young girl who was pointing a long staff toward the sky.

"Once again we walk by you, our silent heroes. Let our deeds be as fair and brave as yours," Tynia said as she placed her hand on the pedestal. A mark glowed briefly on the statue's neck.

We walked by many other pedestals as we climbed stairs. Some were empty, and some held proud figures of boys, girls, and other creatures frozen in time in what I always imagined to be the moment that defined their lives.

As we walked through the archway on the top, we stepped into an area that seemed to be the remnants of an old garden built between the walls of a canyon. The place looked ancient. There were a few shy trees and pockets of plants here and there. This place was worlds away from the variety and beauty of the garden down below. Stone benches stood lonely along some old, disregarded walkways that were now winding unevenly around the garden. We followed the center path until we reached a stone bridge over a river that emanated furiously from one wall of the canyon and was forcing its waters into a similar opening on the opposite wall.

Something I always found interesting about that place was that you couldn't hear the water thundering through the canyon until you actually stepped on the bridge. I remember how my ears felt overwhelmed by the stormy sounds of water rushing under the bridge, and then how jarring it was to step back into silence once we left it behind.

The area at the end of the canyon was fairly empty. Once we climbed a set of three steps, there was only a long wall leaning the face of the mountain and a small bench in front of an old, dry fountain on the left side.

Tynia walked to the center of the wall and put her hand on it. "Many years have passed since the last time I stood in front of you. May your wisdom guide us through light and darkness."

Tynia's mark briefly glowed on the back of her hand, and a wave of light emanated from it to every corner of the wall. Tiny flows of dust cascaded from hundreds of crevices along the wall, allowing thin carvings to appear in front of us. Letters, numbers, symbols—all kinds of images took shape in front of us. The only two I was able to identify were Tynia's and Kharlo's marks glowing yellow as they appeared and disappeared around the wall.

Some of the carvings started to merge until an image of a woman molded itself softly into the face of the wall, then gracefully stepped out of it. This beautiful ghost walked past us toward the fountain and sat down on the bench. Tynia walked closer and knelt down inside a circle in front of the woman. I didn't know what to do, so I walked closer and got down on one knee a few steps behind Tynia.

"Who are you?" she asked.

"Tynia. Guardian of the Twin Stars."

The woman placed her hand over Tynia's head and closed her eyes. "Our young Tynia. One of the heroes of Suphrilet. Slayer of Muzpokra and his eight demons. Master wizard and protector of our two most beloved lights." Many images of Tynia casting magic, fighting beasts, and traveling through amazing and frightful sceneries came to life in the air just above her head as the woman said those words.

The woman opened her eyes and looked back at Tynia. "My child, your legacy is as big as the sorrow you now carry in your heart. What is it that you seek?"

"Passage to Kirolcan."

"But why? Your presence there will further enrage the heart of our enemy."

"I know, my lady, but Malok's forces have found a way into this world, and many are dying here too. We can't hide here anymore."

"Where are the other guardians?" the woman asked.

"Artego and Jalyena are hiding in places unknown to me, and our leader . . . he is dying."

The woman put her hands together, and many symbols cycled across her forehead until Kharlo's symbol illuminated her skin with a bright blue color.

"I see him—Kharlo, our Guardian of the South Winds—holding onto a small piece of Jiretal wood, drifting away in the stormy seas of death. Strange, . . . I feel his presence nearby."

"A brave young warrior named Jonek travels with me. Kharlo entrusted his powers and knowledge to him so he could join me on this journey. It is important for our quest to bring Kharlo back to Kelfia, but he won't survive the endeavor without medicine from the elders."

The woman raised her eyes and looked at me. "Young warrior, approach. Let me see who you are."

Tynia stepped back so I could kneel inside the circle. When my knee touched the bricks, the outer edge of the circle lit up.

"Please, give me your hand," she said.

I extended my hand and saw her fingers blending with mine. I didn't see any images or lights above me. In fact, I didn't even feel anything, but something indeed was happening. The woman kept her eyes closed even as tears began to roll down her face and disappear into the air.

She moved her hand away, opened her eyes, and stood to go toward the fountain. "I haven't felt the kind of love this boy harbors in his heart since I was just a young star in our sky. There is so much innocence in him . . . and recklessness. What this boy carries inside is not only vital to aid in our struggle—it could mean the end of it. Our guardian Kharlo is right. It is time to gather those pieces hidden by you and your predecessors and face Malok once and for all."

The lady waved her hand, and water began to pour down from the top of the fountain. She scooped some up with a shell and offered it to me. "You have been touched by a dark wizard. Clean your forehead with this water." She handed the shell to me and sat down again. "There are cold flames guarding your soul. They are so powerful that even I am not able to see what is beyond them, other than a soft melody that will now caress my heart through eternity."

I honestly didn't know what she meant by that. I just resigned myself to looking at the light around the circle fading away as I cleaned my face with the water.

"My lady," Tynia said as I kept myself occupied with the water, "even with the elder's medicine, it will be very difficult to bring Kharlo to the Lost Path."

"Look for the mark of Hykhor on the right side of the wall and place your hand on it," the woman said. Tynia walked back to the wall and put her hand over a brick that had only one symbol carved on it. The brick came loose, and on top were six small holes. Five were empty, and one was holding a small green gem. She carefully pulled it out and brought it back to where we were.

"What you hold is my last marker. Bind it with the orb you carry and leave it by the door. You will be able to bring four more with you directly to the Lost Path. Now, be careful who you bring—this marker will bypass all the challenges our ancestors devised to keep fiends from finding this place."

There was no more light around the circle, so I left the shell on the ground and stood up. The lady bestowed a gentle, glittering rain that landed like a morning mist on us, making Tynia's and Kharlo's marks glow briefly on our hands and weapons.

"Now go and do your part. Our quest is in your hands."

The water in the fountain stopped flowing, and the lady vanished as she walked away. Only her last words remained in the air, making me feel even more lost than I already was.

"Young guardian, do not let Malok capture this boy. It may be our demise."

***

Tynia looked up to see where the moon was.

"Jonek, give me the rope and the key you found on the mountainside. Here comes the hard part."

"The hard part?" I said as I opened my bag. As if the previous molten rock, labyrinth of tunnels, and hordes of enemies around a deadly, thorny tree were the *easy* part. I pulled the rope out and emptied everything on the ground. Tynia walked along the wall reading symbols, glancing at the moon and whispering numbers.

"Seventeen, maybe eighteen measures. Take this end of the rope and stand on that brick that has a triangle on it." She pulled the rest toward the other end of the wall. "We need eighteen times this distance. Let's see how much we have."

I stood still on top of the triangle counting how many times Tynia walked back and forth, laying rope on the ground between her spot and mine. Finally, we ran out of rope, and I calculated.

"Barely seventeen. But that's all there is," I said. Tynia walked along the wall, muttering about finding "the right keyhole for this time of year." Everything had to be so complicated.

"Here it is," she said at last. "Give me the key." Tynia grabbed the key by the ring and pushed it into the hole. Two things disappeared at that moment—all the symbols on the wall, and the stone railings on both sides of the bridge we'd crossed earlier.

"Jonek, listen carefully, because we won't be able to hear each other once we step on the bridge, and this is rather convoluted. Put Kharlo's weapon inside the ring of the key, grab both ends, and turn the top to your right when you see me waving. Once you make a full turn, the key will vanish and you'll have to join me on top of the bridge as fast as you can.

"There is a large ring hidden in the edge of the bridge facing downstream. It will start spinning the moment the key is gone. I will loop this rope into it through a gap on the ring so we can grab onto the other end, dive into the river, and allow the current to carry us as far as this rope stretches—which isn't quite far enough.

"There's no air in that tunnel, so take a deep breath before jumping. If this rope gets us close enough, we'll see a round door opening on top of us that will let plenty of light into the waterway. Remember, this current is violent, and it might disorient you, so keep looking at the light and wait for some metal poles to drop into the water. There are six poles, but only one or two will drop into the water at a time. They have large handles, so grab onto any of them and let them pull you out of the water. Do *not* let go; your life depends on it.

"Let's just hope we can hold our breath long enough to grab a pole, because once the ring completes a full circle, the gap that I looped the rope through will come back around and release it." With that, she rushed away, dragging the rope with her.

My skin still shivers when I write about those moments. In all honesty, I definitely should have asked her to repeat all that, and I didn't truly understand the consequences of failing to correctly do any of those tasks. I knew my ears had heard Tynia saying something about our lives depending on something, but everything was just a blur, and I had a vague idea of what to do. Then I heard a soft voice whispering by the wall.

"Follow the guardian, young man, and don't let go of the rope until you can grab onto a pole. My blessing lives within you, Warrior Eyes."

I have to admit that those few words gave me a better sense of what I had to do than Tynia's not-so-brief briefing. I willed my body to relax, passed Kharlo's weapon through the ring, and grabbed its ends firmly. Tynia put the rope on the bridge, knelt down in front of the ring, and waved at me.

It wasn't as easy as I thought, but I turned the key until a bright flash dazzled me and made me fall. The key was gone a moment later.

There was no time to lose. I picked up my bag and ran toward the bridge.

The ring started spinning, so Tynia passed the loop into its gap as soon as it came out of the bridge. She took the other end, wrapped it around her arm, and kicked the rest into the water.

I couldn't hear anything she said, so I just put my arm inside the loop she made and grabbed the rope with all my strength. There was no time for hesitation. She put her hands around me and pushed us into the water.

CHAPTER 9. THE LOST PATH.

Once in the water, the fierce currents pushed us everywhere. By the time the rope stretched out all the way, I was alone and in complete darkness. At least I was lucky that the rope didn't give in.

I could only really focus on two things—holding my breath and holding onto that rope. My bag certainly wasn't helping. The force of the water pushing it was slowly pulling my arm away from the rope.

It wasn't easy in the oppressive flow of water, but I was able to briefly open my eyes. Nothing. Not even a glimpse of light around me.

Nothing can prepare you to live out something like that. Those few moments where my life depended on the little air in my lungs, how strong my hands were, and all the other things that had to happen perfectly made me feel for the first time that I'd gone too far. And where was Tynia? Was she alive? Or was it just me hanging from this rope? What should I do in a moment or two when my lungs run out of air? Should I keep my hands on the rope until the end or just let go?

I remember thinking, *Mother, guide me with your light.*

I tucked my chin down, trying to keep the ripping currents from hitting my face. Suddenly, I saw light illuminating the area downstream. I struggled to focus on it as I was whipped around by the flow, but I saw something block the light on one side. A large pole made its way down into the waterway probably fifteen or twenty feet away from me.

The pole reached down, stayed there for a moment, then slowly made its way back up.

One thing was for sure—I was never going to reach those poles without letting go off the rope. My lungs really started to burn and my head felt fuzzy, so I decided to let go as soon as I saw the next pole dip into the water.

Suddenly, something hit my head. Fighting the current to look up, I caught sight of a large shadow upstream. I would've cried if I could have. It was Tynia, just an arm's length away from me, rope tangled all around her. No wonder we were so far from the poles.

Two other poles descended and blocked the light, but how was Tynia supposed to free herself from the rope? I looked down and saw the two poles disappearing again, so I knew I only had a moment or two to decide what to do.

I never would've forgiven myself if I didn't try to do something for

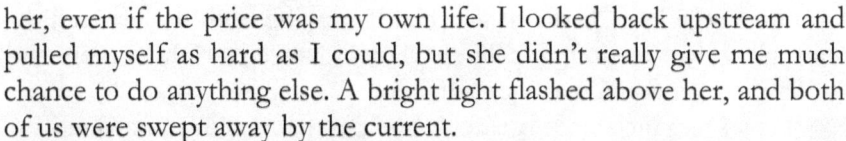

her, even if the price was my own life. I looked back upstream and pulled myself as hard as I could, but she didn't really give me much chance to do anything else. A bright light flashed above her, and both of us were swept away by the current.

I've always assumed that she knew what she was doing when she cut the rope, but sometimes I think about the way our bodies hit each other and how we ended up catching one of the last two poles. That didn't feel like a well-managed plan.

Somehow, my leg got stuck in one of the large handles of the pole, but even as strong as I was at that age, I wasn't going to be able to hold Tynia's weight for too long. As soon as the pole brought me up, I threw my bag to the side and grabbed the rope with both hands.

By the time I heard Tynia coughing and gasping for air, the two sides of the round door slammed closed just a few inches from her face.

The bright light above me started to die, and I had no more strength left, so I dropped her on top of the door and stayed hanging there, completely exhausted. After she caught her breath, Tynia looked up, and in the near-darkness saw me hanging upside down.

"Jonek! Are you alright? Are you hurt?"

"My leg hurts, but I'm fine."

"Thank you for saving us. This didn't go as well as it normally does, but so far, we're alive. We don't have much time, though."

Tynia shook off the rope and approached a wall. She put her weapon in a hole and pushed it to one side, lowering the pole—and me—to the ground. She passed her staff over my legs, and they warmed for a moment.

"No broken bones, but I had to heal your muscles. Stand up and walk around to keep them moving while I set the orb. Just don't light any torches or leave this room."

Complete darkness fell a few moments later, but I could sort of tell that we were in a large room filled with chests, crates, satchels of all kinds, and piles of very old toys and trinkets. On the wall, I could feel carvings and crude drawings of boys and girls holding staffs and weapons all over it. As I walked away from the round door, I saw moonlight coming in through a large opening and landing on a golden bowl sitting on top of a square pedestal.

Tynia retrieved her orb from my bag, left it on the floor in front of the pedestal, and placed the green gem in its hole. She turned her weapon into a long staff and touched it, making both the orb and the staff glow for a moment. Then, Tynia glanced at the moon and touched the pedestal with her staff too.

"Let's see which path is safer." She passed her fingers around the edge of the bowl, and a wall of symbols came to life on each side of the pedestal.

As I walked around it, I noticed some had different colors. Most were gray, a handful were golden, and one was bright white—Tynia's mark.

"Touch the bowl with your hand," she said. I looked inside the bowl as I touched its edge. Imagine tiny waves of liquid gold emanating from the center and dying furiously on the walls of the bowl, as if that miniature ocean was screaming in anger for being trapped there.

Another symbol changed colors in the pedestal, just by my knee. Kharlo's symbol was now glowing white on the opposite face where Tynia's was.

"Here it comes," she said as she glanced toward the moon once more.

The wall behind the pedestal had a large map of some sort carved into it. As the moonlight moved, the bowl began to make a humming sound, and two green gems illuminated the wall—one on the left side and one on the lower right. A moment later, a larger one sparkled to life at the center, and Tynia quickly touched it with her staff.

Slowly, thousands of tiny red dots fanned out all over the map, some in small groups, others in large masses. I will never forget Tynia's face when she saw those large clusters of red dots so bright they turned the room red.

"The dark army is everywhere. The Lost Path could take us to either one of these two places, but we still have to reach Kelfia—this big gem I'm touching in the center—on our own."

She took a last look at the map and pulled her staff away from Kelfia's gem; all the red dots vanished. Two small trays came out of the wall below the green gems, and Tynia emptied the contents of my bag on the ground.

"Gather all the rocks and pebbles and put them here in front of me." I picked up the disk and put it inside my clothes. "You can't take anything with you other than the clothes you're wearing and Kharlo's weapon, so put everything else in your bag and leave it here. Whoever built this pathway made sure that only certain items can make it through—the rest is lost. The doors will open soon, so get those pebbles."

I could see two narrow archways, one on each side of the wall where the map was, but they were already open. At this point, I was getting used to not understanding what was going on. How had Tynia learned all this the first time?

I put all the pebbles I could find in front of her, and she separated them, making two piles and counting them over and over.

"We don't have enough," she said, glancing around for more.

"I don't even know what you're doing, but those are all the rocks I could find."

"Are you sure? Did you look in your pockets?"

I had completely forgotten that I was still carrying the three pebbles the Satolgac gave me for my bow. To be honest, I couldn't believe they had survived the whole journey. I took the pouch from my pocket and gave it to her. "I have these, but I'm not sure if they're what you need."

Tynia spread the pebbles out in her palm and allowed the moonlight to shine on them.

"They're perfect. A Seven, a Two, and even a Ten. I haven't seen a Ten in ages," she said, sorting those as well. "It will be dangerous, but I think we should use the eastern path and travel as close as possible to the Valley of Souls. None of us have seen it, but other guardians have left writings describing a path along the mountain range south of the valley that spans westward all the way to Kelfia's border. It might be our best chance to avoid the dark army. Get Kharlo's weapon; it's time to go." She scooped up the two piles of pebbles and put them on the trays on the right side of the map.

The small green gems on the wall turned blue, and a loud crack resonated from behind each doorway. This is when the ground shook violently for a moment.

Being so close to the fury of the Bhormaks' Dragon's Back, sometimes I wonder how we didn't feel more of those tremors on our journey there. The sudden jolt tossed many things onto the floor, including all those pebbles Tynia had placed in the trays.

Both of us began to pick up as many as we could, but then Tynia yanked me up.

"Forget them! Let's just go or we'll miss our chance." She tossed the rest of hers to the ground and darted off.

Instead of dropping mine too, I put as many as I could on the trays as I followed her toward the doorway on the right. Tynia saw me toss the pebbles into the trays, and for a moment her eyebrows peaked, but she said nothing. Another round door in the ground opened, only this time, it was the water rushing underneath that illuminated the room. My body was still shaking from our recent experience in the other waterway. I glanced at Tynia a few times, eyes begging us not to go in there, waiting to see if there was anything else I needed to know. She never looked back at me. Her gaze was completely focused on the doors opening. Then, as I feared, we plunged in.

***

The eastern pathway. Mountains. The Valley of Souls. Kharlo, Nuthek, Tobho, my mother. Many voices and images whirled through my mind during those moments under water. The light was so intense that I didn't even try to open my eyes. Well, at least until I felt myself falling.

I could still feel water around me, but I could tell I was in the air. I couldn't see much until my body sank deep into those warm waters. I rushed to the surface, gasping for air. Something wasn't right, though—there was daylight. It was midnight a moment ago.

I was swimming in a small lagoon surrounded by dense vegetation. Large trees and tall plants grew all around the edge and into the water. I don't remember how or when, but somehow I ended that brief journey with Kharlo's weapon in one hand and the disk in the other.

Some large rocks dotted the right edge of the shore, so I started swimming toward them. This was when I noticed that something wasn't right with me. My arms seemed longer and . . . hairier. I stopped swimming and looked down through the water. I had no clothes on. Not a single thread.

I reached the rocks and tossed the disk and rod onto them. Then I looked back. Where was Tynia?

I swam back the way I'd come, toward where a waterfall fed the lake, but I couldn't see anyone above or underwater. Heading back to the rocks once again, I saw my ramikha floating on the surface of the water.

Only four things survived that trip with me: Kharlo's weapon, the disk, my musical instrument, and the bracelet I got from Zilhien at the theater. Even though Tynia had said that nothing like that could come through.

I pulled myself out of the water and sat on the biggest rock. I can't even describe what it was like to see all that hair under my arms, on my chest, legs—everywhere. Then I looked at my reflection and jumped back.

"Who's that man, and what am I doing in his body?" was the only thing that came to mind.

My hair felt the same but my face didn't. Suddenly, a pile of clothes landed at my side.

"These may be the right size," a voice said. "Put them on and come over here."

A young woman, maybe twenty years old, was carefully stepping away toward the other side of the rocks. I pulled on the shirt and leggings and took the rest with me as I fumbled across the rocks. The woman was wearing the same sort of leggings and was putting on some kind of soft leather boots. She saw me standing there, bewildered, and smiled.

"You'll grow up to be a handsome man one day," she said as she twisted the water out of her hair and pulled a long skirt over her leggings. She looked up at me again. "It's me. Your Witch of Barkrek. I told you to forget about the pebbles. You could've turned us into babies! Well, at least you got enough aging stones in the trays for us to look about the same age. You look twenty-three or twenty-four, and I'm about nineteen or so."

"Tynia?" I asked.

"Of course it's me. The real me. Not bad for an old witch, huh?" she chuckled. "Even though I'm really thirty-five, my real body looks even younger than this one."

I couldn't believe how different we looked. Now I was older and she was young—and beautiful. "Well don't just stand there," she said. "Look for a pair of boots in one of those crates. I'll look for some cloaks and a couple of satchels."

The place we'd ended up sat in an opening surrounded by rocks with only one small exit to the forest. Many crates, weapons, satchels, and piles of clothes lay strewn everywhere. It took me quite a bit of time to tie the leather straps around the boots once I found some; I'd never owned a pair in my life, much less this fancy kind.

Tynia stuffed clothes and a few other items in the satchels. She made me wear a long hooded cloak and gave me two strips of cloth.

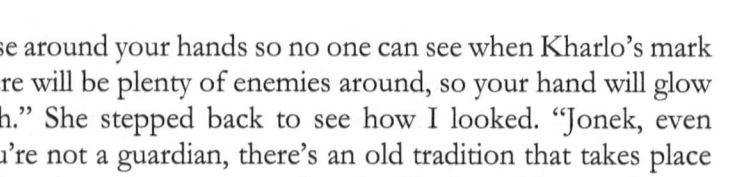

"Wrap these around your hands so no one can see when Kharlo's mark glows. There will be plenty of enemies around, so your hand will glow like a torch." She stepped back to see how I looked. "Jonek, even though you're not a guardian, there's an old tradition that takes place here the first time someone sets foot in Kirolcan. Do you have a mark?"

"A mark?"

"Yes. A symbol—something to identify yourself."

My mind quickly flashed back to the day of my initiation with the soldiers. "I do."

"Draw it on the ground in front of you."

I didn't feel it was appropriate to use Kharlo's weapon to draw it, so I knelt and used my finger. Tynia drew a circle around it, took some dirt from it, and whispered a few words. She poured it over my shoulders and finally put her forehead against mine for a moment.

"We need to look like a young couple seeking refuge in Kelfia. It would be best if we could join one of the groups migrating there. A group of hunters maybe." She pulled two bows from a pile of weapons. "I don't know why the shield and even your ramikha made it through, but put them in your satchel with Kharlo's weapon and keep this bow in your hands. Just help me with the quivers and some arrows."

I found a few old arrows and put them in two quivers that had the Satolgac symbol embossed on them.

"Satolgac?" I whispered.

"Yes. I'll share the story with you later. Let's go—we still have a long road ahead," she said as she walked toward the gap in the rocks leading into the forest. Suddenly, she stopped. "Wait. Someone is coming this way."

Tynia didn't hide. She didn't pull out her weapon or even prepare the bow. She just stood there.

A group of dark soldiers was making its way through the forest. A few were bears, but most of them were men marching in a single line through the woods. Probably patrolling or scouting.

My heart was pounding as they passed no more than five steps away from us. Then, to make it worse, Tynia spoke.

"They seem to just be passing through this area. No sentinels. That means they're not searching for anyone," she said, glancing at me. "Don't worry. They don't even know we're here. This area can only be reached via the Lost Path. Once we step beyond these rocks, we won't be able to come back here, so let's wait for them to go away. Remember, no loud sounds once we're out. Look where you step, and if we encounter someone friendly, let me do the talking."

We waited until the scouts disappeared into the distance, then we pulled the hoods over our heads and left the rocks behind. It felt so unreal to take one step and stop hearing the noise of the waterfall behind us, then turn around and see nothing but an immense forest. No rocks, no crates, nothing. Tynia kept walking, so I rushed to stay a couple of steps behind her.

I was in another world.

Reaching that mountain where my mother and I saw the Carudhan bridge in the distance was probably the farthest I'd ever been from Ferdhen in my life—until now.

The trees in those mountains were fairly similar to the ones we had in the Stapian forest, only I wasn't able to find young ones anywhere. All of them were thick and tall with old bark around them all the way to the top. These woods were old but beautiful. Unfortunately, not all the trees stood proud and undisturbed. We went down a trail and found a number of them torn and burned, with traces of weapons scarring their bark. There were some garments with blood on the ground but no bodies to be seen.

Tynia noticed a small basket stuck in a bush and opened it. "Farmers. Common folk fleeing the devastation of war. This was probably the only food they carried," she said as she pulled out a piece of bread wrapped in soft cloth.

"Put this bread and some of the fruit in your satchel. I'll put the rest in mine."

We left the basket in the bush and followed the trail out of the area. We walked in silence, but I couldn't help making a little noise with my constant scratching—chest, underarms . . . everywhere.

"Are those clothes bothering you?" Tynia whispered.

"No, the clothes are fine."

"Do you have ants crawling on you?"

"No."

"Well what is it, then?" she said, stopping.

"It's all this hair! I was fine without it. Now I feel it rubbing on these clothes and it's bothering me."

Tynia smiled and kept walking. She was silent at first, but she just couldn't help it and burst out laughing, covering her mouth to block the sound.

"I'm sorry, I forgot how it goes the first time. Well, if you think *you're* having a hard time, you should see what we girls have to endure. You don't even have much hair on you, so you'll get used to it fairly quick. Now stop walking like a duck and keep your eyes open."

"Can't you use your magic or give me something to rub over my skin to stop the itching?"

"Not really. This battle is between you and your body. Now be quiet." She stifled one more giggle.

After a long walk, we left the trail and climbed to an area where the forest wasn't as dense. Tynia looked at the sky from time to time and changed directions accordingly until we entered a small clearing with a creek flowing through it. She motioned me to follow her to it, saying only, "Don't touch those plants by the edge."

Tynia crouched to fill her water bag, but I was having trouble opening mine. Suddenly, the symbols on our hands made both of us jolt and cringe. I dropped my water sack to grab my throbbing hand, unbalancing myself and plunging my other hand into the weeds Tynia had told me not to touch. She was right—they really stung. I sucked in a sharp breath. Now *both* my hands hurt.

"Calm down. Close your eyes and focus. Someone is in danger— the dark army is nearby—but we need to see what we're fighting against."

I couldn't keep my eyes open. All the images flooding my mind almost put me head-first into in the water. All I could see was people running through the woods and some awful beasts chasing them. The rest moved too fast.

"They're coming this way! I'd trade all we have for a vial of your mother's red paint right now." She yanked me to my feet. "Get behind that tree. Prepare your bow, but keep Kharlo's weapon ready just in case."

Just beyond the edge of the clearing, we could see someone careening downhill toward the creek. Tynia and I pulled our bowstrings, aimed toward the tree line, and waited. Almost instantly, a young woman and three companions burst through the branches, desperately fleeing from over a dozen beasts and soldiers. Right behind them, one of those enormous soldiers like the one we'd seen by the cemetery shouted commands in a guttural voice.

The men desperately tried to defend the woman. Unfortunately, they didn't last long at the hands of the beasts. Tynia dropped her bow.

"Jonek! Forget the bow! Use Kharlo's weapon!"

I released an arrow and watched it bounce off the armor of the scout running right behind the woman, making him briefly take his eyes off her. I threw the bow to the side and took the disk and weapon. Another scout threw something that looked like a small metal ball with spikes toward the woman. Tynia vanished and reappeared in front of that woman making her stop abruptly. She put her arm around her, and both disappeared as the ball exploded, throwing its spikes in all directions.

An even larger shield burst from the disk, blocking the spikes for me, then turned round again. Behind me, Tynia and the woman were lying on the ground by the tree where my satchel was. The woman had one spike stuck into her side, and Tynia was just staring at me, unable to speak.

It wasn't just a shield that came out of the disk this time. I hadn't even felt anything, but I was now wearing a helmet and some kind of armor of light on my chest and arms. I barely had time to notice the traces of light swirling like water on the braces when a battle axe struck my shield. My knees buckled and I dug in as I took the hit.

Tynia left the woman leaning on the tree and ran toward a group of soldiers storming their way through the woods. Every time she took a step, she left behind another Tynia that engaged a dark soldier using a different weapon. I swiftly dealt with the scout in front of me and walked forward to meet the large warrior, escorted by two wolves, approaching the area.

The wolves moved to the sides, and I hesitated at the sight of a grotesque beast the giant warrior was holding on a chain leash. Some unnatural breed of mountain cat covered with scales instead of fur, dragging a long tail behind it like a lizard.

I never thought of changing weapons, but suddenly my sword turned into two smaller blades coming out of each end of Kharlo's weapon. To be honest, I don't remember much about how I fought and the weapons I used by that creek. I still think Kharlo was in control during those moments. And you know how battle is—blurred, heart pumping wildly as you turn to your instincts to survive.

What I do remember is that the wolves jumped at me just as the warrior released that beast. I ducked low to the ground, putting the weapon against the shield and allowing the blades to show on each side. One wolf crumpled onto my shield as the other ducked around the shield but into a blade. I saw the cat leap over me, but I rolled to the side before his tail lashed down at where I was.

I quickly finished the first, stunned wolf and got to my feet as the warrior got closer to me. The beast also moved carefully, its tail curved around and pointing at me. It paused for a moment, ripping a large bite of flesh from one of the dead wolves as its master pounded the ground with the back of a large axe. Glancing back, I saw there were still five or six Tynias fighting the other scouts.

The warrior lunged into a wide axe swing, and the waves of light rippling from the center of the shield concentrated on the place it landed. The shield melted a bit of his axe, but that blow sent me flying; I slammed down onto my back, my breath knocked out of me. The beast charged, and if it wasn't for one of those Tynias putting an arrow in his neck, the monster would've caught me stunned on the ground.

At the sight of his impaled pet, the warrior howled.

He swung his axe relentlessly, and I kept blocking it with the shield, each time a little less able to regain steady footing. I took a gamble and dropped the shield just long enough to change Kharlo's weapon into a spear and put it through one of his legs. His growl probably echoed for miles.

He crumpled to his side, and I used this opportunity to jump at him and slice his neck with the disk.

I quickly pulled the spear from his leg. Tynia pursued the last two soldiers downhill, but a bear and a pack of wolves suddenly appeared—alerted by the warrior's call—and rushed in toward the woman.

I knew I was going to lose my armor, but I instinctively threw the disk toward the tree with all my strength. The disk got stuck in it just a few inches above the woman's head. Then, I pointed my hand at it and whispered some strange words that even I didn't understand. The shield flickered and reappeared all around her. Two or three wolves crashed into it, their skin bursting in flames. Then I turned Kharlo's weapon into a bow and finished the rest.

I landed on my knees trying to catch my breath, but horns blowing in the distance forced me to stand up and walk toward the woman. I pulled the disk from the tree and the shield disappeared. She was sitting in a puddle of blood.

Why didn't she put pressure on the wound? I thought.

She was looking at me, and I could see so many emotions in her eyes. She whispered something, but I couldn't understand a single word.

"Please don't move," I said. "Tynia will help you."

I thought about pulling the spike out of her side, but then she moved her arm; there, between some of her clothing, a much smaller hand reached out. The woman's arm fell to the ground, and I saw the face of a little girl, barely a few months old, peacefully sleeping on her chest.

I'd never handled a baby before, so I just kept her on top of the woman, making sure she stayed underneath her cloak. Out of all the words she whispered over and over, only one was familiar to me—Kelfia. The woman's breathing grew ragged, so I turned to go and find Tynia.

The woman grabbed my arm and made me look at her. She carefully touched the forehead of the little girl and put her other hand on my face. A warm feeling invaded my body as I saw my skin and theirs glowing with a bright red aura. The little girl opened her eyes and briefly looked at me before yawning and going back to sleep. Tynia suddenly appeared out of a whirlwind and staggered over to the tree. She had a piece of arrow stuck in her shoulder and a look in her eyes that could only mean one thing. Trouble.

Tynia waved her staff over the arrow, making it disappear from her shoulder, and dropped down in front of us, gasping for air. "There are just too many of them. They're going the wrong direction, but they will soon find out I tricked them. We don't have much time."

I said nothing. I just looked at Tynia as I moved the woman's cloak so she could see the little girl. Tynia pursed her lips.

"What's your name?" she asked as she passed her staff over the wound, making the spike disappear. The woman barely had the strength to whisper, but Tynia leaned in to listen and her eyes widened. "We'll take care of your daughter, but you'll have to stay here. I'll make you sleep, but we'll come back for you. Do you understand?" The woman said a few more words and touched Tynia's hand. "Yes. We promise," Tynia said as she turned her weapon into a long staff.

"Take the girl and move aside, Jonek. Look in the satchels for something to keep her warm." Tynia cast a spell, and the roots of the tree crackled and groaned as they and a host of other plants grew around the woman, engulfing her.

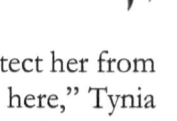

"These plants will not only hide her, they will also protect her from further pain or ill. Not even the wizards will know she's here," Tynia said. She shrunk her staff back down. "We have to reach the top of this mountain. The Valley of Souls is on the other side, so the trail must be just beyond these peaks."

The mountain range before us spanned as far as my eyes could see. We weren't that far from the top, but there were now three of us climbing the steep paths.

**

We crossed the creek and kept going as fast as we could. I wasn't sure if I was holding the girl the right way, but she bounced off my chest enough to make me realize that she must've been put under some spell that kept her sleeping.

We could hear horns, howling, and growling all around the base of the mountain, but our eyes were fixed on the top. I was happy we weren't carrying those bows and quivers anymore. That would've made our climbing even harder.

We left the trees behind and reached the rocks. Once out of the cover of the treetops, I took a moment to drink in the amazing sky of that place. Their sun was shining as bright as ours, but there were two large moons out there as well, moving low on the horizon, one behind the other as if they were racing.

Tynia climbed on top of a flat rock, and I offered her the baby so I could climb up too.

"If I take her, she'll wake up," she said. "Give me your hand. I might be able to pull you up."

"Are you worried she might cry and alert the dark army?"

"The mother bonded this girl with you. If she doesn't feel your touch, she will wake up."

"Bonded? What do you mean by that?"

"Well, it's probably best for you to know, I suppose. This little girl now feels that you're her father."

"Her father? But I'm not even thirteen!"

"Remember you don't look thirteen. The mother saw you as a man who could take care of her child, so she bonded her with you so she feels close to her own blood. Now give me your hand. Hurry!"

Carefully, I pushed myself up while I held the girl with one arm.

"What happens if she wakes up?" I asked as we rushed onward.

"Two things. One, she might get hungry and we have no milk for her. And two, she'll need all the attention a baby requires. Who knows—the mother's spell may be protecting her in ways I don't even understand."

Once we reached the crest of the peak, we paused to catch our breath. The sight on the other side of the mountain was unreal. A large valley surrounded by mountains as tall as the Bhormaks extended west as far as I could see. A thick layer of dark clouds covered everything below the peaks of the mountains. The sky above us was all clear, but those stormy clouds covering the valley below us weren't a good sign. Lighting illuminated the clouds here and there as they roiled around like a boiling soup of darkness. But there was something missing, though. I couldn't hear any thunder.

Tynia glanced at me. "Those clouds down there are not only a sign of danger, they're deadly. Your skin will decompose if you touch them. No one can survive in them for more than a few moments—not even the dark soldiers."

"So why are we getting close?"

"The trail I've told you about should take us west around the valley just above the clouds." She pointed to the side of the mountain. "If we find it and travel carefully, it will take us almost to the outskirts of Kelfia. The dark army would never risk getting that close to the clouds."

"How do you know they won't follow us?"

"I don't. I just remember that Jalyena told me about the dark army avoiding this valley at all costs. We'll have to start searching those—"

An arrow zipped between us, cutting Tynia's thoughts short. We ducked our heads and rushed down toward the clouds. A thin patch of forest clung to the rocky hills below us, so we slid down to get some cover.

We hid behind some trees and looked back at the rocks at the top of the mountain. That was the second time in my life I felt truly, genuinely terrified. A mass of soldiers and beasts too thick to count swarmed the area, almost changing the landscape at the top of the peak.

"They won't risk coming down into the valley," Tynia whispered.

She was right—the long line of soldiers didn't venture down, but suddenly, a group of wizards appeared. They argued for a moment and then cast a spell. Like a writhing tidal wave, hundreds of sentinels appeared in front of them. The snakes quickly made their way down, following our scent.

"We'd better move. Follow me."

I could tell by the look on Tynia's face that she couldn't believe how desperate they were to hunt us down. We left the trees behind and ran as far as we could—out to a lonely tree standing by the edge of a cliff.

There was nowhere to go. All we could see was the thick layer of clouds moving ominously maybe fifty feet below the edge. Tynia turned around and looked at the trees we'd left. She changed her weapon into a long staff but stood still. I could tell that she wasn't sure what to do.

Out of nowhere, the image of us climbing the Patriarch Tree with the chain rushed back to my mind. I took Kharlo's weapon and squeezed its grip, recreating the ball with hooks and a chain, which clattered to the ground in front of me. I swung the chain around the base of the tree and held the little girl in my left arm as tightly as I could.

"Tynia, I'll go over the edge and hang from the chain. Do the same, and let's just hope they don't see us."

She didn't turn her weapon into a chain; she didn't even say anything. She simply stood behind me, put her arms around my neck and pushed us over the edge.

I was grateful for my large, grown-up-Jonek muscles supporting the weight as we whipped to a stop above the clouds. Tynia wrapped her legs around my waist and pointed her weapon up toward my chain.

All my strength was focused on holding onto the chain and keeping the baby as close to my chest as I could. Tynia conjured some vines that burst from the edge of Kharlo's weapon all the way to the tree, covering the entire chain.

"Lower us closer to the clouds," she whispered.

The chain stretched until we were two or three feet above the thin wisps of clouds moving on top of the darker mass. Suddenly, I noticed a large opening on the wall of the mountain hidden underneath the cliff we were hanging from.

"Do you see that cave?"

"Stay quiet, Jonek," she said, calling the vines down to cover us too.

I can't describe how difficult it was for me to hold all that weight and still try to stay still. I glanced up without moving my head to see shadows of scouts and sentinels roaming the edge of the cliff.

Maybe I lost concentration. Maybe my muscles gave in. I really don't know what happened. But even now, if I hold my left arm over my chest, I can still feel that little girl slipping away from me.

The way my hand flew down, desperately trying to grab one of her arms or a wad of her clothes made the chain rattle from end to end. I missed.

For a moment, I didn't care about the howling up there letting the rest of the dark army know where we were. The only thing I could think of was the image of the mother entrusting that little girl to me.

I was frozen, looking down through those vines in complete agony. Even as burning spit from those beasts began to rain over us, I couldn't move, didn't feel it. It wasn't until I heard a feeble cry and saw Tynia hanging upside down holding the little girl by her clothes that I came back to life.

"We have to get to that cave you saw. I won't be able to hold on to you much longer!" she said.

I took the disk from my clothes and made the shield cover all of us. For the first time, it was on me to get us out of trouble. Tynia was barely keeping the girl from falling, and I could feel her legs slowly sliding down my body.

I closed my eyes and let those voices guide me.

"Breathe Jonek, breathe . . ."

All the images of moments I've never lived myself flooded my senses until I saw a strong young man holding a disk like mine pushing away a large beast without even touching it. It wasn't Kharlo, but the images were the clearest I'd seen until then. I looked down through the vines.

"Hold onto that girl for your life! We might land hard!"

I blocked a few arrows coming from the far side of the mountain before I pointed the shield toward the cave and said more words I didn't know I knew. A sudden blast pushed us away from the cave, and made the chain rattle the tree on our way back.

"Don't let go!" I yelled as I felt Tynia's legs digging deep into my sides. Tynia pulled the little one up and wrapped her arms around her just before we rolled into the cave. That landing really hurt.

This time, we weren't lucky. I felt the bones in my leg and foot snap as I came down, and cuts and bruises covering my body oozed blood and made me stiffen in pain. Tynia ended up with deep cuts in the back of her arms and elbows as she protected the baby.

Other than a small scratch on her head and being covered in dirt, the little one was fine.

I dragged myself closer to Tynia and took the girl from her. She stopped crying as soon as she felt my arms. "I think my leg and foot are broken," I said, my voice strained. I felt like throwing up.

"Every part of me hurts right now, Jonek," she responded, equally wheezy. I took Kharlo's weapon and passed it over her, illuminating her mark on her neck.

"You'll live," I said, leaning back against a wall. "Can you fix my leg?"

Tynia transformed her weapon into the long staff and pointed it to the top of the cave. A thin layer of clouds blossomed into existence until they covered most of the cavernous roof. Tynia tapped on the ground, and a small, glimmering light shot up from her staff and got lost in the clouds. A soft mist began to cover us.

Those tiny drops soothed our pain and healed our wounds. I pulled my leggings up, letting the healing rain land on my legs. I didn't feel anything, but I could see how the bones went back into place. Tynia held her arms and face out under the mist. Even the little girl opened her hands, trying to grab the beads of dew that were making her laugh as they healed the scratch on her head.

The clouds eventually blended with the dusty air and vanished.

"That's it. That was the last healing stone I had. Rubzilet gave me three, and I was saving this one for a time like this."

Even though we both felt weak, the pain was gone, at least. Tynia made her blue flames appear, and we walked deeper into the cave.

It wasn't long before we found an archway made of bricks that marked the entrance to a massive cavern inside the mountain. Not even Tynia's light could illuminate the immensity of that place. She pointed her staff toward the top and shot out a large flame, which burst into a flash of light that briefly allowed us to glimpse a long set of stairs going down along the wall.

"We have no option—we need to find a way out of here. The dark army will follow us into this cave, so we can't stay."

I kept the baby in one arm and held a staff with flames in the other. The little girl kept making noises, playing with her hands and sneezing from time to time, but she never let out a single cry as long as I kept her in my arms.

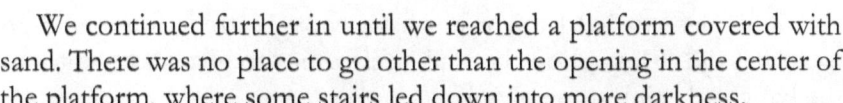

We continued further in until we reached a platform covered with sand. There was no place to go other than the opening in the center of the platform, where some stairs led down into more darkness.

Tynia tried to read the writing carved on the first step, but even she couldn't understand its meaning. She was about to open her mouth to say something when two flaming arrows landed in front of us.

We both looked up and saw a rain of fire coming at us.

"Get in there!" she yelled.

The little girl and I went down first. Tynia was a few steps behind when a blast made us fall.

The last I remember is seeing Tynia buried under a cascade of rocks and the baby landing on the sand close to the dying flames of Kharlo's weapon. We were shrouded in complete darkness, but I could hear her crying fairly close to me. My head was throbbing and I felt disoriented, but I extended my arms and started touching everything around me. I couldn't get to the little girl or Kharlo's weapon, but I still had the satchel by my side.

I reached inside and grabbed the disk and the bag of water. I poured some water on the disk, and its glow slowly illuminated everything around me. The air was still dusty, and rocks were strewn everywhere. I looked up and saw that our staircase had collapsed, so it seemed that at least for now, we were safe. I followed the baby's cry and found the little girl wedged between two immense rocks. I picked her up, doing my best to comfort her.

Tucking Kharlo's weapon into my clothes, I made my way around the rocks to where I'd last seen Tynia. Her legs were pinched under some big rocks, but to our good fortune they weren't crushed. Her face was covered in blood pouring from a large wound on her forehead.

I pulled her out and passed her weapon over her mark. She was alive, but I couldn't wake her up. I sat down, cleaned her wound, and wrapped her head with a strip of cloth I'd torn from the bottom of my shirt.

I was deciding what to do next when another blast shook the ground above us.

So much for safety. I used some of the clothes and our satchels to keep the little girl by my chest and then hoisted Tynia over my shoulder. I was propelled forward by the sense of responsibility—their survival completely depended on me. I didn't even try to sit down and rest, as I was worried I might not have enough strength to stand up again if I did. I leaned on the wall a few times to give some water to the baby and drink some myself.

After what seemed like an eternity, we reached the bottom and went through an archway illuminated by two large torches. My muscles burned with each step, but I carried them on into a large hall with an enormous door on the other side. The hall was well illuminated by torches on both sides and the remnants of a large fountain stood lonely at its center, completely dry.

Those last few steps before I put Tynia next to the door felt endless. I collapsed by her side as soon as she was on the ground. I waited for my heart to slow down before taking a look around.

That door must've been made by giants—it was almost twenty feet high. I would've never been able to reach its lock, so I was grateful to see the door slightly open. Too narrow to fit through, though.

We had nowhere else to go, so I had to open it somehow.

The little girl cried as soon as I left her on Tynia's legs. I put my back against the door and pushed with all my strength, but a hinge at the top had come detached and was making the door drag on the ground.

I took Kharlo's weapon and transformed it into a long pike. I stuck it underneath the door and pushed it forward. The monstrous door moved two or three inches at a time, creaking and moaning all the way. After toiling at it for longer than I probably realized, it opened wide enough for me to slide my body to the other side.

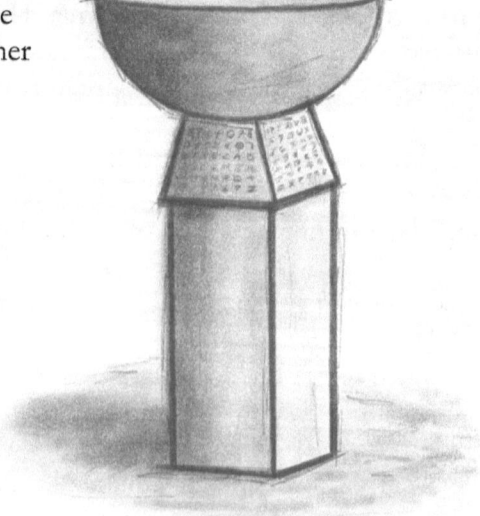

CHAPTER 10. THE BARRIER.

The clouds in the sky were a refreshing change of pace from being underground, but the feeling didn't last long; the lightning reminded me where I was. The Valley of Souls.

Imagine walking into a vast area where a large army is making its way to the battlefront. Weapons, armor, battle carts, wagons with provisions, and many other tools of war were spread everywhere in front of the door I slipped through. I could see all these military artifacts lined up in long trails into the distance. Everything was primed and ready for a full assault—but there were no soldiers.

Other than a few goats roaming the area, I was the only living thing. Even the foliage was scarce and the grass yellow. I walked closer to the edge of the bricks outside the door and suddenly heard a sound behind me, as if someone had snapped a dry piece of wood.

Right there, under the long vines covering the recess around the door, was a man sitting on the ground, a sword resting over his legs.

The man pulled away the weeds covering his face, allowing me to glance into his deep brown eyes trying to get used to the light. No doubt he was a soldier—most likely from this army—but what was he doing there under the vines? And where were the rest?

I kept Kharlo's weapon and the disk in my hands as the man stood up and took some shaky steps toward me. I really thought he was going to fall, but he stabbed the tip of his sword in between two bricks in front of me and leaned on it.

He slowly raised his head, looking at my boots, my clothes, and then the weapons in my hands. He opened his mouth, trying to say something, but he couldn't. Every sound he tried to produce got drowned in his throat, and he took a hand off his sword to put his fingers on his neck. Unfortunately, that made him lose his balance.

I lurched forward to grab him and help him lay down. I took his helmet off and put his sword back in his hand. Then, motioning for him to wait, I ran through the door to get the water bag. The girl saw me and began to cry again, so I took her with me.

I sat down by his side and left the little one on my legs. Lifting his head gently, I poured some water in his mouth. The man was parched. He waited for the last few drops to land in his mouth before he closed his eyes and rested his head against the bricks with a heavy sigh.

The little girl began rustling and wriggling on my lap; she was putting her hands in her mouth. "Oh no; you're hungry, aren't you? I knew this would happen eventually."

I left the man again and went back to see Tynia. She was still unconscious, but her forehead wasn't bleeding anymore. I looked inside the satchel and took tiny pieces of the softest part of the bread and put it in the girl's mouth.

"I should've left some water for you," I said as I passed my hand over her fuzzy hair. "Your mother certainly chose the wrong caretaker."

Suddenly, a soft voice echoed from the door. "Hulez sjomt. Brukhwoldhin zemot," the man said.

"I'm sorry, I don't understand what you're saying," I responded as the man walked closer, using his sword as a walking stick. "But I'm glad you can talk again."

"Brukhwoldhin zemot . . ." he said again.

"Zemot?"

The man nodded.

"What's a zemot?"

The man touched his chest and pointed at me.

"My chest?" I asked as I put my hand over it.

"Brukhwoldhin zemot," he repeated, tapping on his chest.

I didn't have the slightest idea what he was talking about, but as I held my hand over my chest, I felt the disk inside my clothes. I took it out, and the man nodded as he got closer and knelt in front of me.

I put my fingers inside some holes and moved it closer to him. The man tried to take his battle glove off, but the old, rotten leather was stuck to his hand. I reached out to help him, but he pushed two fingers through the decaying leather and touched my disk with his bare skin.

A bright light circled around the edge of the disk, then the man collapsed on the floor, exhausted.

"What just happened?" I said, dropping the disk and grabbing the man's head to see if he was breathing.

"Your armor, my liege," the man whispered.

"My armor? What armor? Wait, I can understand what you're saying."

"Thank you for letting me touch your armor, now I can understand your words. So many years have passed since I've spoken to anyone. Please, what age is this?"

I wasn't sure how that worked. I was convinced that both of us kept speaking in our own languages, but from that moment on, I was able to understand and be understood by anyone speaking his tongue.

"Age? I don't know. How long have you been down here?"

"I don't remember anymore. Our commander left us here guarding the door before taking the legions to face Sulibhor's army."

"Sulibhor? I heard that name just yesterday, but it sounded like someone who lived many generations ago."

"Is Sulibhor dead? My soul would rest in peace if he is."

"I don't know if he is, but I know Malok is alive, at least."

"Malok? Prince Malok? Heir of the throne of Zukreya? He was just a newborn when we marched into this valley! He must be dead by now." He paused. "No, Sulibhor is the darkest and most wretched spot of evil that has ever walked under our sky."

His last words stirred many thoughts in my mind, but I had more immediate challenges to face. "We need water. Do you know where we could find some?"

The man grunted as he tried to sit up a little. "There's a creek flowing along the base of the mountain on the north side of the valley, but I wouldn't dare go beyond those bricks outside. The clouds out there brought a curse on us. They came out of nowhere, and once they covered the skies, lightning rained down on everyone and made them disappear. Horses and other animals were spared, but their numbers declined through time. Goats are the only thing left." The man paused. "There were three of us guarding the door. We don't know why, but our lives were spared during the rain of lightning that took away our brothers."

"Three? Where are the others?"

"We ate what we could—rodents from the cave, a stray goat that ventured onto the bricks from time to time—but then we gave up. The other two surrendered their minds and decided to challenge the curse. They stepped beyond the bricks and lightning took their lives long ago. Then I decided to sit down and sleep so the shadow of death could take me to join my ancestors. Then you woke me up, my liege."

"You don't owe me any allegiance. I'm not even from around here," I said as I put Tynia's satchel under his head.

"I may be just a soldier, but I know the hands that carry these weapons. Your clothes deceived me, but your eyes can't. This is the first time I've been this close to one of you." He put his hand over his chest, looking at me intently.

"There has to be another way out of here," I said, diverting the conversation to a topic I could actually understand.

"There isn't, my liege. The curse won't allow us to reach the stairwell around the main cave. Once the clouds see your skin, you can't cross the gateway of sands in the cave."

"Well don't worry about that option. The entire floor collapsed on our way here. What's most important right now is finding food for this young one."

"Can't the mother feed her?"

"Oh, Tynia is not her mother, and I'm not her father. It's a long story, but for now, let's focus on finding some food for her. I was thinking that goat milk could be our only option."

"They're not easy to trap, and it could take a while before we find a female with milk."

"We have to try. You can rest here while I look outside."

"I'd rather stay with you and hear your voice, my liege. I've had enough silence to fill many lifetimes." I gave him his sword, and he pulled himself to his feet. Together, we slowly walked to the edge of the bricks.

"You'll have to sit here so I can leave this little girl with you," I said. "I'm glad you don't want silence, because she may cry until I take her back."

"I think I can manage, my liege," he said with a hint of a smile.

I left her in his arms, and even though she looked nervous, she didn't cry this time. The little one even looked curious about the man holding her. But she made sure he knew who was in charge by pulling his long beard and holding it tightly.

I walked along the edge until I saw a small herd roaming over a patch of grass in the distance. There was no way to get to them without stepping off the bricks. I threw a few rocks and even extended my arm beyond the bricks, but nothing happened.

Maybe lightning strikes when you touch the ground, I thought. *It would've been great for Tynia to make us walk in the air like she did before we reached the Patriarch Tree.*

I glanced at the clouds rolling slowly overhead and contemplated another way to test the curse. I stepped away from the soldier and the girl, and transformed Kharlo's weapon into a long bow. I shot a silver arrow across the valley. We followed its path until it vanished in the distance. Nothing happened. I released a few more in other directions with the same result.

Then I aimed toward the sky and let another one loose, defying the clouds themselves. I kept my stance as I watched it disappear into the clouds. Then it streaked back down, glowing with a bright green glare until it stuck into the ground by some wagons. A large dome of light erupted around it—and everything inside came back to life.

They were far from us, but I could clearly see the soldiers take form once again, riding on the wagons, others marching off to the side. They were surprised and began to trip over each other.

I could see them opening their mouths, but no sound broke through the silence.

"Your fellow soldiers are still alive," I said, turning back to offer my hand so the man could stand up and see. He didn't say a single word, but his eyes flooded with tears when he saw them alive out there in the distance.

"But . . . how could this be?" he managed at last.

"I'm not sure, but I have an idea. Let's walk both of you back to the door so you can take cover behind it." I left them sitting by Tynia and returned to the edge of the bricks. I sent an arrow flying into the clouds almost on top of me and ran back to the door. Unfortunately, the wind made it land somewhere on the mountain behind us.

I released another one, and this time it flew a bit farther into the valley. Another dome surged out of the ground, and a line of soldiers leapt to their feet maybe fifty paces from the edge of the bricks.

This one didn't last long, though. I wasn't sure why, but the dome vanished a moment after. Once it was gone, the clouds poured lightning on top of everyone, leaving piles of lifeless armor on the ground once again.

I aimed again toward the clouds right above me and followed the arrow until it landed maybe four or five feet beyond the bricks. This time, the dome covered me too. Suddenly, I noticed two soldiers standing a few steps away from me. They were both facing the valley and had their swords in their hands.

"You! Step back onto the bricks," I said, changing Kharlo's weapon into a sword. Both men turned and saw me holding that shimmering blade in my hand. They were startled but lowered their weapons.

"Our apologies, my liege," one of them said.

"It's fine. Just walk toward me." Slowly, they stepped onto the bricks and tried to kneel in front of me. "No need to kneel. Please touch my hand." Both hesitated, but they did it. I was so relieved when I realized they were real.

"Follow me," I said. "There's someone you may want to talk to."

The soldiers didn't recognize him at first, but suddenly they rushed forward through the giant doors and engulfed the man holding the little girl. None of them could contain their emotions as they saw each other again.

"Don't ever leave me behind again, you stubborn dogs!" the man shouted, teary-eyed. One soldier shook his head.

"I don't remember much after we ran into the valley. Everything feels like a dream."

"Maybe for you. I went on for ages debating if I should keep guarding the door or just run into the valley to end my misery." The old man paused. "I don't know what happened, but I fell into a very long sleep. Then this great knight woke me today."

"My liege," the other soldier said with a bow. "We can never repay you for bringing us back from the dead."

"I don't think you were dead," I said. "This could just be magic. Dark magic."

"The valley is cursed. Sulibhor must have done this to prevent us from reaching the town of Kelfia and fighting his army."

"The dark army is in Kelfia?" I asked.

"They invaded the settlements around the lake to stop its waters from reaching the farmlands. Crops were lost as far as the eye could see. We survived on famine rations."

"I've never been to Kelfia, but in this age, it's not a town anymore. It's one of the largest cities, and from what I've heard, it's the last safe haven from the dark army."

"Kelfia has been liberated? What age is this?"

"She's the only one who knows," I said, pointing at Tynia.

"Is she ill? Does she need a healer?"

"Indeed she does. I'm not even sure what to do to help her."

"There are many healers traveling with our legion," a soldier said, pointing out toward the field beyond the bricks. "They usually stay close to the wagons."

I nodded. "Another thing I'm worried about is feeding this little girl. I need to find some milk for her."

"There are very few women marching with us, but none with

younglings."

"At this point, our only choice is to try to get some goat milk."

"There used to be plenty out there," the soldier said. "The challenge is to get close to them. You'll need a rope and fast feet."

"My liege," the other said, "remember to boil the milk or it will make your daughter sick. It sure made mine sick once!"

"This little one isn't my daughter. You would probably never believe me if I told you how old I am."

"It doesn't concern us, my liege. Just tell us what to do and we'll help," the old man said.

I pursed my lips, thinking. "The little girl seems to like you so stay with her. Both of you follow me. I have an idea."

I took the water bags and pulled the disk from my clothes. We went back outside through the door and saw the dome from my arrow still glowing by the edge of the bricks. We walked into it.

"I'll cover myself with my armor and shield and walk beyond the bricks," I said as the chest piece, braces, and helmet of light covered my skin. One of the soldiers stepped in front of me.

"Let me do it, my liege. You've saved me once; you may be able to bring me back again if something goes wrong."

The man didn't let me answer. He pulled his sword out and faced the valley. I stood behind him and pointed the shield toward the clouds just in case. His foot touched the ground, but nothing happened. He kept walking until he reached the arrow at the center of the dome. I was going to tell him not to touch it, but his curiosity was faster than my voice.

The dome collapsed the moment he touched the arrow, and the clouds roiled and shot the man with a swift stroke of lightning. The other soldier and I were dazzled by the light and sparks landing around us.

"Step back!" I shouted. "I need to shoot another arrow."

That was the first time I didn't put the shield away to use the bow. As soon as I touched the bow with that hand, the disk became translucent, snaking through my fingers like water to rest on the back of my arm. The arrow landed very close to the first one. The dome appeared around us, and we were able to see the soldier still leaning down as if trying to grab the first arrow.

"What happened?" he said when he came to.

"Don't touch the arrow! Just walk back to the bricks," I said as I changed Kharlo's weapon into a spear and the disk moved back to my hand before turning solid again.

Once I made sure that all of us were standing on the bricks, I reached out and nudged the arrow with the spear. The dome didn't disappear. I pulled it closer and the dome moved with it. I was able to pull it all the way to the bricks and then pick it up. The dome remained around us.

"Maybe the arrow and the dome haven't disappeared because I was the one who shot the arrow into the clouds." I said as I turned back to the soldiers. "Stay here. If something happens to me, please take care of the women." I slung the water bags around my neck and walked into the field.

Just as I'd hoped, the dome traveled with me as I ventured into the valley. Every time I got closer to soldiers and the dome revived them, I walked away as fast as I could so they didn't have time to react. I felt bad seeing them getting struck by lightning once the dome left them behind, but I wasn't sure bringing them with me—or trying to explain to them what was going on—would've been the best idea. I reached the area where my first arrow landed, but there was no dome standing anymore. Most likely because someone touched the arrow.

I approached a wagon that had a piece of rope hanging off one side. I grabbed the rope as I passed—we'd need it later for the goats. I quickly ran around and noticed a man sitting on the back wearing light leather armor and no helmet. He had two satchels hanging from his shoulders.

"Are you a healer?" I asked as I stopped in front of him. He was fairly surprised to see me, but he nodded. "Come with me. Do you have provisions? Food?"

"I have some in my satchels."

"Follow me and help me fill these water bags in the creek. Quickly!"

The man slid off the edge of the wagon but kept looking at the dome around us. "What is this light on top of us? What kind of magic is this?"

"Just stay right behind me and don't talk to anyone. Do you understand?"

"I do, my liege."

We filled the bags in the creek and walked back around the columns of soldiers until we reached the bricks.

"Please go through the door and help the injured woman on the other side," I said, leaving the arrow stuck in the ground by the edge of the bricks.

The other soldiers greeted the healer with joy—apparently they knew him well. At first he didn't recognize them, but after a few moments of thought, he called them by their names.

"What happened to you? You look different," the healer said.

"Well, this is what happens when you get old," the old man chuckled.

"What are you talking about? I just saw you this morning when I gave you provisions to stay and guard this entrance."

"My dear friend," the old man said, putting his hands on the other man's shoulders. "It must have been a moment for you, but it has been centuries for us. Don't dwell on this—we will explain it later. Please take care of this woman. She is in dire need of your services."

The healer knelt down in front of Tynia and asked me to hand him a bag of water. The soldiers took the other satchel and unpacked it— bread, dried meat, and some pieces of fruit that I didn't recognize.

"We can give the little girl some of the softest parts of this fruit, but she still needs milk," the old soldier said.

"I need someone to catch the goat while I keep the dome of light up to protect us from the clouds."

One of the soldiers stuffed a piece of dry meat in his mouth and stood up. "I'll do it, my liege. Just keep those clouds from reaching me."

***

It wasn't easy. By the time we came back with a fairly large female goat and two young ones following her, the soldiers already had a fire going, and the healer had Tynia sitting up with her eyes open.

A soldier used a helmet to boil the milk and then mixed it with some water to cool it down. I was going to feed the girl directly from the helmet when I heard a familiar voice behind me.

"Don't you dare do that. You'll end up bathing her in milk. Give her to me."

I have to be honest—I was so happy to hear Tynia's voice that I almost cried. I placed the girl in her arms and left the milk by her side. Tynia took a piece of white cloth and soaked it in the milk, then she put it in the little girl's mouth and let her suck all the milk she could from it.

"I think it's best to let them be by themselves," the old soldier said from over my shoulder as I watched. By that time, we'd used most of the water we brought from the creek so the healer, a soldier, and I ventured again into the valley to fill our bags again. When we came back, Tynia was talking to the soldiers with the little girl asleep in her arms.

"I've only heard tales, merely fragments of what happened to your army. Sulibhor gathered mercenaries from all over the northern territories so they could face you in battle while he ordered his main army to march in secret toward Zukreya. That was almost a thousand years ago, and there is no memory of you ever marching into this valley. It is now known as the Valley of Souls."

"Sulibhor wasn't in Kelfia?"

"No, my dear friend. From what I've read from old writings, Zukreya was always his main objective."

"Our families, our people—are they gone?" a soldier asked.

"The people you knew are indeed long gone. But your descendants are still here, fighting for their lives in Kelfia and a few other hidden places," Tynia said, glancing sidelong at me.

The soldiers remained composed, but I could feel the weight of their sadness and shock. The old man walked closer to the door.

"If you want to reach Kelfia, you'll have to pass Sulibhor's mercenaries at the far end of this valley. From what we know, they are over ten thousand strong. But they must be in shadows, like we were."

"My liege," a soldier said, "allow us to escort you to the other end." Tynia looked down at the little girl asleep in her arms.

"We need all the help we can get," she said.

There was nothing else to say. We gathered our things and everyone walked into the dome.

I took a deep breath. "Remember—don't leave these walls, and don't talk to anyone as we cross the valley. Just follow me as quickly as you can. One more thing." I paused. "Never touch the arrow I'm holding." With that, I raised it over my head to make the dome larger.

Even Tynia was surprised to see the thin wall of colors moving with us as we ventured into the valley. The soldiers took turns helping the old man keep up with us, sometimes even carrying him on their back. We tried to stay away from the main columns of soldiers, but we couldn't help seeing some coming back to life as the wall of the dome

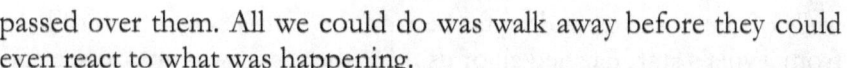

passed over them. All we could do was walk away before they could even react to what was happening.

Eventually, we reached the battlefront. The area wasn't spoiled with artifacts of war and looked peaceful, even beautiful. But just a bit further, beyond a thin line of trees, a large group of catapults clearly indicated where the enemy forces waited.

Two lonely battle carts were facing each other in the middle of the empty area. Our plan was to keep walking along the side of the mountains, but the old man stopped us when he saw the carts.

"They're talking," he said. "Our commander is talking to the enemy." We all waited in silence. "Can't you see?" the old man continued, holding out a hand toward the carts. "Our army was deceived, true, but if the ten thousand souls at the end of the valley are indeed mercenaries, they got it even worse. They were utterly betrayed. Seeing their legions lifeless in shadows like ours makes me think that Sulibhor never intended to pay them for their allegiance. They were sacrificed."

"How does that help us?" I asked.

"They may let us pass without fighting. There are just too many of them, and we don't know how many are hiding in the valley."

"What do you want us to do?" Tynia asked.

"Let's get closer and see if we can get our commander inside this dome and talk to him."

Tynia and I looked at each other. Both of us knew it was worth a try. "We'll follow you, but be ready to push anyone that's not your commander outside the dome," I said.

Tynia took me by my shoulder. "Jonek, I have an idea. Let's approach the cart from the back so you can jump on it and hold the arrow as high as you can. Try to make this dome wider." She turned her weapon into her long staff.

"What will you do?"

"I'll cast a spell. Anyone standing within thirty feet won't be able to move. Unfortunately, that will include all of you. It won't last long, but it will give me enough time to do what I'm thinking." We didn't ask more. We moved around the area until we were ten or fifteen steps behind the commander's cart. "Are you ready?" Tynia said as the head of her staff began to glow brightly.

I didn't even look at the others. I just held the arrow as high as I could, jumped onto the cart, and stood at the highest point. I saw the walls of the dome extending far beyond the cart. Then, a flash of light from Tynia's staff dazzled all of us. Like the rest, I was able to see and hear but couldn't move.

The battle carts were empty, but there were three soldiers standing on our side facing three warriors wearing different kinds of armor. Tynia put her staff away and walked closer to the group. One by one, she took all their weapons and threw them beyond the walls of the dome—even the ones our four companions were carrying. Everyone must have been quite confused. What was the dome they were under? And how could a woman carrying a baby disarm them so easily? She took out her weapon but didn't transform it as she walked between the soldiers and the mercenaries.

"Listen carefully," she said, holding up her rod. "I will allow you to move, but don't try to harm anyone. Do you understand?" She looked intently at both leaders standing in the middle. "Both armies have been deceived and betrayed by Sulibhor. Commander, marching into this valley was just a trap. Sulibhor was never interested in Kelfia, and your bid to liberate it was in vain. His main legions marched south toward Zukreya and were never going to reinforce the army here." Tynia then looked at the leader of the mercenaries. "And you. Neither you nor your bloodline would ever see whatever Sulibhor promised you for your services. Kelfia is already free and has been for almost a thousand years." Tynia walked closer to the cart I was standing on and leaned back on it. "Gather around me once you are able to move." She uncovered the girl's face and allowed her to yawn away her sleepiness.

"What kind of sorcery is this?" the commander asked Tynia as he regained control of his body.

"This dome of light is the only thing protecting you from dark magic looming up in the clouds. Look out there." She pointed to the battlefield. "Where are your armies? Are you going to fight a war with just these men around you? Just don't try to walk outside this wall. Lightning will swiftly take you back into the shadows if you do."

The commander pursed his lips and walked closer to our companions. "What are you doing here? You look sick."

The soldiers saluted him. "Not sick, commander, just old. What this lady is saying is true. You left us guarding the entrance to the caves. But that happened hundreds of years ago—she says almost a thousand. What we thought were just rain clouds that day was an evil curse. Lightning wiped out everyone. Us, them—only the beasts survived, but not for long. Look at your battle cart; not even the bones from your horses exist anymore."

The commander pulled out the old reins of his horse from the dirt. "But we just marched into this valley before sunrise. This morning you were my son's age, now you look like my grandfather."

The old man bowed his head. "In a way, I would've preferred for these clouds to have pulled me into shadows with you and my brothers. But you ordered me to guard the door. And I did . . . for centuries." His voice trembled a little as he spoke.

Those few words swept away the rugged features on the commander's face. The fierce leader took his helmet off and put his forehead against the old man's.

"My brother, no matter what our destiny is, I will never leave you behind again."

Off to our side, the leader of the mercenaries, who had stood in silence this whole time, approached Tynia.

"Are you a witch? Are you Zerkial?" he asked nervously.

"I've been called a witch before, but I am not Zerkial. Sulibhor corrupted their sages long ago, and we've been fighting them for generations."

Something odd happened when the mercenary got closer to us— both my face and the little girl's started glowing red. His eyes widened.

"Who are you?" he said. "What are your names?" I was going to answer, but then his own face began to glow too. "Only my bloodline, the house of Serthoz, has fire skin."

"This baby was entrusted to us by her mother," Tynia said. "We were attacked in the mountains by the dark army and she bonded her with Jonek so we could take her to Kelfia."

The mercenary took off his gauntlet and softly touched the little girl's forehead. Her skin resonated red under his touch.

"There is no doubt. Her skin glows as bright as my own daughter's did when I said farewell to her not a month ago. Do you know her mother's name?"

"We don't. But she's still alive and well protected with powerful magic. We promised her that we'd go back for her once this little one is safe in Kelfia."

The mercenary's face fell and his brow furrowed. The same evil he had sworn to help—for riches and power, of course—was now hunting his own bloodline. He scowled.

"She bonded her with you. Do you know what this means? It means that she will always love you. This honor belongs to her father, not a stranger!"

"I didn't ask for it," I said softly. "I didn't know what she was doing."

"A mother will do anything to save her young ones," Tynia interjected. "Anything. Even if it's against her most sacred traditions." The mercenary took a step back, but his frown remained. "We'll take her to safety. There must be other family members in Kelfia."

"Just make sure they have fire skin, you hear?" he said, pointing at us. Then, he sighed deeply. "I still don't understand what's happening here, and I don't believe most of what you're saying. For all I know, this could be a trick from the enemy. But I can't deny that you two are protecting my own blood, my kin." He paused, motioning for his two fellow mercenaries to join him. "These two men will escort you to the end of the valley. You can follow the main road to Kelfia or walk along the river from there."

The commander stepped between me and the approaching men.. "We won't leave them alone with your thugs," he said defiantly.

The mercenary yanked his gauntlet on with a snap. "My dear commander, I would fight against your entire army and Sulibhor himself to protect this little one. My men will defend them with their own lives."

I looked at the commander and nodded. He frowned but backed off.

"Please get closer, everyone. I need to step down from this cart, and the dome will get smaller," I explained.

Both commanders faced each other, their soldiers standing a couple steps behind them. Tynia walked closer to the old man and our other companions.

"Your kindness will live in me forever. We are in great debt to you," she said as she softly placed her hand on their faces.

"It was our honor, my lady," the old man responded as he briefly bowed his head. Tynia returned to my side and looked at both leaders.

"You will be struck by lightning the moment this dome leaves you behind. I assume you won't feel anything, but I think it's best you know." She paused. "I don't know if the dark magic boiling in these clouds will let us leave this valley. But if any of you want to walk out of this valley with us, you are welcome to."

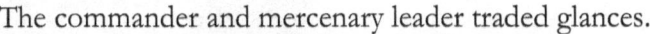

The commander and mercenary leader traded glances.

"We would never leave our brothers behind."

"Very well said," the commander responded.

For once, they didn't argue.

***

I turned around and looked at the soldiers and the leader of the mercenaries one last time.

"We won't forget you. All of you," I said before taking a few steps toward Tynia and our two new companions.

None of us had the courage to look back as lightning took those men. Even the two mercenaries remained quiet as we took our first steps toward the line of catapults.

"Try to avoid areas with many soldiers," Tynia said. "If you see someone appearing inside the dome, walk away or push him out as quickly as you can. That's probably the best thing we can do for them."

Our escorts guided us closer to the creek on the north side. We followed it for some time, but then we took a trail that merged with the main road.

It took hours, but eventually we reached the end of the valley. The ancient road would've taken us through a pass between the mountains, but there was now an enormous pile of boulders and rocks blocking it. Even our escorts were astonished by the sheer size of the devastation.

"The road was clear this morning! We left five hundred men guarding it," one said.

Tynia put a hand on his shoulder. "That was a long time ago. Is there another way to get out of this valley?"

"I only know this road," he answered. The other mercenary pulled out an old piece of parchment from his clothes.

"The creek we followed earlier flows into some caverns and then into the main river coming from Lake Kelfia. Not many know, but thieves from a village nearby use these caverns as their hideout. Here— one of them gave me this map a while back because they thought I'd be a good fighter for their guild and asked me to meet up with them. There must be a way for you to reach the other side through these caverns. Just be careful in there." He handed the piece of parchment to Tynia.

Tynia opened it and walked closer to me so I could look at it too. The drawing was rough, but it clearly marked the valley and the creek splitting in two inside the caves. Their hideout was in the cave on the right side, and there were some markings we couldn't understand on the one to the left. There was nothing connecting the creek to the main river, so it was on us to find out if that even existed.

We had no other option, so we followed the edge of the mountain until we saw the creek pouring its waters into a large pond some twenty feet below. Down there, on the wall of the mountain, a large cave opened wide as if thirsty for the water. Some crude steps were carved on the left side to reach the pond, but they were narrow and slippery.

We approached the area, and suddenly the round wall of the dome of light in front of me flattened exactly at the edge of the first step. Tynia grabbed my arm to stop me from walking any farther.

"The curse ends there," she said, looking at the mercenaries. "We don't know what could happen if any of us cross that wall. Jonek and I have no choice, but you'll have to decide if you want to join us or stay."

"We gave our word we would escort you to the end of the valley, and we have. Our allegiance is to the Serthoz clan, so we must stay here. Take your satchels and water, and may the souls of our people protect you."

"Thank you for keeping your word," Tynia said before turning around and walking closer to the wall.

She transformed her weapon into the long staff and took a deep breath before stepping beyond the wall of the dome. My breath caught in my throat. She slowly turned around and let all the air in her lungs out as she leaned on her staff. She was still alive.

I left the arrow on the ground and picked up our bags.

"My friends, all you have to do is touch this arrow and the dome will disappear. Don't be afraid—I don't think you'll feel anything as you go back to sleep."

"If you don't mind. I would like to smell the grass a little more before we go," one said.

"Do it when you feel it's time," I responded.

I transformed Kharlo's weapon into a sword and crossed the wall. Other than the wind touching my skin and the sound of the waterfall finally reaching my ears, I didn't feel anything different. I waved farewell to our escorts and made my way down toward the pond. Tynia was looking into the darkness of the cave. She glanced at me as I joined her.

"The only way in is this narrow path on the left side. This isn't a creek anymore. The water is calm, but it looks deep." Tynia stared at the water. "I don't know if you can see it, but there's something moving at the bottom. We better stay dry this time."

We both looked at the dome of light at the top of the steps one last time, then walked into the cave.

***

The cave on the left was a dead end, but we were able to lash together a makeshift raft from scraps of crates we found in it. Tynia and I clung to it as we careened with the current down the right-hand tunnel. Tynia tried to illuminate our surroundings, but every time she reached her staff out, she had to grab hold of the raft again as we dropped deeper and deeper, vaulting over the edge of one of the many small waterfalls. At long last, it seemed like we'd passed the rapids and were out onto still water. She held out her staff, and her blue light almost instantly vanished among thousands of long vines hanging from the top of the cavern. There were so many that we couldn't see anything beyond the small pool of open water we were in.

We slowly glided toward the vines and moved them aside to allow the raft to drift forward. It took a lot of work for us to move through that dense forest. Some of those vines were as thick as my leg.

"Tynia, I can't see anything! I don't know where to go."

"There must be a way out. But can you hear that?"

"What?"

"That sound coming from way out there. Let's keep moving toward it."

"I don't hear anything," I said after listening for a moment.

"It's just straight ahead," she said, pointing her staff (and its blue flames) between my legs.

Even though the little girl was well protected inside Tynia's clothes, she knew something wasn't right. She wasn't loud, but she wouldn't stop crying.

"I can't really say if it's another waterfall or not, but we're getting close."

I pushed away two or three thick vines in front of us and felt the raft sink slightly under my feet. She was right—there was another waterfall and our raft was balancing on its edge. We couldn't hear its waters crashing at the bottom, because the opening on the face of the mountain was hidden by immense vines that silently carried the water into the river, maybe a hundred feet below. Both of us quickly grabbed onto a vine as the water pushed the raft out from under our feet. We slid down the long vines, fighting the water. Haphazardly tumbling to the bottom, we walked out into a very wide river that carried the waters from Lake Kelfia along the base of the mountains. We slowly crossed the waters to the other side and sat by some rocks.

"She's cold," Tynia said, wrapping her arms around the baby. "We need to dry her clothes. Ours too."

"Should we make a fire?"

"No, it's too dangerous. It will be night soon, and we can be spotted from high ground. I can dry them, but not while we're wearing them." Tynia carried the baby behind a bush and put all their clothes on a rock. "Give me your clothes and empty our satchels so I can dry them too. Don't worry—I won't look this time."

I snorted and tossed my clothes and satchels over the bush, then sat on a rock massaging my legs. That reminded me of that night when I pulled my bag out of the river. The disk was wet, so it began to glow as the last light of day left the sky. I quickly used sand from the riverbank to dry it.

"How about the food? Is there anything left we could eat?" Tynia asked from behind the bush.

"Everything's soaked," I relayed to her. "The fruit looks edible, but I'm not sure. I don't even know how to eat fruit like this."

The satchels and my clothes landed on my head a moment after, completely dry and even warm to the touch.

"Put your clothes on. We can't stay here."

We threw the rest of the food in the water and followed the river upstream. Tynia gave me pieces of that fruit and I let the little girl taste them while I kept her hidden under my cloak. Tynia changed her weapon into a staff and looked at me.

"Kelfia is protected by a barrier created by our elders long ago. Their own souls dwell within the magic protecting the city, from its underground all the way to the skies above it. For many generations, Malok's forces have destroyed themselves trying to breach it, but they still make attempts from time to time. They know that the only way to destroy Kelfia's defenses is from inside, so for the last few centuries, they have been trying to infiltrate the city as one of the many souls seeking refuge.

"There are four entrances to the city, and all of them have one or two portals that look like mirrors made of water hanging on a wall. Everyone must walk through them to enter the city. There will be a few soldiers pointing their weapons at anyone trying to cross the portals. Don't talk to them. Don't even look at them. Whatever they do, just keep walking and enter a portal. Remember, we are just a family fleeing from the dark army."

"They won't ask us who we are? Where we're coming from?"

"They don't care who we are. Their only concern is seeing who can't get through the portals. If the dark mist flows strongly in your veins, the portals won't let you pass and the soldiers will use their weapons immediately, without even saying a word."

I respected the reasons for devising such a harsh method of protecting the city, but I couldn't help thinking about those poor souls who may have made serious mistakes in the past but worked hard to straighten out their lives afterwards. Would they dare to pass through the portals? Who or what decides how much dark mist makes someone good or bad?

I was pondering those questions when we saw the first moon rise again and cast its light over the mountains. Tynia looked at the moon and pointed at the stars above us.

"It must be early summer," she said.

The light from that moon wasn't as bright as ours, but it was good enough for us to walk safely once our eyes got used to it. We were crossing a small clearing when we saw five or six people rushing toward the river with more than a dozen children following them, like birds chasing their mother. Two men stayed behind and kept looking at us, maybe trying to determine if we posed a threat to them.

"Don't say a word. Just keep walking," Tynia whispered.

We left the clearing and saw more and more pockets of people joining us in the same direction. Even though our group grew to the hundreds, only whispers spoken in strange tongues briefly broke the silence. A group in front of us stopped at the top of a hill and looked at the sky.

"Azthule Komgrothe," one said.

Tynia glanced toward the sky, then looked at me. She smiled.

"Jonek, I think you will like this."

Some kept walking, but many of us stood there looking up. Kirolcan's second moon showed itself over the mountains, chasing her younger sister. That alone was a marvelous event to witness, but it was dwarfed by the spectacle of color it created once its light landed on the barrier over Kelfia. Similar in shape to the dome protecting us in the Valley of Souls, but of gigantic proportions. When the second moon illuminated it, a wide spectrum of lights burst into the sky over the city like sunshine through colored glass. It didn't last long, though. Some kind of burst of fire shot up from an island inside the barrier and made it lose its brilliance moments after.

It took a few moments for our eyes to get used to the darkness of the night once more. Tynia took the girl and covered her with her cloak. We walked downhill and merged into two long lines that took us inside a tunnel. I don't know why, but once in there, everyone went dead silent—even the children.

Although there were torches on both sides of the tunnel, the brightest light was coming from the far end. The tunnel became wider, and the two lines separated as we entered a maze of blocks of stone that led us to the main cave.

Tynia had said there were going to be a few soldiers pointing their weapons at us, but that place had dozens on each side, most of them aiming toward the two round portals with golden frames where long lines of people were disappearing into.

I'm not sure why, but I was nervous. I kept my head down, looking at Tynia's skirt. We were maybe ten paces away from the portal when I suddenly felt the back of my hand burning.

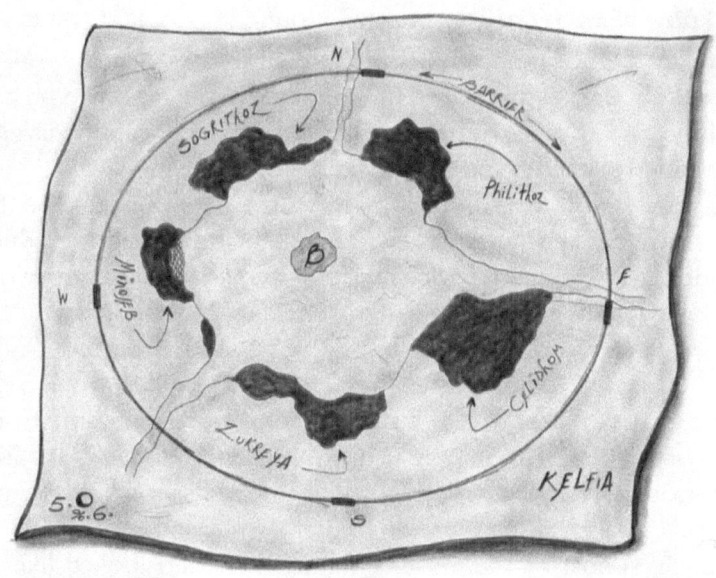

CHAPTER 11. SHADOWS AMONG US.

I didn't know what to do. Tynia turned around and looked at me.

"There are a lot of innocent people around us."

That's all she said as she pulled me to the side and got down on one knee behind me. By the time the light from her weapon dazzled everyone, arrows, spears, and swords were already flying at us.

All those weapons would've hit many of the people around us if it wasn't for the barrier Tynia made with her staff. I dropped everything and grabbed the disk and Kharlo's weapon. Shield, armor, and sword briefly shone around me as I walked out of Tynia's barrier.

Families ran toward the walls and even landed by the feet of the soldiers. And just in time.

At first, I couldn't tell where a sudden rain of fireballs came from, but three or four crashed into my shield, pushing me backward in a cloud of sparks. Then I saw him through the waves of light on my shield.

Way back, almost by the maze, a skinny man who looked like an old farmer was pointing a staff at us. Both he and the woman standing by his side quickly morphed into old rotten figures, much like the man Tobho hit with an arrow outside my house. The man blasted fireballs in all directions while the woman turned to sand and reappeared by my side, bombarding my shield with a sword that moved like a snake in her hands. Tynia cast a force spell, pushing the man against the wall and buying just enough time for the soldiers to pepper him with arrows.

The woman saw his demise and took a couple steps back. She pointed at me with her bony fingers and yelled one word before bursting into flames and disappearing.

"Hokdhanet!"

There was a lot of confusion after that. People screaming, soldiers pointing their weapons at everyone; many around us, including our little girl, couldn't stop crying.

As the chaos died down with the two dark enemies gone, a group of soldiers walked closer and knelt in front of us while their leader sent others off to tend to the wounded. He then approached us as well, took his helmet off, and knelt with the others.

"I never thought I would see this day," he said, head down. "Our people have been waiting for your return since the days of our fathers."

Tynia changed her staff back into a rod. "There are no more wizards or dark army soldiers here. Take care of the wounded and have someone escort us to Barthenoz." Tynia waited for a moment. "Please stand up. We are no royalty, just soldiers like you."

I put my weapon away as two soldiers picked up our satchels and guided us through one of the portals.

Maybe it was the lack of rest or just that brief battle with the wizards, but something made me feel lightheaded as I crossed into Kelfia. Of course, the feeling faded quickly when my eyes saw the landscape on the other side.

Kelfia doesn't look anything like the image of it you see through the barrier. That must've been another illusion to protect its dwellers; from the outside, you could only see a few lights on the western side and a castle to the north. The landscape in front of me, though, made me think of not one, but four or five cities built around an enormous lake in the center.

And there, high on an island in the middle of the lake, a castle of great size and beauty stood proudly with its walls and towers, commanding respect and admiration.

The soldiers guided us away from the roads being used by the refugees and extinguished their torches in one of the ponds by the river. We kept walking in the dark until we reached the top of a hill above the shores, where the lake poured its waters into the north river. Down there, two boats guarded by soldiers waited for us. I knew the lake was large, but reaching the south side of the island certainly took longer than I expected.

The boat entered a pass in the cliffs so narrow that it would be nearly impossible to find with untrained eyes. The two soldiers kept rowing until we reached a secret cove. One of the soldiers escorting us made a very peculiar sound with his mouth and hands, and many torches flickered to life on the shore and the cliffs behind us.

We tied the boat to the dock and disembarked. The soldiers escorting us talked to someone on shore and left our bags with him. Then, they walked back to where we were and knelt down in front of us.

"Please stand," Tynia said again as she offered her hand to the soldiers. "We are the ones who should be kneeling in your presence. You have given blood and family to protect this city."

The soldier raised his eyes toward Tynia. "If half of what our people say about the guardians is true, the price we pay is nothing compared to yours."

"Don't believe everything you hear. What you do is as important as our tasks. Thank you for bringing us here safely."

Some soldiers guided us uphill until we reached a stone stairway that took us to a small door at the outmost barrier of the castle. There, an old man stood silently holding an old oil lamp by his side.

"Oh no," Tynia sighed heavily. "He's still here."

"What? Who is he?"

"The most bothersome man in the history of both worlds."

Even the soldiers couldn't stifle a smile.

"I heard that!" the old man grumbled in the distance. "I am old, but my ears can still hear your annoying voice from afar, young lady! Oh dear, my days of peace and quiet are over."

The soldiers put our satchels by the door and left us with the old man. He rubbed his nose and narrowed his eyes to look us over. "What are you doing here with a child in your arms? You better have a good explanation, or the next task the elders will give you is scrubbing floors for the rest of your life."

"I thought that was your job," Tynia said as she lowered her head, saluting him. "Jonek, allow me to introduce Peprokh, the steward of the castle of Barthenoz."

"I'm more than the steward of this castle—I'm the rightful owner!"

"Indeed you are," Tynia said, her expression bland as if she'd had this conversation a hundred times. "You're just allowing the king and council to use it temporarily. How generous of you."

"That's right! I made a promise to take care of them."

"A promise? To who? One of the many ladies in your life, perhaps?" Tynia sneered.

"Yes, well, . . . I don't remember anymore! But I prefer a battleground to talking with you. You've grown, but you're still a spoiled little girl in my eyes." The old man waved the lamp at me. "And who's this? The father of your child? And why is this man carrying a guardian's weapon?"

"It's Kharlo's. It's a long story, so I need to talk to Rubzilet as soon as possible."

"Your master and the council have been busy for the last three seasons. I rarely see him anymore." The man pointed at the lights in the distance. "As you can see, this is not the city you left behind. We now have many other problems to take care of besides the war outside. Look over there. Refugees first settled on the outskirts, but then they wanted to be closer to the lake, taking every spot they could in our towns around the water. Some found a way to live together, but many Kelfians are not happy about what's going on in here." He leaned in closer. "Sometimes I wonder what's worse—staying in here or taking our chances outside the barrier."

The little girl cooed from inside Tynia's cloak, and the old man paused.

"Well, don't just stand there," he rasped at last. "Follow me and let's see if we can pull your master out of the main chamber." Tynia waved her staff over our satchels and they drifted into the air behind us.

"You can do that? Why didn't you do that on our way here?"

"It's very dangerous to use magic outside the barrier. Dark wizards can sense magic at great distances. Here in Kelfia, though, people that know magic use it in their daily lives."

The old man stopped and glanced at Tynia. "Yes, but some are still not very good at it," he said.

"Well, it all depends on who their teacher is. Some masters are patient and caring, and then there are others who are sulky and lazy."

The man left the lamp floating in the air and pointed his finger at Tynia. "I am the best magic teacher this castle has ever seen! Twice as good as Grekozte and way better than your beloved eminence, Rubzilet. I just don't like to work with useless apprentices, and absolutely not before midday." The man ended those words with a loud sneeze. He cleaned his nose with his robe while Tynia and I just glanced at each other.

"Let's make sure no one sees you," he grumbled. "The rumor that guardians have returned must be spreading by now, and it's best we control it as much as we can. We can't use the main door. Many hallways stay crowded day and night with folks seeking audience with the council. Annoying buggers—they don't mind sleeping in my hallways so they don't lose their place in line."

We left the outer wall and followed a path around a wing of the castle that led us into a secluded garden.

"Let's use your hall to enter the castle," the man said as we walked into a circle of bricks where four large pedestals stood empty around it.

Tynia approached one of them and touched it with her weapon. Her symbol briefly appeared on it as a translucent stairwell flickered into existence around the edge of the circle. Those stairs took us to a bridge high above that ended in front of a large window made of colorful glass that caressed my skin as we crossed through it.

"The Guardians Lair," Tynia whispered. "How I missed this place."

"Just don't get too comfortable. I'm fairly sure your master won't let you stay in here for long. I'll go and find him." The old man waved his lamp and vanished into thin air.

"Why didn't we just use magic to get in here?" I asked.

"Ancient magic protects this castle. It's so powerful that it prevents even the mightiest wizards, good or evil, from using spells or charms to get in here. The only way in or out of the castle is to walk through a door, the same as anybody else. This window is the only exception, but only guardians can open it."

Even though I had only seen one window from the outside, we were now standing in a large round hall with dozens just like it looking out every twelve or fifteen steps. It was the light of the moons that made me notice all the shapes and colors dancing in the glass in all windows.

Bright blue water poured from four or five pillars into a pool in the center of the room. There were chairs, benches, and chests of many types, as well as countless items filling tables all around the hall. Tynia waved her staff and the satchels dropped softly to the floor.

"Follow me. I want to see something before they come back."

We walked to the far end of the room and got closer to a line of windows that had no colored glass.

"These empty windows belong to the guardians who will eventually take our place. The four to the right are ours. These two belong to the siblings Jalyena and Artego. This one is Kharlo's, and this one here is mine."

The little girl was sleeping, so Tynia left her on a low bench and covered her with a soft cloth. She walked back to her window and placed her weapon on a small cradle at its base.

The shapes and colors on the window began to change until they created an image of Tynia and I standing in front of a similar window. Tynia moved to one side, and the shape of her in the window followed her movements—not like a mirror, but as if someone was viewing us from behind. I raised my hand and my shape did the same.

"Now let's go back in time."

Tynia passed her hand over the window from right to left, and the shapes changed quickly until we saw the two of us walking out of the river earlier that evening. She did it a few more times, and I watched us walking on top of that narrow bridge over the sea of molten rock.

"How can you do that?"

"These weapons carry our memories, Jonek. Don't ask me how. I just know that we can see what we've lived in these windows. Now, take Kharlo's weapon and put it under his window."

I placed his weapon in the cradle and the shapes of the window began to change. I was expecting to see us standing in front of the window, like it happened with Tynia's, but the image we saw was very different. People were sleeping in a very small place. Tynia and I walked closer, and she pointed at the figure of a man lying on a bed on one side.

"This can't be," she said in wonderment.

"We never told you that your weapons kept your memories," a voice said behind us.

There he was—an old man with long white hair but whose beard and thick, pointy eyebrows were black as the night. He was leaning on a walking staff, Peprokh standing by his side.

"Placing your weapon under your window will allow you to see your past, but it is the mark that hangs from your neck that actually keeps track of your deeds and everything around you."

"Master Rubzilet!" Tynia said as she ran and hugged him briefly, then stepped back and saluted him more formally. Tynia tried, but she couldn't hold back the tears.

The castle steward just rolled his eyes and sighed. "I can't take this emotional nonsense," he said, walking away and sitting on a bench.

Master Rubzilet spoke softly, "It's been a long time, my child. What are you doing here? These are very dangerous times, and your presence may just complicate things."

"I know, master. But Kharlo has found what we've lost. He says it's time for us to come out from hiding and retrieve it." Tynia walked closer to Kharlo's window and pointed at his image lying in that cot in the tent. "He's dying. He stepped in the way when Malok cast an evil curse at me. He's been able to handle the pain, but the curse is consuming his memories. I've tried my best to help him, but his body has begun to decay. Malok's scouts attacked us just yesterday morning, and I had to cast a Jiretal spell to keep him alive."

"Jiretal? I didn't know you'd learned that magic. What color was Kharlo's mark when you left him?"

"Blue."

"Blue?" He smiled. "I'm proud of you. Unfortunately, that won't give him more than two or three days under that sun. We need to bring him here. You said Malok's soldiers have reached your world?"

"Wizards, scouts, sentinels—even some of his blackguards."

Rubzilet frowned. "It's worse than we thought."

Peprokh stood up. "I've been telling you, but no one listens to the crazy old steward."

The old master then looked at me. "And who are you?"

"His name is Jonek," Tynia said before I could speak. "Kharlo used some magic I'm not familiar with to share his skills and knowledge with him. He helped me travel to Kelfia. The protector of the Lost Path said that Jonek is carrying something inside that could end this war."

"Is that so? Well then, let's see what Kharlo hid in you. Walk with me, young man."

The old wizard guided me to the pool in the center of the room and asked me to take my cloak, shirt and boots off. "Please follow the steps into the water. Don't worry," he added with a smile, "it's not cold."

I splashed in and saw Tynia and Peprokh standing by the master's side. Rubzilet tapped the floor with his staff. "Submerge your head and stay calm for a moment. This won't take long."

In my mind, all I did was take a deep breath, dunk my head underwater, and then get out a moment after. But when I opened my eyes, only the steward of the castle was standing there by the edge of the pool.

"So that's who you really are," he said. "Oh get out, would you? That's enough water for you."

Peprokh lowered his staff and touched the water with it. When he pulled it away, there was a leather string with a golden pendant hanging from it.

"Don't just stand there, hurry up! I have my own duties to attend to." He wrapped up the pendant and walked away.

I swam to the steps, but when I pushed myself out of the water I noticed something—all the hair covering my body was gone, and my face was as smooth as a river pebble. Other than my left hand, which was now dark red all the way to my wrist, I was back the way I was before I left Ferdhen.

I was having a hard time walking up the steps with my long leggings still on me, so by the time I caught up to Peprokh, I had no clothes on and was using the leggings to cover myself. The old steward turned around and looked at me dripping water, my hands holding the leggings in front of me. He shook his head and scowled.

"I'm too old for this. Another immature boy with no respect for my floors or myself. Go over there and find some clothes in those baskets. And don't touch anything! Everything in here belongs to the guardians."

"What's wrong with my hand?" I questioned.

The old man glanced at it. "That's what happens when you don't do as you're told. The guardian said not to touch those plants by the creek, remember? Your whole arm would be red by now if you would've waited a few more moments to lift your hand. You better get used to it—it'll take a long time to fade away. Now stop dripping water on my floor and find some clothes!"

I wrapped the leggings around me so I could cover my behind. I tried to run toward the baskets, but it didn't take more than a few steps for me to trip, stumble into a table, and send all the items on it cascading to the floor.

Peprokh just closed his eyes and took a deep breath.

"Don't touch them!" he snapped when I reached to clean up the mess. "Leave them there and keep walking. Just make sure you don't disrespect any more of our heroes' belongings."

Maybe to give me some privacy or maybe just to deal with his frustration, the man opted to walk away and look at the pendant under the light of a window. I was able to find clothes in my size and walked back to where he was. Even though I saw light streaming through the windows when I walked out of the pool, it didn't occur to me until then that it was now daytime.

"Where's Tynia? How long did I stay underwater?"

"Four days," he said as he turned around.

"Four days? But I only submerged my head for a moment."

"Well, that's the way it works. Follow me. There are too many questions left unanswered. The memories you carry make no sense. I don't know what Kharlo did to you, but Rubzilet and Tynia are searching for some answers."

"Are they working with the council?"

The old man stopped and pointed at me with the hand holding the golden pendant. "Listen to me very carefully, young man. The council knows nothing. It is best they never know that either you or Tynia are here. Do you understand?" He paused. "Rubzilet gave me clear orders to keep you away from everyone. Unfortunately for me, the best place to hide you is in my quarters. There goes my privacy and the well-being of my pets."

The old man turned away and kept walking toward the far end of the hall where a pedestal and a golden bowl (similar to the one in the Lost Path) stood in front of a staircase. I chose to stay quiet and glance at the stairs going down into the floor. I looked around the entire hall and realized there wasn't a single door in it.

This must be the way out, I thought.

Peprokh dipped the pendant in the golden liquid and allowed it to dry for a moment.

"That's not my symbol," I said softly.

"Of course it's not. You're not a guardian. But it is indeed a very unique mark. Kharlo must have hidden it in you for a reason. I wonder who it belonged to."

It was a convoluted figure—three small circles inside a larger one, all touching each other as well as the larger one, with a triangle extended from the center of each of the areas outside the small circles.

The old man kept staring at it, so I left him standing there and went down the stairs a couple of steps.

"Where are you going?"

"Isn't this the way out?"

"No, it's not. You will only find more halls like this one down there. Now get closer to me."

A bright light from Peprokh's staff took me by surprise, and when I opened my eyes, I was standing in a narrow passageway in front of an open door leading outside. Out there, Peprokh waited for me in the middle of a stone bridge connected to a flanking tower. As I made my way there, he walked to one side and looked down through the battlement.

"Come here. Do you see all the people below?" I looked down and saw hundreds of people walking around tents similar to the way the streets of Ferdhen looked before I left. "There must be a relative of that irritating girl you both brought with you down there. We must find someone to take her soon; I can't keep her in my quarters much longer." The old man looked at me, then grabbed me by my shoulders and shook me. "That little bugger won't stop crying, and now my pets are beyond restless! Almost going wild!"

I couldn't believe I'd forgotten about her.

"Is she alright? Has she eaten?"

"Your nosy friend is the only one who's made her eat and sleep, but the guardian can't look after her day and night. That's why I summoned the baby's tribespeople to set up their market in this area of the castle. You and I will find someone to take her. Either we accomplish that soon or I'll join the legions bringing survivors to Kelfia. I'd rather join the battle than spend more time with that vicious creature."

I let him take a deep breath, but then I said it. "You do know that the vicious creature is just a baby girl. Right?"

The old steward opened his eyes wide. "No, she's not! She's small, I'll grant you that, but her powers over me and my creatures are devastating."

"What powers? The sounds she makes?"

"All of it!" he said, throwing his hands in the air. "The way she cries, drools, and smells is just unbearable."

"I can make her stop crying," I said softly.

The old man didn't say another word. He dragged me through the door, conjured his staff, and all I remember is feeling a gust of air for a moment. When I opened my eyes, we were standing in front of a large opening high on the wall of a tower. My feet were just a few inches from the edge, and the wind played gracefully with our clothes. It was so high that I could see the shores on the far end of the lake and the mountains in the north. The people on the ground looked very small, so I moved back a step or two. Didn't want to join them.

"Now don't be shy. Get in there! You said you can make her stop crying."

"Get where? Fall down?"

"Oh please. Don't tell me you can't fly!" A wicked grin spread over his face. "My own master always said that there's no better way to learn than by doing it!" He grabbed me by the back of my shirt and pushed me through the opening.

I don't remember flying. In fact, I can't remember much of

anything before I tripped over some broken barrels and landed on a pile of sacks of grain. The sudden lack of light quickly made me realize I was now indoors. Then I understood. That dreadful opening on the wall of the tower was just a doorway to a place that, to be honest, looked more like a dungeon than someone's quarters.

There were windows in some walls, but none of them were open, so the only light came from the many lamps and torches hanging on the walls and floating in the air.

"Well, get up! Let's go tame the beast." The man took a couple steps, then stopped and remained silent. "This can't be," he muttered. "Can you hear it?"

"Hear what?"

"Oh, this is beautiful."

"What is?"

"The silence," he said as he closed his eyes and took a deep breath. "Isn't it more precious than gold?"

I followed the man through a maze of crates and endless stacks of dusty old items. Once my eyes got used to the light, I realized that the place was neglected, but it wasn't lifeless. Almost everywhere I looked, I could see birds, rats, lizards, and many other creatures unknown to me coming out of their hiding places to look at us.

"You have a serious infestation here."

"Stay quiet, young man! Some of my friends are very sensitive and won't like your attitude."

We reached a place where large quilts were hanging from a rope to separate the far end of his quarters. Peprokh made a signal for me to stay quiet, and we went under the sheets.

The area on the other side didn't look as…frumpy. There was a long table and some chairs on one side and a large fireplace with pots and other cooking items on the far left. Countless rugs covered the floor in the middle, thrown rag-tag over each other, and to the right were a few more quilts with many strange symbols sewn on them hanging from another rope. I followed the old man through those quilts too, and there she was. The little girl was sleeping quietly on the old man's bed, wearing nothing but a soft white cloth covering her bottom. The little girl had her hand wrapped around Tynia's finger, who was also sleeping by her side.

The old man walked up and batted Tynia's foot, startling her awake. "If that thing wets my bed, you will pay for it."

Tynia carefully left the bed and pushed us out to the main area. "Don't make so much noise! And besides, the smell in there will greatly improve if she wets your bed," she said with a snide chuckle. Looking over at me, Tynia passed her fingers through my hair. "This is the Jonek I remember. Welcome back, Warrior Eyes. I assume there's no more itching, huh?"

I certainly blushed as she finished that sentence, so she smiled and looked at the old man. "Were you able to retrieve it?"

"It wasn't easy," he said as he pulled the golden pendant from his sleeve and showed it to her. "Remember, he will need this when he goes back to his world. Kharlo may not heal without these powers and memories."

Tynia took it and walked closer to a lamp floating nearby. "This mark is unique indeed. I have a feeling I've seen it before, but I don't know where. Jalyena would know for sure."

Peprokh sat on a chair and allowed a white snake to climb up and curl on his lap. "I looked at every symbol on the pedestals and it wasn't there. It doesn't belong to a guardian."

"My master has been searching for it in the council's vaults but hasn't found anything yet. The only thing he said is that Kharlo must have seen this mark long ago."

Suddenly, I realized something. "You said I stayed in the water for four days," I said, ducking under a floating lamp as I came closer. "What happened to Kharlo? What happened to my mother and friends?"

"I saw them this morning in Kharlo's window," the old man said. "The image has barely moved."

"Jonek, do you remember when I said that time works differently here? You and I have spent almost five days in Kirolcan, but your mother and friends are still sleeping in the tent on the same night we last talked to them. That's why their image in Kharlo's window seems to be frozen for us. They're moving, but it's just too slow for us to notice. Jalyena once said that we could live one month in Kirolcan for every day in our world."

"Wait. Are you saying that time is slower there? I'm confused."

Peprokh smiled. "No one really knows, but this is only evident when you travel between both places. Your life would be normal if you stay all your life in either place." The man paused and looked at Tynia. "The only thing we haven't been able to understand is why your bodies never age when you're in Kirolcan. Well, on the other hand, we do live longer lives here compared to yours over there."

Tynia looked at the old steward. "Peprokh, I know you and I have had our differences, but you know I trust your instincts and loyalty. What's happening in the council? Why is Rubzilet keeping us hidden from them?"

The old man rested his head on the back of the chair. "Why don't you ask him?"

"I did, but he just said that for now, it's best if everyone thinks that the guardians didn't come back. I understand why it might be good to make it sound like another rumor. But there's something different about him. He's behaving oddly."

"Listen to me, young lady. Many things have changed since you and your friends left. There are thousands of people crowding this city, and more walk through the barrier every day. You would think that all of them being refugees, they would find a way to get along, but unfortunately that hasn't been the case. Nowadays we need almost as many soldiers keeping peace in here as we do in our battlegrounds out there. Kelfia is not one city anymore; I would say there are now six very different cities under our barrier."

"But how is this affecting Rubzilet?"

"You don't understand. Every king, queen, religious leader, and patriarch that has walked into this city leading their refugees is now part of the council. The last time I counted, there were over thirty chairs in our main chamber." The man put the snake down on the floor. "Giving their leaders a voice in our council is the right thing to do. The problem is that their own laws and traditions are not always aligned, and this has caused debates between them. Nowadays, getting them to agree on even simple things takes weeks. To make matters worse, even King Himret has changed. His behavior has become erratic. For the last two seasons, he's barely offered more than a few words while the others joust with monologues for days."

The old man walked closer to us. "The tone in there became so polluted that the elders left the council during the last eclipse and secluded themselves in a secret place. Only your master remained in the chamber, but I suspect it's only to keep the elders informed of what takes place in there. It wasn't until recently that the elders requested my services again. I can't share a word about my task, but I think it's important for you to know that there could be members in the council who are not who we think they are. We might have shadows among us."

"The enemy is in Barthenoz?"

"We can't prove that yet. But there are many unusual signs and behaviors. Two days ago, one of the messengers I use to get food for my pets saw a crowd gathered in one of the markets. Every person in that group took a piece of parchment like this from a message posted on a wall."

Tynia opened the parchment—which I later learned was just one of an infinite number of magically replenishing copies you could tear from messaging walls—and we saw both of our faces with a message saying, "No more hiding. The guardians are back." The old man put the parchment back inside his sleeve.

"We know many saw you fighting the Zerkial wizards at the north gate, but your hood and this boy's armor covered your faces most of the time. We just don't know how someone was able to draw these pictures so accurately."

He was right. Other than the color of our skin, the drawings looked identical to us, even our hair. Well, in my case, to my older self. Peprokh glanced at me. "Well, this boy does look different now, but with parchments like this being passed all over the city, the last thing we want is for anybody to confirm that some guardians really came back."

"But where should we hide? And for how long?" Tynia said.

There was a long moment of silence. Suddenly, Peprokh's pets rushed back into their hiding places. The old man conjured his lamp into his hand and walked toward the quilts by the entrance.

"Someone's coming. Go and stay with that creature in my bed and be quiet."

He moved the quilts to go out, but someone was standing right behind them. We all tensed up but were relieved to see Tynia's master walking out of a cloud of dust he was making by patting his robes vigorously.

"I can't believe how dirty this place is. How can you live like this, Peprokh?"

"That's the way I like to receive uninvited guests. I hope you didn't touch any of my treasures on your way in. My pets will not appreciate it."

"You and your sick love for unintelligent creatures."

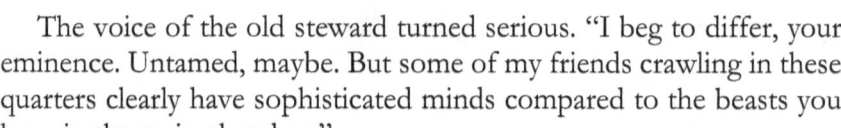

The voice of the old steward turned serious. "I beg to differ, your eminence. Untamed, maybe. But some of my friends crawling in these quarters clearly have sophisticated minds compared to the beasts you have in the main chamber."

"Well, unfortunately, I can't argue with that," Rubzilet said. "Did you tell them about the parchment?"

"I just did."

"The situation is worse now. The parchments have reached the council, and now that they've seen your faces, various factions are questioning the king and accusing him of not revealing why you are here and your whereabouts. The king knows he could lose control of the council if he doesn't act quickly, so he has ordered everyone to find you and bring you in front of the council."

"But the guardians respond to the elders, not the king," Tynia said.

"Yes. But like his predecessors, King Himret sees the elders as very important advisors still under his will. In any case, the boy will stay with Peprokh and you'll go see the elders. They will continue your training and give you what you need to bring Kharlo to Kirolcan."

Peprokh whirled toward Rubzilet. "Wait! That wasn't the agreement! Why can't you take both?"

"It wasn't my decision," Rubzilet said, raising a hand. "The elders want to keep Tynia and the boy separated for now." He turned his attention to me. "I apologize, young man. You haven't done anything wrong. This is what they told me to do."

"How long do I have to keep him here?"

"I don't know. Besides, he needs to stay with the infant until her family is found. Just make sure no one discovers who he is."

"Allow me to say goodbye to the little girl. I might not see her again," Tynia said.

"Do it quickly. The elders are waiting for us."

The three of us stood there in silence while Tynia went under the quilts to see the girl. It didn't take long for her to come back, but she wasn't alone. The little girl was yawning, but her eyes were wide open.

"She was just waking up when I approached the bed. Here, take good care of her."

I took her in my arms and both our faces glowed red for a moment. Tynia smiled and looked at Peprokh and her master. "Don't worry, they aren't sick. It's just a trait from the little girl's family." Both men sighed.

Tynia stood by her master's side and waited.

"I am ready."

"Ready for what?" Rubzilet responded.

"To go see the elders with you."

"Well, thanks to this old stubborn steward, we can't travel to other parts of the castle from this chamber—like any respected wizard has done for millennia. We will have to walk out of this dirty old dungeon hoping we don't get bitten by some ugly hairy creature on the way out."

"You shouldn't worry about that, your eminence. My pets only get close when they see something interesting."

"You haven't changed since the day I met you. Shouldn't you be using your charm and legendary powers to find someone?" Rubzilet said, and Peprokh frowned.

"I *will* find him. He won't be able to hide from me much longer."

"You'd better be as good as you think you are. I'll update the elders on your lack of progress," Rubzilet said as he turned around. Tynia and her old master ducked under the quilts and disappeared into the maze behind them.

We stood there for a moment, but then I felt something warm dripping down my arm. The old steward quickly stepped away from me.

"Can't this creature remain dry? This rug was a gift from the royal family! You! You are going to clean this. Yes you will."

"Well, she didn't do this on our way here. It must've been the spell from her mother."

"I would give many of my treasures to learn that spell and cast it on her right now," he said. The little girl responded by sucking her own hand and looking at him with her big green eyes. "Of course, the beast is hungry again. There are clean pieces of cloth by the bed. Throw the dirty ones in the fire and keep her away from my bed until I come back with some milk."

The man passed through the quilts, but I could hear him ranting as I walked to his bed. In my short life, I'd never needed to hold a baby, much less change its clothes or clean it. Yilian, Nuthek, and I always said that we would rather haul rocks on our backs for a month than clean a baby. Now I had no choice.

I took a few pieces of cloth and covered one side of the bed. I tried to scare away two rats that were looking at me from the other side of the bed, but they just stood there as if they were eager to witness my struggles. I left the little girl on top of the sheets and took a deep breath as I opened the cloth covering her bottom.

All I can say is that I wasn't prepared for what she was hiding in there. First of all, Tobho was right. Boys and girls are very different down there—I just didn't know how much. To make matters worse, the little girl left more than just wetness in her cloth. But I was even more surprised to see the leather string and golden pendant Peprokh gave to Tynia inside all that mess.

I'm going to need water and more cloth. Lots of it, I thought.

I found a pot with water by the table and brought it with me. I carefully pulled the pendant out and set it off to one side. Then I took a piece of cloth, poured some water on it, and began to clean her the best I could.

The little one even smiled at the faces I was making during that ordeal. By the time I finished, I was lying by her side, sweating like a horse, and there were no clean pieces of cloth or water left.

"You'd better be gentle with me," I whispered as I dried the sweat on my forehead. "I'm not sure I can do this too often."

The little one just stretched her arm toward me. I took the pieces of cloth I used and threw them in the fire. Then I sat by the bed and looked at the pendant. "Why would Tynia leave this behind?" Somehow my thoughts flew back to that moment in my room when I pulled Kharlo's pendant from inside his clothes. "Peprokh said it doesn't belong to a guardian, but it sure does look like one of theirs."

The little girl responded with one of those sounds she made when she sucked her hand.

"What do you think? Should I put it on?" I was thinking about it, but my hands were already doing it.

My body hit the floor, and an endless flow of images flooded every sense in my body. The images slowly faded, but then I started to feel pain in my back and hips. I knew I was in Peprokh's quarters, but when I opened my eyes, the light of the sunset made me look down toward the grass I was now lying on.

A bright symbol was glowing on the back of my hand, very close to my smallest finger—a mirror image of the pendant hanging from my neck. I heard the sounds of the little girl, so I raised my head again and saw the last light of the sun shining vividly on a disk just like mine that was stuck on the ground three or four feet away from me.

I reached for it, but it was too late. Once the sun went away, the only light around me came from the lamps around Peprokh's bed. I was back in his quarters.

Where was that place? Whose memories had I seen? Why did Kharlo carry them with him? I could've stayed on the floor debating those questions, but the pain in my body was intensifying—my clothes didn't fit me anymore.

I took my shirt off and saw my chest and arms covered with hair again. I loosened my leggings and went to the opposite corner of Peprokh's fireplace, where water poured from the wall into a stone basin.

Not knowing what else that pendant was doing to my body, I felt immense relief when I saw my reflection in the water showing the face I'd had when we crossed to Kirolcan.

"Good. At least I don't have someone else's face."

I walked back and sat in front of the girl, looking at the back of my hand. There was no symbol burning on my skin—neither Kharlo's nor the one hanging from my neck. I hesitated, but I knew I had to take that pendant off, so I closed my eyes and removed it. When I opened my eyes, my body was small again, this time with no images and no pain. I stood up to tighten my leggings just before Peprokh walked in.

"This is disgraceful! Completely unacceptable! Not only do I have to keep the creature here, staining the dignity of my sacred place, but now I've become her servant." Peprokh stared at me. "And you? What happened to your clothes?"

I quickly pointed at my shirt rolled up on the floor while I hid the pendant in my other hand. "I had to clean the girl and my shirt got dirty. The smell was unbearable."

The old man glanced at the shirt and gave me an angry look. "Well, don't just leave it there! Throw it in the fire and find something else to wear in one of the chests. Don't take long; you'll have to use this contraption to feed the creature."

When I came back, the old steward handed me an odd-looking cup made of clay with a white piece of cloth as thick as my finger sticking out at the bottom. I just stared at him.

"Don't look at me," he said, rolling his eyes. "Just pour some milk in it and give it to her. Do it while it's warm. And don't spill a single drop on my bed."

It took longer than I thought, but eventually the little one was full. I will always remember that moment when we went under the quilts and saw Peprokh sitting by the table with his pipe in his mouth. The man laughed loudly when he saw the front of my shirt drenched in milk and the little one smiling.

"So, young man, I guess you can't wait to have your own children, eh?" The little girl didn't let me answer. Her hand slapped my nose as she turned to one side. "We have to search for her relatives. Find another shirt and let's walk through the market."

The little girl began to cough as she smelled the smoke from Peprokh's pipe.

"I don't think she likes the smoke."

"Too bad for her," he grumbled. "If she doesn't like it, she can sleep outside." He paused. "But she may not have to if we find her family today. Let's go."

***

We gently merged with the flow of people heading like a river through the market.

"Well, young man, how are we going to find her family?"

"As you saw in your quarters, her face glows red when she's close to a member of her clan."

"Very distasteful indeed. I just hope it's not contagious."

"They called it fire skin."

"Fire skin? Who told you that?"

"The leader of the mercenaries from the Serthoz clan."

"I've never heard of them. Who is he?"

"Didn't you see him in my memories from the Valley of Souls? The giant door. The soldiers in the shadows. Didn't Tynia tell you about that?"

The old man stopped and looked at me. "Young man, I have no idea what you're talking about. All we saw in your memories is you carrying the guardian and this creature all the way to a big door. You opened it and once Tynia awakened, the three of you went through. The river from our lake must have been right on the other side, because we saw you walking out of it after that."

"You didn't see the valley covered in clouds? What about the domes of light?"

"Oh boy. We probably hurt your head by keeping you in the pool that long. Look up. Do you see a dome on top of us right now?"

I briefly looked up. The sky was as blue as ours, with only a few clouds moving slowly here and there.

"No, I don't see any dome."

"Good. You may still recover. Now, let's separate to cover more ground. I'll ask around to see if someone has heard about people with fire skin. You will have to go tent by tent to get this bugger as close to the people as you can. Hopefully someone's skin will glow. Start here on the right side. I'll see you back by the door at sunset, when you hear the sound of the horns seven times."

With that, the old man walked away. Even though there were many people around, I felt very lonely and confused. What he said about my memories from the Valley of Souls made no sense. Was he lying? Why would he? There was only one person who might know what was going on, but she was now far away, hiding with the elders.

That little hand touching my face brought me back from those thoughts, so I kept walking. I visited every tent I could and walked by hundreds of people. Even though many looked like me, some of the races I saw out there reminded me where I was—in another world.

There were times when I was just too tired from carrying the girl, so I sat in places where people gathered to eat or watch their children play. I was asked a few times if I was taking care of my little sister while my parents were buying goods nearby. That became our story. Some women shared food and water with us, and one of them even gave me a set of clothes for the little one, for free. I would've liked to give her something, but I didn't have anything in my pockets, nor did I know the value of the coins being used.

By the time the soldiers at the top of the tower blew their horns seven times, I had barely walked through half of the tents standing on the right side of the grounds.

I made my way back to the door, where Peprokh was already waiting with two small cages and some sacks by his feet.

"Any luck making someone's face glow?"

"Not a single one."

"Not even a weak blush?"

"Not even."

"Were you actually looking for her relatives or just buying food and clothes for her?"

"I couldn't have bought anything. I don't have any coins."

"Ah, so you stole all this? Interesting."

"I am *not* a thief. These were gifts."

"If you say so," he said as he walked back into the castle.

"You don't have to believe me. My conscience is clear, so I'll have no trouble sleeping tonight."

"Well, I'm not so sure about that," he said as he carried the cages inside.

"What's with the empty cages?"

"Who says they're empty?" The old man made his lamp appear in his hand. "What's that smell?" he said, nose wrinkled.

"I have to change her clothes again."

The man just looked away and waved his lamp.

Back in his quarters, I took care of the little one and even gave her some milk while Peprokh put a cauldron on the fire and left us to attend his duties around the castle.

"I wonder where I'll sleep tonight. Where have you been sleeping the last few days?" The only answer I got from the little one was a long yawn. "There's only one bed in here, and I don't see Peprokh letting you sleep close to him."

I took her in my arms and began to hum my mother's lullaby as we walked around. I searched everywhere for a place where the old man could've left the little one at night.

She would've fallen from the table, and he couldn't have left her on the floor with all these creatures roaming around, I thought. Then I looked at the quilts separating his living area from the entrance. *Did he actually . . . ?*

We slid under the quilts and left the center path, making our way around crates, baskets, and endless piles of parchments and relics from old times. Most of the stacks were so tall and fragile that they could've easily buried anyone who tripped over them. And if that wasn't dangerous enough, some of the creatures living there would've made anyone's survival doubtful.

I was grateful that the little girl slept under the spell of my mother's song as we risked our lives in there. Some of the spiders, rats, and lizards were just the sort of creatures to give nightmares to anyone.

When I saw the head of a snake by my face, all I could do was close my eyes and hold the girl tightly against my chest. For a moment, I could even feel his tongue flicking through my hair. I waited, but nothing happened. When I opened my eyes, the viper was slowly going in the opposite direction.

Then I realized—the creatures in there looked vicious, but their behavior wasn't. *Maybe if we don't bother them, they will do the same,* I thought hopefully.

I didn't see anything touched recently, so I made my way back to the center of the room and ventured over to the other side. I walked around some old crates and saw light coming from the far corner. We made our way through a narrow passageway between the wall and stacks of barrels, and there it was—an improvised sleeping area with more stacks of barrels acting as walls all the way to the ceiling. The space wasn't large, but it had a bed, a small table with two chairs, and a wooden chest in one corner. A single candle traveling slowly through the air was the only source of light. It was actually clean and the bed seemed comfortable—at least it must've been for the dozens of lizards lying on it.

For some reason, all of them were sleeping. Not a single one had its eyes open. Bodies and tails of all shapes, sizes, and colors quietly stretched out among each other. A few of them even laying on their backs, bellies bulging as they breathed. Other than those little creatures, I couldn't find anything else roaming the area.

"This can't be the place you've been sleeping. Maybe I'm misjudging him and he's the one sleeping here? Yes, that must be it. I should go back and put you in his bed."

I walked back into Peprokh's sleeping area and moved the bedding to put the little one in.

"What are you doing?"

I jumped a little at his voice. "She's asleep. This is where she sleeps, right?"

"My dear boy, this creature will sleep in this bed when my last bone turns to dust in my grave."

"But there's nowhere else! Where did she sleep last night?"

"She's been sleeping in the Guardians Lair with your friend. I told them that keeping her here would be a problem, but they didn't listen."

"I don't have a place to sleep too. Can we both sleep in the Guardians Lair?"

"Are you a guardian? Do you carry a mark with you?"

I hesitated to answer, as I did have the pendant in my pocket.

"I'm not a guardian, but I carry the memories and powers of one. I can even use his weapon. Isn't that enough?"

"Not anymore. Everything that Kharlo passed to you is now inside that mark that Tynia took with her. You can't even use his weapon without it."

My mind went in two directions immediately. One part of me felt intense relief knowing that I was a normal boy again. The other part felt sorrow realizing that I didn't have all those powers in me anymore.

"Don't tell me we're supposed to sleep with your lizards."

He turned and glared at me. "So you've been snooping around in my absence. That was a dangerous mistake. I'm not sure how my pets allowed you to enter, but don't push your luck. Some of my creatures can kill a hundred men with a drop of their venom."

"Give us some blankets and we'll sleep on the table."

"And where would my snakes sleep?"

I sighed. "Your snakes sleep there?"

"Well, not until midnight; then they just stay there until sunrise."

We stared at each other silently for a few moments. I refused to break eye contact with him. Finally, the old man made his lamp disappear and walked toward the fireplace.

"I'll ask the lizards to sleep on the floor. Both of you can use that bed. Don't worry, they won't bother you."

Ask the lizards? Can he talk to animals? I wondered.

I didn't say anything else. We only exchanged pleasantries (which were decidedly not very pleasant) as we ate stew and some pieces of bread. Once we finished eating, I followed him back to the corner room. He asked me to wait by the entrance as he took each one of the lizards and placed them on the floor.

The creatures gathered in the corners and went back to sleep almost immediately. Peprokh waved his lamp, and a stack of clean blankets appeared on the table.

"The water in the pot is clean. We'll keep searching for her family in the morning, so try to sleep." The old man walked away, but he stopped by the crates.

"It's been a very long time since I've seen a shield like the one you carry. We have much better weapons nowadays, but the feats our warriors of old accomplished with those disks are legendary."

Peprokh disappeared in the maze and I walked closer to the table. I pulled the chairs out and felt a deep moment of happiness and longing for my mother and friends when I saw my ramikha and the disk on one of them.

I prepared the bed and left a blanket rolled up on the far side between the little girl and the barrels. I pulled a chair closer and left my boots on it to prevent the lizards from getting in. I rested by her side and closed my eyes as I softly passed my fingers over my ramikha.

The next thing I remember is hearing Peprokh's voice. The room was in complete darkness, and I felt something heavy on top of me. Peprokh walked in and waved his lamp to light the candle that was now lying cold on the table.

"Well, I see that you've already become friends. Did you sleep well?"

My heart lurched. There wasn't a single lizard on the floor—all of them were lying on top of me and around the little girl. Two of them were even sticking out of my boots, now lying on their side on top of the chair.

"You both should get out of bed. We need to eat and go back to the market."

"Could you get these beasts away from me?" I whispered, reluctant to move.

"You'll have to do that from now on. Just be careful—some of them are a bit moody. Let's go. I've already boiled some milk for the creature."

One by one, I put them on the floor until I was able to get out of bed. The little girl was far more valiant, as she slept holding the tail of one of the gray ones that slept on its back.

We cleaned up, ate, and walked into the market again. The second day, Peprokh stayed with me and taught me the names and traits of some of the races of Kirolcan. He explained to me that all newborns in Kirolcan are given a drop of water from a secret well protected by the elders in Kelfia so they can understand all tongues. In my case, I was now able to understand everyone because of my stay in the Guardians Pool.

We couldn't find anybody with fire skin on that second day, but Peprokh allowed me to bathe the little girl in the Guardians Pool that evening. Both of us needed that bath.

That became our routine for the next ten weeks. Every now and then I asked Peprokh if he had any news from Tynia and the elders, but he always claimed I knew as much as he did. He never said it out loud, but he was also worried about Kharlo's Jiretal spell running out, allowing the dark army to find him and the others. I guess there was nothing else for us to do but wait.

Peprokh summoned merchants from other regions to set up their markets on those grounds, but we were unable to find anybody with fire skin.

I tried many things, but every morning I woke up covered in lizards, the little girl holding the tail of the same gray one. It wasn't until a few days later that I realized something unusual. I couldn't remember a single dream or even waking up at night while I slept with those lizards. In fact, I felt rested and invigorated every morning when they spent the night on top of me.

Peprokh had to free up the grounds so the last group of merchants in Kelfia could set up their market there. It was sad to watch some of them leave, as we'd become very close friends.

We were standing at the same spot on that bridge where he first showed me the market, watching them leave, when I finally said it. "What if no one from her family has made it to Kelfia?"

The old steward kept looking at the long lines of people flooding the road to the docks. "In that case, you'll become the youngest father I've ever known."

"But I don't even know how to raise a child!" I paused. "You're probably the only person who will ever hear me say this, but look at me! I'm still a child too!"

The old man leaned on his staff and looked at me. "Someone told me long ago that we are just leaves tumbling in the winds of life. You'll never know where you'll land or whether something will land on you. The mother of this child probably never thought she would have to bond her with a stranger, but she did. Now, you know this creature will have a very difficult time living with anybody else unless they carry her blood. So you'd better accept the possibility that she may have to stay with you."

Those words made me restless that night. I left the little one in the bed and sat at the table, looking at the candle moving through the air. It grew so late that I saw for the first time how the lizards made their journey from the floor onto the bed. One by one, they carefully got on top and took their places. It was so curious to see the one that always slept by the little girl actually place its tail in her little hand.

At some point, the candle made its way down to the table, making its flame die as it rolled. I touched around the table and put my hand in the pot with water, then rubbed it on the disk.

I'm not sure why, but this time, only a very faint light came from it. Once my eyes got used to it, it was good enough for me to see my surroundings. I stayed there thinking, then I saw all those lizards sleeping in my place and thought it was too late for me to try to get into bed.

I decided to get something to eat, so I silently made my way to Peprokh's fireplace. I was taking a piece of bread from the table when I heard his voice and some strange noises coming from his sleeping area. I hesitated, but as always, my curiosity made me hide the disk in my clothes and quietly move the quilts to look inside.

Peprokh was sitting on a stool with his back toward me. He was wearing some strange white leggings, and his hair was partially covering the skin on his back. Even though he had many scars, the most astounding thing was the many beasts and creatures inked on his skin. Every one stood proud in its place covering most of his upper body all the way to his shoulders.

I was going to leave, but then he leaned forward and unlocked the chains of a strange wooden cage. He whispered some words as he opened a small door on its top and put his hand inside.

His scream must have reached every part of the castle.

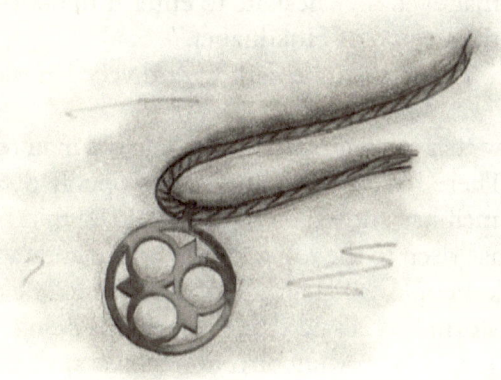

CHAPTER 12. LOST WHISPERS.

I rolled onto the floor and started crawling back to the lizard room. I could hear the old man cursing as things hit the floor everywhere.

"You ungrateful monster! I should've let you face your demise. I don't know how I let you fool me. Don't run away from me!"

With all the racket he was making, he probably didn't hear when I stumbled over a pile of old helmets in the dark.

"That wasn't our deal!" he roared. "Are you breaking your word now? Get in the cage! We'll try this again tomorrow."

Those were the last words I heard as I wove through the maze back into my room. This time, I didn't hesitate to take the lizards from the bed and get under the bedding as quickly as possible.

I woke up the following morning covered with lizards as usual. I tried my best not to look suspicious, but Peprokh was unusually quiet during breakfast.

"We will have to visit some of the cities around the lake to continue our search while the new market settles in on the castle grounds. We just have to be careful out there. Our soldiers patrol most places, but there are a few that even they hesitate to enter. I think it's best for you to know about the Legion of Hokdhanet."

"Hokdhanet? That's what the dark wizard yelled at me at the north gate."

"Yes. We saw that in your memories." The old man rested his back on the chair. "There have been many voices openly disagreeing with the way the council has chosen to fight Malok. Within that group, an obscure figure has risen to the top and now commands a large number of common folk. People called him 'Hokdhanet,' an ancient word that means "winter storm." It is said that his legion is being trained in the arts of war and magic in very unconventional ways; all this in order to face the savagery of the dark army. Unfortunately, many have lost their lives training under these dangerous methods, but we've also heard they've been successful conducting raids along the eastern front, keeping Malok's forces scattered in that region.

Rubzilet and I believe those Zerkials at the north gate thought that you and Tynia were part of this Hokdhanet legion, not real guardians. At least that's what we hope.

As far as Hokdhanet, it's hard to say what is true and what isn't.

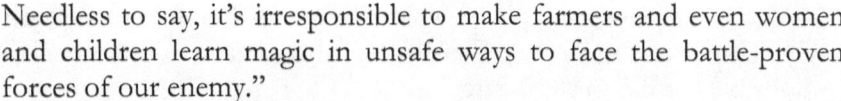

Needless to say, it's irresponsible to make farmers and even women and children learn magic in unsafe ways to face the battle-proven forces of our enemy."

"Well, your guardians are children too."

The old man looked at his empty plate. "True, but they endure a long period of training before they face the enemy. I'll be honest with you—I don't know why the guardians start that young. I've even asked the elders about it a few times, but all they've given me is silence."

"And the leader of this legion—is he a child too?"

"Nobody knows. All we've heard is that he is well versed in the arts of magic." Peprokh stared at the symbols covering the quilts from his sleeping area. "He is good, but I'll find him." He left the table and brought a set of clothes for me. "Put these on. Today we'll visit the area west of the lake where the refugees from Minojeb established themselves. Remember, Hokdhanet has eyes everywhere, so let's not use our names or make ourselves too visible. Let's just blend in with the crowd. Hopefully we'll find someone with fire skin in that area."

We merged with the people at the docks and took a boat to the west. I was worried that the little girl wouldn't feel well as we rocked on the water, but she remained calm, even curious about all the sparkles on the water's surface.

I couldn't see the city at first. But once the sun took care of the fog, I was astonished by the view—hundreds of boats of all sizes crowding the entire western shore.

The old steward looked at me. "Be careful as we move from boat to boat. Some of the walkways are slippery, or rotten."

"We're not stopping at the docks?"

The old steward chuckled. "I don't even remember the last time a boat was able to reach the western docks. All these vessels are now permanently tied to each other, and many more join this floating city every season." He paused. "Minojeb is very far from Kelfia and is covered by scorching deserts. Water is so scarce that it's more precious than gold in their clans. When they reached Kelfia and saw the waters of our lake, they eagerly moved into the town and used any available space to be as close to shore as possible. When the people from Kelfia complained, they didn't hesitate to build boats and move into this floating city. Most of them still travel through the Kelfian town to reach the western lands every day, though."

"Why? What do they have on land?"

"Mainly farmlands and places where they keep their livestock. Each city is tasked with protecting their side of the barrier, so they are also responsible for the western gate."

I felt our ship slowing, and Peprokh took a pouch from his sleeve and gave it to me. "Use this to buy food. Be careful—don't let anyone steal it from you."

The boat stopped alongside a much larger vessel, and we walked up a wooden ramp onto it. Many people greeted us by offering their merchandise and inviting us to follow them to their boats. I covered the little girl and followed Peprokh as he squeezed himself through all the merchants trying to make a living. Eventually we made it to a boat with far fewer people.

"Jonek, walk through these four boats on the right, and I'll ask questions on these ones on the left. We'll meet back here in this boat selling fish. If you don't see me, just wait here. Don't wander around."

"Wait! Could we meet somewhere else?"

"Why?"

"Let's just say that I don't like to be around fish that much."

The old man didn't answer. He just turned around and stepped away with a shake of his head. The little one and I walked by every person on those boats without any luck. Against my will, we headed back to the boat selling fish and waited for the old man. Even the little one turned away from the baskets filled with fish of all kinds.

"So you don't like them either," I chuckled. "Maybe we are indeed related."

Peprokh eventually returned, and we walked further into the city. It was amazing to see some of the impressive structures built so high on top of the boats. Many times I looked down to see if the boats holding the buildings were on the verge of sinking, but they weren't.

As we walked through a narrow boat, we saw two elderly women asking a merchant for some bread. They didn't have coins to pay for it, but I heard them saying that the bread was for the Lost Whispers. The merchant gave them two loaves and the women offered him their blessings before walking toward an old boat at the far end.

"What are Lost Whispers?" I asked Peprokh as we walked onto the next boat.

"Not what, *who*. The Lost Whispers are children who have lost their families in the war. Well, a few may still have someone fighting out there, but at this point they are entirely alone in the city. The adults pass the news of the fallen by whispering the names of the boys or girls who have lost someone, usually when children are not around. As you just saw, the older women take care of these younglings who have lost everyone and everything—the Lost Whispers."

"We have our own Lost Whisper here with us."

Peprokh frowned at me. "Not we, *you*! Don't think that because I haven't said anything for some time it means that I am a happy with this creature—or you—being close to me. By the way, this little bugger is living a life of privilege compared to what the Lost Whispers endure every day. Remember that."

He was right, so I just followed him in silence. Even though he was always loud while reminding us what a huge burden we were for him, sometimes he couldn't help but show glimpses that he really didn't hate us as much as he claimed.

We kept walking from boat to boat until the afternoon. We found a vendor who sold us milk for the little one, and Peprokh and I had a plate of a very tasty soup. When I asked him what was it made of, the old man just whispered that it was best if I didn't know.

"Jonek, do you see that mast with three flags in the distance?" he said, changing the subject. "That boat will take us back to Barthenoz. Make sure you board it before the horns sound six times. You'll have to give them three coins like this one." He held up the kind he meant. "I still have one more thing to do, but it's best I do it alone. Just don't be late."

Peprokh returned his soup bowl and walked away, leaving us at a long table with many strangers. I left a piece of bread by my plate and stood up. I was going to take the plate back to the vendor when a girl, not older than five, ran by us and took the piece of bread with her. For one brief moment, I saw her face as she glanced at me and offered me a single word that I couldn't understand. I never saw her again, but her big, lovely eyes, dirty face, and untamed hair will forever live in my heart.

I wish I could've given her more, I thought as I made my way to the next boat.

I was still thinking about her as I walked by the place where the two elderly women had asked for bread. I stood there staring at the loaves and baskets full of fruit, then turned around and looked at the old boat at the far end. I opened my coin pouch, separated five or six coins, and put the rest on top of the merchant's table.

"How much bread and fruit can you give me for these?"

I certainly didn't know the value of the coins, as the man took one of the two gold ones in the pile and said, "You can take everything I have for just this one."

I gave him the coin and put the rest back in the pouch. "Put everything in sacks and follow me."

The man and three of his sons carried the bread and fruit and followed me to the old boat. An older woman washing clothes by the edge of the ramp down by the water saw me standing by the side of the boat. She walked closer and extended her arms, offering to take the little girl.

"No, my dear lady. I'm not here to give you another mouth to feed. In fact, I brought something for the ones you already have." I pointed to the merchant and his children.

They showed the food to her, and she quickly called others. Three or four ladies joined us and started crying and offering us their blessings when they saw the food. Many children also gathered around and began to shout and celebrate as they saw the feast.

I turned to the merchant and his sons. "Leave the sacks here. I'll see you back at your boat; I might need other things from you."

"We'll wait for you. We don't have anything else to sell today anyway. We thank you for what you did for us, as well as for these children."

I couldn't help them carry anything because my hands were full, but there were plenty of little hands quickly shimmying everything inside. I couldn't believe how many children lived on that boat. Fifty, maybe more. I have to say that even with that many living there, those ladies kept everything very clean. It's true that many parts of the boat were old and rotten, but I didn't see any water leaking anywhere. Rudimentary beds of all types were built in every open spot, even hanging from the sides of the boat.

The elderly women didn't know how to thank me. They offered me anything they had on hand. I told them that I didn't want anything in return. My problems began when one of them asked me what my name was.

I didn't know what to say, so I quickly changed the subject. "How long do you think this food will last?"

"We will share some with other boats that have more children than us, but we can make it last for three or four days."

"I will arrange for the merchant to bring you the same amount of food in three days. You can use the time you would've spent looking for food teaching these children how to read and some trade skills. Fishing, maybe?"

"Some of the older children know how to read, but they're out there helping us gather food."

"I'll think of a way to keep the food coming for these Lost Whispers. You should find a way to educate them. Make them see a world beyond the sorrows of war."

A very old woman left a chair hidden in a corner and slowly walked toward me, her white knuckles gripped around a walking staff. She briefly touched the little girl's hand, then moved my hair away from my forehead.

"You have the face of a child, but you speak the words of a king. Who are you?"

I couldn't answer. The brief red glare illuminating our faces interrupted me. The old woman made a signal, and her companions took everyone to other parts of the boat.

"Only another Serthoz could've made my skin burn." She said.

"I am not, but this little one must have your blood."

"But your face burned too."

"We'd better sit down so I can tell you why."

I followed her to the small area where she slept and shared with her how the mother bonded the little girl with me so we could bring her to Kelfia. She told me how the Serthoz clan was the most powerful in their region but fell into disgrace many generations ago for reasons already lost to time. Unfortunately, their family had been persecuted and killed since then, so they had to change their names and hide in places far beyond their homeland to survive. Families were usually separated to avoid being discovered when their fire skin burned. It was really sad to hear that her oldest son wasn't even six years old the last time she saw him.

"The mother must've really been on her last breath to bond her with a kid like you. You could be her brother. I wonder who the mother is. Bring the child closer to me." She separated the top of her walking staff and took out a piece of parchment rolled in it.

I felt bad that I couldn't share with her that I looked much older when the mother bonded her with me, but I thought it was best for her not to know those details.

Many symbols and lines connecting them covered most of the parchment. She took the hand of the little one and passed it over each symbol starting from the top.

Some of them changed colors as she touched them, but they stopped changing as she reached the bottom.

"She belongs to the fourth branch, the Serthoz from the south. Unfortunately, I haven't seen any of them in many seasons. When we encounter someone with fire skin, we draw a symbol on these parchments with their blood so we can keep track of them and share their whereabouts with others."

The old woman took the little girl's finger and put it over a circle drawn on the top of the parchment. When she pulled it away, a tiny drop of blood was left inside the circle. Then, she took a quill and drew a symbol on the lowest part of the fourth branch using the blood in the circle.

"Our writing is not easy to translate, but in plain words, this reads 'girl with green eyes carried by a boy.'" The old woman opened a small bottle of ink, drew the same symbol on another piece of parchment, and added a few more around it. "Visit the market across the lake where the people of Celidhom settled. Find a woman as old as me selling spices and give this to her. She keeps a small bird on her shoulder that seems to be blind—you can't miss her. Just don't get too close to her so you don't make her fire skin burn. She might know where to find this girl's family."

"What color is the bird?"

"That will depend on her mood," she said, smiling.

The old woman touched our faces one last time and wished us farewell. I told the others outside that the merchant would bring the same amount of food in three days and walked away.

I gave the other gold coin to the merchant, and he even offered to bring an extra sack of bread to the Lost Whispers. I told him that this could become a regular trade for him if he kept the children happy with his goods.

I couldn't see it from a distance, but when I finally reached the boat, I couldn't help but be astonished by its size. It was so big it could've challenged the treacherous waters of our Garpodian Sea. I boarded it after paying the three coins and walked to the other side so the little girl could see the sparkles on the water one last time that afternoon. I kept looking around, but Peprokh was nowhere to be found.

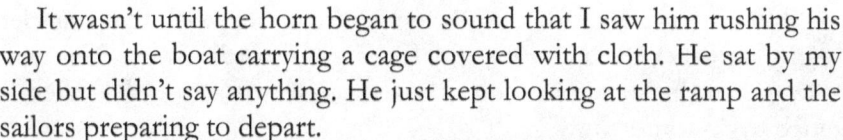

It wasn't until the horn began to sound that I saw him rushing his way onto the boat carrying a cage covered with cloth. He sat by my side but didn't say anything. He just kept looking at the ramp and the sailors preparing to depart.

"Why are they taking this long?" he whispered under his breath.

I looked at him, then glanced at the men doing their job. "Well, this is a big ship. What's your rush? Running from someone?"

"What did you hear?" he said nervously.

I glanced at the cage. "Nothing. Don't tell me you took something that doesn't belong to you."

"This is an important matter."

"Is this part of what you're doing for the council?"

He paused. "Yes, indeed it is." He turned around and looked at the sailors.

"So, the council asked you to steal an animal?"

"Keep your nose in your own affairs. You wouldn't understand anyway."

The ship's bow was already pointing toward the island when we heard voices yelling back by the ramp. Even though he grabbed my arm to keep me from looking back, I was able to see two men wearing dark cloaks lowering their bows as we moved away.

"They didn't look happy."

"I know," he said as he released my arm.

"Dark cloaks and long hair. They must be Satolgac."

The old man looked at me, surprised. "Indeed they are."

"I've never seen any of them raise their voices."

The old man pulled the cage closer to him. "Well, I don't blame them. It's unfortunate but necessary."

"I have some good news for you."

"Let's talk about that later," he said, cutting me off.

We reached Barthenoz and walked into his quarters, then I told him that the little girl needed a bath.

"Is that necessary? I'm really busy tonight," he grumbled.

"It was a long day. I need one too—I smell like fish."

He pushed the cage into his sleeping area and took us to the Guardians Lair. He paced around the pool until he finally made his lamp appear and waved it toward me. As he gestured in my direction, the silver bracelet Zilhien gave me at the theater briefly turned blue on my arm.

"I don't have time for this. When you're done, touch that bracelet with your other hand and just say 'Barthenoz north tower.' That will take you to the stairs outside my quarters. Go to sleep early—there's much to do tomorrow."

"Wait! I haven't told you the good news. I found a woman with fire skin! She's not directly related to this girl, but she gave me—"

"Excellent! Great news indeed," Peprokh interrupted. "You can tell me more tomorrow." The man waved his lamp and disappeared, leaving me utterly confused.

"I thought he was going to be elated to hear we might have found your family," I said as I looked at the little girl splashing her hands in the water. The echo of her playing reminded me of the size of the hall. For some reason, Peprokh always stayed with us by the pool and never allowed me to get closer to Kharlo's window again. With him gone, I crept over and looked into it. I can't describe how surprised I was to see that image. The entire window was dark with just a few glimpses of light here and there.

"We've been in Kirolcan for over two months and we left on the night of the second day of the fair. If every day there is about a month here, it must be around noon of the fifth day of the fair. Why is the image this dark then? Where could they be?"

I thought about confronting Peprokh and make him tell me what he knew, but I had to find the right moment to do that. I didn't want him to get angry and restrict my liberties for snooping around again. Furthermore, he'd been acting strange lately.

"I know Tynia and the elders wouldn't leave them unprotected. Maybe they moved Kharlo into a cave." I said, looking at the little one. "One thing is for sure, though, we better be back before the fair ends and all the warriors in town leave."

Then I wondered if I could pass my hand over Kharlo's window (like Tynia did in hers) to see what happened before the image went dark, but decided not to try. I didn't want to risk doing something to the image.

The little one must have felt how my heart longed to see them; she softly rested her head on me and put her hand around my neck. I smiled.

"You must be missing your mother too. Don't worry—we'll bring her back from the mountains."

I walked away from the window, but there was one last thing I had to do before we left the hall.

I headed toward the pedestal with the golden bowl and went down the stairs to the floor below. The little girl just grabbed onto my clothes and hid her face in my neck as we ventured into the darkness. Only the light coming from the hall we'd just left allowed me to see where I stepped. There were moments when I thought that this wasn't a good idea, especially carrying a baby in my arms, but I kept going.

I took the last few steps almost in complete darkness, but lamps and candles began to illuminate my surroundings the moment I stepped away from the stairs.

When the little one opened her eyes, the astounding view certainly distracted her from her worries—a round hall as magnificent as the one we just came from, only this one had two pools in it with various closed tents erected around them. Another golden bowl rested on top of a round pedestal just a few steps from where we were. I looked to the left; a lonely lamp floating nearby illuminated the entrance to another staircase in the floor.

"How many halls are in this lair? And how many guardians have walked through them?" I said to myself, looking at the long line of windows with changing images around the hall.

I went down another level and walked into a similar hall, but this one had a waterfall flowing from its highest point into a large pool in the center. The pedestal in this room looked like the trunk of a tree but was silver in color. A long torch stuck on the floor illuminated yet another staircase to my left.

"I can tell you how many guardians have walked in these halls if you let me touch your bracelet."

I whirled around but didn't see anyone. "Who is this?" I said, my voice echoing loudly. "Is that you, Peprokh? Where are you?"

"The steward doesn't know I'm here," the voice said.

"Where are you?"

A round pebble rolled from under a pile of trinkets all the way to my feet.

"I was once a guardian. I should've stayed sleeping forever, but your voice woke me up a few weeks ago. I think the question is, who are you?"

"Why do you want to touch this bracelet?" I said, cautiously tucking it close to me.

"I'm not sure. There is something familiar about it. Maybe touching it will help me remember."

"Come out. Let me see you."

"I am here, by your feet."

I looked down at the pebble and saw it moving back a little. "You are quite small for a guardian."

"The size and shape of your body can't show who you are—only your actions can."

I hesitated, but then I remembered where I was. "May I pick you up?"

"If you want to." I took the pebble from the floor and walked closer to the long torch. "If you are trying to find a face on it, don't waste your time. It's only a pebble. I put myself inside this rock in order to stay alive. I don't even remember how long ago that was. We faced Sulibhor on Mount Nijithok, but we were betrayed by the Zerkials. The wizards turned against us at the last moment, and we couldn't contain the wrath of Sulibhor and his beasts. I protected the other guardians as they escaped, but it was too late for me. All I could do was to use my last speck of magic to pour my life into this rock. Unfortunately, this magic is so ancient that no one alive knows how to undo the spell. I learned it myself by mere chance, but I now regret reading that scroll."

"This pebble looks perfectly round," I said, flipping it over in my hands.

"It wasn't like this when I cast the spell. A few guardians have tried to help me through the centuries. One of them polished the pebble this way so I can move around. It wasn't easy learning how, but time is all I have."

"What about the elders? Can they undo this spell?"

"None of the elders, or even their masters before them, know that I'm still here. When we were betrayed, there were rumors about one of them possibly being loyal to Sulibhor, so the other guardians thought it was best to say that I perished in the battle and hide me here.

"For many years, the wizards among the guardians inherited the task of finding a way to get me out of here, but eventually the war took their minds away from me and I was forgotten. The last guardian who held me in his hands cast a spell to make me sleep forever. I'm not sure why your voice awakened me, but it's great to see another guardian again."

"I'm not a guardian," I said as I moved the pebble away from the little girl's groping hands.

"You sure look like one—a warrior, maybe. Who is this young one you carry in your arms? Your sister?"

"I don't have any brothers or sisters. She is just a little one I've been entrusted with."

"If you're not a guardian, what are you doing here?"

"A real guardian is dying. He gave me his powers to help his friend, a wizard, travel back here to get some medicine for him."

"I'm sorry to hear that. I've never heard of a guardian sharing his powers with others. It must be a new kind of magic."

The little girl slapped my hand, making me drop the pebble. I rushed after it and picked it up before it tumbled down the stairs in the floor.

"Sorry! Are you alright?"

"Don't worry," the voice said with what sounded like a hint of a smile. "This rock is as sturdy as the iron from my islands. Believe me, I've tried to shatter it myself a few times."

"You were born on an island? What's your name?"

"My real name is long and difficult to say. The elders called me Kolikuj, like the islands I come from. I'm the Guardian of the Falling Water."

"I've heard of those islands. They make the finest blades and shields a warrior could wield."

"So you come from there too. The land with only one moon in the sky."

"Yes. I'm from Ferdhen." I crouched down and sat on the floor, the baby in one hand, the stone in the other.

"Ferdhen? I've never heard of the place."

"It's west of the Stapian Forest, just south of the Bhormak Mountains."

"I know the area south of the Bhormaks. It's where the sages planted the Patriarch Tree. One of the entrances to the Lost Path. I never liked that entrance. Too long and dark."

"You mean long and hot! The molten rock almost killed us when we crossed the narrow bridge a few weeks back."

"That never happened to us. There was an enormous abyss under that bridge in my time. It was dark and cold for sure."

I sat the little girl on my legs, took the pebble, and touched my bracelet with it. "So, do you remember anything?"

"Not really, but I still feel I've seen this piece of jewelry before."

I sighed. "Well, I have to go back. Peprokh might be looking for us. Where do you want me to leave you?"

"Just leave me here on the floor. I'll hide myself."

The pebble stayed there, maybe looking at me as I stood up. "You never told me your name," he said.

"Jonek."

"There are very unusual flames burning in you, Jonek. That's why I thought you were a guardian."

"Other people have said that, but I don't really know what it means."

"It means there are powers in you. Guardians, elders, and other beings have flames in them. They are usually hard to control, so it takes many years before they can be used without causing more harm than good. Not everyone can sense them in others, but I can tell you that yours burn bright and cold, as if you've already tamed them."

"But I don't even know how to cast a spell."

Kolikuj chuckled. "That's easy. It only requires good memory and practice. Stay safe, Jonek."

The pebble slowly rolled back into the pile of trinkets. "Don't worry, Kolikuj. I won't tell anyone you're here, and I'll come down to see you when Peprokh isn't around. I promise."

I touched the bracelet with my hand and said the words. It didn't feel as smooth as the times Peprokh brought us back there, but we made it to the tower. We quietly walked into his quarters and made our way to our room. The little one was more sleepy than hungry, so I took the lizards from the bed and left her under the bedding. I went to Peprokh's area and called for him a few times, but there was no response. I poked my head through the quilts and noticed that not only was he not there but that the new cage he brought onto the boat with him was also gone. I was going to go back to my room, but then I heard a sound off in the far corner.

I walked over and saw the cage he'd opened the previous night covered with empty sacks. I could almost hear Yilian's voice in the back of my mind saying, "Jonek, leave that thing where it is and get out of there!"

I should've done that, but as always, my curiosity made me pull those empty sacks to the side and open the small door on the top.

I quickly stepped back, waiting for something to jump out, but nothing did. I carefully walked closer and glanced inside, but it was way too dark to see anything.

I was reaching out to take a lamp from the wall when the cage rattled abruptly, almost tipping to the side. I hurried to close the door and threw all the sacks on top of it, bolting to my room and diving under the covers with the baby. I even covered my head with the bedding that time.

At first, I slept as deeply as always, but soon I was engulfed in an endless thread of nightmares. In the beginning they were horrible moments happening during or after a battle. Later, I saw countless faces of innocent people falling under the wrath of horrendous beasts. In the end, I saw myself lying in a large, muddy pit with two arrows stuck in my chest. Just when I felt like I was going to take my last breath, a small creature crawled out of the mud and bit my hand viciously.

That's the last thing I remember before waking up sweating, the little girl crying by my side. I lit the candle and comforted her in my arms. It took some time, but eventually she stopped crying.

"You must be hungry," I said as I searched the floor, looking for my boots.

It was only the two of us on the bed. All the lizards were piled in the corners with the usual two or three sleeping in my boots. That was odd, but I didn't have much time to think about it as Peprokh burst into the room a moment after.

"I'm glad you're up," he said breathlessly. "Both of you need to leave my quarters immediately. A very dangerous creature escaped from its cage, and I have to find it before it hurts or kills someone."

"But this girl hasn't eaten, and you need to take us to the market on the eastern shores. You haven't even let me tell you what I found out about her family yesterday."

"Buy milk for her in the market," he said dismissively. "You have enough coins."

"Actually, I used the gold coins to buy food for the Lost Whispers."

"You did *what?* These are times of war, and coins are scarce!" He shook his head. "Here's another one—use it carefully. We'll talk about this later. Now go!"

"But how am I supposed to get to the entrance of the castle?"

"Once you leave my quarters, touch your bracelet and say 'Barthenoz Old Hall.' We use that place to store old items. Make sure no one sees you as you leave, and this time, don't touch anything! Just make sure you're back before nightfall."

The old man barely gave me time to put some clothes on and grab my satchel. He pushed us out of his quarters, and this time, he filled the hole in the wall of the tower with bricks.

"I just hope it's not my fault that creature escaped," I said to the little girl, "although, I didn't see anything coming out of the cage last night."

***

We got out of that dusty hall full of books and parchments and waited for the right moment to merge with the flow of people leaving the castle toward the docks.

I asked around, and eventually we boarded a ship that took us to the docks on the southern shores. We were supposed to take another one from there to the eastern shores, but we heard some people at the docks talking about the great food they sold, so I bought milk for the little one and had a plate of a very strange dish made from mushrooms, spices, and eggs the size of my head. One thing I can say about the people from Zukreya—their bread is the best.

We were waiting for the boat to arrive when a man walked by us saying that a group of wagons would leave toward the eastern city of Celidhom and had room for twelve more. They were charging less than the boats, so I saw that as an opportunity to save some coins and see the landscape around the lake. We joined two families on the last wagon and left the city just before midday.

I will always remember the woman sitting nearby looking at us as if she couldn't comprehend how two younglings like us could be traveling alone between cities. "Our parents are waiting for us in Celidhom," I said to her. She never said a single word. She just pulled the little boy sitting on her lap close against her chest and offered me a brief look of sadness.

The road from the south shores to the eastern city is something I encourage you to travel if you ever have a chance. In those days, the rolling hills were covered with crops of all colors stretching all the way to the barrier. Children counted aloud the many bridges crossed when traveling that road. I tried myself, but I lost count.

Unfortunately, the landscape changed dramatically once we

approached the hills surrounding the city. Long lines of refugees slowed down our pace as they poured into areas on both sides of the road, where soldiers built rudimentary tents day and night to provide them with some shelter. Peprokh wasn't lying when he said that the situation in Kelfia was becoming as challenging as the war outside.

The wagons slowly made their way uphill, and as we passed between the trees crowning the hilltop, I was finally able to see the oldest and largest settlement around the lake. Maybe the others traveling with me were used to the majestic view, but for someone like me who'd never had the opportunity to visit a large city before, the experience was unforgettable.

The wagons left us at a street far away from the market, but I overheard some people traveling with us saying they were heading that way, so I ended up following them. At first, all we did was wander and try to see if we could find anyone selling spices, but there were too many. I had no choice but to start asking merchants if they knew an old lady with a blind bird. Most of them didn't answer or told me to stop wasting their time, but one finally pointed toward the far end of the street.

There she was, in a small tent full of baskets with powders and herbs all over the floor. The old woman was walking toward the back of the tent, but the red bird sitting on her shoulder turned around. Even though its eyes were covered by a tiny piece of cloth, it moved its head as if looking at us.

The woman slowly turned around and saw us standing there. I was careful to keep my distance as I stretched out my arm to give her the piece of parchment. She looked at it and quickly put it inside her clothes.

The bird suddenly flew toward me, stood on my shoulder, and then carefully hopped toward the little girl. I'm not sure why, but she wasn't afraid of it. She actually moved her hand closer and touched it, making its feathers turn white as salt. The bird flew back to the old woman, who looked at me.

"Come back here when the drums sound at three in the afternoon. Now go!"

That's all she said before walking away to help some customers.

We went back to a street that was less crowded and looked around for some more milk. Unfortunately, the closest place was quite far from there so I ended up buying a bowl of soup and gave a few spoonfuls to the little one. She actually liked it.

Drums, bells, horns—what else do they use to announce the time of the day in this world? I thought as I heard the drums in the distance pounding twice. In all this time in Kirolcan, I never saw a sundial or a water dropper like the ones keeping time in my world. *How do they even know what time of the day it is?* (I later learned that this was the sole responsibility of the "Time Keepers," a small group who observes the position of the moons and sun throughout the day to keep exact time across the land.)

We walked back just as the drums beat three times. The old woman was standing outside her tent and walked toward us. "Follow my bird," she said as she walked right past us.

Her bird turned blue and flew to a nearby tent to wait for us. He kept hopping from place to place until he took us to an alley full of empty cages. The bird guided us to the far end, where a small door stood partially open. The bird swooped in, but I honestly hesitated to walk into that dark place.

The door closed abruptly as soon as I entered. Someone took the girl from my arms, and a large man put a dagger to my neck. Too late for me to reach for my disk.

The only light in the room came from a hole in the roof. Someone took my satchel and emptied it on the floor under the light. The little one was crying loudly as the bird flew nervously all over the room.

The man holding the girl brought her into the light, and a young woman ran from the other end and took the little girl from him, lighting their faces vividly with a bright red glare.

"Mizjial! I thought I'd never see you again!" the woman said, her eyes filling with tears. "Where did you find her? Where is my sister?" she said, looking at me.

I couldn't really answer with the blade against my neck, so she called the man off. I landed on my knees and started scooping everything back in my satchel.

"The mother and her companions were attacked by the dark army in the mountains," I said as I wrapped the top of the sack closed again. "The mother was badly injured, but my friend kept her alive and hid her with a spell. She asked us to bring her daughter to Kelfia, so that's what we did. It took me a while to find you, by the way."

"What happened to the others traveling with her?"

"We saw three others, but they gave their lives to protect them."

The woman's face fell. "More than fifty started the journey with her," she said as she offered me her hand. My face glowed brightly as she touched me, and everyone in the room began to whisper.

"I don't understand—who are you?"

"Just another traveler. Your sister thought she was going to die, so she bonded this little girl with me before she was hidden."

"She bonded Mizjial with you? But you are just a boy."

"I don't know why, but she did. Believe me, I don't even know how to be a father. I never even knew mine."

"Well, somehow you have been taking good care of her. She looks healthy, even bigger since the last time I saw her."

I felt both happy and sad to see the little girl wrapping her arms around her aunt's neck. She was finally back with her family. It was time for us to go our separate ways.

"Does your skin burn when you're close to anyone from my clan?" she asked.

"Yes. I've met some already, and my face glows just as bright as yours."

"If you don't have Serthoz blood, my sister can make it stop with another spell. But your skin will always burn when you touch my niece. I trust you know by now that she will always love you. I'm not sure if she will ever see you as a father, but you will always live in her heart."

I clearly remember fighting back tears as I struggled to respond. ". . . my heart will always remember her too."

The little girl must have felt something; she stretched her arm toward me.

"You need to let us know where my sister is. We have to bring her back."

"You take care of your niece, and I'll bring your sister to Kelfia. It may take some time, but have no doubt that I'll do it."

"But you are just a child."

"Someone told me last night that the size and shape of your body can't really show who you are—only your actions can. Don't worry about me, just tell me how to find you."

"Stay here in the light. Don't move," she said as she stepped back into the shadows. All I heard was crates being dragged and things falling to the floor, then silence. I stood there calling out to the lady for some time, but no one responded. I pulled the disk out to pour water on it, but the armor appeared around me as soon as I put my

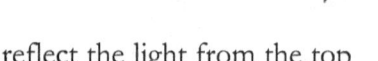
fingers in the holes. I used the shield to reflect the light from the top of the room only to confirm that I was alone in there.

I found my way back to the door and put the disk back in my satchel. Reaching the street, I merged with the people crowding the market.

She was gone. The beautiful little girl with green eyes was now back with her family. I wandered through the market lost in thought when the old woman's bird suddenly landed on my shoulder carrying a piece of parchment. I unfolded it to see some symbols unfamiliar to me, so I put it away and headed to the docks.

The boat left me back on the island, and I felt empty and alone. I was ready to go back to the tower, but I didn't want to be by myself. I touched my bracelet.

"Barthenoz Guardians Lair."

I appeared by the pool on the top floor, then walked down two levels.

"How are you, Jonek?" Kolikuj said as he rolled out from under a bench.

"It's been an interesting day, Kolikuj. Here, I want to show you something."

"What is it?"

"A parchment with symbols I don't understand. Maybe you can read them."

"I can try. Put it down and let me look at it."

I unfolded the parchment on the floor and Kolikuj rolled on top of it. "I can read it, but I don't know what it means. The symbol in the middle always tells you the main part of the message. This one says 'Dome of Trials.' On the left is Celidhom, and the one on the right is Philithoz. The three symbols below are 'Azthule Komgrothe,' the name of the large moon. The last two mean Satolgac and blue. This makes no sense—the cities of Philithoz and Celidhom are weeks away by horse and are very far away from each other." He rolled away from the parchment so I could pick it up.

"I don't know how long you've been sleeping, but nowadays there are settlements around Kelfia's lake where refugees from most major cities live. People from Celidhom settled on the eastern shores, Philithoz on the north. I think this message means there is a place in between those two settlements that is called the Dome of Trials."

"If that's true, then you are supposed to be there when the big moon shows up in the sky. Around midnight."

"Satolgac blue. What could that mean?" I asked.

"There are many myths about the Satolgac. I've even heard that their forefathers were created by the sages by striking a bull with lightning."

"Is the color blue something special for them?"

"I don't believe so, but I've seen some wearing dark blue cloaks."

"Maybe that's what it means. I need to wear a dark blue cloak to get in there."

The pebble rolled a few tumbles forward. "I know where to find one, but it might be too big for you."

Kolikuj took me to the other side of the hall and directed me to a large chest. I actually found two blue cloaks, but he was right—both were too big for me. I used a dagger to cut one and put the other one and the pieces back in the chest.

"Now my biggest problem is to find a way to get there tonight. I can take the last boat from the island this afternoon, but then I'll have to find a place to sleep out there."

"It would be easier if you can go out of the castle through the guardians' window and use your bracelet. Have you walked through the window before?"

"Not since I walked into Barthenoz the first time. But I'm not a guardian, what makes you think I would be able to open it?"

"A guardian shared his powers with you. You might be able to."

I pondered his words for a moment.

"Well, there's only one way to know . . ." I said as I picked him up.

I was thinking about the pendant in my pocket as we made our way there. Maybe I'd have better chances if I used it. I left Kolikuj on top of my satchel, loosened my leggings, and took my shirt off.

"What are you doing?"

"I'll wear this mark around my neck and see if the window will let me pass," I said as I showed him the pendant.

"Does it belong to the guardian who shared his powers with you?"

"No, it's not his. I don't really know whose mark this is, but it now carries his powers."

I put it on and my body morphed back to my older self. Then I turned toward the window and walked out onto the bridge of light.

"It worked!" I said, looking at the sun shining on the garden below. I walked back inside and put the pendant away.

"I remember using aging stones to change the way we looked as we crossed the Lost Path, but I've never heard of a guardian changing his appearance with a mark. That is powerful magic," Kolikuj said as he rolled down the satchel.

"I don't know how this works either, but it will surely help tonight. Now I just need to think about what I'll tell Peprokh."

I left Kolikuj in the top hall. I touched the bracelet and appeared at the tower just as Peprokh was casting a spell toward the opening. He walked a few steps down to where I was and glared at me.

"I don't like it, but you'll have to sleep in the Guardians Lair for the next few days. I haven't been able to find the beast, so I'm closing the opening to make sure nothing comes in or out."

"What kind of creature is it?"

"It's just a fat lizard."

"Like the ones I sleep with?"

"It's small, not even the size of my hand but deadlier than a hundred vipers. I've searched the rest of the castle, but now I have to cover the rest of the island. I'll even go to the mainland if needed." He paused. "Speaking of creatures, where is the smelly beast?"

"I have good news—I found the girl's aunt. She's with her now."

"Great! Some good news at last."

"There's one thing, though," I said carefully, the wheels in my brain turning hard. "She asked me to stay with her in Celidhom for a few nights until she gets used to her new family."

"I'm not sure about that. Rubzilet might not like having you out there without protection."

"I'll be fine," I said, trying to project confidence. "It's just for a few days, and I'll be back in Barthenoz every morning. I may need more coins, though."

The old steward mumbled as he gave me another pouch. "I want to see you every day around midday. Now go."

I touched the bracelet and went to the hall of scrolls to make him think I was going to take a boat to Celidhom, but then I touched it again to go directly to the Guardians Lair. I grabbed the blue cloak and put the pendant around my neck to cross the window.

"Wish me luck, Kolikuj. If the bracelet doesn't take me there, I'll have to rush down to the docks to catch the last boat to Celidhom."

I walked through the window and took off the pendant. I put on my shirt and cloak and touched the bracelet, saying, "Road between

Philithoz and Celidhom."

It was a rough ride. I felt my body bumping around hard until I landed in a field very close to a crossroad.

I wasn't sure if anybody saw me land, as there were still travelers walking and riding wagons both ways, so I casually got on my feet, patted the dust off my cloak, and approached the road. At first, I didn't know where to go, but I soon spotted a small group wearing cloaks walking away from the main road toward a hill.

I followed them until the night covered the sky. I was starting to think I never should've followed them, but my hesitation went away when we reached a small valley where the head of an enormous warrior statue was sticking out of the ground. It didn't have any openings around it, but everyone just disappeared as they walked into it.

Like the soldiers guarding the city portals, a large number of archers wearing black cloaks and masks aimed their arrows toward the statue, ready to dispose of any uninvited guests. I pulled the hood over my head and approached the torches. I saw the people in front of me disappearing into the statue, so I took a deep breath, closed my eyes, and kept walking.

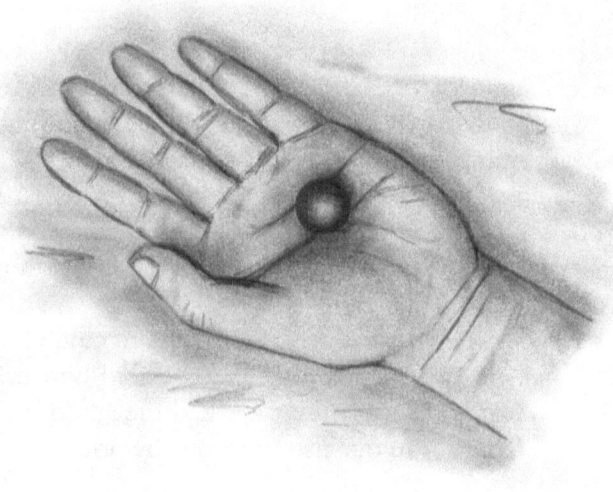

CHAPTER 13. THE DOME OF TRIALS.

If I would've kept my eyes open, I could've avoided bumping into the group in front of me. It was like walking into a Satolgac city. Everybody in there, young and old, was wrapped in long cloaks of all colors everywhere the eye could see.

Most of them uncovered their heads as they arrived, so I was able to admire—and sometimes get just a little startled by—the very unconventional ways people painted and shaped their hair and faces.

I assumed we were in an enormous cave, as everything was pitch black high above me, but it was hard to say, as glimpses of light could be seen here and there.

I followed a group into a crowded path that circled the entire cave. On both sides of it, merchants used every trick in their pockets to pull you closer and convince you to buy their goods—very much like Ferdhen's market. The only difference was that the vendors in there also offered all kinds of weapons and magical artifacts. Some even claimed to be selling guardians' weapons.

Approaching one of them, I saw no less than twenty wooden rods in all shapes and colors with intricate leather grips and straps wrapped in the middle. *These look even nicer than Kharlo's and Tynia's,* I admired as I picked one up and looked at it.

"Ah, you have a great eye," the merchant said as he walked closer. "I would've chosen that one myself. Crafted from a branch of a thousand-year-old Triklepo tree. Cut and carved only during twilight hours; go ahead, touch the grip." He paused. "Winter elk. There is nothing as soft and durable anywhere north of the eternal ice. You won't find a better weapon! And just because I have a feeling one day you'll become a great warrior, I'm willing to part ways with it . . . for just ten silver coins."

I glanced at the man and smiled. Somehow he reminded me of the way Da Klarismek negotiated with us when we sold him fish during the fair, only backwards. Klarismek always had the smoothest way of pointing out imperfections in our fish to lower the price.

"Is it real?"

"What do you mean, dear boy?"

"Could it be used as a weapon?"

"Absolutely! You can throw it and hit someone really hard with it."

"So, it's not a guardian's weapon."

The man took it from me and cleaned it with his robes. "Well, no. But it *could* be, if you ever become one." The man looked around to ensure no one was listening, then leaned in close. "Look, I don't really know how that works. I just make these to feed my family." He pointed at the woman sitting in one corner holding a baby in her arms.

"I can't give you ten, but I'll give you four silver coins for it."

The man narrowed his eyes at me as if he was trying to read my mind. "Five and it's yours," he said.

I gave him the coins and put the weapon in my satchel.

I kept visiting merchants until drums began to pound around the cave, one after the other. I followed the crowd away from the wall and briefly stopped at the top of some stairs. This is when I realized that I'd only been walking around the highest level. The actual Dome of Trials was a circular arena way down in the center.

I followed the crowd down and found a place to sit somewhere in the middle. The arena had columns and some other structures, but most of them were torn to pieces. There were countless weapons lying around—some new, some rusty and useless. It was easy to see that bricks had covered the entire arena at some point, but now most of it was sand.

A man walked to the center of the arena. He pulled his hood back and struck his staff on the sand. His voice echoed everywhere.

"Before the trials begin, all of you should know that Malok must be burning in rage tonight. The legion pushed the dark army all the way to the great rift this morning!" He paused. "Nine wizards burned, four captured, and half of the dark army's beasts and soldiers ended up at the bottom of the rift. Kelfia's warriors took care of the rest." The crowd roared, and I had to cover my ears. "Unfortunately," the man shouted, quelling the noise, "this wasn't without sacrifice. Some of our brothers gave up everything so we could achieve victory today."

The man put one knee on the sand and rested his forehead on his staff, conjuring the faces of the fallen, one by one, high above the middle of the arena. There were ten or twelve boys and girls among them.

The man stood up. "Remember! We, the ones that know, must honor them every time we witness a new morning, feel the touch of a loved one, or are blessed with the briefest sound of life." The man pointed his staff at the crowd around the arena, making tiny white petals rain on us. "Are you ready for the trials?" He yelled, raising his arms and making the audience roar. "You know the rules. Fifty gold coins to whoever defeats three warriors in a row. Use any weapons you like and fight any way you want. Just remember—you take a life, we take yours."

The man turned around and walked out of the arena.

***

The first warrior was a very strong-looking man. He walked to the middle of the arena and climbed on top of a large piece of column, waiting for a challenger from the audience. A man sitting fairly close to me left his seat and jumped in. He picked up a sword and fought valiantly, but the warrior was superior. At the other side of the arena, a woman jumped in and crossed the edge of the circle. She looked harmless, but suddenly she invoked a spell that threw up a cloud of sand around the warrior. She quickly ran behind him and hit him in the head with a club.

The warrior was dragged out of the arena, and then a boy walked in. This one cast a spell that dazzled the woman (and most of us). When we opened our eyes, there was an enormous bear reared up in front of the woman, paw already flying toward her face. She tried to move backward, but the boy had already tied her feet with vines and she tumbled to the ground. She was also dragged out of the arena.

Many others jumped in looking for gold and glory. Some fought in ways I was familiar with, but most used weapons and magic like I'd never seen before. They were very good, but none of them were able to defeat three in a row. I have to admit that I enjoyed the trials almost as much as I liked watching the Vothras.

It wasn't until an old man cast a spell that blasted flames in all directions that I realized why it was called the "Dome of Trials." Both the old man and the female warrior in the ring were severely burned, but the flames never reached the audience—they simply bounced off the edge of an invisible dome around the circle.

Eventually a boy whose face was covered with green paint and leaves was able to defeat three warriors, one after the other, by summoning dreadful beasts to attack them. The creatures weren't real, but their appearance was so terrifying that the warriors were distracted long enough for the boy to immobilize them in ice.

The man who had opened the trials walked into the arena and gave the boy a bag with the gold coins. He announced that the next trial would take place in four days and asked for everyone who fought in the arena that night to follow him.

"They're taking them to see Hokdhanet!" a man sitting behind me remarked to his friend.

I turned around and looked at him. "So the person who gave out the coins isn't Hokdhanet?" I asked.

The man smiled. "Hokdhanet rarely attends the trials. I think I've seen him two or three times since I came to Kelfia."

"What does he look like? Is he a boy?"

"I am fairly sure he's not a boy. He is tall, but I wouldn't know what he looks like. Very few have seen his face, because he always has something wrapped around his head or uses a helmet." The man stood to follow the rest to the highest level. "But you can't miss him—he carries his staff around his neck most of the time."

"What do you mean?"

"His staff is made of wood, but it behaves like a snake."

Those words made me remember how the sword of that Zerkial witch moved like a snake when she hit my shield at the north gate.

I followed everyone to the upper level. The merchants were making their last efforts to sell their goods, so I stopped here and there to see what other wonders were for sale. I was looking at a table full of colorful frogs when I heard a familiar voice behind me.

"Don't turn around, just keep looking at the frogs." She paused. "Mizjial didn't sleep well last night. She misses you."

"I miss her too. How is she doing? Is she eating well?"

"You even sound like a father. It'll take some time, but she'll do fine. I have to go now, but if you ever need to see me, we will meet here in front of this merchant at the end of the trials. Just one thing— I'll only stop by your side if you're wearing a blue cloak. Do you understand?"

"I do, but when can I see the little girl?"

"Soon. Stay safe, and remember your promise. My sister is still out there."

"Don't worry. I will bring—"

"Bring who?" said a man standing nearby. I turned around, but she was already gone.

I walked off toward the exit and noticed that everyone was taking a

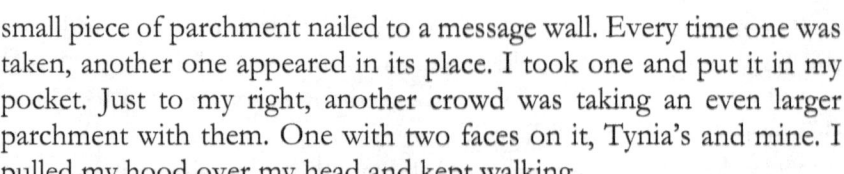

small piece of parchment nailed to a message wall. Every time one was taken, another one appeared in its place. I took one and put it in my pocket. Just to my right, another crowd was taking an even larger parchment with them. One with two faces on it, Tynia's and mine. I pulled my hood over my head and kept walking.

There were four or five lines disappearing into the feet of the statue whose head I'd entered earlier. This time, I didn't hesitate to walk into it and appear back in the valley between Philithoz and Celidhom. I followed the trail with less people and then ventured into the woods until I was sure I was alone.

"Guardians Garden," I said, touching the bracelet.

Traveling far is quite rough. I rolled into a bush between two pedestals in the garden, and it hurt just as much as my fall the night our horse ran wild on the bridge. I got to my feet and looked up. There was no staircase or bridge. I took my shirt off and loosened my leggings, then put the pendant on.

I touched each one of the pedestals with the pendant, my hands, my forehead, and even my feet, but nothing made the staircase and bridge appear. All I could do was spend the night in the garden and wait until the soldiers opened the doors in the morning.

I kept the pendant around my neck but covered myself with the cloak, then sat on my shirt with my back against one of the pedestals.

Watching the moons traveling the sky reminded me of the night I pulled my bag from the river. I had nothing to lose, so I took the disk from my satchel and touched the pedestal above my head. I didn't even turn around to look at it, just kept my eyes on the bricks, waiting for the staircase to appear. No luck. I opened the satchel to put the disk back in and felt the rod I'd bought at the trials. I took it out and wondered. "Why not?" I said as I touched the pedestal with it. Nothing.

I exhaled in frustration and rested my head back on the pedestal. I closed my eyes and passed my fingers over the rod, exploring every part of it. The merchant was right about one thing, its grip was as soft as flower petals.

I don't know when, but at some point I fell asleep.

The grass poking my face made me open my eyes. I lifted my head, and there I was again—lying on the top of a hill moments before sunset. The symbol with circles and a triangle glowed brightly by my little finger and the disk was still there, stuck in the ground in front of me.

Dream or not, I pulled myself forward, put my fingers in the disk, and pulled it out of the ground.

Armor of light and a shield appeared around my body as I rolled to look up. I remember seeing the sky through the shield, but there was something different. The symbol was glowing on the shield too. It didn't last long, though. A silver axe crashed into the shield, and sparks rained everywhere.

It happened so fast that it's hard to describe, but I do remember that the one holding the axe was wearing dark clothes. He slowly circled me, but then a shadow jumped from one side, tackling the man to the ground.

I passed my right hand over the grass until my fingers touched the grip of a rod. I raised it above me and it illuminated my surroundings as a short sword and a thin axe appeared on each end.

Everything went black.

I was lying on my back, my hand holding the weapon above me, but I was back at the Guardians Garden. There was no axe or sword, just the wooden rod.

I lowered my hand and looked up. It was still night, but there was now something that wasn't there before—the staircase and bridge. I looked around, but nobody was there.

I didn't know who made the staircase and bridge appear, but I didn't hesitate to grab my satchel and run up to the window. I walked into the lair, put the pendant in my bag and hid it with the cloak inside a chest. I quickly found a place to sleep and closed my eyes. I was thankful I didn't have any more dreams.

The sound of a bell and a voice woke me up at first light the following morning.

"Wake up, Jonek!"

I soon realized it wasn't a bell, though. Kolikuj was rolling in and out of a silver cup right by my head.

"You may be a boy, but you sure snored like a bear last night. I thought maybe beasts were attacking us! Tell me, how did it go in this Dome of Trials?"

I reluctantly opened my eyes, only to close them again to avoid the glare on the windows.

"Wait!" I said, jumping to my feet. "This is one of the first sunrises I've seen in this world. The windows in Peprokh's quarters are always closed so I can't miss this opportunity." I opened the chest and looked for my ramikha in my satchel. Walking to the closest window, I held it out under the first light of day.

"Why are you doing that?" Kolikuj said as he rolled closer to me.

"It's just something I've done since that old woman gave this to me. She said I should feed it with the light of sunrise whenever I can so the sounds it makes remain true to my heart."

"Well? Are you done? I want to know about this Dome of Trials."

***

I shared every detail of my ordeal with Kolikuj. He told me that the parchment I took from the wall said that the next Dome of Trials would take place in four days, and the entrance would be somewhere around the south spring. He was also very surprised to hear about what happened to me in the garden the previous night.

"I forgot about the staircase. You can only make it appear using a guardian's weapon. Let me see that rod you bought at the trials."

I placed the weapon on the floor. Kolikuj was rolling around it when I heard Peprokh's voice on the other side of the hall.

"Are you here, boy? You'd better not be touching anything!"

I walked to the other side, stretching and yawning as if I'd just woken up. I told him that I ended up not going to Celidhom the previous night, but I would have to go that day. He looked distressed. He'd probably realized that I'd seen Kharlo's window by now so he told me that sometimes those windows behaved like that for no reason. True or not, he did share with me that he was getting worried about Kharlo's Jiretal spell running out. He still hadn't heard from Tynia, so he was going to try to talk to Rubzilet that morning.

I asked him if he had found that dangerous creature he was looking for, but the man just huffed and left me standing there, puttering off with a shake of his head. I walked back to the other side and sat on the floor by the weapon and Kolikuj.

"Jonek, this is a real guardian's weapon. Look at the symbol by the grip."

I picked it up and took it closer to the sunlight streaming in from the window. It didn't make sense. The mark that Peprokh pulled out the water, the one Tynia hid in the little girl's clothes, the symbol that burned on my hand in those dreams—it was now carefully carved onto that weapon. A weapon that cost me five silver coins.

"The mark is there, but how do we know if it's real?" I said, walking back to Kolikuj.

"You can put the pendant on and try to use it, but there is better way to know for sure. Pick me up and take me to the pedestal with the golden bowl. Bring the mark too."

He asked me to put the pendant on, so I took my shirt off.

"Put the weapon in the golden water. Make sure it goes all the way in."

"I don't want to touch that odd liquid."

"Don't be scared. Unless you have plenty of dark mist flowing through your veins, it won't do anything to you."

"What's going to happen if the weapon isn't real?"

"If it's a real weapon, it will float back to the surface. If it isn't—well, we just won't see it again, and you'll lose your five coins."

I kept Kolikuj in my hand and submerged the weapon. I pulled my hand out and waited. Suddenly, the golden waves crashing on the walls of the bowl subsided and the entire surface remained flat as a mirror.

Not even Kolikuj understood what was happening. The weapon floated back to the surface, but instead of wood, it looked as it was made of gold.

"Look at the mark!" he said.

The symbol on the rod was changing so rapidly that it was impossible to identify. I instinctively stepped back and looked at the pedestal. Every symbol around it was being illuminated one at a time. Once it went through all the symbols, the mark on the weapon stood still, showing the circles and triangle.

"What did that guardian put inside of you?" Kolikuj said breathlessly.

"I don't know." I stared at the golden rod.

"Take the weapon. Let's see if it works."

I reached out to take it, but the rod suddenly vanished into the liquid, and the waves began to storm the surface again.

I stood there like a statue and Kolikuj didn't make a sound. Suddenly, we heard a loud sound coming from the staircase in the floor. I rushed down to the hall below and looked in the bowl. There it was.

The golden fluid was now frozen, and the rod was lying on top of it, its symbol changing rapidly again. It didn't take long for all the marks around the pedestal to glow on the weapon.

One by one, the weapon traveled from floor to floor until it reached the bowl on the seventh (and lowest) level. Finally, the original symbol on the weapon stood still, but I hesitated to take it. We waited, but this time the weapon remained on the surface.

Kolikuj moved in my hand. "Now you have the answer to that question you asked when you walked down to my hall the first time. There are seven halls in this lair, and I've counted five hundred and twelve windows with moving images so far."

"Five hundred guardians?"

"Yes. It's hard to believe, but the quest to defeat Sulibhor is as old as time itself."

"Still, five hundred is way too many."

"Unfortunately, many didn't last long in the beginning. It wasn't until the last five or six thousand years that we started earning significant victories against him. Go ahead, take the weapon." The rod turned into wood the moment I took it out of the bowl, but the symbol glowed golden a bit longer. "Let's see," the pebble said, "try a sword."

I swung the weapon and it changed into many different swords as I sliced through the air.

"Amazing! It's like it's trying to see which weapon is best. Now let's try a bow."

I stood still. "Kolikuj, I'll be honest with you. I've had a hard time using Kharlo's weapon. I couldn't make it change as quickly as I wanted."

"Well, you need someone to train you. Guardians don't have a Dome of Trials, but we have a dungeon. Touch the edge of this bowl with the sword."

I did as he asked, and we appeared in a small room in front of an old door with a rusty ring hanging in the middle. The only light came from the top and was illuminating a pedestal and a bowl right behind us, similar to the one I'd just touched.

"Before you walk through this door, you must hear the words said to all guardians the first time. 'Your choices should always protect those with light in their hearts. Don't let your eyes and ears deceive you.' " He paused. "Now, open the door."

I pulled the ring and the door creaked menacingly as it pushed away the dust piled on the floor. On the other side, a long hallway loomed cold and quiet, and torches illuminated every other door on each side.

"Usually, you'd have two or three elders walking with you through the dungeon. I'll try my best to guide you, but not knowing how warrior guardians train, don't feel bad if we fail many times."

I paused. "Could you teach me how to defeat others without killing them? That way I could fight in the Dome of Trials, and win gold for the Lost Whispers."

"What are the Lost Whispers?"

"Children who have lost their families in the war. They need food."

Kolikuj hesitated to answer. "That's not how this works. Most of what you'll learn in here could harm or take the life of someone. You'll have to follow your instincts and use these skills wisely." He paused. "But you will have one advantage."

"What's that?"

"I am a wizard. I can teach you spells that a warrior or an elemental guardian will never be taught. That might help you in the trials."

"What's an elemental guardian?"

"Those guardians have very different skills. I'll tell you more as we go. Now, do you see these doors? There are men, beasts, wizards, and all kinds of enemies waiting to fight you—or stand ready to hurt others. You are the only one who can save them. Some foes will be beaten by weapons, some with magic, but there will be a few that you'll just have to outwit. The most important skill you'll ever learn is to quickly decide the best way to deal with them—don't be surprised to hear that sometimes the best option is to flee. Now let's open the first door."

***

For the next two days, all I did was learn spells, summon weapons, and heal cuts and bruises in the Guardians Pool. It felt amazing casting magic for the first time. It's hard to control, especially when you have to cast it for long periods of time, but it is certainly a powerful ally in battle.

"The trials will be tomorrow night, and I need to wear the pendant to use this weapon. How am I going to hide my face so they don't recognize me from all those parchments posted everywhere?"

Kolikuj rolled closer. "You'll have to wear different clothes, and I was thinking you could spread mud on your face and neck. There's a pond in a hall four levels down that has some. Let's go there and try it."

I picked him up and walked down. It was somewhat surreal to see a pond surrounded by trees, shrubs, and bushes inside a hall. I took my boots and shirt off, then walked around the edge of the water looking for soft mud. When I felt some squish between my toes, I scooped up a little and put it on my forehead.

"What is that!" Kolikuj yelped as he rolled closer to the water.

"What is what?"

"That thing on your skin!"

I sucked in a breath. "Where? What are you talking about?" I leapt out of the mud and looked all over my arms and chest.

"There! It's moving to your back!"

I touched my side, smearing some mud on it, and saw something crossing my belly from side to side. It wasn't on me, it was *in* me. I won't lie—I shrieked.

"What is it?" I asked desperately.

"I'm not sure. It looks like a small dragon!"

"A dragon?"

"Well, not exactly, but it does have a long tail. Whatever it is, it doesn't like the mud. Try to trap it."

"Trap it? This thing is in my skin! What if he gets angry?"

"He might bite you, but he may also choose to get out."

I didn't like his answer but I also didn't have a choice. I sat by the edge of the water and put mud on my legs and inside my leggings. I put my back on the mud and then rubbed more on my neck, arms, and sides. Mostly by accident, I ended up trapping the creature inside a circle of mud around my chest and belly.

I never felt anything. My skin didn't even move, but the shape and colors of the thing raced furiously between the walls of mud. Maybe it was my desperation or just the honesty of my plea, but I never thought the beast would listen.

"Please stop!"

The shape and colors slowed down until I was able to see a wide-bodied lizard with a long tail panting heavily, tongue sticking out of its mouth. It was exhausted. Sitting still, it looked very much like the painted beasts Peprokh had all over his back.

"Oh no—this must be the dangerous lizard that Peprokh is looking for!"

"Other than the tip of his tail looking like a fiery arrowhead, this creature doesn't seem evil to me," Kolikuj said as he rolled closer.

"It may not look evil, but what is it doing inside me?"

The lizard stared at me, and my hand suddenly moved closer to the mud and began to write on it using a finger. I couldn't stop it, even though I was fighting with all my strength. The marks read, "Going home. No harm." —in my language.

"Are you going home? Is that what you mean?"

The lizard nodded.

"What do you mean by 'no harm'? That you won't harm me, or that you don't want me to harm you? I hope it's the first." He nodded again. "Why are you running away from Peprokh?"

My hand erased the words in the mud and wrote four more.

"Wizard took from family."

"Peprokh separated you from your family? Where are they?"

"North. Beyond barrier."

"So you want to get out of Kelfia. Why can't you go on your own?"

"Wizard finds."

"So he can't find you if you are in me." I moved Kolikuj back to dry ground as I wondered what to do. The lizard even looked timid as he waited for my response.

"I didn't like the way Peprokh treated you the other night. I'll take you with me when I leave Kelfia, but it might take a few more days. Just promise you won't harm any part of my body."

"Promise no harm. Help."

"Help? How?"

The lizard put his tail in his mouth, and I was forced to close my eyes. Somehow, the lizard made me see myself walking back to the top hall and cleaning my body in the pool. When I opened my eyes, the lizard was staring at me waving its tail.

"I think the lizard wants me to get in the pool to clean my body," I said, looking at Kolikuj.

"What makes you say that?"

"I just saw myself doing it."

I picked up Kolikuj and my clothes and went to the pool in the top hall. Once I got rid of the mud, I sat on a bench and put my leggings on.

Kolikuj rolled up to my feet. "Well, now that you're clean, tell me again how we're going to disguise your face?"

"Right," I mumbled. "I need the mud, but the lizard can't have it."

The lizard put his tail back in his mouth and made me see myself walking in front of a mirror nearby. "Hang on; he wants me to stand in front of that mirror."

I walked over to it and kept Kolikuj in my hand as I saw the lizard moving from my belly all the way up to my face. He moved around a few times and began to change the appearance of my face.

I can't even describe how strange it was to see my forehead, chin, and nose grow wider. Then my hair shrunk so short I could even see the skin on my head. The thick eyebrows were a nice addition, but then he made the skin around my head and neck turn dark red, as if I'd spent all my life living in the desert. Once he finished, he made the rest of his body disappear. My face was unrecognizable.

"Well, that'll work," Kolikuj said. "Your face is now as red as your stung-up hand. By the way, you may want to wear gloves so nobody sees that your right hand isn't red." I nodded. "Now, we just have to keep practicing how to keep your weapon from changing. If you use your staff like I taught you yesterday, you won't need anything else. We'd better get back to the dungeon—there is still much to do."

"Just let me eat something. I'm starving," I said.

"My apologies. It's been so long since I had a piece of bread in my mouth that I keep forgetting you need food to survive." Kolikuj paused. "I have an idea. Why don't you go to the castle grounds and buy something to eat at the market, but do it just as you look right now. Let's see if someone can recognize you from the parchments. If someone does, just rush inside the castle and use your bracelet to come back here. I'll wait for you by the pedestal."

I hesitated, but then I realized it was a good idea. Better to be recognized now by one person when I wasn't the center of attention. I took a pair of gloves and touched the bracelet. Once in the hall of scrolls, I put the gloves on and headed to the market.

I walked around for a while, but other than the merchants pushing me to buy something from them, no one really had much interest in me. I ate a nice plate of boar and potatoes and a handful of berries. I was heading out of the grounds when I saw a maybe a dozen young men pushing each other as they ran away from soldiers and a few old ladies rushing behind them.

Petty thieves, I thought as the soldiers surrounded them.

But then I noticed two things that gave me pause. First, none of the young men had anything in their hands, and two, one of the old ladies was pointing at me.

Great. Now they think I'm a thief just because of the way I look, I grimaced.

The soldiers quickly surrounded me. "Show me your hand!" one said. My heart started to beat hard in my chest as I thought about the different color of my hands. But lucky for me, he pointed at my left hand. "Take your glove off! Do it now!" Another soldier said.

I showed them my hand, and one of them poured some liquid on it. They waited for a moment and then pulled me in with the others.

I didn't understand what was going on, but I also didn't want to say much. Other young men joined us where we were, a few walking quietly on their own, others being pushed by soldiers or some elderly women holding sticks.

This must be an entire guild of thieves, I thought.

They made us walk beyond the outer wall and then into the hills to the southwest. Most men looked worried, and some even cried as we began to go uphill.

"They aren't taking us to the cells in the guardhouse. Are they going to execute us?" I asked a young man walking by my side.

"It's worse than that," he sniffled. "And I'm not even twenty-two."

"But why? What did we do wrong?"

"I guess it's our time."

I tried to ask something to a soldier nearby, but he just pushed me back in line. Turning around, I caught sight of the group of old ladies walking behind the last soldiers, all of them holding those long sticks in their hands.

What did these men do to those ladies? I cringed to think about the possibilities.

We formed a single line as we reached the top of the only hills on the island. I had no idea what they would do to us, but I was thinking that they would probably make us jump from the top of the cliffs— what a horrible way to die. My only plan was to touch the bracelet and appear by the Guardians Garden once I was in the air.

Two old ladies waiting at the top gave us a purple leaf as big as my hand as we reached the edge—not of the cliffs, but of a spring. This beautiful pond nestled in the hills fed the only creek on the island. The water left the basin, gliding gracefully over the hills and into the waterways of the castle, eventually reaching the lake somewhere west of the docks.

Many in front of me were cutting small branches or picking up thin sticks before sitting down by the edge of the pond. I saw the man I had been walking with nearby, so I sat by his side.

"What is this? What are we doing here?"

"I told you already. They think it's our time. To find a wife."

"A wife!" I exclaimed.

He quickly motioned me to lower my voice. "I know! It's worse than death. I was able to hide last season, but I couldn't this time. These old ladies keep track of every man, and they start hunting you when you reach twenty—if you're unmarried and aren't a soldier, of course."

I looked around and saw others crying quietly as they used the branch or a small stick to write something on their leaves.

"What do we do with the leaf?"

He glanced at me and kept writing on his. "You must be new in Kelfia. When did you leave Minojeb?"

"How do you know I'm from Minojeb?" I bluffed.

"Your skin. It's burned so badly, you must be from that area." He put his hand on my shoulder and looked at me. "My friend, you fled from the war to avoid being made a slave only to meet your real master—a wife—maybe even tonight."

"Tonight? What do you mean?"

"I'll tell you everything, but first, put the leaf on the palm of your hand and use something to write your name on it. Just don't move it— do it softly so you don't tear the leaf. Hurry up! They're watching us."

"Who?"

"Look beyond the edge of the pond."

I got on my feet to cut a small branch from the bush behind us and glanced over it. Elderly ladies marched like soldiers beyond the bushes surrounding the pond, keeping an eye on each one of us.

"Write your name as I told you!" he whispered as he pulled me down. "Your name will stay on your hand until one of these ladies erases it with a potion. Don't even bother trying to clean it off yourself—only they can do it. Once you're done, put the leaf on the ground and draw or write anything you want around your name so it looks decorated."

I didn't know how to write in their language, so all I did was draw the same symbol I drew for my initiation. I peeled the leaf off my hand and then drew anything that crossed my mind on it—a cloud, the moon, my ramikha, and even a bow and arrow.

 264

The horns sounded by the castle, announcing it was an hour before midday. Everyone took a small flower or just a few petals from the many varieties around the pond and began to walk into the water. Once they passed the belt of plants floating by the edge, they carefully placed the leaves on the surface. I was surprised to see those strange purple leaves curving their sides upward and their stems downward into the water, making them look like tiny boats without sails.

Everyone put their flowers or petals on their leaves and released them so the current could take them downstream.

I took three petals of different colors and walked into the water. I did feel the lizard moving briefly on my face when my feet touched the mud around the pond, but he calmed down as the water reached my waist. I looked back and saw two older women following everything I did, so I left my leaf on the surface, placed the petals on it, and let it go.

"That's it. The only two things that can save us now are if no woman chooses our leaf, or if she decides to break up the courtship before the marriage," said the man I was talking to.

He explained to me, as we walked down the hills, that women would gather at midday in the south gardens and walk into the pond one by one, look at the leaves, and choose one if they liked it. If they did, they would come back to the gardens at night to meet the man whose name was on the leaf. If she liked him and wanted to start the courtship, then the man must agree.

"But what if the man doesn't like the woman?" I asked.

"Men can break the courtship. But you are only allowed to do it once in your lifetime. So if you like the second one even less, bad luck. These old ladies keep track of everyone."

"This doesn't seem fair. Nobody can force us to like someone we don't."

"I know, but this war has made it difficult for women to find husbands and raise a family. Some say we are less than half of the population that used to roam this world three thousand years ago."

"So what am I supposed to do now?" I asked.

"We'll have to go to the south gardens tonight. If we're lucky, our leaves will still be in the water. If they aren't, then we'll have to wait for the women to walk into the gardens sometime around midnight so we can meet our future wives."

"But how would they know who we are?"

"Your name on your hand will glow under the moonlight. You're supposed to show your hand to any woman who walks near you. If you are who she's looking for, she'll take your hand and you will go someplace nearby to talk and get to know each other. You'd better be there. If a woman chooses your leaf and she can't find you, the elderly women and soldiers surely will. Remember, they are the only ones who can erase your name from your hand. And even so, they have a potion that shows if your name has ever been on it. As I've told you, they keep track of everyone."

The man wished me farewell and I quickly made my way back to the Guardians Lair.

"You can move away from my face now, Arrowtail," I said to the lizard as I left my boots and shirt by the edge of the pool. I took the pendant off, jumped in and stayed underwater as long as I could. I didn't look at it, but I kept rubbing the palm of my hand until I walked out of the pool and sat on the floor.

"Arrowtail? Is that what you're calling that creature now?" Kolikuj said as he rolled closer to me.

"Well, I don't know his name, and the tip of his tail sure looks like an arrow to me."

"What's wrong? Did someone recognize you?"

"No, but I have bigger problems now," I said, showing him the symbol on the palm of my hand. "I was hoping the waters of the pool might get rid of it, but they didn't."

"What is that?"

I shared with him everything that young man told me. Kolikuj was very surprised to hear there was such a ritual taking place in Kelfia. He rolled over the purple lines on my hand, then stood still.

"Jonek, I know we just met a few days ago, but someone has to tell you this—first you reach Kelfia carrying a daughter, now you might end up with a wife. You're doing things backwards!"

I chuckled. "I know. And I'm not even thirteen!" I said as I rested my head on the floor. "Just wait until my mother finds out. It might be best if I stay in this world."

"Well, there's no way around it. You'll have to follow this ritual, and if some poor woman made the mistake of choosing your leaf and wants to start the courtship, you'll have to be the one breaking it."

Kolikuj knew I was worried, so he made me train hard in the dungeon in order to forget about my problems for a while. It was late in the afternoon when I cleaned up, changed my clothes, and asked Arrowtail to change my face again.

"Remember to keep the glove on your right hand so no one notices that it isn't red," Kolikuj said as I watched the night eat up the light in the windows.

"I'd rather fight beasts with my bare hands than break the heart of a woman," I said as I pulled my hood over my head.

Kolikuj rolled closer. "I know what you mean, but it's best for you to know that sometimes you'll end up breaking a heart without even knowing it. Keep in mind that it could be far worse to let a grown woman fall in love with a boy who's not even thirteen."

"Wish me luck," I said before I walked through the window.

I went down into the Guardians Garden and hid my weapon in a thorny bush nearby. I made my way around the castle and into the south gardens. Most of the men I had walked with that morning were already there. A few roamed the pathways nervously, and others sat quietly on the many benches around the garden. But a large number of them were crowding together on one of the bridges at the far end. My instincts told me I should join them.

It was challenging to get closer at first, but once some of them left the bridge, I was able to look down and see five leaves floating on the surface. The markings on them glowed brightly under the light of the first moon, so there was no confusion who they belonged to.

My heart filled with joy when I saw mine floating bashfully off to one side.

Probably no women understood my symbols. Or maybe they thought I wasn't right in the head, I imagined.

I can't describe the great sense of relief I felt as I walked away from the bridge. I knew I had to stay until the ritual ended, but now I had nothing to worry about. The women began to walk into the garden, so the men raised their hands to them. No words were exchanged until both confirmed that the symbols on the leaf and hand matched.

Most of the couples separated from the main group and sat on benches or just kept walking as they talked, but there were a few who got lost in the immensity of the garden after a while.

I glanced at their faces whenever I could, trying to read if those first moments together brought them happiness or not. Honestly, it was hard to tell. I saw a few women who seemed to be the ones suffering because of their choice.

As time passed, I was very curious to see if the man I talked to that morning ended up with someone, so I searched for him. As I walked by the entrance, I learned that once a couple agreed to start the courtship, the woman presented the man to the elderly women as they left the gardens. The elderly women wrote their names in a book and then poured a potion on the man's hand to erase their markings.

"But what happens to the ones who still have their leaves floating in the pond? Should we bring them to the entrance so they can pour the potion on our hands?" I wondered.

I was pondering those questions when I saw the man I was looking for walking with a woman by the edge of the pond. One thing was for sure—I wasn't going to leave the gardens without seeing the face of the woman who'd snagged him.

I quietly made my way along a pathway behind a line of tall bushes, but even though there were many lamps floating throughout the entire garden, I didn't notice two steps going down in the middle of the path. All I remember is a brief moment when my body was in the air, and then when I hit the bricks. Even Arrowtail bounced across in my face, changing it briefly as I hit the edge of the grass.

"Are you alright?" a voice said nearby. Everything was still swirling around me, but I shakily looked up to see the shadow of a person standing by my side. "Can you hear me? Are you hurt?"

"I'm fine, I just need a moment." I grabbed my head, taking a deep breath and keeping my gaze on the ground to steady myself. "I didn't see the steps. I'll be on my way now," I said as I slowly stood.

"You're supposed to show me your hand," the voice said. I froze.

"I'm . . . deeply sorry," I said as I raised my hand.

Maybe it was the darkness, but somehow the symbol on my hand illuminated that woman far more brightly, allowing me to see the tip of her nose peeking out of her yellow hood.

"That symbol on your hand. What does it mean?" she asked.

I knew I couldn't say much, but I also felt that lying wasn't the right thing to do. "It's just something I drew on the ground a few years ago."

"Does it mean anything? Is that your name?"

"It's just a symbol I use to identify me. My real name is—"

"No, please don't tell me your name! I just wanted to know what all these symbols mean," she said as she took her hands out of her cloak, allowing the moonlight to fall on my leaf.

I can't even describe what that felt like. I was fairly sure I saw my leaf floating on the pond earlier that night. I was free. But for reasons I couldn't fathom, I was now back in the same quandary I'd endured all day.

"I was late to the ritual, so I chose your leaf just moments ago. Please follow me—I know a place where we can talk." She made her way through a gap in the bush line, motioning for me to follow.

"Where are we going?" I asked as I pushed the plants away from my face.

"Lower your voice. We're almost there."

There was a small opening in the wall hidden behind the plants. We crawled into it and emerged in another garden to the east. Water flowed from the south garden into this one, but the pond in there was smaller.

"Where are we? What if the guards see us?"

The woman chuckled briefly. "There are no guards in here. No one can enter this garden."

"How do you know?"

"My father takes care of these gardens. My ancestors have worked for the royal family for a very long time. I know every tree, plant, and bench in here. When I was six, I planted my first flower right over there, on the other side of the water."

She asked me to sit on one of the benches around the pond. I didn't do much after that other than watch her walking back and forth, as if there was something really troubling her. The first thing that crossed my mind was that she didn't like me. Maybe she was expecting someone more handsome (or less clumsy).

Eventually, she stopped. "Tell me something about you," she asked.

"What do you want to know?"

"Anything. Do you have a family?"

I didn't know what to say, but then I thought that if I just answered as the boy I was, she would most certainly become discouraged and stop the courtship.

"Just my mother and I. I never knew my father; but I do have a few friends that I see as brothers."

"Why? What makes you see them as brothers?"

"Well, one of them is great at buying and selling anything. He can even convince you to buy the clothes you're wearing right now from him." She chuckled at my humor. "The other one has a great memory and can tell you stories day and night, especially if you ask him for

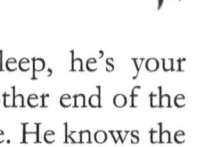
some involving wizards and magic. If you can't sleep, he's your answer." The woman kept giggling as she sat at the other end of the bench. I continued, "The last one is in love with nature. He knows the name of every plant and creature that crosses his path. I saw him talking to a spider once and thought he had some contagious illness. That's the only time I took three baths on the same day."

The woman laughed merrily.

"We are very different," I went on, "but we hunt, fish, fight, and protect each other, like brothers."

"You have very interesting friends. What about you? How do you think they see you?" she said.

"I don't know. I believe some of them think I'm somewhat reckless. Some days I'm the leader, other times just the stubborn one."

"Are they still in Minojeb?"

I paused. "They are very far away. I just hope they're doing fine right now." I glanced at the moons traveling the sky.

"What is love for you?" she asked softly.

"I don't know. I always thought love was just a word older people use to explain why they're together."

The woman left my leaf on the bench. "I was told once that love is like a flow of warm water that rises through your body when someone touches your heart. It drowns your mind and could even burst through your eyes," she said.

"Then it might be best if I don't touch your heart. I wouldn't want to see warm water pouring out of you."

She chuckled again and traced the edge of my leaf with her finger. "Don't worry—I won't make you continue the courtship. I apologize if you were ready to find a wife. I just can't marry you."

I didn't know what to say. One side of me was screaming in happiness knowing I wasn't the one breaking the courtship. But the other side was truly wondering what the story behind this woman was.

"I'm sorry that I wasn't what you expected," I said.

"No. Don't be. I think these few moments with you have been the best I've had in a long time." The woman put her hands inside her cloak.

"Why don't you share it with me?" I asked.

"What do you mean?"

"The great sorrow you harbor inside. You and I may never be destined to be husband and wife, but that doesn't mean we can't become friends. Please trust me."

She couldn't offer more words. I didn't know what to do as she cried, so I just sat there until her sobbing grew softer. I left the bench, knelt in front of her, and offered her my hand. Her hand eventually peeked out of her cloak and touched mine. She even followed the symbol on my hand with a finger.

"Just tell me. The secret will stay with me," I assured her.

The woman pulled her hood off, and what I saw under the moonlight was something I wasn't ready for—a woman of immense beauty, not older than twenty, with an enormous scar crossing its entire face from the top left part of her forehead, passing over her eye, around her nose, and over her lips all the way down to the lower right part of her neck.

Even under the shadows of the night, the gruesome remnants of that devastating injury made my entire body shake. She must've felt it in her hand, as she immediately reached up to cover her head again.

"Please don't do that. I'm sorry for my reaction," I said as I reached out and held her hand again. "We all carry scars, and some are even more devastating than yours."

"But not like this one." She paused. "This is not only a scar—it's a curse."

"Please tell me what happened."

"I can't tell you much, but this was done by an evil wizard when I was just a few years old. Many have tried to help me, but this magic is just too powerful. I might stay like this forever."

"Is this why you can't marry anyone?"

She pursed her lips. "In part, yes. But I always wanted to marry a man who truly loves me, one who would make my heart drown when he touches me. I have no desire to force anyone to be with me."

I was going to say something, but Arrowtail bit his tail again and made me see myself licking the woman's scar, first from her neck to her lower lip and then from her forehead to her upper lip. I fell backwards.

"Are you alright?" she asked.

"Yes, I'm fine. I must've hit my head harder than I thought. Just give me a moment." I got to my feet and stumbled toward the pond.

"Are you crazy? You want me to lick her scar? She's going to think I am deranged!" I whispered as loud as I dared.

Arrowtail bit his tail again, and I saw the face of the woman with no trace of the scar after I finished licking it. But there was another problem—my face wasn't red in those visions. I even had my hair back. That meant that Arrowtail would have to stop changing my face and do something else in order to heal her.

The risk was too high, but just realizing that we could have the means to heal her convinced me it was worth it.

"Listen to me," I whispered. "If you don't heal her and make me look like a fool, I will cover my entire body in mud so thick I can't move. You hear me?"

I walked back to the bench and sat by her side. "You've said many have failed to heal this scar. If I tell you that I might be able to cure you, would you let me try?"

"What do you mean? How would you do that?" she asked.

"You'll have to trust me. You may not like the way I'm going to do it, but please remember, I've nothing but respect toward you."

"What are you going to do? You're scaring me."

"Don't worry. There are only two things I need you to do for me. First, no matter what you feel, try not to move your head. But the most important thing is to keep your eyes closed until I say so. You have to promise you'll do that." She probably thought she had nothing to lose. She offered me a brief smile and closed her eyes. "Remember, I'm going to touch your face. Please try not to move."

I took the glove off and kept her hands between mine. Arrowtail moved away, making my face and hair go back to normal. I don't know what he did, but I started to feel like ants were crawling inside my tongue.

"Please move your head back. I have to start on your neck."

She slowly faced the sky. I wasn't sure what she would do the moment my tongue touched her neck, so I felt better holding her hands right then.

I couldn't stall any longer. I got closer, closed my eyes, and touched her neck with my tongue, just below the scar.

I certainly felt her reaction. Her hands moved abruptly, but I kept them between mine and continued. Even though I tried to go faster, Arrowtail wouldn't let me. I didn't know what he was doing, but I have to be honest with you—it felt gross.

My tongue got dry, so I had to close my mouth. I kept my lips touching her skin so she didn't think I was done, then kept going. The good news is that she became less tense as I kept going. Her hands felt warm inside mine, and she even helped me by moving her head down as I reached her chin. My tongue felt numb, so I moved my head back for a moment. I can't tell you how happy I was to see that the parts I licked didn't have a single trace of that horrible scar left on them.

"Please forgive me. You'll have to open your mouth slightly so I can put your lower lip between mine and lick around it. I'll do it as fast as I can. I promise."

She was probably so disgusted with everything I was doing that she didn't answer. She just took a deep breath and exhaled slowly.

She opened her mouth, so I placed her lip between mine and softly passed my tongue over it. That scar was thick and course in that area, so I was grateful when I felt it disappearing.

I took a few moments before I started on her forehead. I released her hands, as they were sweating a little bit.

"I'm sorry. I won't hold your hands if you promise to keep them inside your cloak."

"No, it's fine. Please hold them," she said with a soft voice.

By the time I licked her forehead, eye, and around her nose, my tongue was really hurting. I just wished I had some water to drink.

"Same thing as before. I have to put your upper lip between mine, so please forgive me."

I was so thirsty when I finished that I left the bench, walked to the pond, and put some water in my mouth. The woman didn't move. She sat there with her eyes closed and her hands still held in the position I had them the entire time.

"Are you alright?" I asked as I sat back down on the bench.

The woman sighed. "Well that was an experience I'll never forget."

"I know, I truly apologize for making you go through this ordeal. But please, touch your face. Or even better, go and see your reflection on the water."

"I feel lightheaded. Could you please take my hand and put it over my face?"

"I sure can." I took her hand and softly passed her fingers over where the scar used to be.

It was the tears that made her open her eyes. I didn't even realize that Arrowtail never turned my face red again; the woman didn't care. She threw her arms around me and held me so tightly that I couldn't breathe for a moment.

"I have an eternal debt to you. My heart made the best call when I chose your leaf." She pulled away and looked at me. "You're one of the guardians that came back. I saw the parchments."

I took her hands again. "No one should know we're here. Please promise me you won't tell anybody, not even your family. Do it for what I did up here," I said as I softly touched her face.

The woman's voice trembled as she looked into my eyes. "No." She paused. "I'll do it for what you did in here," she said, putting a hand on her chest.

I didn't understand what she meant, but I smiled and stood. "You need to help me with the elderly ladies. I need to erase this symbol. It's dangerous for me to carry it."

The woman dried her tears. "Change your face and let's walk to the entrance. I'll tell them something."

Arrowtail couldn't change my face after he healed the woman because he was exhausted, so we waited a while for him to regain his strength. He managed to change my face almost to the way it was when I walked into the gardens. I covered my head with the hood and we both approached the ladies and soldiers at the entrance.

"What is your choice, my dear?" an old lady asked the beautiful woman by my side. For some reason, she remained quiet. "What do you have in mind? Tell me, dear."

I glanced at her and saw her hands trembling as she held my leaf.

"I . . . I don't want to continue the courtship with this man," she said, letting some tears roll down her face.

The old woman's glare burned into me. "You brute. What did you do to this poor woman?" I didn't answer. "Don't you worry, my dear. You'll find someone with a bigger heart next season," the old woman said as she reached to take my leaf from her.

"No. I want to keep this leaf as a reminder of this night," she said, pulling the leaf away from the old woman.

"You're right, my dear. Make sure you don't make this same mistake again."

"I only wish," she whispered.

I extended my hand, and the old lady poured some potion on it with all the anger in her heart. "Now go! Before I ask the guards to throw you in a cell, you insensitive barbarian."

I walked away and hid in the shadows of a bridge. I looked back and saw the yellow cloak moving toward an archway. I don't know if she knew where I was, but she stopped before going in, turned around, and casually raised her hand, wishing me farewell.

"Barthenoz Guardians Garden," I said, touching the bracelet.

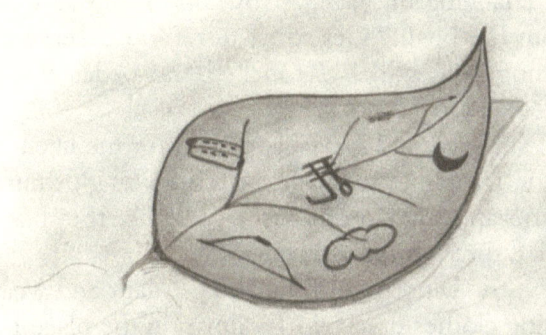

CHAPTER 14. BETRAYAL.

I appeared right at the center of the garden, and for the first time, I landed on my feet. I wasn't even lightheaded like the previous times. The only thing hurting was my tongue.

"You can stop changing my face, Arrowtail," I said as I carefully pulled the rod from the bush. "Get some rest. You deserve it. Now let's see if this thing will work." I touched the pedestal with the weapon.

The translucent staircase and bridge appeared for me like it did for Tynia, only this time I couldn't tell which symbol was glowing on the pedestal. Many marks appeared one after the other like they had on the weapon as it traveled through the golden bowls.

I walked through the window and put the pendant and weapon in my satchel. Changing clothes quickly, I lay down in the place I usually slept. I could barely keep my eyes open.

"So, my young heartbreaker, how did it go?"

I heard Kolikuj's voice so close to my ear that it made me jolt, pushing into a table and a pile of armor nearby. The ruckus must've echoed in all seven halls.

"Are you crazy, Kolikuj? My heart is pounding a hole through my chest!"

"I've got to know what happened! I've been in this pebble for centuries, but the last few hours have been the worst."

"You could've waited until morning."

"Absolutely not! You can't leave me like this."

I breathed deeply. "Just let me catch my breath." I took in deep gulps of air, calming my heart from the fright he'd given me. As the candles nearby went out, I shared with him everything that took place that night. When I finished, he sat quietly. I thought he was finally letting me sleep, so I closed my eyes and rolled to one side.

"So, you kissed her," he said.

"No I didn't."

"Yes you did."

"I just healed her with my tongue—or maybe it was Arrowtail's. I don't know."

"But you touched her lips . . . with yours."

"Yes. One at a time."

"I see." He paused. "So you kissed her *twice*."

"Are you deaf? I didn't kiss her. That wasn't a kiss."

"Well, I don't know how to tell you this, but in my time, that would be considered a kiss."

"Well, it wasn't. Now go to sleep! I'm tired."

"Alright, I'll let you sleep," Kolikuj said. "But I just hope that young woman thinks the same way you do. In my time, if a woman kissed a man before marriage, it meant she was promising not to marry anybody else and wait for him."

Those words gave me pause. "I believe she thinks like I do," I said softly.

Kolikuj rolled into a crease in a rug nearby. "Well, if she doesn't, wait until her family finds out why she isn't getting married. They'll hunt you down like a mouse in a kitchen."

"I don't think that'll happen. She must be so happy to have her face healed that she's probably forgotten by now that I even touched her lips."

Kolikuj chuckled. "Indeed. And you've just proven to me you're twelve years old."

"Almost thirteen," I whispered as I struggled to keep my eyes open.

"Have peaceful dreams," he said.

Those were the last words I remember.

***

When I felt Peprokh smacking my feet with his staff, it was almost midday.

"Well, you've become as indolent as a bear in the winter. I can't believe you're making me miss that smelly creature. At least she made you wake up early to clean and feed her." He grumbled when he noticed the pile of armor I tripped over last night. "Did you touch these? I told you not to touch anything!"

"It was dark and I tripped," I said as I rubbed my eyes.

"Well, I need you to stay here all day. Something happened this morning that has everybody under the barrier in a tizzy," he said as he used magic to reassemble the armor.

"What is it? Is it the dark army? Did they cross the barrier?"

"That I could live with." Peprokh said. "What I can't stand is all this nonsense taking place all over Kelfia because she was up in her terrace this morning."

"Who? What are you talking about?"

"The princess! The heir to the throne of Kelfia. No one has seen her since she was but a few years old, and this morning, she was up there, waving at the crowd on the grounds. I saw her myself."

"So why is this causing such a big commotion?" I said as I got to my feet.

"Many thought the princess was dead. She was last seen when she was a child, just before the royal family was attacked on their way to Sogrithoz. Some even say Malok himself took part in that ambush, so nobody knows how they were able to escape. With no other heir to inherit the throne of Kelfia, some kings (now hiding in the city) had hopes to annex this kingdom into their own once the king and queen were no more. That is, of course, if Malok and the war allowed them to. Now that she has proven to be alive, many will see those hopes vanish."

"So if nobody has seen her since she was that young, how do you know it's her?"

"There's no doubt. Long black hair and beauty like nothing you've seen before. She looks just like our queen before she married; she must even be the same age by now. Just one thing didn't seem right, though."

"What was that?" I asked.

"For some reason, she wasn't wearing a royal dress; she had an unusual yellow cloak on. It's not even that cold." I remained silent. "Many will want to see her, so there will be large crowds visiting Barthenoz today. Even some of the elders might come back, so it's important for you to stay out of sight. I'll send food to that table over there so you don't have to leave this hall. Just stay here . . . and don't touch anything!"

Peprokh turned and vanished and I just stood there, frozen. Kolikuj rolled out from the crease in the rug as soon as he was gone.

"A beautiful woman with long dark hair, wearing a yellow cloak. Where have I heard that before?"

"Oh no," I said as I leaned back on a table.

"The good news is that you didn't kiss her," he said, a hint of sarcasm in his voice. "You just put your lips on hers."

"I'm doomed," I said, sliding to the floor.

"I think the king will be merciful. I wonder if the honor of his only daughter would be important for him?"

"Quiet, Kolikuj! Let me think."

"You may want to find a pebble like mine and use the same spell that put me in here."

I paced around the hall. "She said she couldn't marry me anyway," I said as I looked down at Kolikuj.

He rolled closer. "Who? The woman who said those were the best moments she'd had in years? The one who promised to keep your secret for what you did in her chest?" Kolikuj stopped rolling. "Please, just tell me you didn't lick her there too."

"I did not! Don't even say that."

"Can't you see? She was talking about her feelings! The steward is right—you should stay hidden here, at least for the next few centuries."

Needless to say, that was a long day. Kolikuj and I trained the rest of the day, and I only left the dungeon to eat what Peprokh made appear on the table. The night was still young when I put on the large blue cloak and swung the satchel over my shoulder. I walked to the other side of the hall and saw my image in a mirror—very little hair, my entire face and neck burned by the sun, holding the staff in two gloved hands.

"I shouldn't leave the lair, but I need those coins for the Lost Whispers," I said, glancing down at Kolikuj.

"Just remember your training, and don't let your eyes deceive you," he said as he rolled back into the crease in the rug.

"I should be back before sunrise."

"Jonek, don't let anybody find out you're a guardian."

"I'm not a guardian."

"True. But other than not having the elders training you, and the protector of the Lost Path not giving you a name, you are no different than any of us." He paused. "Just try not to kiss anybody this time!"

"I did not kiss her!" I said as I walked through the window and touched the bracelet. This time, I appeared in the middle of a creek with water up to my knees. I walked out and waited for my eyes to get used to the moonlight. It didn't take long for me to see others wearing cloaks going uphill along the other side of the water.

I crossed the creek and followed them until we reached the lagoon at the top. I wasn't far behind, but I somehow lost the group by the edge of the water. I hid behind a tree, carefully scanning the edge of the lagoon, and eventually saw others putting out their torches as they walked into the water.

I hesitated, thinking of my clothes and everything I carried in my satchel, but this time I wasn't going to leave anything behind, so I walked into the water and went under.

I didn't know where to go, but then I saw light coming from the depths. Far below, the statue of the warrior was glowing at the bottom of the lagoon. Well, at least the upper part of his body was—the rest was underground.

I returned to the surface and swam to the center of the lagoon. Then, taking a deep breath, I swam to the bottom as fast as I could. I don't know how the others did it, but I was practically drowning when I touched the statue and appeared by the merchants inside the Dome of Trials.

A man selling food walked toward me as he saw me coughing up water.

"Is everyone in Minojeb as crazy as you are? Next time, keep the parchment in your hand as you walk into the water. Like everyone else," he said, pointing at the rest coming in, all dry and ready to see the trials.

An old woman saw me walking toward the wall with my clothes drenched, and she slowly approached me. She didn't say a word, just pointed her staff at me, drying my clothes and warming my body.

"Thank you so much," I said as I looked inside my satchel.

"You're welcome, young man. That will be three coins."

"Three coins?"

"You do know that old women have to eat, don't you?"

"Yes, of course I do. I just wasn't expecting you to charge me."

"Well, would you like me to make you wet again for free?"

"No, please . . . my apologies. Here, take them." I handed the coins to her.

"Thank you, and enjoy the trials, young man," she said as she walked off toward a man who'd just landed nearby, all wet like me.

That's a clever way of earning coins, I thought.

I walked by the merchant who sold me the weapon and noticed that he only had two more left sticking out of a pot on the floor. I took both to see if they had anything unusual, but the man swiftly made his way around the table and joined me.

"Welcome! Long ways from Minojeb, my dear friend. I see you like fine craftsmanship. If you like them, you can have both for two gold coins. Those are my last two until next season."

I couldn't believe he was asking two gold coins for them, especially since I got one from him for five silver coins just a few days back. But I was truly tempted to accept his offer, knowing what happened to the first one.

I looked at them one more time and made my offer. "I can give you one gold for both."

"I can't do that. I know they're just pieces of wood and leather, but I still have a family to feed."

"I understand. Thank you," I said, leaving the rods in the pot.

"Enjoy the trials," he said as I walked away.

I stopped by the merchant where Mizjial's aunt was supposed to meet me after the trials. I was looking at the frogs on the table when I felt someone pulling the back of my cloak. A woman with a small child in her arms was holding the two rods by their straps.

"You can have them for one gold. We need the coins," she said.

I gave her the coin and put the rods in my satchel. I walked the rest of the way around the cave, watching all kinds of mysterious items and foods exchanging hands everywhere. This time, I went down to the edge of the arena but stayed close to the stairs. Soon, the crowds filled every available spot.

"Did you hear that the princess sat by her father's side in the council today?" a woman said behind me.

"I did. People say the king and queen never looked as happy as they were today."

"Why do you think it took this long for her to appear again?"

"For her own protection, of course. But I think she is now ready to find a husband."

"But who could she marry? The only two princes left are not even fifteen. I don't think she would even consider someone that young. She needs a real man. Maybe a knight."

"I don't think that'll happen. King Himret would never accept someone with no royal ancestry. Not with our traditions."

"And his temper too," the other woman said.

My blood chilled.

The same man who opened the trials the last time walked into the arena, followed by two large warriors.

"Before the trials begin, everyone should know that Kelfia's soldiers were just defeated in two battlefronts in the southwest. Thousands were lost, and many more could've perished if it wasn't for us. The legion covered their retreat, allowing them to reach the main river early last night.

"Hokdhanet himself battled with our brothers and brought the bodies of the fallen with him. He is here with us tonight. Let us welcome our true leader!"

Everyone around the arena stood up and cheered as a tall man with torn, dirty robes walked down the stairs on the other side of the arena. Step by step, the man helped himself with his staff while the two large bears in front and a dozen warriors on his sides and back kept everyone from getting too close to him.

He pulled his hood back, allowing us to see a long piece of red cloth wrapped around his head, covering everything but his eyes. The warriors sat down at the lowest level while the bears and Hokdhanet jumped into the arena and sat on the sand just below them, inside the circle. Hokdhanet's staff began to bend, and he let it rest around his neck. He and his bears turned their attention to the man opening the trials.

"These are the brothers who are no longer with us," the man said as he put one knee on the ground, making the faces of the fallen appear again high above in the middle of the arena.

"Remember! We, the ones that know, must honor them every time we witness a new morning, feel the touch of a loved one, or are blessed with the briefest sound of life," the man said as he made tiny white petals rain down on us again.

The man stood. "Fifty gold coins to whoever defeats three warriors in a row. You can use any weapons you like and fight any way you please. Just remember—you take a life, you won't keep yours."

The first warrior was a large fellow carrying a club in one hand and an axe in the other. A young woman jumped in and defeated him handily, making a cloud of smoke swirl around his head until he fell unconscious from lack of air. The woman defeated two others, but couldn't deal with a skinny man that bounced rocks off the dome itself, making them rain down on her relentlessly. Even Hokdhanet had to use his staff to protect himself and the bears from those rocks.

That was when I jumped in.

I left my satchel by the wall and crossed the circle toward the center of the arena. The skinny man was leaning on a column with rocks floating all around him. I didn't walk more than a dozen steps when the man blasted a part of the column to pieces and sent them hurtling toward the top of the dome. I ran to one side and cast a spell that turned the ground he was standing on into quicksand, which swallowed him.

Only one of his rocks hit me on the leg as I took cover. The whole arena remained silent as I walked closer, put my staff into the sand, and pulled him out.

I would've loved to use a sword to fight the next one, because the man didn't use any magic. In many ways, I truly appreciated his efforts to use traditional weapons during the fight. I even felt bad as I melted his sword in his hands before defeating him.

The third warrior was a woman who fought the same way as the boy who won the previous trials. Only she didn't even move as much. She sat down in the middle of the arena and made me fight beasts so real that even though I knew they were an illusion, I still see them in my nightmares from time to time.

It wasn't until I blinded her (and most of the people around the dome) with a spell that Kolikuj called "The Dying Star" that I was able to get behind her with my staff pointing at her head.

What I didn't know was that Hokdhanet was also standing behind me, pointing his staff at me.

I had won indeed, but no one was celebrating my triumph. Everybody was dead silent. I slowly turned around and saw him staring at me without moving his staff from my face.

"Who are you?"

"A warrior from Minojeb," I responded.

"Your spells. Where did you learn them?"

"From an old wizard. He raised me, but he is now long gone."

Hokdhanet lowered his staff but kept looking at me as if he were trying to determine if I was lying.

"Be careful with this magic. It is too powerful to be used here. Look at what you did to my guards," he said, pointing at the bears.

Both beasts were rolling on the ground, pawing their eyes. Hokdhanet made a signal, and the man who opened the trials walked into the arena and gave me the bag of coins. It wasn't until then that the crowd finally roared, celebrating my triumph.

I can't deny that it felt great. Many times, my friends and I dreamed about winning a competition, even becoming an Olikant Warrior. But I never thought that the first time I would actually win a competition would be in a different world.

The man who gave me the coins called for everyone who'd fought on that night to follow him, so they began to join us in the middle of the arena. I told him I had to go back and get my satchel, but my plan was to pick it up, climb out of the arena, and merge with the crowd back to the statue.

I was a few steps away from my satchel when I saw four men jumping into the arena. Something wasn't right, though—out of the eight of us who had actually fought that night, six were already with the man who opened the trials.

I dropped the coin purse by my satchel and quickly headed back to the center of the arena. Out of the corner of my eye, I saw someone wearing a yellow cloak jumping into the arena with a bow in his hand. The next few moments seemed to happen very slowly.

The four men pointed their staffs toward the top of the dome, making the walls turn red. We were trapped. Balls of fire burst out of their staffs as their faces and hands turned bony and decrepit.

The fighter with the yellow cloak began to shoot arrows toward the Zerkial wizards as he ducked for cover in the dome. The man who gave me the coins and the warriors behind him were surprised at first, but they also took cover and began to defend themselves soon after. Unfortunately, one of them tried to cross the dome, and his body exploded into flames as it touched the red wall.

Two of the Zerkial wizards conjured large beasts that quickly engaged Hokdhanet's bears and destroyed some of the columns in the arena. One of them rushed toward me.

I didn't know what to do. I knew I couldn't change my weapon, so I pointed the staff to the ground and made the beast fall into quicksand. Hokdhanet took his staff from around his neck and cast a spell that deflected the balls of fire back to the Zerkials. The person with the yellow cloak kept shooting arrows at an incredible speed while Hokdhanet walked in front of the warriors to protect them.

Suddenly, one of the Zerkials walked toward me and changed himself into a snake maybe twelve feet high with two heads on each end. Balls of fire blasted toward me from each mouth.

I avoided them as best I could. I pointed my staff at the beast and summoned a barrier of light in front of me similar to the one Tynia used at the north gate. I held the beast as long as I could, but with each ball of fire I deflected, I was being pushed closer and closer to the red

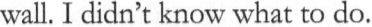

wall. I didn't know what to do.

I was holding the staff with both hands, keeping the barrier in front of the beast. Suddenly, I felt Arrowtail moving away from my face toward my hand. My glove burned away and the little lizard jumped right out of my skin. He blasted through my barrier, growing into a ferocious horned lizard creature as big as the snake in front of me. As I covered my head with the hood and walked away from the red wall, his tail cut off one of the heads and pierced another one from side to side. Then he just used his fanged mouth to rip the other two to pieces.

All of us fighting in the dome and the hundreds watching as they fled to safety couldn't help but be astonished by the sheer power of that mighty creature. Even the balls of fire from the other Zerkials bounced off of Arrowtail's skin.

Hokdhanet and the others dealt with the remaining Zerkials as Arrowtail pierced the red wall of the dome with his tail. We barely had time to take cover as the entire dome turned solid and crumbled down on us.

I was lying on the sand in a cloud of dust, but I was able to see a small lizard jumping through the debris toward me. He stopped for a moment to catch his breath, his tongue sticking out to one side. He looked at me, then jumped into my hand and got lost in my skin.

Arrowtail bit his tail again and made me see myself running up the stairs as a boy. That could only mean that he didn't have strength to change my face anymore. I took the pendant from my neck and rushed toward my satchel.

The screams and noises of people fleeing from that place were overwhelming. I picked up my satchel and the bag of coins and climbed out of the arena. It was hard, but I merged with the flow of people and managed to reach the place where the merchant sold the frogs. Everyone was pushing me, but I stood there until I finally heard the voice of Mizjial's aunt.

"Don't just stand there. We have to leave this place," she said.

I gave her the bag of coins. "Please give some coins to the Serthoz woman who takes care of the Lost Whispers on the west shore. You'll find her in an old boat on the southern side." The flow of people pushed us toward the statue, and we were too close to each other. Our faces began to glow red, so we pulled our hoods over our heads and rushed toward the statue. At that point, I was more worried about people not stepping on my cloak—now that it was too long for my size—than wondering why most of them had a piece of parchment in their hands.

By then, it was too late. The flow of people barely allowed me to take a deep breath before I was pushed into the statue. The next thing I remembered was swimming as fast as I could toward the surface. By the time my face burst out of the water, all I could do was gasp for air and cough.

It took some time for me to slow down my breathing and look toward the edge of the lagoon. Many lights suddenly came to life as people walked out of the water and disappeared into the forest. I headed toward a place that seemed to have the least lights, then stopped by a tree to catch my breath. I heard someone walking my way.

I didn't look back. I made my way through the woods, picking up my pace to lose whoever was following me. I went downhill and ducked behind a tree. I was going to touch the bracelet but decided to look back. Just there at the top of the hill, I saw someone following my trail.

The person lit a torch, and I was able to see the yellow cloak he was wearing. The shadows of the night and the color of the cloak reminded me of my previous night with the princess. Was she the one who jumped into the arena and fought those wizards? Was she some kind of warrior? Maybe even a guardian?

I stayed behind that tree, but I could see that the person was having difficulty going downhill. The unknown traveler slipped and rolled down a short distance, and the unmistakable voice of a woman yelped in pain. She was injured.

I left my hiding place and picked up her torch. "Allow me to help you, princess."

"First I'm a witch, and now I'm a princess? Your stay in Kirolcan has really improved your manners, Warrior Eyes."

Tynia's voice sounded like a gift from heaven. I flung my arms around her and didn't want to let go.

"I missed you too," she said as she ran her fingers through my hair. "I briefly saw you behind that creature that took care of the Zerkial viper, and I've been following you since then. I don't know how you were able to conjure that kind of magic, but it's beyond anything I've seen or heard of."

"It wasn't me, it was Arrowtail. It's a long story, but I think you need to take care of your leg first."

"Jonek, many things have happened since the last time I saw you. Help me get up; we need to find a safe place so I can heal my leg."

I didn't ask her, nor did I know if it was going to work, but I put my arms around her and touched the bracelet. "Barthenoz Guardians Garden."

It worked, but we landed hard.

Rolling into the pedestal probably hurt her leg even more. Tynia didn't say a word, though. She took her weapon, turned it into a staff, and made clouds appear like she did in that cave where I broke my leg. I took off my cloak and allowed the mist to land on me as Tynia tore the leggings she was wearing under her skirt.

"When did you learn to transport?" she said as she sat back against the pedestal.

"Peprokh cast a spell on the bracelet. That's how I've been traveling lately."

"Just don't try to do it outside of Kelfia. The Zerkials will find you quickly." She paused. "Come here and sit by my side. I'd better tell you what's happened while my leg heals."

I sat on my cloak and pulled my satchel closer, listening intently to her words.

"The first thing you should know is that your mother and friends are fine, but the dark army knows where Kharlo is, and they're on their way to attack the competition grounds. Unfortunately, I know this because we've been betrayed."

"Betrayed? By who?"

"We don't know, but it's someone who's been close to the guardians. Maybe for generations."

"But how do you know?"

"One of the elders woke me up one night and made me follow him into the waters of a secret grotto. Once in there, he showed me a parchment that had Kharlo's face on it, just as he looks nowadays. The parchment had blood on it. The elder put one of the corners stained with blood in the water and I was able to see Kharlo in the water, sleeping in the tent while your mother and friends talked and ate around him. Apparently, the parchment was taken from a Zerkial wizard not even a month ago."

"I don't understand," I murmured.

Tynia covered her leg and looked up so the mist could land on her face. "Zerkial wizards can make these parchments if they have two things—a necklace with a mark just like Kharlo's and some of his blood. Now, blood is something we've spilled on many battlegrounds, but our marks can only be forged in the golden bowls in the Guardians Lair or the Lost Path." Tynia looked at me, a little bit of worry behind her eyes. It startled me. "Someone made another mark and gave it to Malok. Kharlo can't hide anymore—the dark army will find him anywhere as long as he carries that mark around his neck."

"But he'll die if he doesn't reach Kirolcan."

"Not if we give him this," she said as she passed her hand over her staff and a vial containing green and blue colors emerged from it. "The elders used their strongest magic to create this potion. It will make every speck of magic in Kharlo's body disappear. We just need to make sure he drinks it before the Jiretal spell fades away and he dies."

"But who could be the traitor?" I asked as we felt the last drops of mist falling on us.

"An elder? Peprokh? Who knows? It has to be someone with access to the Guardians Lair or someone who has found a way to reach the Lost Path."

"What if the traitor is an elder, and that person did something to the potion you carry?"

"That's not possible. I was there when they made the potion, and none of us took our eyes away from the vial until I took it." She paused. "One thing is true, though. Whoever is betraying us is getting desperate. I think Hokdhanet and his legion is making Malok furious, so they are trying to kill him and disband his legion at any cost. The same elder who showed me the parchment with Kharlo's face asked me to follow him to the forest this afternoon. He shared with me that someone had briefly opened a gap in the barrier to allow four Zerkials to get inside. He said the rest of the elders will find out who the traitor is, but he wanted me to follow the Zerkials and see what they were after before coming back for you and going back to help Kharlo. I followed them to those trials you were in, and you know the rest."

I took my weapon from the satchel and gave it to Tynia.

"Whose weapon is this?" she asked.

"Look at the mark," I said as I pulled the pendant from my satchel.

"This . . . it's not possible. Where did you find this?"

"I didn't find it, I bought it for five coins. It had no symbol when I bought it, but I woke up one morning and it was carved onto it. By the way, why did you leave the mark with the little one?"

"For some reason, I didn't want either my master or Peprokh to keep it. Rubzilet said that if Peprokh was successful in retrieving the mark from you, we should immediately give it to him and keep its existence a secret, even from the elders. I didn't like that, but I didn't say anything. I decided to tell him that Peprokh wasn't able to retrieve it, but at the same time I wanted Peprokh to think that I took it to the elders." She paused. "By the way, where's the little girl?" She handed the weapon back to me.

"It took me weeks to find her family. She's now with her aunt, but I made a promise to bring her mother back from the mountains."

"Yes. I made that promise too, but we need to go back and save Kharlo first. Is his weapon still under the window?"

"Yes, I saw it there a few days ago."

"I think it's best for Peprokh not to see me, so I'll stay here while you go back and bring Kharlo's weapon. It's time for us to go back to Ferdhen," she said.

I left my satchel by her side and walked all the way to the window. I put the pendant on and got into the lair. Candles and lamps began to light as I walked toward Kharlo's window.

I took the weapon and headed back.

"What happened? Where are you going?" Kolikuj said as he rolled out in front of me.

"I have to go, Kolikuj."

"Why? Did someone recognize you? Don't tell me you changed your weapon and they found out you were a guardian," he said.

I picked him up and held him in the palm of my hand. "Many things happened. I won the trials. I gave the gold coins to the little girl's aunt so she can give them to the Lost Whispers. But then we were attacked by Zerkial wizards."

"Zerkials in Kelfia?" he said.

"It's a long story, but unfortunately it's time for me to go back to Ferdhen, our world. Tynia is down at the garden. We must leave as soon as possible."

Kolikuj rolled closer to my face. "Jonek, please take me with you. I don't want to stay in here alone any longer. I would rather see my world one last time, even if I do it from this pebble."

"But what if you can't cross back like this? You may die."

"Better to die than stay alone in here. It will be my last adventure. I can be of help—there are many things I can still teach you." He paused. "Please don't leave me. You are my only friend."

I just couldn't say no. "Alright, I'll take you with me, but you'll have to stay in my pocket for now."

"I won't be able to see anything, but that's fair enough. Now go back down to the hall where we met the first time."

"What for?" I asked.

"For my weapon. I'm not leaving it here. I promised myself that I'd keep it until the day I die. Now don't waste time. Go!"

We ventured down, and he directed me to a pile of rugs. There, right in between them, was an old weapon with thin, dark stripes from end to end. I took it and made my way back up. I was crossing the window when I heard Peprokh's voice coming from the far end of the hall. I rushed down the staircase and joined Tynia by the pedestal.

"Peprokh just entered the hall," I said, catching my breath. "He probably saw me crossing the window."

Tynia slung my satchel over my shoulder and held my hand. I didn't feel much as we appeared on top of a barren hill. Checking to make sure I came through fine, Tynia noticed I was now holding two weapons in my hands.

"Who's the owner of the other weapon?" she asked.

I was still trying to catch my breath, so I held both rods by their straps and pulled Kolikuj's pebble from my pocket.

"The weapon with black stripes belongs to me. I am Kolikuj, Guardian of the Falling Water," he responded.

Tynia took the pebble from my hand and looked at it under the light of the moons. "Kolikuj? I thought you were just another myth from the old guardians."

"I am very much real. Another wizard made me sleep for many centuries, so I was forgotten. I don't know why, but Jonek's voice awakened me a few weeks ago. I am a wizard guardian, just like you. I can tell you more, but I think this is not the time or place to do so."

Tynia took Kolikuj's weapon from my hand and touched it with the pebble. Slowly, a mark that looked like three mountains burned vividly on its wood very close to the grip.

"Well, it's your weapon alright. It's great to meet you. I am Tynia, Guardian of the Twin Stars." She looked over at me. "Jonek, why are you taking him with us?"

"I promised him I'd take him back to our world. His world."

"But he might not make it through the Lost Path inside this pebble."

"He knows, but he's willing to take the risk."

Tynia gave me back his weapon and leaned on her staff. "Let me see your bracelet." She pointed her staff at it and magically reforged some of its silver links into a small round cage. She placed Kolikuj's pebble in it and made sure it was secure inside. "The metal of this bracelet might be able to protect you. If it made its way here, maybe it can take you back."

"At least I'll be able to see where we are from here," Kolikuj said as he made the bracelet move around my wrist.

Tynia looked downhill. "The barrier is down there. Once we're outside, I'll transport us to the dune maze at the edge of the Minojeb desert. Zerkials will sense us, so we will be surrounded in moments. Stay right behind me so we can lose them as we enter the Lost Path. Keep your shield and weapon ready, but don't use them unless you have no choice."

I put both rods in my satchel and readied the shield and weapon I used at the trials. "Oh, Tynia, there's one more thing. That creature that killed the Zerkial's serpent in the Dome of Trials is hiding in my skin. I promised him to release him as soon as we cross the barrier. So please don't take us to the Lost Path until he's on his way."

Tynia huffed. "Are there any more promises I should be aware of?"

"None that I can think of. Once he's out of my skin, we can go home."

Kolikuj rattled his cage. "It might be best for Jonek to leave Kirolcan as soon as possible. Very soon, the dark army will not be the only one looking for him."

"Why is that?" Tynia asked.

"Well, let's just say that the king might want to hold Jonek responsible for what he did to the princess."

"The princess? What did Jonek do to her?" Tynia said, whirling inches from my face.

I covered Kolikuj with my hand. "Nothing! I just helped her by healing the scar on her face."

Tynia's face relaxed. "You healed the curse cast by Malok himself? And how did you do that?" she said as she pulled my hand away from Kolikuj's pebble.

"He kissed her," Kolikuj said.

"He did *what?*" Tynia said, scowling.

"I did not!"

"Jonek says they weren't kisses, but he put his lips and tongue over her neck, face, forehead, and yes—on her lips."

For some reason, Tynia was furious. "So your lips have healing powers now? Eh, Warrior Eyes?" She whipped back around and started walking downhill.

"It wasn't me! I just did what Arrowtail told me to do."

Tynia stopped and glared back at me. "So now you do what any creature tells you to do? I'm just glad it didn't tell you to jump from a cliff."

"He didn't. In fact he helped me make it through the marriage ritual," I said in my defense.

Tynia turned around again. "You went through the marriage ritual?" She jabbed her staff right toward my face. "I leave you alone for a few weeks and you start courtship, kiss a strange woman, and end up with creatures roaming in your skin. That doesn't say much about your character. Wait until I tell your mother." Tynia turned around and kept walking.

"But I didn't kiss her," I said meekly as I followed her.

Tynia didn't say much the rest of the way down to the barrier. We reached the bottom of the hill and hid behind some rocks.

"Once we go beyond these rocks, we'll be outside the barrier. Release the creature roaming your skin and meet me by that bush over there. Do it fast."

I darted out quickly, knelt down, left my weapons by my side, and put my hands on the ground.

"Arrowtail, we are beyond the barrier. It's time for you to go back to your family. Thank you for helping the princess and saving me at the trials. Be safe, my friend," I whispered.

Arrowtail must've put his tail in his mouth, as I saw an image of him moving to my face and licking my cheek. I remember seeing something in my hand, then watching tiny footprints appear on the sand in front of me.

"Farewell, my friend," I said as I picked up my weapons.

"I'll miss him too. He certainly made you look better," Kolikuj said.

"Oh shut up, Kolikuj. I'm not happy with you right now. How could you tell Tynia about my ordeal with the princess?"

"I was just trying to make a point that you did kiss the princess."

"How many times do I have to say it? That wasn't a kiss. I never kissed a woman. I don't even know what a kiss feels like."

Tynia suddenly left the bush and ran toward us. She didn't even offer warning before she took my hand and both of us appeared in a maze made of walls of dirt and rocks. She covered my mouth and pulled me behind a wall as a small horde of dark soldiers roamed the maze with torches and weapons.

Tynia used her staff to send out a mirror stone, which touched a scout and flew back to her. She put it in her mouth and turned into a scout. She did the same for me, but in my case, she made me turn into a bear.

"Just follow me and avoid any sentinels or wizards," she whispered.

We walked by many dark soldiers, and I couldn't believe how aggressive they were, even with their own kind. Another bear challenged me to move aside, and I felt Tynia's hand on my back pushing me to stand my ground. I stood on two legs and growled at him. I don't know how we managed to do it, but we made our way out of the maze through a secret doorway hidden in a dead end, just as dawn began to break. We sat down to rest our legs, changing back to our old forms, and even though there was no sunlight touching us yet, I took my ramikha from the satchel and held it up.

After a good while of walking, we reached a ledge that overlooked a very deep chasm. Even in broad daylight, the bottom was just a black shadow. There were countless satchels, crates, and bags piled on the left side of the ledge and a pedestal and golden bowl standing in front of a wall on the right side. It looked quite similar to the one on the cave on the Lost Path—a map was carved on the wall, but this one had the unmistakable shapes of the Bhormak Mountains and the Garpodian Sea in the south. The map had three gems encrusted on it very close to each other.

Tynia took out her weapon and looked at me. "There is no moonlight, so we won't be able to see where the dark army is in our world. Jonek, I'm not sure which weapon you should use to touch the bowl. I think it should be Kharlo's, but you need that mark around your neck to look the same as when you crossed last time."

"Touch it with all of them, even mine," Kolikuj said.

Tynia touched the bowl first, and one stone tray came out of the wall just under the gems.

"Why are there three gems on the wall right over Ferdhen?" I asked.

"Many of us have asked that question before. No one really knows why, but I know that Artego once asked the elders, and he was told that the sages who made the Lost Path must've had too many gems in their pockets," Tynia said.

"What a way to avoid the question," Kolikuj said.

I touched the bowl with the three weapons (Kharlo's, Kolikuj's, and mine) so there were now four stone trays below the gems.

"Let me try something," I said as I held out the two weapons I bought the previous night. I touched the bowl with them, but nothing happened.

"Where did you get those?" Tynia asked.

"I bought them from the same merchant who sold me the one I'm using. How many stone trays can you open on the wall?"

"One time we opened five," Kolikuj said.

"Five guardians?" Tynia asked.

"Yes. An elemental guardian from my islands stayed with us until the new guardian completed his training. Those were desperate times," Kolikuj said.

"The trays won't matter this time, because we won't use any aging stones. When we cross back, we will look as old as the years we've spent under our sun." Tynia said as she took the dust from the top tray, now showing her symbol.

"So how am I supposed to keep all these weapons, the disk, and my ramikha in my hands as we pass through?"

"Hold the weapons by their straps and keep your shield in your other hand. Leave the rest in your satchel and put it in that pile over there," Tynia said.

"Wait, my ramikha made it to Kirolcan. I should be able to take it back with me."

"You may lose it, but it's your choice. Let's go—we have to leave."

I put my fingers through the straps and clung tightly to the disk and my ramikha. I was walking toward the crates to leave my satchel there, but something made me change my mind. I closed it tightly and joined Tynia by the edge.

"Jonek, you probably know what has to happen, so don't think about it too much. If you want, I can push us the same way I did on that bridge," she said.

I didn't say a word.

Tynia put her arms around me and pushed us over the edge.

That fall felt endless.

CHAPTER 15. TWO PROMISES.

I kept my eyes closed as Tynia held me tightly in that darkness. I instinctively took a long breath just before Tynia and I plunged deep into the water.

The fall disoriented me, but I followed the light and swam back to the surface. The view of the steep wall of the mountain almost made me cry—we were at the top lagoon. Tynia swam closer to me, and I could see that her face looked even younger now. For some reason, she seemed surprised.

"This doesn't make sense," she said. "You look the same as you did before we jumped off the ledge. We didn't use any aging stones, so you should be back to normal. Look, even the satchel made it through. That never happened to us." She paused. "There are clothes hidden in a small cave behind the waterfall. Follow me. And please don't look; let me get in there first."

Tynia hopped out of the water and crawled into the small cave as I looked at the daylight filtering through the waterfall.

"You can come in now," she said a minute later. "Don't worry, I won't look."

I pushed myself out of the water and crawled into the small opening. The blue flames from Tynia's staff were already illuminating the place, so I quickly looked for clothes.

"Don't bother trying to dry yourself. Usually we use magic to leave this cave, but we can't risk doing that now. We'll have to get in the water again and swim out of this lagoon. This time, keep your weapons ready," Tynia said as she tied a strap on her belt that brandished a unique hook to carry her weapon.

I put some clothes on and found a pair of soft leather gloves. Then I saw a leather chestpiece sticking out of a crate. I pulled it out and put it on to see how it looked.

"It may not be as effective as the one coming out of your disk, but it might still help," she said as she tightened its straps on my sides.

I put everything in the satchel and kept my weapon and the disk in my hands. We dove into the water, swam toward the edge of the lagoon, and crawled over a pile of rocks to look down into the gorge leading out. Tynia was right. Down by the edge of the lower lagoon was a group of scouts and a large soldier like the one we saw by the cemetery the day we left—a blackguard. Two enormous beasts sat by his side, ripping pieces of flesh off what seemed to be a dead horse.

We would've been spotted easily if we tried to climb down or jump into the lower lagoon, so we decided to use bows to take care of them from above. The armor of light appeared around me as we pulled back the strings of our silver bows. Our first arrows took care of a soldier and a wolf. Unfortunately, we never noticed the wizard walking behind the trees to the right. A ball of fire exploded just below the rocks we were standing on, so we were already falling when we shot our next arrows.

We didn't plunge into the water this time—Tynia kept us floating above the surface while we reached the edge. She shot arrows as I blocked their attacks and the balls of fire with my shield. We kept moving until we'd left the lagoons behind.

The blackguard pulled his swords out and summoned his beasts toward us. One of them crashed into my shield and sent me flying backward while Tynia blasted flames out of her staff, burning the other beast.

The creature cried in pain, but the Zerkial sent his own wave of flames toward Tynia. Both streams of fire collided, roaring over the beasts and me. I was lucky that my shield deflected most of it (and that my clothes were still wet). Arrows continued flying toward us, so I ran toward Tynia.

"I'll deflect the fire with my shield. Move away!" I said.

My shield grew larger and turned bright red as it absorbed the wizard's fire. Tynia turned her weapon into a bow and kept shooting arrows from behind me. Many of her arrows flew so close that I could feel them touching my clothes and hair.

My shield suddenly turned black, and some instinct made me push it into the ground. A massive blast sent everyone in front of it flying a great distance. Even the trees were torn to pieces.

I pulled it out and looked at Tynia.

"To the river. Run!" she said.

We ran as fast as we could, but the two beasts intercepted us. I was facing the one that got burned when an arrow pierced my leg from side to side and made me stumble. Tynia was dealing with the other one, and I could hear the scouts and wizard getting closer. The beast lunged.

"The Dying Star!" Kolikuj shouted.

I turned my weapon into a staff and cast the spell. Tynia fell to one

297

knee and closed her eyes as our entire area burst into white from the light of my staff. Unfortunately, the beasts weren't dazzled, but the soldiers that came out of the bushes were. Even the Zerkial was caught by surprise.

Tynia still had her eyes closed when one of the beasts rushed toward her and opened its mouth around her head. I threw my shield in between them, and the beast crumpled into it. Almost immediately, the other one jumped at me. I didn't have time to react, so all I could do was close my eyes.

I was expecting to feel unbearable pain as the beast drove its slimy teeth through my skin, but the only thing I felt was some pressure in my hand. When I opened my eyes, I could barely believe what I was seeing!

The beast was there, maybe six feet away from me, but it now had something stuck in its mouth and was coming out the back of its head.

Whatever that was, it was emanating from my hand. Slowly, a large creature emerged from my hand walking backward and grew almost twelve feet high.

To my surprise, Arrowtail was still with me, and it was its tail that took care of that beast.

"Break the arrow and pull it out!" Kolikuj said as Arrowtail threw the dead beast toward the other one to protect Tynia. Tynia picked up the disk and rushed to my side. I grabbed the disk, broke the shaft of the arrow, and pulled it out. Tynia stopped the bleeding almost immediately.

Arrowtail tore the other beast to pieces and stood behind Tynia as she faced the Zerkial while the rest of the dark army fled back into the woods.

I stumbled to my feet just as she conjured a spell that turned the wizard's staff molten. Arrowtail turned around and shrank as he approached me. By the time he reached my feet, he was the size of my hand and was panting as he always did, with his tongue sticking out one side of his mouth. He was exhausted.

I put my hand on the ground and he disappeared into my skin. In the distance, the blackguard was making his way through the devastation I caused with my shield. Tynia rushed back toward me. "Jonek, we have to reach Dragon's Breath Lagoon as soon as possible. The fastest way should be to let the river take us downstream to the shallow banks. Let me carry your satchel."

"But what about my mother and Kharlo?"

"I talked to them some time ago, and we agreed they would hide Kharlo in the lagoon."

There was nothing else to say. We made our way into the water and began to swim downstream. It didn't take long for the waters to turn furious as they rushed through the sharp turns in the riverbed. Tynia and I were quickly separated, and I completely lost her just as I saw Ferdhen.

As soon as I could, I clawed my way onto the riverbank on top of some rocks. I was catching my breath when I saw the blackguard running out of the woods on the other side of the river. He pointed one of his swords at me as he stopped by the edge of the river. I knew I couldn't run, so I just slid off the rocks as the blackguard walked into the water. I looked around and saw the Satolgac camp to my right, just across the river, and then the bridge further down.

I turned my weapon into a sword as the shield and armor appeared. The warrior snarled and charged, his swords a flurry against my shield.

People in the distance began to notice we were fighting, so I had to stop using my shield and armor—with those lights moving all around me, I would've been seen as an evil sorcerer by many, and that could've made those moments even harder for me. I stuck the disk inside my clothes and hobbled toward the north side of the market. I saw a helmet on a table, so I put it on as I dodged the blackguard's frenzied swings. Many people ran away from us, but soldiers from Da Grokpel's garrison noticed and formed up ranks.

I told them to stay away, but the blackguard cut some down swiftly. Our fight led us around the market and into the competition grounds. Lucky for me, most of the arenas were empty—everyone was assembled in the largest one watching the warriors fighting in the last event of the games.

I saw an old shield leaning by some crates, so I grabbed it and kept fighting. Hundreds of people began to scream and run away from us. Even some warriors who competed in the games moved back, appalled by the appearance and size of the blackguard. A few brave ones engaged him, but they lasted moments at most. After that, I tried my best to keep him focused on me.

"Arrowtail, can you do something?" I whispered frantically as I kicked a large pot and spilled boiling soup on the blackguard's feet.

Arrowtail didn't even answer—he was still exhausted.

Some archers aimed at us, but most hesitated to release their arrows knowing they could hit the people around us. The blackguard pushed me deeper into the competition grounds and finally into the arena for the Vothras. The swordsmen in there were still fighting to become the next Olikant Warrior, oblivious to what was happening outside. I've always wondered what they thought in those moments where, without any warning, they became part of my own fight.

I have to say that all of them fought valiantly and even managed to make the blackguard drop one of his swords. We fought together, but he stormed the warrior who took his sword. Thankfully, I was able to stop his blow before he could strike that brave man down.

Our swords kept colliding as we stepped on the many falcon feathers still lying on the Gronsvoh. I taunted the warrior, giving the others a chance to escape. Everyone around the arena looked like they wanted to leave, but many ended up staying to watch us.

It wasn't until I saw a young five- or six-year-old boy with an injured leg, dragging himself behind some barrels, that I realized I had to stop this dark warrior, even if that meant my own life.

That voice traveled again through my mind. "Breathe, Jonek. Breathe. He is just a fish in the river."

Most people around the arena gasped as I dropped the shield. I took my sword with both hands and walked toward the blackguard. My blade sliced the air so fast that even I couldn't tell where it was most of the time. The symbol on my hand was shining so brightly that I could see it through the glove. The blackguard did manage to make a long cut across my chestpiece, but it barely grazed my skin.

I kept pushing him until he rammed up against the second pole. For just a flash of a second, he took his eyes away from me. The force of my sword getting stuck in the pole made the plates on top shake vigorously, as if a Vothra had hit them. I reached up and pulled the sword from it, and the head of the blackguard rolled down as both his body and mine landed on our knees.

At first, no one made a sound. Then, suddenly, the place erupted into deafening cheers as the soldiers and warriors rushed out to see if there were more brutes like him around.

I walked toward the boy and carried him out in my arms. I was looking for someone who could take care of him when I saw the members of the council and a few soldiers walking toward me carrying the golden bell on a tray.

The leader of the council stopped in front of me. "No one can deny that you are the best swordsman this town has ever seen. Not only do this bell and the title of Olikant Warrior belong to you, but you have our eternal gratitude for facing this wretched soldier from the evil hordes of the west. What is your name?"

Many began to walk into the arena. Then I spotted a group of Tromzils using this opportunity to get close to the place where the falcons are kept during the games. All of them, including their children, began to pick up the scraps of food left by the contestants as they fed their birds. My heart ached more than my wounds.

"Arrowtail, leave no hair on the top of my head. Do it quickly," I whispered as I walked away from the members of the council.

I turned around, approached the leader of the council, and left the boy in his arms. Then, I picked up a broken sword and threw it toward the top of the halfway pole, making its shattered blade pierce one of its plates from side to side. The fury of its sound must've echoed across town. Everyone became dead silent.

"You want to know my name? I have no name!" I bellowed, my gaze burning into him. "I didn't face this creature for gold or fame, much less a title. I did it to defend life! This boy's, yours—everyone's." I took my helmet off and threw my gloves on the ground. "Look at your Olikant Warrior!" I yelled as I raised my hand, still tinted red by those flowers at the creek. "An insignificant Tromzil. One of those poor beings that some of you deem less important than dogs. And why? Just because we look different and our skin has a different color."

I turned back to look at the many listening to my words. "Your eyes are deceiving your hearts. There is good and evil in any race, even yours. Nobody can tell what a man carries in his soul just by the way he looks or the blood he carries in his veins." I paused. "Every living being has one light inside, the same size, the same color. Only by respecting life and helping each other will be able to maintain its brilliance . . . the only treasure we'll keep when we die."

I walked toward the leader of the council. "Respect and help anyone in need. Give us a chance to live a decent life. You never know who might be helping you, or who might be saving the lives of your loved ones tomorrow." I paused. "Melt this bell and divide the gold among the Tromzils and the families who lost someone today," I said as I bowed toward him and walked away.

Da Grokpel was standing in front of his soldiers nearby. I stopped in front of them and gave them a soldier's salute. Da Grokpel and his men were very surprised, but he responded accordingly.

"Not bad for a boy who falls out of trees, eh?" I whispered to him before I ran toward the family of Tromzils picking up food scraps.

"Do you know Zatioke?" I asked the man when I reached him.

"Yes, I know him and his family," he said as he took his hat off.

"Tell him that Jonek asked you to work with him cleaning his fields southeast of Ferdhen. Your family can stay there for the winter," I replied.

The man was certainly confused hearing those words from another Tromzil, but he nodded in agreement. His youngest son, still learning how to walk, stumbled his way toward me and put his arms around my leg.

"Holpoka, come here!" the mother said, pulling the boy away from my leg.

I put my hand on the boy's head before leaving through the crowd. Then, I ran south as fast as I could.

"Well, you certainly have a way with words," Kolikuj said as I bolted down the south road.

"I just don't like how most people treat the Tromzils," I said as I looked back quickly to see if anyone was following me.

"In my time, we were afraid of them," Kolikuj said.

"Why is that?"

"They had the largest fleet west of our islands."

Those words puzzled me, but I had no time to talk about it. "Arrowtail, there's no one around us. You can change me back to the way I was earlier," I said as I turned the sword back into a rod. The sun was dying when I left the road and crossed the river on the shallow banks so I could take the south trail toward the lagoon.

The landscape I saw when I reached the lagoon was as grim as that scene I'd watched at the theater when the princess reached the front lines searching for her loved one. Countless dark soldiers, beasts, and even Zerkials laid on the ground lifeless while my friends and a group of Satolgac warriors walked around them cutting their skins with arrows and swords covered in red paint.

I walked on top of the fallen trees to cross the entrance of the lagoon, and my heart swelled with happiness when I saw my mother and Zilhana walking with Tynia on the other side of the lake. Tobho and Nuthek saw me but didn't recognize me.

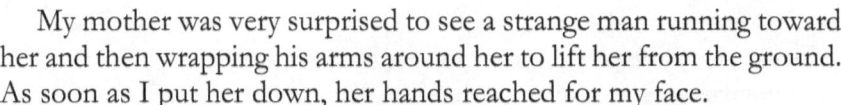

My mother was very surprised to see a strange man running toward her and then wrapping his arms around her to lift her from the ground. As soon as I put her down, her hands reached for my face.

"The body is not familiar, but these eyes have given life to my heart since the day they looked at me for the first time," she said as she moved my hair from my forehead.

"You were right, mother. I miss my warm nest," I said as tears rolled down my dirty face.

We hugged again, and even Zilhana put her arms around us. My friends and the others got closer.

"You look very handsome, but where is my boy?" my mother said as she dried the tears on my face. I took the pendant off, turning my body back to normal. The clothes didn't fit me anymore, so I threw the chestpiece on the ground, tightened my leggings, and tossed the boots to the side. My mother smiled. "This is my boy. Happy birthday, my son."

"Oh mother, I may look the same to you, but I feel way older than thirteen," I said as I buried my face in her neck.

"Maybe if Jonek would've remained like this during his stay in Kirolcan, he wouldn't have gotten into trouble," Tynia said as my friend's rushed in and hugged me.

"What do you mean? What did he do now?" my mother asked, giving me a serious look.

"Well, to start with, he almost promised to marry someone," Tynia said.

"You were getting married? To who? Was she beautiful?" Yilian asked. My mother scowled.

"She's a princess, maybe ten years older than him," Tynia said.

"You lucky dog," Tobho said, giving me a playful punch.

"It's not true, though, mother. Well, it's true she was that old, but I wasn't going to marry her," I stammered to explain.

"But you kissed her," Tynia said.

"Yuck, you kissed her?" Nuthek said, wrinkling his nose.

"From the neck to her forehead, with a couple of stops by her lips," Kolikuj added. Everyone stepped back, surprised.

"You stay quiet, Kolikuj!" I said, lifting my arm to look at him in his cage.

"What did you do to my grandmother's bracelet!" Zilhien said behind me.

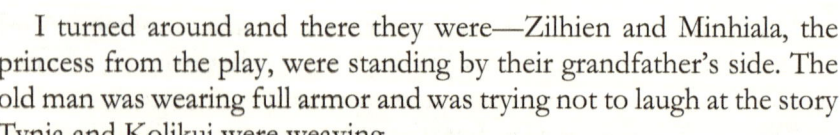

I turned around and there they were—Zilhien and Minhiala, the princess from the play, were standing by their grandfather's side. The old man was wearing full armor and was trying not to laugh at the story Tynia and Kolikuj were weaving.

"Don't mind my granddaughters, young man. I want to know more about your future wedding to that princess. I look forward to the invitation," he said as he leaned on a sword fully covered in red paint.

"We needed help, so we invited them to join our fight," Yilian said.

A few Satolgac warriors approached. "There are no more dark soldiers in sight. You may want to use your staff to confirm, my liege. We will tend to the wounded, but we'll stay in the outskirts just in case." Tynia nodded.

I turned to my mother again. "Mother, really, I wasn't going to marry the princess—"

"And Jonek has a daughter too," Kolikuj interjected. Tynia and the others laughed as I ducked behind Tobho to hide from my mother.

"Her mother asked me to take care of her, and I did for a few weeks. That's all," I said, though I doubted anyone was even listening.

This is when Tynia's staff burst into light.

"Kharlo," she muttered. "We have less time than I thought. The Jiretal spell is running out!"

Tynia motioned for us to follow her, and everyone rushed to the fallen trees by the entrance. Yilian untied a rope hidden where we used to fish and dragged it back to shore. Slowly, Kharlo's body emerged from the depths.

His mark detached from his skin just as we laid his body on the ground. Tynia made the elder's potion come out of her staff's head and poured a few drops in his mouth.

We waited.

Suddenly, Kharlo's eyes fluttered open. He smiled weakly.

"How are you, Tyn? Thank you for bringing me back."

Tynia smiled slightly and asked someone to bring her my satchel. "Kharlo, we don't have much time. We've been betrayed, and the dark army has the means to find you anywhere you go." She paused. "Unfortunately, this means that your role in our quest is over. Someone has to take your place—right now." She carefully dried Kharlo's face.

"But who? Have the elders trained another guardian warrior?"

"The elders can't train anyone until the traitor is found, and unfortunately, it may very well be one of them. We will use this potion to transfer your powers to someone else. We can't pass your memories and knowledge on as you did with Jonek, but someone else can carry your mark and use your weapon. The dark army won't be able to track that person, because the new guardian won't have your blood."

Kharlo looked over at me. "But I didn't pass my knowledge to you. Only my powers."

Tynia and I were confused, but she leaned in and took Kharlo's mark from around his neck.

"I can replace him. I already have his powers," I said.

Tynia shook her head. "The elders told me that the mark will decide." She put Kharlo's golden mark inside the vial. Tynia dangled the pendant on top of the vial as the potion dripped back into it. Kharlo's mark suddenly moved to one side.

"No one move!" Tynia said as she stood and followed the direction of the pendant. She walked in a jagged, wavy line, but Kharlo's mark eventually guided her to Zilhien. Her sister immediately jumped in front of her.

"My sister is too young. Take me instead—I know how to use a sword," Minhiala said.

Tynia smiled. "I have no doubt you do. Your eyes are both fierce and beautiful. But your age prevents you from this task."

Zilhien took her sister's arm. "Don't worry, Min. I might not be as good as you, but I can hold my own in a fight. Remember, our grandfather's blood runs through our veins."

Tynia took her hand, and they both leaned down closer to Kharlo. "Is there anything she needs to know in order to continue our quest?" Tynia said.

Kharlo looked up at Zilhien and smiled. "The book that Jonek took from me . . . ten drops on page seventeen and three drops on page five." He paused. "Be strong, young girl. You are not alone." He took his pendant from Tynia's hand and put it around Zilhien's neck.

Kharlo's mark glowed on Zilhien's neck as he closed his eyes and rested his head on the ground. His body began to change until he looked as young as Tynia.

Moments later, he awoke without any recollection of who he was, who we were, or even what had happened all his life. He began to fret in his confusion, but a voice behind us calmed him immediately.

"Your name is Kharlo. You are my grandson, and you just fell and hit your head. Don't worry, we'll take care of you. Minhiala, come here and help your 'cousin' onto the wagon." The old man quickly squeezed Tynia's shoulder. Minhiala helped Kharlo stand up and walk a few steps. "You take care of my granddaughter. I'll take care of Kharlo as if he were my own son," the old soldier said to us.

Tynia ran and wrapped her arms around Kharlo. Even though he didn't know who she was, he offered her a smile and nodded his head. Tears flooded her eyes, and she couldn't bite them back. Two young guardians, survivors of countless battles, friends sharing a single heart, had just become strangers in front of our eyes.

Minhiala left Kharlo resting on the wagon and joined us again. Tynia took Kharlo's weapon from my satchel and gave it to Zilhien. Slowly, Kharlo's symbol began to glow brightly on the back of her hand and on the weapon.

"It worked. This weapon is now yours." She paused. "Now it's my turn," Tynia said as she looked at me.

"What do you mean?" I said, my heart already sinking.

Tynia cupped my face in her hands. "I'm very sorry, Warrior Eyes, but I thought it was best to wait until the last moment to tell you this. Do you remember that parchment that had Kharlo's face on it? The one that was taken from a Zerkial wizard and was covered in blood." She paused. "Well, it not only had Kharlo's face—it had Artego's, Jalyena's . . . and mine too." I shook my head, willing it not to be real. "It's now up to you to find Artego and Jalyena before the dark army does, and make them pass their powers to someone else. Just make sure they look at the clues that Kharlo left behind. They should be able to find a way to defeat Malok once and for all. I know you've already made a promise to bring back the mother of that little girl, but I have to ask you to make another one, for me. Please save my friends, Warrior Eyes."

My eyes began to burn with tears. "I promise. But I don't even know how to train guardians, and there are many things I still don't understand. Whose memories am I holding? Why did Peprokh say we never crossed the Valley of Souls?"

Tynia's did her best not to cry as she wiped the tears from my face. "Unfortunately, I have no answers for you. But it's true that when Rubzilet, Peprokh, and I saw your memories, there was no image of us walking through that battlefield. This and other questions, like why this red paint is lethal to the dark army, will require all of you working together to solve. But don't despair—I know in my heart that you and your friends will find your way, just like we did when we started this journey. Now let me see who will take my place." She opened the vial once again, put a few drops of the potion in her mouth, took her mark from her neck, and put it in the vial. The pendant pointed at Nuthek.

"Magic must flow strong in you," Tynia said.

"At least in his head," Tobho quipped.

Nuthek spent a good minute opening his mouth to say something, then closing it again, baffled. He looked at me a few times, but I had nothing to say. "My family won't understand why I'm gone," he managed at last.

My mother put a hand on his shoulder. "My heart is dying knowing that I might not see Jonek for a long time, but I now understand that the evil upon us won't stop until all of us bend to its will. Nuthek, take care of my boy. I will tell your mother that royal artisans visiting our fair invited you and Jonek to become woodworking apprentices in the capital. Your parents may not like that, but I don't think they'll challenge a request from the king's court."

Tynia approached Nuthek. "Nuthek, I wish I'd had time to train you in the basics of magic. Now you'll have to learn the hard way."

"I can train him," Kolikuj said, jangling the cage on my wrist. "I am a guardian wizard, after all. In fact, I can train all of them on the basics of being a guardian."

"But Kolikuj, I thought you wanted to see your islands one last time," I said.

"I still do, with all my heart. But the last few days have made me feel alive again. I can't fight anymore, but maybe my new task in this quest is to train you and your friends. Besides, I can't wait to go back to Kelfia and find out what the king will do to you once he finds out you kissed his daughter."

"I did not kiss her!" I repeated emphatically.

Tynia couldn't help but chuckle. "Very good then. My staff is linked to an orb that has a special binding gem in it. It will take five of you directly to the Lost Path, but I don't know if Kolikuj will count as one inside that pebble. You will have to decide what to do next." Tynia paused. "Jonek, you need to find two more who might be able to take Artego and Jalyena's place. They can't be older than fifteen when they wear their marks for the first time. Remember, find Artego first; his location is hidden in the pages of the fifth journal. Only he knows where Jaly is."

Tynia untied the strap of the hook she used to carry her weapon and put it on Nuthek's belt. She handed him her staff and asked him to lower his head to put her pendant on him. My mother reached out to grab Tynia's arm.

"Young lady, you are now part of our family. Zilhana and I will take care of you until life takes us apart. Just try not to give me as many headaches as Jonek, please?" New tears flooded Tynia's eyes.

Tynia put her pendant on Nuthek, making her mark glow on his neck, Nuthek's hand, and her weapon. Tynia's body collapsed, but my mother and Zilhana caught her and helped her to the ground. She remained there, sleeping.

Everyone walked closer and stood around her. "Tynia said that Artego and Jalyena have very special powers—he controls the elements and she has mind powers. I don't know what that means, but who could replace them?" I stood, staring at everyone, awaiting a response from someone.

"I want to go with you," Yilian said.

"Me too," said Tobho.

"I know," I said, looking at both of them, "but one of you has to stay to tell us what takes place in this world, and most importantly, to protect my mother and the rest."

"I should go with Jonek," Tobho said, turning to Yilian. "I know more about nature and the elements."

Yilian couldn't debate that much, so I turned to him for support.

"Yilian, you know this region and its people better than any of us. If there is any danger, you can lead my mother and the rest to any of our hideouts," I said.

Zilhien's grandfather put his hand on Yilian's shoulder. "You won't be alone. I deserve a respite from traveling with the theater, so I'm thinking of buying some land around here to settle down for a while."

"And I can help you polish your skills with the sword and bow," Minhiala said.

Yilian nodded, and Nuthek gave him the gold coin he used to communicate with Tynia and me.

"That settles it. Tobho is coming with us. We just need someone to learn Jalyena's mind skills," I said.

None of us had the slightest idea who could take her place. Only the sound of torches being lit by the Satolgacs nearby broke the silence.

"I can do it if my elder allows it," a voice said from the edge of the forest. All of us looked at her, but only I knew who she was.

Khatzika appeared from behind a group of Satolgacs carrying a bow in her hands. Her voice reminded me of that cold night in the woods when the old man threw her bow in the fire.

"For countless generations, our task has been to protect them, not fight on their behalf, Khatzika," an elderly man said.

"Isn't that the same, grandfather? Look around you! This entire battle took place just to protect them. These new guardians will need protection too," she said, pointing her bow at us.

"These boys are not guardians," the old man muttered.

"They may not be guardians, but I am!" Kolikuj said. "I know the sages saved your ancestors from annihilation, and in return, you promised to protect us until Sulibhor is defeated. Well, seeing that I can't use a weapon, fulfill your promise and allow the girl to protect me. Let her join us."

"I will honor our beliefs at all times, grandfather," Khatzika said as she took an unusual necklace from her neck and gave it to him.

The old man scowled but took it and softly allowed their foreheads to touch.

Suddenly, a cascade of images pounded into Nuthek's head.

"Jonek, something is happening," he warned, waving a hand to get my attention. "I can see soldiers and beasts rushing through the forest." Zilhien braced him to keep him from falling.

"My liege, you have to leave. We'll take care of your family and fight what's left of the dark army," the old Satolgac said to me.

Khatzika and I walked away from them, but a single Satolgac stepped into our path. The man pulled his hood back, allowing his torch to illuminate his long red hair. Khatzika bowed with deep respect. The man looked at me.

"I'm not sure you understood me when I told you to use the Seven and Two wisely. Our days of peace are over, and somehow, you seemed to be in the center of the storm." He paused, then reached into his cloak. "Make sure you use these ones to unwind the stride of the dark army," he said as he tossed a pouch full of stones to me.

"I will," I said, putting the pouch in my pocket. "Just take care of my bow."

"Keep my granddaughter safe, Warrior Eyes," the old theater man said as he bid me farewell using the soldier's protocol.

"Don't worry. She's braver than I am," I said as Zilhien hugged the old man one last time.

I approached my mother, a knot in my stomach. "Mother, I asked two families of Tromzils to work for us this winter. Zatioke is the name of their leader. Please don't be mad," I said as I put my arms around her.

"My dear boy, how can I be mad at you? Right now, we need all the help we can get. Don't worry—Tynia left me enough gold to feed us for a few seasons." She kissed my face and head tenderly, then very slowly let me go.

"Jonek, I think it's best if you put the bracelet on Nuthek. Right now, he needs me more than you do," Kolikuj said.

"Let me do that," Zilhien said.

She took the bracelet from my wrist, and I gave Zilhana a quick hug before she burst into tears. The Satolgacs disappeared into the shadows of the forest moments later.

"Nuthek, take your weapon but don't look at it," Kolikuj said. "Think that you have a long staff in your hands and tap the ground with it. Do it quickly! The rest of you, listen. There are six of us, and Tynia said that only five can go, so there is a chance that one of us will stay behind. If that happens, stay with Jonek's mother. We'll find a way to come back for you." Horns echoed in the depths of the forest.

"Mother, you'd better leave," I said as I picked up my satchel.

"Take this vial of red paint with you. It may help," she said.

Yilian, Zilhana, Minhiala, and the old man picked up Tynia and carried her to the wagon where Kharlo was.

Somehow, Nuthek was actually able to make a staff appear in his hand. It looked different than Tynia's but had similar lights floating around its head.

"Everyone grab onto the staff and don't let go!" Kolikuj said as the lights flying around the staff became brighter. A strong wind began to blow around us.

Tobho, Khatzika, and Zilhien put their hands on it.

My mother moved away but kept her eyes on me.

"Come back to me, my son."

"Don't worry, mother. I'll always protect you from wolves and bears," I said as the wind blew stronger around us. I couldn't hear her voice, but I clearly read two words on her lips, "I know."

I put my hand on the staff and a flash of light illuminated the entire lagoon.

Bell—

OUR YOUNG GUARDIANS

SEVEN & TWO

ABOUT THE AUTHOR

Rodolfo "Rodi" Szoke was born in Mexico City in 1967. His ancestry blends Hungarian and Mexican heritages across generations. He earned his bachelor's degree in information technology in 1991 and has worked in that field ever since. Early in his life, Rodi developed a keen interest in fantasy and sci-fi adventures, making him grow into an avid moviegoer and casual gamer. In 2004, he conceived the idea for the Our Young Guardians series as one avenue to teach some key "life lessons" to his daughter once she reached middle school.

Our Young Guardians: Seven & Two is his first novel.

Rodi currently lives in Texas with his family, but you can visit him at:

www.rodibooks.com

 http://www.facebook.com/rodiszokeofficial

 http://www.twitter.com/rodiszoke

 https://www.goodreads.com/rodiszoke

 313

www.ingramcontent.com/pod-product-compliance
Lightning Source LLC
Chambersburg PA
CBHW030530270626
47155CB00024B/2648